HOUSE OF FATE

Praise for Barbara Ann Wright

The Pyradisté Adventures

"[A] healthy dose of a very creative, yet believable, world into which the reader will step to find enjoyment and heart-thumping action. It's a fiendishly delightful tale."—*Lambda Literary*

"Barbara Ann Wright is a master when it comes to crafting a solid and entertaining fantasy novel…The world of lesbian literature has a small handful of high-quality fantasy authors, and Barbara Ann Wright is well on her way to joining the likes of Jane Fletcher, Cate Culpepper, and Andi Marquette… Lovers of the fantasy and futuristic genre will likely adore this novel, and adventurous romance fans should find plenty to sink their teeth into."—*The Rainbow Reader*

"*The Pyramid Waltz* has had me smiling for three days…I also haven't actually read…a world that is entirely unfazed by homosexuality or female power before. I think I love it. I'm just delighted this book exists…If you enjoyed *The Pyramid Waltz*, *For Want of a Fiend* is the perfect next step…you'd be embarking on a joyous, funny, sweet and madcap ride around very dark things lovingly told, with characters who will stay with you for months after."—*The Lesbrary*

"This book will keep you turning the page to find out the answers…Fans of the fantasy genre will really enjoy this installment of the story. We can't wait for the next book."
—*Curve Magazine*

Thrall: Beyond Gold and Glory

"[I]ncidents and betrayals run rampant in this world, and Wright's style successfully kept me on my toes, navigating the shifting alliances…[*Thrall*] is a story of finding one's path where you would least expect it. It is full of bloodthirsty battles and witty repartee… which gave it a nice balanced focus…This was the first Barbara Ann Wright novel I've read, and I doubt it will be the last. Her dialogue was concise and natural, and she built a fantastical world that I easily imagined from one scene to the next. Lovers of Vikings, monsters and magic won't be disappointed by this one."—*Curve Magazine*

"The characters were likable, the issues complex, and the battles were exciting. I really enjoyed this book and I highly recommend it."—*All Our Worlds*

Paladins of the Storm Lord

"This was a truly enjoyable read…I would definitely pick up the next book…the mad dash at the end kept me riveted. I would definitely recommend this book for anyone who has a love of sci-fi. An intricate…novel one that can be appreciated at many levels, adventurous sci-fi or one that is politically motivated with a very astute look at present-day human behavior…There are many levels to this extraordinary and well written-book…overall a fascinating and intriguing book."—*Inked Rainbow Reads*

Coils

"Greek myths, gods and monsters and a trip to the Underworld. Sign me up. This one springs straight into action…a good start, great Greek myth action and a late-blooming romance that flowers in the end…"—*Dear Author*

"A unique take on the Greek gods and the afterlife make this a memorable book. The story is fun with just the right amount of camp. Medusa is a hot, if unexpected, love interest…A truly unexpected ending has us hoping for more stories from this world."
—*RT Book Reviews*

By the Author

The Pyradisté Adventures

The Pyramid Waltz

For Want of a Fiend

A Kingdom Lost

The Fiend Queen

Thrall: Beyond Gold and Glory

The Godfall Novels

Paladins of the Storm Lord

Widows of the Sun-Moon

Coils

House of Fate

Visit us at www.boldstrokesbooks.com

HOUSE OF FATE

by

Barbara Ann Wright

2017

HOUSE OF FATE

ISBN 13: 978-1-62639-780-4

This Trade Paperback Original Is Published By
Bold Strokes Books, Inc.
P.O. Box 249
Valley Falls, NY 12185

First Edition: August 2017

CREDITS
EDITOR: CINDY CRESAP
PRODUCTION DESIGN: STACIA SEAMAN
COVER DESIGN BY SHERI (GRAPHICARTIST2020@HOTMAIL.COM)

Acknowledgments

As with all my books, this one wouldn't be possible without Mom and Ross. Another big thank you to Angela, Deb, Erin, Matt, Natsu, Sarah, and Trakena. You're the best readers anyone could ask for.

A continuing thank you to Bold Strokes Books, Radclyffe, Cindy, Sandy, Ruth, and Sheri. You're forever awesome.

Thanks to Carsen Taite and Melissa Brayden for letting me bounce ideas off them during our writing sessions at the BSB Retreat. Good times.

And to anyone who took the time to read this, thank you. Secret snuggles to you all.

For my friends. You know who you are.

CHAPTER ONE

A s the hour of emergence grew nearer, Judit turned away one glittering courtier after another from the airlock of the *Damat*. She could have assigned the task to a lackey or one of her crewmen, but there was always a chance one of the visitors would be House Meridian Blood, and they wouldn't speak to anyone but family. Lucky her.

At least gazing at the courtiers gave her something to do besides mope. She'd never seen gowns of so many materials: feathers, lace, leather, fiber optics, plastics, glass, and metal. The wealthiest were clothed in nanosheen, fabric made of tiny bots that restructured the outfits as they walked, turning them into living art. It was hard to focus on the people past the clothing. Some faces and bodies she couldn't even recognize. But that was the reason no one was allowed to see the chosen one before the emergence: assassination would be all too easy.

She turned away another courtier riding on an antigrav sled pulled by huge butterfly-shaped bots. He'd tried to bribe her, and she'd almost sputtered a laugh before she politely declined. Being the guardian of the chosen one wasn't a demanding job, but it was better than being an ordinary guard. She could count herself lucky that she only had to keep her cousin Noal from harm. She didn't have to settle disputes or listen to the many claims of heredity that stood between calling oneself a member of the populace of House Meridian and a member of the Blood.

When the antigrav sled departed, she looked out on the assembled masses milling about the platform. It was a small space, devoid of any structure save the airlock housings. White pedestals held pieces of art but nothing large, nothing anyone could hide behind. Neutral territory made everyone feel safe, though Judit didn't know how safe she felt under the glassteel dome, all that shielded the assembled throng from open space on this lonely satellite platform. She supposed it was only natural that the courtiers were bored. All their ships had departed—docking during the emergence was reserved for the two heirs—though the berth for House Nocturna remained empty. House Meridian's heir couldn't emerge until both heirs would be vulnerable at the same time. It should have made her feel more secure, more sure of Noal's safety. As the guardian of the chosen one, that was her duty, but her thoughts kept straying to the Nocturna heir. She'd been trying and failing to keep Annika Nocturna off her mind for years.

She told herself to watch the crowd, to do her darking job. Even through the throng, Judit detected a separation, an invisible line between the courtiers and Blood of both houses. She couldn't blame them. They'd been at war for almost a hundred years, would still be at war if the rest of the galaxy hadn't tired of how the fighting impacted their resources. The other houses had demanded that Meridian and Nocturna find a way to end their feud or be annihilated.

Judit snorted. Fat chance. She had no doubt that the combined military might of Meridian and Nocturna would be more than a match for every other house, but she supposed that was the problem. They weren't united, but they would be soon. When Noal Meridian wed Annika Nocturna, they would be unified into one gigantic, unstoppable house. She wondered if the rest of the galaxy had really thought about what it had done.

Cana, another of Judit's cousins, slinked up the gangplank toward the airlock of the *Damat*. Judit straightened and pulled her lightweight uniform jacket tighter across her body. On this day of outlandishness, Cana had gone against the grain, as she always did. She wore a simple gauze shift, completely see-through, and her hair cascaded down her back, silvery white like Judit's own, the natural color of a Meridian Blood. No one who had genetics on their side bothered with dyes, not with a color so striking against dark brown Meridian skin.

Cana smiled as she paused. Even her feet were bare. "Cousin."

Judit nodded. "Cousin. What can I do for you?"

"You can hurry this darking thing up!" She laughed. Lenses made her eyes gleam like liquid silver, her nod to the pageantry of the day. "Go in there, grab Noal by the ear, and drag him out."

Judit grinned. "You know the heirs have to come out at the same time."

"Then fly out there and bully the Nocturnas until they get *their* asses in gear."

"I'll get right on that," Judit said, not moving.

Cana groaned and rolled her eyes. "It's so boring, and I'm starting to get cold."

"You should have worn clothes."

Cana stepped closer, her smile going licentious. "Can I borrow yours?"

Tempting, and they weren't close enough in blood for it to matter—cousins far removed—but Judit simply shook her head.

Cana stepped back with a dramatic sigh. "If Noal were here, he'd jump at the chance." She winked. "I hear he jumps on everything."

Judit shrugged, letting Cana think whatever she wanted to. She felt the skin tingle along her cheek before a voice spoke in the comm implanted in her jaw, for her ears only. "Jude, they're coming in." Lieutenant Beatrice's voice from her monitoring station on the bridge of the *Damat*.

"Acknowledged, Bea," Judit said. She nodded toward the crowd. "Nocturna's coming in, Cana."

"At last!" Cana strolled back down the gangplank, and Judit ducked inside, letting one of her crew take her place, though she doubted anyone else would come calling. The crowd would know of the arrival soon enough.

Judit clacked her back teeth together, reactivating her comm, and then spoke the name of the signal's recipient. "Bea, anything out of place?"

"Nope, one ship, same as ours. Their guns aren't hot, though their engines seem primed in case they have to make a quick getaway."

They snorted a laugh at the same time. Nocturnas, suspicious as always. As if the eyes of the entire galaxy weren't on this little meeting. "Keep me posted." She clicked her teeth again, and the line went dead.

Within a few steps, she was at Noal's quarters aboard the ship that had been designed to ferry the chosen one about. She rang the chime. After a beat, the door hissed open, letting a loud argument spill into the hallway.

Noal turned from where he was standing in the middle of the

room, surrounded by fussing servants. They'd dressed him in a suit of white feathers, trousers hidden beneath a jacket with a train so long it spread behind him like a bird's tail. "Judit!" he said. "Will you please tell these children of the dark that I cannot deal with this cape! The dark-eating suit already has a train. Now they want a cape, too!"

It was a majestic cape, she'd give it that. With long feathers of red, blue, and yellow, it made a nice contrast to the white. "What's a few more feathers between friends?"

He gave her a nasty look, waved the servants away with another slash of his hand, and turned to the mirror. He'd colored his hair dark blue, a deliberate rebellion against his family, who wanted everyone to look as Meridian as possible that day, but Judit knew who it was really for. Blue was Annika's favorite color, and he wanted their union to work. They all did. Annika wasn't like any other Nocturna, and she deserved happiness.

Judit told herself to stop that line of thinking. Noal applied last-minute cosmetics above his brown eyes and picked at his outfit a few more times before declaring he was ready. She escorted him to the gangplank, signals were passed, and the two heirs emerged from their ships at the same time.

No matter what Judit told herself about her duty, her eyes found Annika at once. Her hair was undyed, a deep honey blond with so many hints of red it seemed to change color as she moved. Judit had thought she'd known her favorite color before she'd laid eyes on Annika's hair. She wore a figure-hugging gown of deep violet that shimmered as she walked, deepening to royal blue then back to purple as the light hit it. It highlighted every sleek curve.

Judit had to swallow as Annika's gaze swept Noal's party and found her own. She didn't smile, too disciplined for that, but Judit thought she saw a slight wrinkling about the eyes. For the past five years, ever since they'd all reached the age of ascension at fifteen, Noal and Annika had met on neutral ground, coming to know each other before their union. Naturally, their guardians had been with them every step of the way. They'd been the best years of Judit's life.

Annika's guardian Feric followed her as Judit followed Noal. A huge, hulking man, he scanned the crowd as Judit knew she should be doing. She didn't know him at all. Through all the years, he'd never spoken. She didn't even know if he could. Judit had joined in the meetings, talking and laughing with Annika and Noal, but Feric had been like a statue.

Hierophants assigned to both houses led the processions through the assembled throng. Judit kept her eyes on the people, looking for a hidden blade, a subtle weapon, even though there could be none. The airlock scanners, run by security from multiple houses, assured there was nothing. Sentry bots whisked discreetly through the air, recording everything, but security could be subverted. And even if a person had no weapon, there were hand-to-hand techniques that could crush a person's windpipe or interrupt the blood flow to the brain, though Meridians usually went for faster, more brutal weapons that could be used at great distance.

And she couldn't imagine anyone in this glittering throng knowing anything about crushing windpipes. Their eyes were glazed, almost vapid as they gazed on the two heirs with something like worship, all of the nonblood jockeying for position behind the ranks of Blood. The families clapped quietly, almost demurely, as the occasion warranted. When Cana caught Judit's eye, she winked, but Judit kept her expression stern, making a mental note to contact her cousin later and give her a few pointers on decorum.

They reached the central dais where the high hierophant waited. Judit wondered if he'd ever seen this specific incident when he journeyed to the black holes at the center of the galaxy. Willa, the greatest hierophant in history, had seen the birth of the chosen one—a Meridian who would unite with a Nocturna and change the face of the galaxy—but she'd disappeared into the black holes after her prediction forty years ago. Judit wondered if any of the hierophants here had ever seen the same.

The high hierophant intoned the ceremony of engagement, the last step before marriage, and as Annika and Noal joined hands, Judit thought again what a waste of time this was. Everyone knew they were engaged. Their destiny had been set long before their births with Willa's prediction. Why was all this pomp necessary? Why did it feel so much like a dagger in her chest?

When the prophecy had first come to light, House Nocturna had disputed it. They'd argued that they would never unite with Meridian, but one day, they'd changed their stance, claiming they'd seen it for themselves and believed it wholeheartedly. After all, Willa was the only hierophant in history to stay so long on the edge of the black holes, to ride the event horizon before she was finally lost. And her every decipherable prophecy had come true. No one pointed out that Nocturna's backpedaling had come hot on the heels of the other houses' edict that Meridian and Nocturna would end their war or die.

A union gave everyone the swiftest way to end the conflict. And so their many battles and schemes had been suspended, and the marriage set, but still they had to have these stupid ceremonies: one where the heirs met for the first time, one on their eighteenth birthdays, and now one to formally announce the engagement. It was the galaxy's most depressing countdown. Now they only had months before they married. Judit had seen the wisdom in all their secret visits. Nothing would be served if the peace hedged on a couple who hated each other. But Noal and Annika got on well, and they'd drawn Judit into their circle. She'd been happy to see Noal develop feelings for Annika, who seemed to have some affection for him, but Judit hadn't been prepared for the effect Annika had on her.

As the hierophant droned on, Judit's heart felt like lead. She couldn't help letting her eyes linger on Annika, to picture herself clasping those long, pale fingers in her own, to be reciting the words to join them together as she stared deep into those dark, wine-colored eyes. At first, she'd thought them brown, but when Annika had come forward to meet her, Judit had realized they were a deep blue, indigo, and since then she'd seen them in every mood from calm, to delight at Noal's antics, to the one time a petulant Noal made her so angry she'd left early. Her eyes had turned as dark as the fiercest storm on Meridian Prime.

Now she and Noal had reached a relaxed, easy peace. If they didn't exactly set the galaxy on fire with flames of passion, they were at least good friends. Many marriages didn't even start with that. But Judit didn't know how Noal resisted taking Annika in his arms every time he saw her. As far as Judit knew, they'd only shared a few chaste kisses, though they could have done so much more. In Judit's dreams, she and Annika had done so much more.

In real life…Nothing.

The hierophant clapped, signaling an end to the ceremony and snapping Judit out of her reverie. She cursed herself for not paying attention and stood aside for Noal to return to the *Damat*. They would pull away from the platform and retreat to another neutral location where Noal and Annika could speak privately, and everyone else would stay here to party. Judit was glad she didn't have to make chitchat with this crowd. Instead, she'd get to spend time with Annika, with Noal and Feric, too, but it was Annika who mattered. She shouldn't have been looking forward to it. It was foolish. But now that the thought of speaking with Annika had broached her consciousness, it seemed the only thought that mattered. She needed to see Annika again away from the throng, needed to speak with her if only to exchange pleasantries.

Was this what her future was going to be like? After marriage, she'd continue to be Noal's guardian, would have to watch him and Annika speak and act and rule as a married couple, would have to be there when they had breakfast and discussed the plans of the day. She'd stand outside the door of their bedchamber when they made love, waiting for them to go to their separate bedrooms with Feric beside her. Oh yes, a wonderful future indeed.

"Stop moping," Noal said when they were behind closed doors. He shooed the servants out and began changing out of the feathered costume. "Help me with this jacket."

"I'm not moping."

"Like a lovesick poet."

"Shut up." She tugged too hard, ripping the sleeve.

He laughed and tossed the jacket in the corner. The dark knew how much it cost. "If she wants you like you want her, I won't stop you, you know that."

"I'm a member of the Blood, Noal. We are spouses, not side lovers."

"You are so old-fashioned, Judit. No one thinks like that anymore. It's anyone, anytime. Ask Cana. By the dark, ask any of them!"

"You're one to talk. You flirt, and everyone thinks you've got a lover behind every piece of furniture, but how many have you truly had?"

He peeled off the feathered eyelashes and muttered something.

"What was that?" she asked.

"Four. I've had four. Happy?"

"And how many will you have after marriage?"

He gave her a dark look in the mirror and began wiping off the elaborate makeup.

"My guess is none," she said, "because deep down, you were taught by the same grandmother as me, and she gave you the same talks, and you took them in the same way."

"Oh, shut up. You're worse than a poet. And we don't know what the head of Nocturna taught Annika. She could have a fleet of lovers lined up, and I wouldn't care."

She knew he would, but she didn't push it. She cared, and he did, too.

Chapter Two

Annika had hoped her glances at Judit had gone unnoticed, but as she reached her quarters in the middle of her ship, her grandmother said, "First form," and Annika knew she'd been discovered.

"Yes, Ama."

She stripped quickly, and Ama did the same, both of them donning training jumpsuits kept in Annika's quarters for these very exercises. Their attendants fled, all but Feric, who stationed himself in front of the door, hands linked in front of his massive chest, eyes staring at nothing while seeing everything.

Annika stood by her grandmother's side and let her body fall into familiar rhythms, old patterns, limbs flowing from one exercise to the next. She didn't risk a look at her grandmother, but she didn't sense the usual wave of disapproval. Maybe she hadn't noticed the glances after all. Maybe she just didn't want Annika getting distracted by the wedding announcement.

As if she could. She liked Noal; she really did. If circumstances were different, he could have been a good friend, maybe even an acceptable spouse for political reasons. They could have been amicable to each other while seeking physical love from outsiders. Even carrying on their lineage wouldn't demand sex. Science could do everything for them.

She wished he'd been an unlikable stooge. That would have made taking over his mind and eventually killing him so much easier. And if Judit was as terrible as the rest of her family, Annika might not have hesitated at all.

But Judit... Annika nearly closed her eyes at the memory of Judit's shoulders, her muscular arms. She wore her uniform tight so it wouldn't hamper her movements, and it clung to her hips, her breasts, her legs. Annika was strong, but she kept her form wiry to disguise her true strength; Judit had no such restrictions. Annika couldn't count the number of times she'd gotten lost in fantasies of Judit's arms around her, lifting her. She'd imagine them entwined in the sheets of her bed, laughing and wrestling. Whoever ended up on top depended on her mood at the time, but Judit was the only woman with whom Annika ever imagined relinquishing control.

"Spar," Ama said.

Annika fought the urge to sigh. Of course her grandmother had noticed her distraction. Maybe her grandmother had noticed a bloom in her cheeks or a quickening of her pulse. Still, Annika kept her face serene as they took fighting stances. No one outside of Nocturna knew that upper members of the Blood were masters of hand-to-hand combat. Most assumed they were as blunt and violent as Meridian; they'd spent wealth and effort to appear so, but they liked to solve problems more subtly. Why bother with snipers when a well-placed jab to the right nerve cluster did the trick? No need for bombs when a slow-working poison got the job done. Unlike Meridian, Nocturna blustered only for show.

Ama's hand shot for Annika's throat, and she knocked it down, launching her own kick. Ama ducked, her foot arching out almost delicately, but her aim was set to take off Annika's nose. Annika threw herself to the side, rolling and coming up gracefully to find her grandmother still coming for her.

On it went, strikes, feints, dodges, and blocks. They circled the room, hands in front of their bodies with only a gentle curve of the fingers so they were a step away from fists, open palms, or straightened hands. After Noal had outlived his usefulness, Annika would kill him with one of these techniques, and he would never see it coming. She would disguise it as a fall, a rival assassination if she had to, and all the evidence would be doctored so she would appear far away at the time, irrefutably alibied.

"Enough," Ama said, straightening.

Annika followed suit but remained on guard. Her grandmother had tricked her before.

Ama's lip quirked up as she eyed Annika's stance. "Have you perfected the worm?"

Annika shuddered. She might not have to kill Noal. Given time, the worm might do it for her. "As much as it will let me."

Ama frowned, and Annika knew what she was thinking. It didn't matter how good a fighter she was or how irrefutable her alibi. The Meridians would never stop watching her. They would always suspect. So before she could kill anyone and take firm control over their new, joined house, she would have to separate Noal from his family. No seductive charms would do that, but with the worm, he'd do it himself.

"Do you need more mental discipline exercises?" Ama asked. "Time is short."

"I know, Ama." She crossed to a disguised section of bulkhead. There was no keypad, no DNA or retinal scanner. There was only one way to open it. She schooled her thoughts into the proper pattern, and when the scanning device detected the right brain waves, an invisible door swung open.

Swimming in a jar of cerebral spinal fluid swam the greatest, newest piece of biotech Nocturna had ever produced. They were good at poisons, at DNA-specific weapons, but so far, Meridian had found a way to counter everything they made. But no one suspected this. It was tiny, too small to make a noticeable hole once it had entered Noal's ear canal, then burrowed into the brain. Coated in a skin of Noal's own DNA, no scanner would detect it. And inside, the greatest achievement of Nocturna technology: an organic nanobot. A tiny computer made of biological matter that, like the scanner in the hatch, responded to her thought patterns alone. She could command it to restructure Noal's brain slowly, changing him in ways no doctor or scientist would be able to find even with the deepest scans.

Chilling. She'd never liked it, didn't want to use it, but she had to prove she could. She commanded the worm to float to the top of its container, and it obeyed. Ama still frowned. Annika wished the frown was because her grandmother also didn't care for the plan, but no. Ama thought she couldn't do what was necessary. And true, she didn't want to, but if Ama doubted her too much, someone else would be found. Even at this late stage, if Annika couldn't be replaced, they'd find someone to join her retinue who could get close enough to use the worm.

Then Annika wouldn't even be *part* of the plan, but she'd still have to watch. That thought scared her more than having to commit the act herself. At least then she could make sure Noal never suffered.

Judit, though…Annika's family would insist she die, even after Annika pulled her and Noal apart.

Ama sighed. "I know you like the boy."

Annika smiled. Her secret crush on Judit might be intact.

"And his guardian."

Or not. Annika kept her smile in place and shut the door to the worm's chamber. "I can do what's necessary."

"Sacrifice is always necessary. Do you think I liked killing your grandfather?"

A closely guarded secret. Most Nocturna Blood relationships were built on the trading of such secrets, and many nonblood suffered because of it. Annika's own mother had fled before it had happened to her. She'd been declared an exile afterward, but Annika often wondered if she'd gotten out so the family wouldn't kill her, even if it meant abandoning her daughter.

"Grandfather seemed like a good man." She remembered liking his smile.

"Good at being a member of this family," Ama said, "but we needed a high-level death to pin on House Donata."

Annika nodded, wondering if her grandmother had ever loved her good grandfather. Maybe she had. Maybe willing to kill was as strong as their love could be. But as many times as she'd imagined killing Noal, Annika had never imagined the same for Judit. In every fantasy fight, they ended up in bed together instead.

"Oh, just have her and get her out of your system," Ama said as she stalked to the door. Feric moved out of her way before following, letting the door shut behind him and leaving Annika alone.

She wished they'd already had each other, but whether it would make things easier or more difficult she didn't know. All the times she'd flirted with Judit, Judit seemed embarrassed even though Annika could tell their desires were the same. Judit was bound by some cultural norms within her own house, and she didn't take sex lightly.

To the detriment of them both.

While her ship traveled toward the rendezvous with Judit's ship, Annika tried to put such thoughts out of her mind. Most times, her mental discipline was on point, but something about Judit always made it...muddy. Best then if Judit *did* die, maybe, as long as it was someone else who killed her.

Annika's nature rebelled against the thought. Better to destroy all the art in creation, for all music to fall silent. They were silly, romantic thoughts, but there they were. She and Judit were going to have to resolve their attraction someday, in some fashion. That, or Judit was going to forsake her role as guardian and leave Annika and Noal to each other. That would hurt, but maybe then they could move on.

Or she and Judit could become lovers and stay lovers after the marriage. She pictured them eking out some kind of life together in between the parties and trade negotiations. Maybe they could bribe a nonblood scientist to mingle their genetic material and make them a child of their own, and after the scientist disappeared, no one would know who the child really was.

But Judit would notice as Noal grew stranger and stranger, losing his mind until he had to turn all the day-to-day running of the house over to Annika. Judit would want doctors, and not those House Nocturna would provide. And if she discovered the worm, she'd know her house had been betrayed, and then any life they'd built would come crashing down around them.

And Annika didn't think for one second that she could abandon the plan, claim she'd do it, then leave Noal alone so they could rule their joined house in peaceful coexistence. Nocturna wouldn't stand for that. They'd formulate another plan, remove Annika if they had to, and she was certain Meridian wasn't going to be sitting on their thumbs. They had to be planning something, too, the only question was what.

As her ship docked at a small, neutral asteroid station, Annika schooled her face into its pleasant mask and forced herself to walk easily into the lushly appointed sitting room. Noal looked much more relaxed in a blousy, multihued shirt that gaped open at the chest, though his trousers were still so tight, she could have drawn him naked. He hugged her as always, and she gave him a bright smile that she only had to fake because her thoughts were so dark.

Then she made herself look at Judit, still in her military uniform. She had a sudden flash of the only time she'd seen her out of it. They'd all shared this location overnight, and Annika had thought it would be the first time she and Noal had sex, but he'd declined, probably under orders to wait for the nuptials. Something had happened to the air reclamators in the middle of the night, and everyone had spilled into the sitting room in a panic. Judit had been wearing a soft dark shirt that hung to her knees and gaped open at the shoulders, showing her collarbones. Her silver hair had been wild, disheveled, and Annika thought she looked absolutely delicious.

Annika had envied her in that moment. Every item of clothing she wore was carefully chosen to invoke a response in the viewer, even the diaphanous nightgown she'd worn that night. She'd never owned something simple or comfortable. She would have given quite a bit to wear Judit's nightshirt. She'd considered stealing it but didn't like the questions that would bring up. Her grandmother would only have found and destroyed it anyway.

Now Judit gave her a nod, and Annika nearly laughed. Judit prided herself on the way she could school her face, but her body spoke volumes. Her jaw was tight; her shoulders were far too stiff, telegraphing that she was trying to keep calm to keep her mind from wandering. Annika was nearly overcome with the urge to kiss her just to see if she'd politely push away or melt into the embrace. Maybe she'd stiffen like a statue, and Annika would have to feel her desire by the heat that flooded her body or the way she did everything she could not to wrap her arms around Annika's shoulders. An interesting question however she asked it.

"All ready for the wedding?" Noal asked.

"To be put on display like a stuffed pigeon? Can't wait."

He laughed. Judit smiled, some of the stiffness going out of her tall frame. She always took a while to warm up.

Noal chattered for a few moments, mostly about clothing and decorations, two of his passions. No matter what else she had to change about him, she'd leave his passions alone. She thought the afternoon would simply be another visit until she excused herself to go to the washroom, and as she was washing her hands before emerging, Judit stepped inside.

Annika froze, taken by surprise for one of the few times in her adult life. Heat started in her belly and spread low as she wondered if Judit was finally giving in to the impulses they were both feeling.

But Judit's eyes widened. "I'm...I'm sorry. Noal said..."

Her mouth tightened, her face becoming grim. "He said he needed something, and when the door wasn't locked—"

"You thought I'd already emerged?" And there she'd been hoping that stoic Judit had finally cracked.

"Or that you were in the other washroom."

"Well, now that you're here." Annika stepped close. She'd had far too much thinking that day. It was beyond the time to feel.

Judit exhaled slowly, and her gaze wandered over Annika's face. Annika licked her lips.

"I..." Judit swallowed hard, but she didn't run. Annika wondered if Judit would let herself be trapped against the door, a thought that made her shiver.

Annika took a step closer. "You what?"

"We..."

"Better." She was nearly there now, their chests almost meeting. She took Judit's hands, wanting Judit to turn her head, to lean forward, anything to signal that they should take this step. The thought that Annika would have to do all the seduction work was intriguing, but another part of her wanted Judit to lift her onto the sink and make love to her before either of them knew what was happening.

A crash sounded outside as Noal screamed. Judit was through the door like a shot. Annika ran on her heels, wondering what could have happened, if Noal had changed his mind about them being together. When she saw Feric lifting Noal by the neck, she stopped in surprise again.

Judit charged him, but several figures in black raced around him. Their bodies and faces were covered in shroud fabric that concealed bodily dimensions and features. Judit yelled for her ship through her comm and moved to engage one. Another rushed Annika, and she fell into a fighting stance, kicking him in the chin. Annika hopped back, hoping Judit hadn't noticed the move.

The attacker staggered but didn't fall. He didn't have a weapon, couldn't have gotten on the station with one, but how had they gotten there at all? Feric? Someone had to be controlling him.

Another attacker rushed her, and she twisted out of the way. She couldn't let Judit see her defending herself, but she also didn't want to be captured. Had her family organized this? Would she be thwarting them if she got loose? Judit seemed to have herself well in hand with her blunt, brutish, Meridian moves. Feric had hauled Noal out the door. Annika charged after them. Maybe it would look as if she was fleeing.

Judit called after her, and several attackers followed. Annika called for Noal and spotted Feric carrying his limp body. "Feric!"

He turned, but his face bore the same half-lidded look it always did, as if he was two seconds away from sleeping. He couldn't speak. Nocturna had removed his vocal cords long ago, but they spoke in sign language. And she'd learned to read his moods, and he didn't seem angry or upset. Didn't seem fazed at all by what he'd done, and she pictured the worm in his mind, slowly changing him until whoever was controlling him could do this. But who could get so close besides Annika's grandmother?

"Put him down!" she said.

He looked to Noal as if just realizing what he'd done. She stopped out of reach and ducked, letting a pursuer fly past her. He dodged away from Feric, and Annika fended off his blows. "Feric!" Whatever they'd done to him couldn't completely rewrite the programming he'd had since birth. He had to defend her. Even the worm couldn't combat that.

Feric launched her attacker out of the way, and she breathed a sigh of relief. Now all she had to do was convince him to drop Noal, and she could get to the bottom of whatever was happening.

Feric reached out more quickly than she expected and wrapped his meaty hand around her neck. She hit his elbow, dug her fingers into the bundle of nerves near the joint, but nothing decreased the pressure on her windpipe. She stared into his eyes, and something struggled behind his half-lidded, bored expression, something she couldn't fathom, but whether he was struggling to regain the programming he'd always had or resisting the urge to submit to something new, she didn't get to know.

CHAPTER THREE

Judit awoke to the soft white shell of a biobed curving around her like a giant egg. Confusion reigned for half a second before her memory came back. She didn't move, fearing she'd disturb the bed. The seal above her was unbroken, which meant there was still work to be done, but if she was awake, she had to be nearly healed. During the attack on Noal, she'd taken a hard hit to the shoulder, dislocating or fracturing it. Whichever, the pain was now only in her memory.

Feric had attacked Noal. Had he simply betrayed Meridian, or had he betrayed Nocturna as well? Nocturnas were never truthful; that's what she'd been taught, and until she'd met Annika, she'd believed it. And Annika had run after Feric, so his betrayal had caught her by surprise. Judit went over the attackers' appearance and gleaned nothing. She'd gotten a few good strikes in, but she hadn't been able to unmask anyone.

Judit tried to breathe deep and ease her frustration. What awaited her outside the biobed's pearlescent shell? Had security arrived in time to save Annika and Noal? She knew she shouldn't worry about Annika as much, but her feelings tangled together.

The biobed made a soft, sighing sound, and the cover retracted. Judit felt a tug as various IVs left her skin, but there was no pain; the bed took care of that. A hand reached in and eased her upright, and she recognized the medbay on the _Damat_. Dr. Sewell had one hand on her back and another on her shoulder. His silvery hair was shot with red strands, the sign of diluted Meridian blood, but she wanted no one else seeing to her welfare or that of her crew. Having a full Blood doctor would be important to some, but his graduation high in his class mattered most to her; that and he didn't ever fawn over her status, probably didn't know how.

"Easy does it," he said as he helped her stand. "Any pain? Stiffness?"

"No. How long was I under?"

"Beatrice is in the hall pacing the flooring away. She has all the information you need. What I need to know is how you're feeling."

She tried out her shoulders, made a show of stretching. "Fine. Can I have my uniform now?"

He sighed. "On the bench." He turned and fiddled with the bed as she dressed, adjusting its settings for the next patient. Sewell's medbay was cold and austere, all shiny implements and counters, interrupted only by the twin biobeds taking up most of the space. It was small, but the *Damat* only had a crew of twenty. The chosen one didn't need a warship to ferry him around, just a fast ship.

"Take it easy for the next forty-eight hours," Sewell said. "There might be some dizziness, some stomach upset. You had a broken collarbone. Let me know if it twinges. I'll be here pretending you'll take my advice while knowing you won't."

She snorted a laugh though her belly was twisted up in knots. If he heard any hysteria, he didn't mention it. Instead, he gave her a wry smile over his shoulder and waved her out the door.

Beatrice waited in the hall, right where Sewell said she'd be. She sighed heavily when they saw each other, and the dark circles under her eyes said she'd done nothing but worry for at least a night.

"Noal and Annika have been missing just over twenty-four hours," Beatrice said before Judit could ask. "We're heading for Meridian Prime."

Darkness, which was worse: the time she'd been out of commission or the fact that she'd soon have to face her family? "How long until we get there?"

"Let's put it this way; it would be easier to head for the shuttle than the bridge."

With a sigh, Judit changed course for the shuttle bay, shoulders back, ready to face the ire of her grandmother, of the rest of her family. She tried to wrestle down her worry, not wanting to show weakness. If her family thought she was too emotional to head up a rescue mission...

But she wouldn't leave this in the hands of anyone else. The

Damat's sleek little shuttle waited in the small bay, the door open. Judit had to duck all the way to the two seats in the cockpit, and she didn't protest as Beatrice took the copilot's seat, both of them strapping in. Judit passed her hands over the console, and it flared to life under her fingers.

She primed the engines. "Tell the bridge we're ready for launch when we're within range." She could have done it herself, but Beatrice passed the words on. Judit wanted to save all the calmness she could muster for her grandmother.

"We're clear," Beatrice said.

Judit shut the door of the shuttle and heard a hiss as the air reclamators started up, pumping atmosphere through the small space.

"Life support looks good," Beatrice said.

The seat under Judit heated slightly, the whole shuttle growing warmer as it prepared for the cold of space. Judit keyed the huge outer doors of the airlock, and they slid open, a warning light coating the bay with a wash of orange. The maglocks on the landing struts held the shuttle in place as the atmosphere was jettisoned from the bay before the inner airlock doors opened. The floor slid outward, heading for open space, and Judit's stomach did a little lurch. The platform carrying them out always put her in mind of the world's highest diving board, and she had to shake the feeling that if they fell, they'd keep falling forever.

She disengaged the maglocks as the platform stopped, and the shuttle drifted gently forward. Judit guided them free from the *Damat* with little puffs of air before they were in clear space, and she could fire up the engines. They glided away from the *Damat* and turned toward the bright riot of greens, blues, and purples that was Meridian Prime.

How long had it been since she'd been back here? At least two years, as the Meridians counted time. The family preferred to keep Noal moving from place to place. Their ship was their home more than any planet could ever be. Still, seeing the twin moons around the planet's curve and picking out landmarks like the massive Paltross Island or the near perfect oval of the Shuttered Sea coaxed a small smile from her. This was the birthplace, the nerve center of her house, the jewel in the crown of House Meridian.

"I like it, too," Beatrice said. She gave Judit a shy smile. Beatrice's dark curly hair didn't show a hint of white, but she was dark-skinned like most people born on Meridian Prime. She wouldn't be counted as

Blood by most, but she was the best copilot, navigator, and aide that Judit could ever hope for. It didn't hurt that they'd known each other from childhood or that serving Judit and Noal had been all Beatrice ever wanted.

"I'm going to have to talk to them alone, Bea."

Beatrice nodded. "I'll keep the shuttle warm in case you want to make a quick getaway."

Judit chuckled and headed straight for Meridian City, the capital. Uninspired, she knew. Meridian City on Meridian Prime in House Meridian, but she supposed her family didn't want anyone to doubt whose territory they were in. All steel and glass, Meridian City shimmered in the sun, and the light reflecting off the nearby bay gave everything a purple tint.

Judit headed for the city center, submitting all the right codes to land at the dock reserved for high-ranking members of the Blood. At the tallest building, where Meridian ran their empire, she glided to a stop at the open bay. After she landed and stepped out, she submitted to the bot that came forward and gave her a quick DNA scan. Only then did the doors leading into the large government building open.

From the outside, it gleamed like glass, even crystal, but the inner corridors had no windows, even ones made from glassteel. Nocturna spies were keen and everywhere, and there was no way Judit's grandmother would give them a glimpse into the inner workings of Meridian. Instead the walls were a uniform gray, as was the thickly padded floor. Maybe the leaders of Meridian thought the gray kept everyone moving; people might stop to admire bright colors or decorations.

The halls bustled with people, all of them wearing the uniform of the Meridian military, just like hers, with trousers that fit through the hips and flared only slightly above knee-high boots. The jacket fit the same across the shoulders and then flared beneath the belt that secured it around the waist. Gray, of course, the uniforms only differed in the color of the buttons and the stripes around the cuffs. She saw many brass buttons go by, a few gold, but she was the only platinum; only the highest military tier for the woman charged with guarding the chosen one.

Still, it meant nothing, save that it caused people to scramble out of her way. In the history of her house, she was unique. She had the highest honor of being guardian of the chosen one, but she made no decisions for the house or its people. Every other person she saw, no matter their tier, had stripes at the cuffs of their uniform, white against the gray denoting their rank within their tier, their level of responsibility within the military. Her sleeves had none. It used to make her angry, as if the military was saying she wasn't really one of them, but she supposed she deserved it today. She'd had one job to do, and she'd failed.

The command hub was another riot of activity, a sea of pale heads bent over consoles or talking to the spectral faces of holo displays. Many held their hands to their ears to better hear the comm signals in their heads. Judit caught snatches of code as she weaved through the room. Short-range transmissions could be made secret, but any long-range messages had to be sent over the same gates that enabled ships to fold space and travel thousands of light-years. Any such transmission could be intercepted, and any code could be cracked, though they often worked for the short term. Like every other house, Meridian only sent long-range transmissions that they knew would be cracked. And like every other house, they had computers and people whose only task was to listen to what everyone else was saying.

And Judit wished all of them were talking about Noal and Annika and how they were alive and safe and waiting for her to come get them. She reached the central console where her grandmother was speaking with a holo projection of Noal's mother. Judit took a deep breath then cleared her throat.

Her grandmother turned, and her eyes bored into Judit's, though her face was as calm and composed as ever. "Here she is now," Grandmother said in the latest code. "Judit, speak to your aunt Cecily."

Noal's mother switched her gaze to Judit. Like all holos, hers had a green cast, making her seem alien. And unlike Grandmother, her brows were drawn in anger, and Judit could feel her rage through the light-years that separated them. "Aunt Cecily, I apologize—"

"We need your assessment, not your apology," Cecily said. "Do you know who it was?"

"I don't…I've been in a biobed and have yet to study—"

Her grandmother waved her away, the barest hint of annoyance flickering across her features.

"Find them," Cecily said, inclining her head. At least she had the specter of politeness. With her son raised apart from her, Judit wondered if she was worried for him or simply concerned for the family, as they were all supposed to be.

"Your parents are in my office," Grandmother said.

Judit's stomach dropped even further. Just what she needed. She usually looked forward to seeing them. Well, to seeing her father, but why did they have to come now? But the answer was simple. They couldn't share what they knew over the comm, so they had to do it in person. Her grandmother probably had ships streaking toward every listening post and mining operation, desperate to compile whatever information they could. Judit straightened her shoulders as she headed toward the office, ready to hear whatever they had to say. She'd do whatever she could to find Annika and Noal, even if it meant being berated by everyone in Meridian.

As she passed the small door into her grandmother's personal office, leaving the noise of the command hub behind her, she let out a breath. Calm, looking calm was important. Behind the desk, a projected image gave the appearance of a window, a live feed of the outside. The sun was slanting down over the bay, turning the sea to silver and gold.

Her parents rose from the sleek black couch next to Grandmother's desk, and Judit looked as she always did for the resemblances between them and her, tiny markers of who they really were, but so many of the Blood shared so many features. Her mother had the silvery white Meridian hair and the dark eyes, but Judit saw her own chin in the slope of her father's jaw. She'd gotten his broader shoulders and sense of humor. His hair was a deep copper, and she'd always admired him for not dying it to match the Meridian Blood. His green eyes smiled at her, but her mother was as calm and put together as ever in her military uniform.

"We've spoken to Nocturna," Judit's mother said. "They deny responsibility."

Judit nodded. She leaned on her grandmother's desk, and her parents resumed their seats. "Annika seemed surprised by her guardian's actions," Judit said. "And it seemed opportunistic."

"What happened?" her mother asked. "The scans showed you weren't in the room when the attack began."

"If you've seen the scans, you know what happened. I was…in the washroom."

Her father shook his head. "Jude, it's not your fault."

Judit fought a blush even though they wouldn't see it. With the rush she'd been in upon waking, she hadn't had time to think of the washroom, to think of Annika gliding toward her with unashamed lust. "I should have been there, but Noal told me Annika needed help."

"Then you should have let her guardian help her," her mother said. "She is not your responsibility."

Judit curled her hand into a fist. "They're going to be married. How can she not be my responsibility if she's Noal's wife?"

"She's not Meridian Blood," her mother said.

Judit thought she saw a flicker of pain cross her father's face. He wasn't Meridian Blood, either. If their lives were in danger, who would the guards rescue first? But Noal and Annika were different. They were joining their houses. She stayed quiet, knowing that would never truly matter to most Meridians. To them, people who weren't their own Blood could be replaced.

"How did they escape the security net?" Judit asked.

Her father sat forward. "The shuttle they used had Meridian codes, but when it pulled away, the exit codes weren't right. The drones went into action with our ships not far behind. We shut down the nearest gate, but they engaged an antimatter drive."

Hope bloomed. "Then they should still be close enough to track!"

"We're working on it," her mother said. "They covered their tracks well, using transmission shadows, keeping close to stars so they're harder to see. It's Nocturna trickery at its finest."

"Why would the Nocturnas kidnap their own heir?" Judit asked. Word would spread far faster than any ship. People would be looking for them halfway across the galaxy if not all the way on the other side. "I need to join the search."

"One moment, Judit," her mother said.

"The longer I sit here—"

"Your grandmother wants a word."

And Judit knew what that word would be. She braced herself for more recriminations, for ways she could and should have handled things differently. Her grandmother had always firmly believed that one had to be constantly criticized if one were to better herself.

Judit stood before the door opened. Without looking at anyone,

Grandmother took a seat behind her desk and gestured to the chair in front of it, letting her eyes fall with a grimace on the spot where Judit had rested before. Judit sighed and sat in the chair. She didn't know if her grandmother had been watching the feed from this office, or if she'd left some invisible butt mark that only her grandmother could see.

Her grandmother fixed her with a steely silver gaze. Eyes that matched Meridian hair were rare but happened occasionally. It was said to be a harbinger of great things. Judit did her best not to squirm under her grandmother's gaze, but the old woman could unnerve a brick.

"Your cousin," she said at last.

Judit waited for more, tales of Noal's importance, how he must be found, but nothing came. Would she allow Judit to take part in the search, even lead it, or was Judit to be punished by having to stay behind? Maybe she wouldn't even be a guardian anymore. Would they let her roam the halls in her uniform with no rank, trusted by no one?

She had to head that possibility off. "Grandmother, please, I can find them, him—"

"Finding him will not be your responsibility."

Judit's heart sank, but she was already making plans. No matter what backwater they assigned her to, her crew was still loyal. She would send them a message; they could retrieve her, and then go looking on their own.

But now she had to put up at least a show of a fight. "I'm best equipped—"

"You will lead the attack on House Nocturna."

Judit blinked several times. "We don't know that House Nocturna is behind the kidnapping. And we can't restart the war! The other houses will destroy us."

"The other houses care only that there is peace. With all of Nocturna dead, there will be peace. That is the job of the chosen one."

"His kidnapping will bring peace through destruction?"

"You are the chosen one, Judit," her mother said. "You always have been."

Judit stared at her, the words echoing in her head, but she didn't believe them, could barely hear them. "What?"

Her grandmother drummed her fingers on the chair, casting one look toward Judit's mother before her eyes rested on Judit again. "We knew this day was coming. We knew Nocturna wouldn't honor their agreement. You and Noal were born hours from each other, but you were the one born first. We hid that from Nocturna because we knew they would betray us."

Judit sat back heavily in her chair. She was the chosen one? Were they lying? But they didn't lie. Nocturnas lied. She shook her head, trying to get a grip. "You knew this would happen?"

"Something like it. We've been building a fleet in secret, waiting." She had a small smile lingering on her lips. Her grandmother loved nothing better than a good campaign. "And you will lead them as the chosen one."

Judit swallowed past the lump in her throat. "And Annika? Is she the real Nocturna heir?"

Grandmother shrugged. "We will retrieve Noal, and if the Nocturna is still alive, we may take her also. But first, we will punish her house for behaving as we always knew they would." She tilted her head. "And so the prophecy will be fulfilled. You will bring us peace by seeing Nocturna destroyed."

Before Judit could stutter any more questions, her father cleared his throat. "She is a Nocturna, Judit. She was probably privy to this plan all along."

"No! She was surprised. She ran after Noal—"

Her grandmother waved a hand. "In the end, it doesn't matter."

"So, while the galaxy looks for Annika and Noal, you want me to take the fleet and destroy Nocturna?" So many deaths, billions of them. How could they?

"It's your destiny, Judit. Predicted by the hierophants, seconded by so many other houses. The chosen one will bring a final end to the war, and what could be more final than Nocturna's destruction?"

"Marriage! We're supposed to bring about peace with a marriage, not another war!"

Before her grandmother could respond, her mother sighed loudly. "We only planned for Nocturnas acting like Nocturnas. Just because we knew this would happen doesn't mean we caused it."

The room started to spin, and Judit had to curl her hands into fists to still it. She wondered if they would have ever let any marriage take place. If this hadn't happened, would they have found some other excuse to launch their secret fleet? If she really was the chosen one, and they'd hidden her from the start, they must have been planning to use her even if Nocturna had gone along with the marriage.

But Feric had attacked both Noal and his charge instead. But why would Nocturna create their own destruction this way? They had to know Meridian would come for them.

And she was the chosen one. All her life, it had been her. What did that make Noal? A decoy? And she could have been with Annika all this time? The questions added to the mishmash of feelings, and she felt as if she was floating above the floor with no way down.

Her grandmother and parents spoke of plans to spread rumors, to make sure Nocturna was actively involved in the search so they'd be unprepared for an attack. They wanted as many Nocturna ships as possible out of the way, but speed was of the essence. Once the fleet started to assemble, Nocturna would know. They would prepare defenses, which was why Judit had to hit Nocturna while they were scrambling. With everyone gathered for the wedding, maybe they could get many Nocturna Bloods in one sweep.

"Won't they be thinking the same?" Judit asked, hearing the breathlessness in her voice. "Aren't you afraid they're already on their way?"

"We've been preparing defenses, too," her grandmother said. "And no doubt Nocturna's spies will know that. However, our spies, even those at the deepest level, report no extra defenses on Nocturna's part."

She wondered if that deepest level meant Feric. Maybe this had all been Meridian's idea. But she couldn't dwell on that. She kept circling back to the fact that she was the chosen one. All the heartache she'd been through, the sleepless nights she'd had thinking about Noal and Annika, knowing she and Annika could never be together; they'd all been for nothing. All her training had been for nothing.

Well, not for nothing. Her family was counting on her to kill billions of people. Or were they? Maybe they only wanted a figurehead because of a stupid prophecy they were paying lip service to. Maybe they laughed at a destiny she'd always felt hamstrung by.

Her grandmother gestured toward the washroom. "Take a moment and compose yourself, Judit. Then get back to your ship. It's time you were gone."

She staggered to the washroom. She didn't dare contact Beatrice, not yet, but plans were trying to form in her mind. Chosen ones didn't matter. Prophecies didn't matter. Only one thing was certain: Noal and Annika hadn't kidnapped themselves. They were counting on her.

After she'd splashed some water on her face, Judit walked out of her grandmother's office without another word. What was there to say? Leaden steps carried her back to the shuttle bay, and once she was behind closed doors, she cut any of the feeds inside the shuttle, leaving Beatrice and her in privacy.

Beatrice watched in silence, and as they pulled out of the dock, she said, "What's up?"

"We're off to attack Nocturna."

Beatrice nodded slowly, but her expression was filled with questions.

"Has the *Damat* been looking for Noal and Annika while I was talking to my grandmother?"

"As much as we can, but so far, nothing." Beatrice looked to the controls of the shuttle. "Do you want me to fly?"

Ashamed that her hands were too shaky, Judit nodded. They sped back to the *Damat*, and the coordinates for the rally point were waiting for them. A few other ships from Meridian Prime cruised with them toward the nearest transmission gate. At other gates, more ships were lined up, waiting for Judit to lead them into battle. How many captains were ready to take her place if she gave the order to stand down? But no one could replace her. She was the chosen one, and only she could lead the Meridians to peace. They all believed it, even her grandmother, or the fleet would have already launched.

At his console on the bridge, Lieutenant Roberts frowned over his data, his dark eyes wide with questions.

"What is it, Roberts?" Judit asked, looking over his shoulder.

"I've been going over the data from the ship that took the heirs, Boss, and well, I don't want to disagree with the Blood."

"I won't tell if you won't."

He smiled slightly. "If my calculations are correct, Nocturna can't be the kidnappers. These engine signatures are all wrong. These trajectories are wrong. Even the possible destinations. It had to have been someone else. The math doesn't lie."

Annika and Noal in unknown hands. No wonder Judit's

grandmother had hurried her so much. She knew. And other people would be analyzing the same data. Grandmother had to know Judit's crew would figure it out, but maybe she thought her granddaughter would be so focused on her mission that she wouldn't bother. Or maybe Grandmother thought her completely incompetent and wanted Nocturna destroyed before anyone had the chance to find out that Nocturna wasn't responsible. Which meant Annika was in as much danger as Noal. They couldn't wait until after a full-scale attack. What could happen to them in the meantime?

"Bea, tell the fleet to hang back. We're going through first. What's your math say about the trail, Roberts?"

He squinted at his data again, pointing at a set of coordinates. "Best place to start is here, Boss."

"Send that data to the gate, and then use our command codes to shut it down behind us."

Beatrice glanced at her. "The family will have it up again in no time, Jude."

"By then we'll be long gone." And once her grandmother figured out where she went, no one would follow. They'd be too busy trying to figure out another way to wage their war.

CHAPTER FOUR

Consciousness came back with a snap, but Annika forced herself to remain still, to listen and feel. The surface under her was soft, but she felt nothing against her sides, head, or feet. Probably a mattress rather than a sofa or any other piece of furniture. Slight heat coming from her left side told her she wasn't alone, but whoever it was wasn't moving, either. By the faint odor of cologne...Noal. She heard the hum of air reclamators and smelled a slight tang of antiseptic. Possibly a medbay, though she didn't hear the sound of biobeds or other equipment. A slight vibration carried through the bed, humming ever so slightly in the surrounding walls. They were aboard a ship.

Ama would tell her to stay cautious. She heard nothing else, no one shifting around, but even if they were alone, there could be cameras or other sensors. She flexed the muscles in her calves and back. She was wearing clothing, but not the dress she'd been taken in. The feel and pull of it indicated some kind of bodysuit with a tighter fit. Whoever had taken her probably feared a concealed weapon in her own clothing. They were prepared, but they couldn't know everything she could do; not even her grandmother knew *everything*.

Time to put on a show.

She rolled her head to and fro, moaning and frowning in mock pain and confusion. She sat up slowly, squinting at her surroundings and blinking in what she hoped passed for surprise.

They'd taken pains to make a comfortable room, at least. She and Noal lay side by side on a bed, both of them dressed in soft jumpsuits of black fabric, something lightweight that they'd have a hard time making a weapon out of, though she suspected her captors considered that a dubious possibility. Her family would have known she didn't need a weapon.

The mattress underneath them was bare, a solid piece of foam. All the other furniture had the sheen of plastic, and she noticed bolts securing it to the floor. She looked to Noal and shook him as a panicked person might. He'd be a helpful distraction and make whoever was watching them have to look in two directions at once.

He snored loudly then smacked his lips before sitting up, and either he was a far better actor than she could ever hope to be, or his surprise was genuine. "Where…" He launched off the bed and slipped, turning a full circle before looking at her with wide eyes. "Your guardian attacked me! Where are we? Where is Judit?"

"I don't know," she said, making her eyes fill with tears. "Feric grabbed you, and I ran after." She blinked so the tears would dribble down her cheeks. "Judit was fighting, and I told Feric to let you go!"

His face softened, and he approached the bed gently. "I'm sorry, Annika. Don't cry. You didn't know?"

"Of course not! Poor Feric. He had to have been…manipulated in some way, but by whom?"

Together, they looked around. She didn't recognize anything from their surroundings, but maybe he would. He tiptoed through the room and tried the door controls, but of course, it didn't budge.

He knocked on the metal surface and called, "Hello?" It almost made her chuckle, and she knew she would have had a very hard time doing anything nasty to him if all had gone according to plan. And then, even while not knowing anything about where they were or what was happening, a sense of relief washed over her.

Noal hugged his elbows. "There's no window, but I can feel the engines through my feet, so I think we're on a ship."

She nodded slowly, and her estimation for him went up a notch. She'd half expected him to collapse into a puddle and cry his eyes out, but maybe that was still her grandmother talking.

"Keep calm, and you will not be harmed," a female voice said over a hidden speaker.

"Who are you?" Noal called.

The voice fell silent. If their kidnappers needed leverage, the hostages needed to remain alive and in one piece, at least until they'd outlived their usefulness. Annika didn't intend to let things get that far.

She looked to Noal and saw the complication there. To escape, she'd have to betray some of her skills. Of course, if this was her family at work, the marriage was probably out the window, and she could show Noal who she really was. But if the kidnapping wasn't the work of Nocturna, the marriage might still continue.

Ama's wisdom was silent on the matter. Of all the times she'd had Annika fight her way out of various situations, there'd never been anyone she cared about with her. But Ama didn't expect her to care about anyone. When she'd first met Noal and Judit, Annika hadn't anticipated coming to care for them, either. But Noal had been open and friendly, far different from anyone Annika had ever met.

At first, Annika had only noticed Judit's attractiveness, but their second meeting had come after a particularly brutal training session. Annika had been clumsy, leaving an opening, and Ama had broken her rib. Leaving it broken for a day was her punishment, and though she'd tried to hide it, her pain had shown through her expression.

She'd told Noal and Judit she'd fallen, that she didn't want to admit her clumsiness to her doctor. They'd argued with her, but when she was adamant, Judit had tenderly bound her ribs, saying she'd learned how in battlefield training. Her hands had been steady and sure. Even with the pain, each time Judit's hands had grazed the bare flesh beneath Annika's bra, little jolts of flame shot through her. When Judit had finished binding the ribs, her gaze traveled up Annika's body as if she'd been fighting the urge to let her eyes wander and had finally lost. When their eyes met, Judit had looked away quickly, but Annika had seen the desire there.

Noal had told her silly jokes to make her smile, and she'd thought, how could she hate these two enough to destroy them? But as her grandmother often reminded her, it wasn't about hate. It was simply necessity.

In the room now, Annika looked at Noal and grinned. Escaping was also a necessity and now an opportunity as well. She would save herself *and* Noal. And if her family didn't like it, well, they should have guarded her better or filled her in on this part of the plan.

Noal stared at her. "What is it? Have you recognized something?" He swallowed. "Please don't tell me you've gone crazy. I don't think I can handle that."

If the door wouldn't open, Ama would get someone to open it for her. Annika crossed to the door and examined it. Someone would have to come in to give them food and let them out to use the washroom, but she didn't want to wait. Always better to catch people off guard.

She turned to Noal. "I'm sorry. I'm afraid I have gone crazy."

He took a step toward her, reaching out. "Please, don't worry. I'm sure our—"

When he was within reach, she slapped him. He staggered back, grabbing his cheek, and she pounced, trying to seem unskilled. It was harder than she thought. He left so many openings, she could have killed him six ways over. She wanted to whisper that she was sorry, but she didn't know how good the listening devices were. He squirmed in her grip, crying out for her to stop, but she persisted, yelling things like, "This is all your fault," and, "Your family is behind this!"

She scratched and bit him, going for pain without damage, trying to make him cry out. The voice came over the speaker again, repeating its message for calm, but it seemed less sure of itself.

When the door hissed open, Annika kept up her attack as she sneaked a look. Nice, they'd only sent two. They were dressed in the same formfitting black with the hoods, still trying to escape detection. They came on slowly, no doubt thinking about some of her moves from before. What they couldn't have known was that she'd been pulling her punches then, too.

She stood and lashed out with a foot, catching one in the solar plexus. The other danced back, brandishing a shock stick. Oh good, they'd brought her a weapon. Ama would have been sickened by them.

With a quick apology, she threw Noal at the one with the shock stick, and they fell together in a heap, their bodies keeping the door from closing.

Annika knelt and swept the legs from the injured one, then delivered a swift kick across his neck to finish him. She slid across the floor as the other was trying to disentangle himself from Noal, whose glazed eyes said he'd been hit with the shock stick. She planted both heels in the kidnapper's hood, and his head rocked back. She neatly flicked the shock stick from his grasp and leveled it against his chest until he stopped twitching.

Annika stood and pulled Noal to his feet. "What happened?" he asked, his voice a slur. "Why did you—"

"Keep moving." She hurried into the hall. "More will be coming."

As she hurried them down the smooth, curved hallway, she scanned the walls for maintenance hatches, any clue as to what part of the ship they were in. Conduits ran along one side of the wall. They were either near the engines, or it was a smaller ship. Maybe both.

"Why did you... Did you kill them?" Noal asked.

Her grandmother's voice demanded she leave him, but she told it to keep quiet. "Better them than us." She followed a line of conduits to a hatch in the wall and eased it open.

"What are you doing?" Noal asked, his voice getting steadier by the moment.

She scanned the wires and chips inside. "Most ships are designed more or less the same, did you know that?" She was mostly talking to herself, but maybe it would keep him from asking so many questions. "It makes them easier to repair but also easier to sabotage, but there's nothing to help us here." She looked up and down the hall. "We have to be near the engines. Come on." She hurried him down a bend in the hallway.

"We're going to sabotage the engines?" he asked.

"No, better to take the ship if we can. Though we have to make ourselves as hard to catch as possible." They reached a small door marked Environmental Controls. "Perfect." And it wasn't even locked. If her family had hired this ship to kidnap her, they needed to demand a refund.

She hurried inside a room packed with machinery and didn't stop until she found the mechanism that controlled the artificial gravity. There was no time to sort out wiring, and she had nothing to cut with anyway. She jammed the shock stick into the tangle. "Ready to be a pain in the ass?"

He stared at her confusedly, and she resisted the urge to roll her eyes. She turned the shock stick on before running from the room, hauling Noal with her.

The shock stick hummed for a moment before the whole mechanism began to groan, and smoke leaked from the open mouth of the door. A shudder passed through the ship, and the sound of popping wires and the smell of burning electrics filled the corridor before a *thunk* sounded around them.

Annika pressed herself and Noal against the wall before the gravity gave way, and they began to float, their hair drifting. Noal struggled impotently, and she let him go. A thump came from a connecting corridor before a door hissed open, and two guards drifted on the other side where they'd bounced off the door.

"Stay here," Annika said. The way Noal was flailing, it didn't seem as if he had much choice.

She turned to the guards. They may have searched her for weapons, but they hadn't found the last gift Annika's mother had given her, a weapon no search or scanner could detect. Annika pressed along the inside of her forearm, massaging until the thin, bone stiletto slipped through the pocket of skin created to carry it. A few drops of blood floated free, and she rolled her sleeve over the tiny cut. Stiletto in hand, she braced her feet against the wall, made sure of the angle, and pushed toward the guards.

These weren't wearing hoods. Maybe they'd been in too much of a hurry to put them on. A man and a woman, they didn't have the specific hair or eye colors of any of the larger houses. One wriggled in the air while the other floated calmly, looking to the wall, probably waiting for the chance to either grab hold or push off, but neither chance would come.

Annika flew for the flailing one. She moved her head away from his wildly swinging arm and dragged the slender stiletto across his throat. As sharp as the knife was, the contact still sent her to the side as his body floated away from her, trailing drops of blood. She shifted and tucked so her legs would be beneath her.

The female guard was trying to keep Annika in view as she reached the wall and scrabbled for something to grab hold of. As she rotated, she fumbled with a pouch on the side of her trousers and pulled a small pistol, one of the ship designs that fired sonic force, designed to damage organics but not harm anything else. To shield against such a shot, a person had to take cover behind thick metal or plastic, and a shot that landed close could still wound.

Annika came at the guard fast, trying to reach her before she could fire, but she pulled the trigger wildly, the deep thrumming sound of the pistol filling the small space. Down the hall, Noal yelped, and Annika gritted her teeth, resisting the urge to look. She grabbed one of the woman's legs and stabbed her behind the knee.

The guard shrieked, pushing off from the wall and taking Annika with her. Annika pulled up the guard's body, jammed the stiletto in her neck, and pulled it free in one smooth motion. She plucked the pistol from the air and turned back. "Noal, are you all right?"

"Bruised. It came...really close."

The bodies drifted away, and Annika had to wait to make contact with another surface before she could push back to Noal. Except for the wild shot, the whole attack had gone like clockwork. She could almost see Ama's small smile of approval.

Noal had ceased struggling and stared at her, his jaw slack, and one hand held to his arm. When their eyes met, his expression turned tightened, panicked, and she knew he'd seen her killing look: the blank expression she remembered from her own training videos. She smiled softly, trying to look like herself again. She hadn't always pretended with him and Judit. Even with all the lies, she'd been able to relax now and again; he'd seen the real her, though she supposed her killing look was another part of her, too. She just had a few...extra facets to her personality.

Now, if she could only make *him* see that. "It's all right, Noal," she said softly. "I'm not going to hurt you." She gestured at his arm. "Want me to take a look?"

He swallowed and stared at her with naked fear. "You killed them."

She decided on half a truth. The whole one would only make things more complicated. "All my life, I've secretly trained as a guardian. My family thought it best that I be able to protect myself and you if necessary." She put on a curious look. "Your family didn't teach you the same?"

He shook his head but seemed a little less panicked. He let her drift close and examine the fast-forming bruise on his arm. Any closer, and the shot would have taken his skin off. If it had hit him directly, it would have turned the whole arm into ruins.

"You really think we can escape?" he asked.

She nodded, smiling wider. "I don't know how we got into this situation, but I'm going to get us out."

His face relaxed a little more. "Did your family suspect your guardian might turn on you?"

She swallowed. That still stung. But she had no real answers. "My family doesn't trust anyone."

Now his face fell, and she saw the same sympathy as when he'd discovered her broken rib. "You can trust me," he said. "And you can trust Judit. I'm sure she's looking for us."

And that was probably true. Maybe her family was also searching, but if they were, it was only so they could find a reason to go to war with Meridian again. Somewhere out in the galaxy, maybe her mother would look for her if anyone bothered to tell her that her daughter was missing. But according to Ama, her mother wouldn't care at all.

"We need to find the bridge," she said. "If we can't take the ship, we'll find an escape pod or shuttle."

He nodded, though he still looked cautious. They floated along the corridors, searching for the bridge. There didn't seem to be many people, but Annika kept herself ahead of Noal, peeking through each door. They passed a large room full of cargo containers secured to the floor by maglocks. A pressure suit hung against the wall, and the window of an airlock gleamed beyond.

Annika pushed inside. "Stay near the door." She drifted to the window and looked out; the light of a nearby planet filled the airlock with a blue glow. She didn't recognize the planet, but she supposed it was a good sign. If it was inhabited, maybe she could signal.

"I'm getting a little…light-headed," Noal said.

She'd noticed the same feeling. "Someone's probably fiddling with the life support, trying to make us pass out."

"Or it happened when you shoved a shock stick into random bits of the ship."

She gave him a wry look. "It's my first time crippling a ship. I think that deserves a little slack." Well, it was her first time doing it for real. But her grandmother wouldn't have given her any slack, either.

He looked as if he didn't believe her. Or maybe he resented the fact that she'd kept such a large secret from him. Well, if he resented that, he was going to hate the truth.

If he ever heard it.

"We need to do something about the air, and I don't know how to fix the ship even if I'm the one who broke it." And there was only one pressure suit. She dug inside a nearby locker and found an emergency canister of air and a mask.

She smiled at Noal before she looked to the cargo containers again. He'd already been wounded, and she suspected that the reason she hadn't seen any other members of the crew was because they were guarding the bridge. That was going to be a hard fight.

She passed Noal the emergency canister then donned the suit herself. "Look, Noal..."

"I'm not staying here and waiting," he said, his voice muffled through the mask.

She breathed a laugh. "I'm not going to leave you behind." The suit was made for cold, low atmosphere environments rather than open space, but it would do aboard the ship. The guards wouldn't be able to turn off the temperature controls without killing themselves, too. "But it's going to be dangerous."

He stayed near the door, watching her with wide eyes.

"And these pistols, they only hurt organic matter, so if you had some kind of shield—"

"You want me to get in the crate, don't you?" he asked flatly.

"It would be safer." And better he get in now than she have to stuff his injured body in later. Maybe if he knew more about the stakes. "You've already seen that a pistol shot won't be stopped by clothing, even a pressure suit. The pulse only came near you, and it left a bruise. It can turn a body to liquid. The crate is thick enough to stop it."

"But..." His mouth worked, and he seemed to despair. "I'm only fit to be cargo?"

She slid a gloved hand along the crate as if debuting it in a showroom. "Once I close the lid, I can fill in the empty spaces with foam. Then you'll be cushioned and safe—"

"And stuffed in a crate."

"Just until I take the ship."

He muttered something about being useless but drifted toward the crate, staring at it. She resisted the urge to stuff him in even as Ama's voice urged her again to leave him behind. He looked from the crate to her and back again, and she knew he was weighing whether or not to trust her.

"I know that finding out about my skills is a shock," she said. "But frankly, I'm shocked your family didn't teach you the same."

"We're not duplicitous and underhanded," he said.

She couldn't even be offended. It was true for her family and probably for his. He'd realize that someday. "If you've got any special skills you're keeping in reserve, now is the time to tell me."

He chuckled, but it didn't have much humor in it. "I'm a pretty good cook."

"You'll have to make me something when we get out of here."

With a grimace, he climbed into the crate. "And apparently I'm good at being cargo."

Annika engaged her suit's magboots and steadied him as he climbed inside. Before she closed the lid, he pressed her gloved fingers. "Thank you for helping me."

She smiled, oddly touched. "You're welcome. Watch your head."

She shut the lid of the crate, filled it with the foam so he wouldn't be jostled around, and disengaged its maglocks. She pushed it into the corridor and then disengaged her boots so she could float after him. Around the bend of a corridor from the airlock, she spotted a pair of lift doors, but when she pressed the panel, it stayed dark, no doubt designed to shut down while the gravity was off.

The lightweight doors slid open when she pulled on them, and she spotted the dark top of the lift car one floor below, blocking that way. There were two more floors above. She drifted upward, pushing the crate to the highest doors and prying them apart. The hallway dead-ended to her left and curved slightly to the right. She pushed ahead, keeping behind the crate. She'd stowed her stiletto and pistol, but when she spotted a contingent of five guards waiting at the other end of the hall, she ducked back, secured the crate against the wall, and drew the pistol.

These guards hovered in front of a large closed door. All wore pressure suits, and she couldn't tell one from another save that two held shock sticks and one a pistol. The others might be armed, but she hadn't been able to tell with a single look.

"Leave the crate and come forward," one called. "We'll put you back in holding. No one needs to get hurt."

She begged to differ, but she said nothing. If she poked her head out, the one with the pistol would have a clear line. And she couldn't get to him fast enough to prevent a shot. She looked to the crate. What was it she'd said to Noal about a shield? It was thick enough to protect them both.

"Hold on, Noal." She put the pistol away, engaged her boots, and clung to the wall. Bending at the knees, she pointed the crate down the hall. When she shoved forward, disengaging her boots at the last minute, she rocketed toward the opposite wall and then pushed off that, the crate between her and the guards. She heard them cry out, voices echoing weirdly through their speakers. The pistol fired, a hollow *whomp* sound, but the shot connected harmlessly with the crate.

Annika released the crate as it crashed into the guards. She caught the back of a guard as he floated past, drew her stiletto, and slashed the hose leading from his air tank to his helmet. The hissing release of air spun him down the corridor behind her. She engaged her magboots and put one foot near the closed door. With her other foot, she kicked another guard, sending him crashing into the wall. The crate knocked into the door and floated her way. She grabbed it, using it to batter two other guards. The last was working to get the door open, and she ignored him, letting his panic get her into the place she most wanted to go. She drew her pistol and shot the one she'd kicked. As one of the others went for his own pistol, she shot him, too, but the last drifted behind the crate.

The one on the door opened it and hauled himself inside. She flung the crate after him, pushing him inside faster, arms flailing as he tried to catch hold of nothing. The last guard caught her leg and yanked, drawing himself closer. He wrestled the pistol from her grasp, and she let it go, slipping her stiletto into his heart.

Inside the now open room, someone in a pressure suit rose from a control console. Annika flicked her stiletto, nicking the suit and sending its occupant careening across the room. She launched toward the crate and secured it to the floor before engaging her boots and pulling the last guard down to her. Stunned, he barely put up a fight as she jerked his helmet off, kneed him into the wall and rammed an open palm into his chin, bouncing his head off steel. He slumped. Only one left, and that one would provide the answers she needed.

Annika reclaimed her stiletto and drifted to the console. She turned the atmosphere back up as the woman in the pressure suit struggled to get her helmet off. She gasped in the thin air, but she wouldn't suffocate, not with everything returning back to normal. Annika eyed her for weapons. When she saw none, she opened the lid of the crate so Noal could struggle out.

The woman in the pressure suit engaged her magboots and clung to the wall, bending at the knees so she could watch Annika and Noal warily.

"Are you the one who told us we wouldn't be harmed?" Annika asked.

The woman swallowed. Her skin was pale, and her curly hair had a bright red sheen. That and golden eyes made her House Flavio. Nocturna used them as occasional allies. But so did other people.

"If I told you the same thing," Annika said, "would you believe me as much as I believed you?"

"I suppose it wouldn't matter if I told you this was just a job." It was the same voice as the one over the speakers, rich and melodious.

"If it was personal, at least I could understand." Annika walked toward her slowly, magboots clunking. "You're Flavio Blood."

Noal gasped, and the Flavio glanced at him but didn't confirm or deny. "I don't have any orders to harm you," she said instead.

"Like the dark you don't," Annika said. "If you're trying to start a war, it'll be a lot more convincing with dead bodies rather than kidnapped ones. You were waiting for the right moment. So, when is it?"

"Will telling you keep me alive?"

Probably not, but she didn't want to say so. "I never throw away anything useful."

The Flavio glanced at the door as if she might bolt. "I don't know who hired us."

Annika nodded. She'd guessed that.

"There was supposed to be a signal, and we were supposed to drop you off. We only woke you because…"

Annika took a deep, slow breath. They were supposed to be asleep for the journey, passed out in their plastic honeymoon suite. That explained a lot. "Because?"

Another swallow, and the skin around her eyes tightened.

"Because you were going to sell us to someone else? No, you would have kept us asleep for that, too. You were going to reason with us, see if you could get us to buy our way out?"

"If that deal's still on," Noal said, "Meridian will pay."

Annika didn't look at him. She'd almost forgotten he was there. The Flavio didn't look at him, either.

"No, that's not it," Annika said, still advancing. "You wanted us awake because…"

"Someone wanted to meet you." She turned for the door again, her magboots coming off the wall.

Annika sprang, leading with her stiletto. She banged into the Flavio, slamming her against the bulkhead. The Flavio cried out as her ankles bent unnaturally. Annika engaged her own boots and pressed down on top of her, knife to her throat.

"Who?" Annika said, voice still calm, but the Flavio had gone limp. Annika grabbed her face, thinking the pain had made her pass out, but her eyes were glazed over, the control panel on her suit flashing red as it detected no vitals.

Annika straightened. "Shit."

Noal gaped at her. "You killed her before she could say!"

"No, I didn't."

"Then what the dark happened?" Noal asked, his face horrified.

"Suicide maybe, or some countermeasure of her house, something that reacts to her vitals." She looked around the room. "Or we're being monitored from offsite." She disengaged her boots and floated to the control panel again. "Whatever it is, we need to get off this ship before whoever wants to meet us gets here."

"Who do you think it is?"

She'd discounted her family because they'd have known she could escape from this feeble attempt, but if the Flavio was supposed to keep her asleep, the bet for Nocturna was back on. They would have kept her asleep until it was more useful to have her as a corpse, then they would have arranged whatever tableau suited them, something pinning the deaths on Meridian. When Nocturna decided to frame someone, they always did an excellent job.

Annika hovered over the comm, wondering if she dared contact her family. It would be nice to hear from Ama's own lips that she planned to sacrifice the Nocturna heir for the chance to destroy Meridian. It was her life's work, after all.

Instead, Annika set up a repeating signal, a distress call seeded with Meridian codes, a clue for Judit, but they couldn't sit around waiting for her. A few quick scans reported that the planet below was inhospitable, but there was a station close by, though this ship was too big to dock there. Annika keyed in a message, again using Meridian codes, telling Judit where they'd gone. They were old codes, well changed by now, but it would give Judit a lead, and if someone else found this ship first, maybe it would slow them down long enough for Judit to catch them.

"Come on, Noal. There's a shuttle below. We need to get out of here."

"What about the other guards?"

She'd already done a scan. The two of them were the only moving things on the ship, but as he stared at her, she didn't know how to put it into words. "They won't be a problem."

He stared at the Flavio as he nodded slowly. His family really had sheltered him. Maybe they'd always known the marriage plan would fall apart. They would have come up with some ham-fisted way to either derail it or overreact to something Nocturna had done. They'd probably never considered the fact that he would actually lead their house one day, so they'd raised him as nothing more than a sacrificial lamb. Ama would have been appalled.

Chapter Five

G oing through the transmitter gates always made Judit feel squashed. In reality, the ship wasn't "going" anywhere. A ship entered the gate, and space folded around them, transmitting them to another gate within the first gate's range. If they wanted to go farther, they had to transmit again from the new gate. Still, it took only seconds. Even with antimatter drives, such distances would have otherwise taken hundreds of years, thousands if one had to actually travel from one side of the galaxy to the other.

Judit was just thankful she'd never had to go near the outer rims. She stuck to the well-maintained gates. She'd heard there were some in the outer reaches that were so poorly kept, it was a wonder they went anywhere, and then not exactly where the crew wanted to go.

Roberts bent over his console, always the first to recover from the mild confusion that came with gate travel. Judit knew he was looking through his data, so she suppressed the urge to prod him. She couldn't hurry him along even if her family might be right behind her once they'd figured out what she'd done. She didn't think they'd launch the attack on Nocturna. Even if her grandmother wasn't the greatest believer in the hierophant prophecies, if the fleet was decimated, everyone in Meridian would think it was because the chosen one hadn't been aboard. That might be enough incentive for Meridian to drag Judit back home, chain her up on some other captain's bridge, and hope that was enough to satisfy prophecy for the attack.

Her patience ran out. "Anything?"

Roberts pressed a hand to his ear as if that would make his comm work harder. "I'm picking up an old Meridian code."

"Head that way."

Beatrice gave her a sideways glance. "An old code could be a trap, Jude."

Judit nodded. Or it could be Annika. And right now, they had to head for the nearest clue. "Keep listening," she said to Roberts. "Let me look at that area of space."

It was sent to her screen, a bright blue planet with absolutely nothing interesting about it. She searched the surrounding area, but saw nothing, not yet. If it was a ship, they weren't close enough for a good look. She zoomed as close as the viewer would allow, looking for darker spots against the stars.

A shadow passed in front of the planet, and she rewound the feed, looking again.

"The signal's coming in and out," Roberts said.

Judit nodded. "Probably the planet's interference. Something's in high orbit."

All three of the bridge crew bent over their scanners. At tactical, Evie brushed her short black hair out of her green eyes and peered at her screen. "I see a dot."

At the helm, Beatrice muttered an affirmative. When they got close enough to move into orbit, Judit saw a small craft with an engine nearly as big as the rest of it, definitely built for speed. Its orbit looked to be in slow decay; that might mean no one was manning the helm. The ship wasn't in danger of falling to the planet anytime soon, but it would eventually when a few small thrusts would have maintained its orbit.

"Any chatter?" Judit asked.

Roberts shook his head.

"They must know we're here," Beatrice said.

Judit nodded. "Go ahead and ping them."

"No response," Roberts said after a moment.

"They've got some pretty nice plate armor," Evie said. "It's blocking scans."

"Shuttle airlock is wide open," Beatrice said. "Maybe they abandoned ship."

"Let's take our own shuttle over. Bea, Evie."

Beatrice called for two other crew members to take their stations on the bridge then caught up to Judit. "Do you need me to remind you that as a member of the Blood—"

"No."

"You shouldn't be going."

"I know."

"But that's not going to stop you?"

"You're going to have to wrestle me to the ground and sit on me, Bea."

"Is that an order, Jude?"

Judit gave her a sideways smile. "If you try it, I plan to put up plenty of resistance."

Beatrice sighed and leaned close. "Running in to rescue your lady love? I don't know whether to swoon or do my darkest to stop you."

"Swooning is safer, but...I need your help, Bea."

Beatrice nodded, all traces of joking vanishing from her face. "We'll find her, Jude, but when we do, well, hasn't everything changed? I mean, Meridian was going to attack Nocturna."

Yes, peace through marriage seemed off the table. Or was it? The only thing that had changed between Annika, Noal, and Judit was the identity of the chosen one. If she and Annika...

Her breath caught at the thought, and her stomach turned a slow circle as the galaxy laid possibilities before her. She could go home with Annika and Noal and tell her family they didn't need the armada; the original peace could still work. *If* they'd ever accept it, *if* either house would accept a peace that didn't end with the other house annihilated.

Once aboard the shuttle, it was a short ride to the unknown ship. It still had atmosphere, though the gravity was shot. No signs of life, though Evie picked up traces of pistol fire. Judit tried not to let herself think of what that might mean.

They donned pressure suits even though the atmosphere was up and running. Judit didn't want to take any chances. Evie took point with a pistol drawn, Judit behind her with Beatrice bringing up the rear, carrying their equipment case.

It was a small ship, only four decks plus a hangar, and it didn't take long to spot the bodies, all of them efficiently dealt with except those who'd suffocated. Judit hurried through the ship, searching for clues of Annika or Noal, expecting to find their bodies floating around every corner, but they weren't there.

"Dig into the computer," Judit said when they reached the bridge. She studied one body stuck to the wall of the bridge that looked to be a member of House Flavio, but someone had already riffled the bodies, maybe looking for clues.

"I've got something," Beatrice said from the command console. "Someone's put in the Meridian distress code from here, but as I said, it's an old one."

Might be Noal. Sometimes he didn't bother with the updates, knowing Judit would memorize all the new codes. "Anything else?"

"Looks like another Meridian code buried in here, a message." She squinted at the display. "Also an old code. Says, 'Judit, we went to the station.'"

"Direct," Evie said, smirking.

Judit took a deep breath and let it out slowly. Noal and Annika were alive and had abandoned ship, but who'd helped them? Where had all the bodies come from? She clicked her teeth. "Roberts, find any nearby space stations."

"You got it, Boss."

She shut down the line and turned to Beatrice. "Copy everything from that computer. We need to get on the trail of that shuttle."

"It's going to take a while…"

"Then leave it. We'll come back after we get Annika and Noal, but shut off the signal and delete the message."

As they pushed back through the halls toward their shuttle, Beatrice said, "This could still be a trap for you, Jude."

"This is a lot of trouble to go through to kill me." But whoever kidnapped Noal and Annika had found all the trouble they could want, if the bodies were any indication. Whoever had killed this crew had probably taken Annika and Noal. They'd either managed to leave a message before they went, or their kidnappers had, and what could that mean?

"Who killed all these people?" Evie asked as they made their way through the dead. "Does the chosen one or the Nocturna heir have some abilities no one knows about?"

The thought of Noal committing such violence almost made her laugh, but someone from Nocturna? She tried to shake the thought away. Annika was Nocturna, but could she have killed all these people so...neatly?

Once aboard the *Damat*, Judit paused. She'd been in such a hurry to get after Annika and Noal, she hadn't thought about asking her crew to disobey direct Meridian orders, but now she ordered Evie back to the bridge and kept Beatrice behind. "I should take the shuttle from here, Bea. This is my quest, not yours, not the crew's. Go back to Meridian, tell them I ordered you off course and then ordered you back. They'll forgive you."

Beatrice shook her head. "I know Meridian might think we can easily wipe out Nocturna, but there'd be heavy casualties, people we know. If we can prevent that..."

"Not everyone on board will feel that way."

Beatrice shook her head. "They'll do their duty. Don't worry about the crew."

Judit smiled and walked with her toward the lift, her heart lighter.

❖

The little shuttle was close quarters, and Annika sighed for the second time as Noal tried to shift away from her. The slender seats forced their shoulders or thighs to knock together constantly, but he kept his head tilted so far away he'd already banged it on the wall.

"There's nowhere to go, Noal," she said. "And I'm not going to hurt you."

He swallowed and didn't look at her.

"We can talk about it if you want," she said.

"No thanks."

"It was our lives or theirs. When you thanked me for helping you, I thought you understood that."

He swallowed. "It was easy to say in the moment."

By the dark, he sounded as if he wasn't Blood at all. "Who raised you? Or do you suppose Meridians never kill anyone?"

"They didn't raise *me* to do it; that's all I know."

"They didn't do you any favors. Maybe they never expected you to survive."

He stared at her. "I don't know you at all, do I?"

And the dark of it was, that was mostly true. "You know...a lot about me. I didn't want you to see this part." And that was true, too.

He studied her before he sighed. "I suppose Judit would have killed them, too, but I don't like to think about it."

She nodded ahead to where the ship's single screen showed the specs of the space station ahead. "We don't know anyone there, and we don't know who might be looking for us. We don't know which house lays claim to this section of space or how tightly they control it. We could find ourselves surrounded by enemies. But even if that's not true," she said before he could interrupt, "they won't be friends. At best, they'll be neutral, and they won't want to give up anything for free. Some might want to hold us for ransom." She patted his arm, and he didn't pull away. "We have to assume we're in danger. It's the only way to be safe."

"Keep my eyes open, that sort of thing?"

"Exactly."

He looked at her sharply. "Should we disguise ourselves?"

It was a good idea. Even with his dyed hair, his looks were very Meridian, instantly recognizable, and though there were some houses with shades like her own blond color, she should probably do something about it. "Let's see what we have."

They found some ration packs, and Noal used a vegetable drink to turn Annika's hair light green. They couldn't do anything about their eyes without lenses. They found a cloth Noal could use as a scarf, and he tied it around his forehead, pulling it low over his eyes. She pulled her hair in a messy bun, wishing she had a hat and hoping she didn't smell too much like vegetables to put anyone in mind of hurried disguises.

The station wanted an ID before they could dock, and she fed them what the shuttle had, telling them she'd come from a freighter that'd had an accident, giving them coordinates far from the original ship. She knew they'd mark it; some would go looking for salvage, and when they found none, they'd come looking for her, but that was fine. She didn't plan to be found. If Judit didn't find them, Annika planned to abandon the shuttle and try to steal or buy her way onto something faster with the promise of creds to come.

After they docked, they gutted the ship of anything saleable, not knowing how long they'd be aboard the station. They'd taken a few creds off their kidnappers as well as weapons and a handheld scanner, but that wouldn't get them far, especially with the station-wide repeating message that no weapons were allowed on board. Scanners wouldn't find her stiletto, but the shock sticks and pistols had to remain behind. Annika tried to put on a relaxed air as they sauntered through the airlock and down a slender tube into the docking ring of the station, joining a few others who meandered toward where the dock opened into the station proper.

She faltered at the door, Noal doing the same, assaulted by flashing lights and a din of noise, the speech of a great many people crammed into a small space combined with the ding and whoop of betting machines and hawkers. It was like an enormous bazaar, with signs in many house dialects as well as the common tongue. With a riot of clothing and hairstyles and just as many places to change an outward appearance, it was difficult to focus on one person, and all of them seemed to be talking at once. Someone bumped into Annika, and she tugged Noal to a spot out of the way of the moving crowd, between a stall selling what looked like bondage gear and one selling some kind of brightly colored dessert.

Noal looked as shell-shocked as she felt. "What is all this?" he cried above the noise.

Even when Ama had let Annika out to practice her skills in the real world, they'd never gone anywhere like this. Most spaces frequented by Nocturna Blood were calm and tranquil. Even their most raucous parties had never been this chaotic. "I don't…" All her careful plans fell apart. She didn't even know where to start in this mess. "I guess we need to find someone to sell things to."

"Any idea where to start?"

Across the crowded space, Annika noticed someone watching them, a shrewd look on his face. She knew what he saw: two newcomers, easily dazzled and easily taken advantage of. Blond, mid-twenties, he was handsome in a rugged, unkempt sort of way. His suit had once been of good quality but had seen better days. The color-changing cravat probably distracted most people from the shininess of his gray cuffs or the threadbare hem of his trousers.

With a smile, he began to work his way toward them, and Annika kept up her expression of wonder, though the arrival of a con man made her relax. A target always put her in the right frame of mind.

"Welcome to the *Xerxes*," he said as he reached them. "You look as if you could use a guide." He put a hand to his chest and gave an antiquated little bow. "I'm Spartan Roulege, at your service."

Annika smiled as prettily as she could manage, nudging Noal to do the same. Any naiveté on his part would contribute well to her disguise. Spartan smiled in turn, and Annika focused on his blue eyes, detecting a tiny movement around the left iris, some kind of implant.

"We're looking for a private place," she said. "Somewhere we can rest."

"I know a few places." He led them into the station, his body tensing, and his cheeks flushed slightly, probably in anticipation. Since he hadn't glanced at either of their bodies, he was no doubt hoping to rob them, maybe sell them back to their families if he'd figured out who they were.

"We're also looking to sell a few things." Best to get all the information they could before she incapacitated him.

"Or make a transmission," Noal said.

Annika kept herself from glancing at him. Surely he wasn't thinking to call Meridian for help? Everyone would intercept a transmission like that and be on them before they could react. And what did he think would happen if Nocturna got to him first? She couldn't protect him from her grandmother.

"There are resale shops on the third level," Spartan said. "The good ones, anyway. All the stuff down here is for users or gamblers needing a quick injection of creds. As for transmissions," he gestured at the vast space, "just about anywhere, depending on who you want to call. Now, if you're looking for something more private, I can introduce you to a few people." He pointed ahead at a looming space, a sign proclaiming it a hotel. "Here we are."

They'd passed several nicer establishments, and she wondered if he got a special commission from this place or if his friends were waiting inside. He led them to the lobby and sauntered up to the counter. "These two need a room, Luis."

So he did know people here. She decided to play along. They had a few creds plus their equipment to sell, and they'd have a few more by the time they'd robbed their new friend and his allies.

"You seem well connected." Noal leaned on the counter, clearly flirting, and as Spartan flushed, Annika had to give Noal credit. A physical attraction might put Spartan off his guard. Her grandmother would have assumed the attraction was genuine, that Noal was as foolhardy about his sexual partners as rumor painted him, but Annika knew that wasn't true. He guarded his heart close. The thought gave her pause. She'd just broken his heart and hadn't thought about it at all. Well, that was something else he'd have to get over, but she told herself to try to be more patient with him. There was no reason they couldn't still be friends.

Once Luis had taken their creds, he jotted down the fake names they gave him. He didn't bother with a DNA sample, not even a fingerprint or retinal scan. So, they were used to people who didn't want to be tracked. Even Ama would have had a hard time not smiling at her luck.

Spartan offered to help them take their bags with an added offer to tell them more about the station. While they rode the lift to the fourth level, Annika slipped her stiletto free. She'd secured it in her arm before they'd left the kidnappers' ship, waiting until Noal's back was turned. She didn't think he'd appreciate watching her do it. They reached their level, and Annika checked to make sure the hall was abandoned before she slammed Spartan into the wall and pressed the stiletto to his throat.

"Keep your hands by your shoulders."

"All right, okay," he said, eyes wide, his empty hands twitching. His breath came in shallow gasps, and his pulse jumped against her blade. "Take it easy."

"I want the info you promised us, starting with who you work for."

"The…the Teagan Conglomerate. It's not a secret."

She'd never heard of them. "A gang?"

He sputtered a laugh and seemed as if he might relax. She dug the knife in until a few drops of blood leaked from his neck.

His eyes widened anew. "They own this hotel. They own a lot of businesses on this station! They pay me to pick up newcomers and steer them toward Teagan establishments, that's all!"

She continued to stare. "And?"

"That's it, I swear!" he said. "Look, don't go to the third level to sell your stuff. What you want is Sal's on second for electronics and the Pawn Emporium on first for everything else. As for sending a secret transmission, there's no such thing. Half the businesses here would monitor you, and there are several high-powered people who'd do the same. You'd have to be in good with station personnel, and there's no guarantee that what started as private would end as private. By the dark, that's all I know."

She spun him around and locked her arm around his throat. "Search him," she said to Noal.

After gawking, Noal did as he was told. Annika tightened her hold as Spartan struggled until he passed out. Noal straightened. "No weapons."

"Any creds? Jewelry or a comm?"

"We are not going to rob the man, Annika!"

"He set us up to be robbed, Noal." She let Spartan slip to the floor. "Watch." She keyed open their room and barreled through, diving behind a piece of furniture so she could better fight whatever was coming.

Nothing. The room was empty.

Noal poked his head inside. "Did you subdue the sofa?"

She glared at him, and looked into the washroom, the closet, both empty.

"That lamp looks awfully suspicious," he said.

"Shut up."

"Not everyone is out to kill us."

She glared. "If we start to think like that, we're dead."

"You and Judit would make quite a pair. You'd have this whole station cowed by now."

She put her hands on her hips. "And I suppose you think we should trust everyone."

"Not trust, but I don't think we should be trying to kill everyone, either. Now, what shall we do with the unconscious man in the hallway?"

They dragged Spartan into the room, and she had to admit, she didn't know how to proceed now that the room wasn't full of hired killers. "I wasn't entirely wrong about him. He was out to get something from us."

"Our business. Like most people, I suspect." He sighed. "Though you are right that people would sell us out if they could. Greed overwhelms a lot of qualms."

"He's got an ocular implant," she said, glad they were finally reading from the same page. "He could be scanning the local net or the news. He might get our pics." She covered the implant while Noal bound his hands. They used the scanner from the kidnappers' ship to look for cameras or listening devices, but all they found was a device for detecting fire or atmospheric leaks. Annika disabled it anyway, just to be sure.

She slowly brought Spartan awake; he blinked sleepily with his uncovered eye and smiled. Maybe he thought they were waking up together. Before she could speak, his eye widened, and he tried to jerk away. "Who...what did you do to me?" He looked around wildly. "Where am I?"

"Shh," she said. "If you're too noisy, you're going to have to go to sleep again, and the way I do it won't be good for you."

He shut his mouth and breathed shallowly. "What did you do to my eye?"

"Covered it. What's the implant for?"

"Gives me all the current odds at the gambling houses. I told you. I drive traffic—"

"Shh." She rested a hand against his neck, fingers over his pulse point. His heartbeat sped up as if in anticipation. "Relax."

"There's no need for this. I'll tell you whatever you want. My... my bosses are going to miss me if I'm not out there doing my thing. I need to get paid. I have a family. I have responsibilities."

Some of that might be true. His heart rate was too all over the place for her to tell. "If you tell us what we want to know, if you're honest, you'll be out of here and back to your family and responsibilities before you know it." She smiled sweetly.

After a deep breath, he nodded. Before she could ask anything else, Noal butted in with, "Which house controls this station?"

Annika kept her face schooled. It was a good question even if it might lead Spartan to think about houses, about Blood.

"Um, it's disputed space, though no one fights over it anymore; it was mined out years ago. This station's all that's left, and three houses take turns managing it."

"Which ones?" Noal asked.

"Atrius, Munn, and Flavio. Are you scouting for another house? Is there something here that the others missed?"

Annika pulled Noal away, but Spartan kept talking. "Hey, if this corner of nothing is going to be worth something again, I'm your guy! I know the place inside and out."

Annika spoke close to Noal's ear. "Flavio was the house who kidnapped us."

"No, there was a Flavio onboard the kidnappers' ship. There's a difference. Atrius has allied with Meridian before. If we can get to them, they can get us back home!"

"And what makes you think Meridian wasn't the one who had us kidnapped?"

His mouth fell open. "My grandmother would never do that! I'm the chosen one, for darkness's sake."

"Chosen to be sacrificed so Meridian can start the war again?"

"It was probably Nocturna," he said, tilting his chin up as if expecting her to argue.

"No, I agree. Probably was but might not be."

Now his haughty, angry look dissolved into shock. "How in the dark do you get anything done if you're so suspicious all the time?"

She waved him to silence. "Can we agree that we need to stay away from Flavio?"

He nodded.

Annika turned to Spartan again. "Maybe you can be of use."

He brightened.

"If you're duly discreet."

He nodded so hard, he almost shook off the towel she'd wrapped around his head. "Soul of discretion, me."

"What about your bosses?" Noal asked. "Responsibilities? Family?"

"Screw them," he said. "I don't have a family; that was a lie. Best to start with the truth." He smiled harder, Mr. Business. "Where do we start? What's the game? Are there minerals nobody knows about? Is one of the houses looking to make this station legit? Turn it into one of those giant casinos? I can see it now," he said, gazing into the distance. "Indoor beach with a view of old Seti-820, the gas giant out there. I always thought it was pretty. You won't be disappointed."

Annika barely kept from laughing. "I can see you're a man with a lot of ideas."

"Inexhaustible, madam. Where should we start? If you're looking to take over quickly, the casino crews are the people you have to watch out for. Station management shouldn't give you much trouble, but the casino bosses—"

Annika held up a hand. "If we end up upsetting things, we might need to get off the station quickly."

"Couple like you, didn't you come in on a fast ship?"

"We were hoping to get something faster," she said. "And less conspicuous than what we showed up in."

He nodded slowly. "There's always a ship to be had for the right amount of creds."

Now that was going to be a problem, but not if Judit got there first, if Judit was even looking...

CHAPTER SIX

On her console on the bridge, Judit watched the station come closer. A disjointed hunk of metal, it nonetheless gleamed against the vastness of space. She searched for anything else of note in the system and found nothing. Who would put a station so far from anywhere unless they had something nefarious in mind?

Judit leaned back in her chair and looked to Beatrice at the helm. "Who owns this?"

"A conglomerate of smaller families," Beatrice said. "Looks like Munn, Atrius, and Flavio."

Flavio again. Did that mean they were at the heart of the kidnapping plot, or were they hired hands? "Anything on the comm?"

"Just coming in," Roberts said. "They're very polite, but it's clear they'd like to know our intentions. They're also reminding us we're too big to dock."

"Literally or figuratively?"

He shrugged. "Literally, definitely. Figuratively? Well, the stationmaster is requesting to speak with you."

"Put them through."

On Judit's screen the stationmaster's skin was nearly as dark as Judit's, though with the tinge of purple that could be House Munn or Atrius; the hue was a result of the bizarre radiation in the systems that had birthed both houses. But a slight golden sheen to her black hair named her as Munn.

Judit inclined her head, and the stationmaster did the same. "Judit Meridian, captain of the *Damat*." Since Munn was a fairly large house, she added, "At your service." Her grandmother wouldn't have bothered, but maybe a little flattery would put the stationmaster in the right mood.

A wan smile greeted her. "I'm Elidia Munn, stationmaster of the *Xerxes*. We don't get many big fish out here. What can we do for you?"

"Oh, we're passing through."

Elidia snorted. "To where? From where? Everyone has a reason to be out here."

Judit blinked, not used to such bluntness from anyone but her own house. It was...refreshing, though her grandmother wouldn't have thought so.

And maybe she should reward bluntness with bluntness. "I'm looking for someone," Judit said.

"Someone to help Meridian buy this backwater? Are you planning to turn it into a luxury vacation spot?"

Judit blinked again, not even knowing how to begin such a process.

"You're not going to cut Munn out if that's what you're planning," Elidia said. "Everyone else in the galaxy might quake at the mention of your name, but we're going to need a big payday."

"Just a moment." Judit silenced the comm before she turned to Beatrice. "What in the dark is she talking about?"

"No idea," Beatrice said while the rest shook their heads. "Maybe someone's jilted them out of some holdings."

Judit rubbed the bridge of her nose. No one in the holdings closest to Meridian Prime acted like this.

"Tact, Jude," Beatrice said.

"Right." She switched the comm back on. "I'm looking for two... fugitives."

"Tell me who and what kind of ship they came in, and I'll be happy to report back."

Well, that pretty much guaranteed that the *Xerxes* had criminals aboard, probably some who were wanted in Meridian space. Elidia was probably looking for a bribe, or maybe Munn took a big part in any criminal activity aboard their station. "It would be easier if I came over and looked for myself."

Elidia paused as if considering. "I'll see if we have a berth available for your shuttle." She cut the comm.

"How much trouble does she think I can get into?" Judit asked.

"If you're planning some kind of hostile takeover, quite a lot," Beatrice said. "She'll probably insist we turn over any weapons if she agrees at all."

"And we don't even know if Annika and Noal are over there," Judit muttered. "And Flavio is probably watching. Let's heat up the forward gun; nothing too showy, a slow build of aggression."

Beatrice gave her a look that asked if she was sure, and Judit returned it with a raised eyebrow. They didn't have time to lose, and it was what her grandmother would have done. As many times as her grandmother's decisions put Judit on edge, the old woman got results.

❖

Annika smiled as she watched Noal walk with his arm around Spartan's shoulders. His voice had taken on a languid, easygoing quality. It seemed they'd found a character he could picture himself as: a member of a rich house trying to schmooze his way into power. Spartan led them to several pawn shops, and they'd sold the items they had. Noal claimed that pawning various items helped them see which businesses were lucrative enough to "make the transition," though he kept it vague as to what that transition might be.

At their fourth stop, Annika noticed an uptick in the clamor. People were walking faster, talking more animatedly. Spartan stopped in the hall. "The numbers just took a nosedive," he said, staring at nothing as his implant fed him information. "People must be leaving the casinos in droves."

Annika caught the shoulder of someone running past. "What's happening?"

"There's a warship come to kill us all!" He twisted from her grip and ran. Several people picked up on his infectious panic and bolted for the docking ring.

Annika's heart thudded. Could it be Judit? Or was it another member of their houses who'd tracked them down to finish the job of kidnapping or killing them? "We need to see outside," she said to Spartan. "We need to see that ship."

"Is it one of yours?" he asked. "They're not really going to fire on the station, are they?"

She picked her way through people, hearing every rumor, but no one had anything certain on the size of the ship or who owned it. They finally fought through to one of the station personnel, someone in the same pocket as Spartan's employers, who assured Spartan it was Meridian.

It had to be Judit. In that case, she might be threatening to fire on the station if she didn't get Noal back. And Annika? Was Judit threatening in her name, too? "We need to get a message to them."

"So it is yours?" Spartan asked. "Are you Meridian? I thought you might be Nocturna." He stepped closer, keeping his voice low. "Does your family not know you're here?"

All day long they'd had to steer him away from any screens or holos broadcasting a news feed. Their pictures were everywhere, and they tried to stay in the shadows, buying hats and pulling them low over their faces. Now, as Spartan peered at them, his eyes went wide, and she knew something must have clicked. Even if he hadn't seen the news lately, Annika's and Noal's faces were often on the holos, just like every high-ranking member of Meridian and Nocturna.

He tried to cover it, but she saw the flash of recognition as the pieces came together, and he realized he'd been duped or pulled into something larger than a simple station acquisition. Annika lunged, but he backpedaled into a crowd of hurrying people. Several tripped over him, serving as a blockade. Annika tried to leap over them, but Spartan took off down a narrow hallway and disappeared from view. The station was a warren of twisting passageways, and he knew them far better than her.

"Forget him," Noal said. "That's got to be Judit out there. All we need to do is get off the station before someone else recognizes us."

"Spartan's probably going straight to his bosses. If they get their hands on us, they'll hold us hostage. They know the ship won't fire with us on board."

"We don't know for sure what anyone will do! Let's hide and think of a way out."

He was right. She headed for one of the places Spartan had shown them, somewhere the cameras wouldn't see.

❖

Elidia came back with a calmer expression, which seemed like a good sign, but she and Judit put each other on hold a lot as they negotiated and threatened and generally proved that they didn't trust each other at all. Judit wondered how often the bigger houses came to this place and threw their weight around. Maybe everyone was tired of seeing their faces on the feeds all the time.

Speaking of feeds, time wasn't on their side. If people on the station hadn't recognized Annika and Noal yet, they would soon. That could even be one of the reasons Elidia was dragging her feet. Maybe she *was* waiting for creds. That edged Judit's admiration down a tick. She hated haggling, and she never knew where to start. One of the best things about having money was that she hardly ever had to darking *think* about it.

A commotion behind Elidia caused her to turn and cut the comm. When it blinked back a second later, Elidia looked smug, and Judit knew her time was up.

"Fugitives, huh?" Elidia said.

Judit thought to feign ignorance, then she sighed, and her temper flared. "Give me who I want. Or let me come get them, and we'll all get out of your hair." Judit pointed at Evie, and the gun they'd been powering fired a warning shot. She knew the rest of the galaxy thought of Meridian as a bully. Well, what good was a reputation if you never used it? "If we can't have them, no one can. You have five minutes." She cut the comm.

Everyone on the bridge looked to her, their expressions carefully neutral, but she read the tension in them. "Oh, come on! We're not going to fire on a bunch of innocent people, but they don't know that."

"We're going to have company soon," Roberts said. "I'm getting several ships on scans. They'll be here in less than an hour. If they fight together, we might have a problem."

"By the dark!" Judit slumped in her seat. "Why can't people just do what they're supposed to?" She thought fast, but this wasn't two commanders facing off on the field of battle. Doubtless this was politics with years of history, and there were civilians thrown in the mix.

But maybe those civilians could be her way around the politics.

"Put out a station-wide message," Judit said. "If we can't scare personnel, we'll get everyone else to give us what we want."

"Transmitting."

"Attention, people of the *Xerxes*," Judit said, "this is the warship *Damat*." Not really true. They were more transport than warship, but their armament was fairly impressive. Meridian couldn't have the chosen one driven about in a skiff. "We're searching for Annika Nocturna and Noal Meridian. Unless they are returned to us, we will begin firing on your station. Implore your leaders and station personnel to turn my people over. You have ten minutes."

Her crew kept their eyes on their stations, and all that was left was to wait.

A voice came over the comm half a minute later. "Judit?"

Her heart leapt at the sound of Annika's voice, but she kept her tone neutral. "Are you both all right?"

"We are."

"Get out on any ship, and we'll cover you. Anyone who tries to stop you gets blown to the dark." That was for the benefit of anyone listening, and she hoped they took it to heart. Unfortunately, it wouldn't help Annika and Noal while they were still inside the station.

❖

Annika felt like leaning into the transmitter. They'd finally found a shopkeeper alone in his store. Everyone else was running, screaming after Judit's station-wide transmission. They were all trying to get to their ships, but station personnel had locked down the docking ring, no doubt trying to keep Annika and Noal in place. And they'd have heard Annika's transmission, but that didn't stop her from loving the sound of Judit's voice, from hearing the slipping of Judit's careful tone. She was about to reply that she didn't know the ship situation when the comm went dead.

The shopkeeper looked at her nervously, wringing his hands. "You'll be leaving now?"

"They'll be coming for us," she said to Noal. "And I doubt they'll be friendly."

She turned to see the shopkeeper disappearing through a back door then looked to the front of the shop. Station personnel filled the doorway, a wall of green uniforms.

She grabbed Noal's arm and made for the back door, but the station goons were quicker, leaping on her and Noal. She got in one or two hits, but there were too many hands grabbing at her, twisting her limbs around. The station scanners hadn't let Annika and Noal bring weapons on board, and she didn't have time to reach for her stiletto. One hand smacked against her temple, and the sounds of the station went quiet, her limbs sluggish. They had Noal away from her in a moment then piled on, over and over, and her hands were cuffed before she knew it.

Her vision was still swimming when they brought her upright, and she stared into the face of the station commander she'd glimpsed on the screens, the one who'd told everyone to be calm, Elidia Munn. It was better than another Flavio. Maybe this one could be reasoned with.

"So, these two are worth all this nonsense?" Elidia looked back and forth between them. She touched the end of Noal's dyed hair. "Nice disguise."

Annika blinked rapidly, trying to clear her vision. "Let us go. Let us get to that ship, and you can go back to normal operations."

"I don't believe you," Elidia said. "So I think we'll hold you until our ships get here, then we can sort things out on an even playing field."

So much for reasoning with her. They hauled Annika and Noal from the store. Noal pleaded, trying to assure Elidia that the station would be safer if they were released. Annika's vision was clearing, but she kept up her stumble, waiting for her moment.

One of the guards called out. Annika lurched to the side as someone bumped into her. A scream came from the pack of personnel, and she glimpsed angry frightened faces, station goers attacking with whatever they had.

"Let them go!" someone cried. "Get them out of here!"

Annika fought to stay near Noal. Some of the guards had shock sticks, but another had a pistol, and that seemed to spur the crowd to greater action. They leapt on him and tried to wrestle the weapon away. The deep thrum of it filled the corridor as it went off, and someone screamed, twisting and shrieking as his organs liquefied.

"Noal!" Annika cried. "Where are you?" She put her shoulder down and rammed a guard out of the way.

Noal was kneeling against the wall, an injured man behind him. Annika hurried to his side, her arms cuffed behind her. "He tried to help me," Noal said weakly, looking to the bleeding man.

Someone pulled Annika to her feet, and she twisted around, poised to kick. She paused when she saw Spartan's frightened face. He pulled back, hands raised, the key to a pair of cuffs in his fingers.

"Let me help, let me help!" When he reached for her cuffs again, she let him. "Get out of here." He nearly snarled as he fumbled with her cuffs. When she was freed, she twisted to face him, and his expression was all dark anger. "I'm sorry I ever thought of you coming here as a good thing. Take your family drama and get the dark out of here!"

The fight was still raging, but she knew how to stop it. "Unlock Noal's cuffs."

Without waiting for his answer, she pushed into the masses fighting for the pistol, kicking and smacking indiscriminately until she found her way to the gun. Once she had it, she cast around, and through the crackle of shock sticks, she saw who she was looking for.

Annika smacked the side of her hand into the back of Elidia's neck, stunning her. When she pitched forward, Annika wrenched her arms around, cuffing them behind her back. She dragged Elidia toward where a heap of junk had fallen off a kiosk and climbed atop it.

Annika whirled the staggered Elidia around. "Noal, get their attention!"

He stuck his fingers in his mouth and whistled a loud, shrill note.

Many people spun, shocked into inaction. Annika jabbed the pistol into Elidia's side. "Station personnel, drop your darking weapons."

They froze, and she gave them half a heartbeat. "Now!"

Weapons fell to the ground. The station dwellers gave a ragged cheer as if they'd forgotten who or what they were fighting for and were just happy someone had won. Several people in the crowd seized the dropped weapons. Noal was frowning at Annika as if he knew she'd kill Elidia if she had to. Well, he'd have to get used to that.

"Take us to a shuttle," Annika said to Spartan. "And we'll pack up our drama and go."

He nodded once, sharply. She looked back to the station personnel who stood surrounded by an angry mob. "Everything can get back to normal once we're gone," she said, hoping that would mollify Noal. "And no one else has to get hurt. Tell the rest of your people that we're leaving. No one gets in our way."

Elidia shook her head as if regaining some of her senses. Annika prodded her into a shuffling jog. With the pistol to Elidia's back and

Spartan leading the way, they headed toward the docking ring. As they rounded the corner closest to the shuttles, someone took a shot, and Annika spotted several figures kneeling down the hall in front of them. She ducked, using Elidia as a shield, and Spartan and Noal ducked behind her, around the corner.

"Get back or I shoot her!" Annika called.

Another shot thumped harmlessly into the wall, close enough to send cramps through Annika's muscles.

"Those aren't my crew," Elidia said. "Someone else is gunning for you."

"Someone's coming up behind us!" Spartan said.

Annika bit her teeth on a curse. "Stay behind me. We're going to run for it."

"Wait!" Elidia said. "Maybe I can—"

Annika fired off a burst of shots and barreled for their airlock, shooting as she went. Spartan yelled for everyone to stop shooting, but no one obeyed. As they crowded into the doorway of the airlock, their attackers fired another few shots.

"Everyone, stay down," Annika said. Elidia squirmed against her chest, but as she was as hidden as the rest of them, Annika didn't see where she had room to complain.

Noal fumbled with the door for a few seconds before shouting, "Got it!"

Annika prepared to step over Spartan, but Noal dragged him into the shuttle, and Annika jammed in behind, hauling their shield with her. She couldn't have the station firing on them once they'd left.

The four of them packed the shuttle beyond capacity, even with Noal taking a seat in front of the controls. Annika dumped Elidia on the floor.

"No!" Spartan said as she secured the shuttle door. "Let me out!"

The shuttle shuddered. "The station hasn't released the docking clamps," Noal said.

Annika pointed the gun at Elidia again. "Tell them to release the clamps."

Elidia glared from the floor. "You won't shoot me."

Annika gestured at the door, at the frantic sounds of someone trying to get in. "They might."

"Let me out!" Spartan said again. "They won't hurt me. I'm nothing to them!"

But they'd get in if she let him go. "Noal, fire up the engines and begin pulling away."

"If we rip the umbilical..."

"We all die," she said, staring at Elidia. "The explosive decompression will open this shuttle like a paper bag."

Spartan was still blubbering about how they had to let him go. Annika pushed him to the floor, too, not breaking eye contact with Elidia. In the cramped shuttle, she'd be stepping on them at any moment.

Elidia looked away. "Put me on the comm."

Noal hit the transmit button, and Elidia gave the order. With a shudder, the docking clamps let go, and they began to drift into open space as Noal steered them toward Judit's ship.

❖

Judit watched the approach of the shuttle with unblinking eyes. "Open the bay."

"We've got company," Beatrice said. "Two of the incoming ships will be here before the shuttle can dock."

"Tell the shuttle to begin evasive maneuvers," Judit said. "They have to keep the station between them and the ships."

"Incoming ships are powering guns," Roberts said.

"Fire a warning," Judit said. "And tell them—"

The *Damat* tilted crazily, and the bright line of the lead ship's cannon arced through where they'd been sitting.

"Nice moves, Bea." Judit sat more firmly in her chair, all her training taking over. This, at least, she knew how to do. "Safety restraints, everyone. Evie, target their engines." Disabling engines was a safer bet than targeting weapons. A damaged cannon could easily blow and kill everyone on board, and Judit wasn't up to killing anyone yet, not when this could still be sorted out.

From her post in the corner, Evie fired the *Damat*'s cannon, making the first ship angle out of the way, but Judit knew she was aiming for the second. She sliced its engine off with the skill of a star surgeon.

"Let's hope they're too busy to fire now," Judit said.

The *Damat* lurched again and shuddered, claxons sounding through the bridge until Beatrice shut them off. "Winged us. Sorry, Jude."

"Fire, Evie," Judit said.

The hull of the lead ship absorbed the blast, glowing cherry red before fading. "They've got thick plates," Evie said. "We'll have to get around them to hit somewhere critical."

A bright spark came from behind the first ship, and Judit squinted at her screen, seeing the shuttle dart through space.

"The shuttle damaged the enemy ship's engines," Beatrice said.

Judit curled her hand into a fist, worry knotting her gut. "They're supposed to be hiding!"

The enemy ship dipped and turned, trying to get a clear line of fire on the shuttle while keeping its plating toward the *Damat*. "Get under her," Judit said.

But the enemy ship turned with them and fired again. At the helm, Beatrice evaded as swiftly as she could, throwing everyone against their safety restraints. The *Damat* rumbled, and Judit knew they'd been scored, though her screen didn't yet show a breach.

But that luck wouldn't last forever.

"The shuttle's keeping at the enemy's side," Beatrice said. "Away from the guns. I think they're trying to get her to turn her back on us."

"Take us toward the station," Judit said. "But keep a target lock on that ship."

When they moved that way, the ship moved with them, forgetting about the shuttle for a moment, just as Judit hoped.

"Fire!"

Evie fired, and Judit noted the shuttle did the same. The ship turned for the station itself, maneuvering to get behind it from the *Damat*'s point of view. The station fired its own cannon, a warning shot that missed everyone.

"Picking up chatter," Roberts said. "The station warning the ship to stay away, and the ship arguing that they're trying to defend the station."

"I guess the *Xerxes* doesn't appreciate being used as a shield," Judit said.

"The shuttle's closing with us," Beatrice said. "We've got a gap while the station and the ship are distracted."

"Pick them up, and let's get out of here."

In order for the shuttle to dock, the *Damat* had to stop moving, making them more of a target. As they halted, Judit whispered, "Come on, come on."

"Got them!" Beatrice said.

"Tell them to hold tight, and get us the dark out of here," Judit said. "Head for the edge of the system." They needed to be far from any gravity wells before they engaged their antimatter drives. Beatrice hit the thrusters, and everyone lurched in their seats. "Take us toward a Meridian transmitter gate," Judit said. "They might not follow us if they think we're headed for our allies."

As soon as the engines were going, Judit was out of her seat and hurrying for the shuttle bay, hoping she found both Noal and Annika in one piece.

CHAPTER SEVEN

When Judit stepped into the bay, Noal left the shuttle, his face haggard. Judit marched forward and hugged him close as he held his arms open for her.

"I'm so happy you're safe," she said. He muttered the same into her shoulder. She looked past him, searching for Annika. Her happy smile froze when she saw Annika leading two people out of the shuttle under guard, one of which she recognized as the stationmaster, Elidia Munn.

Annika smiled, a slippage of the masks their families made them wear, a look Judit had only seen in private. She looked as tired as Noal, and she'd dyed her hair a hideous green. There had to be quite a story there. Judit was about to ask if the man with them was the one who'd rescued them from the kidnappers' ship, but Noal laid a hand on her arm.

"These aren't exactly friends," he said.

Judit clicked her teeth. "Evie, we've got company who'll be needing secure quarters."

The man looked stunned, but Elidia stepped forward. "You have no right to take me prisoner!"

"Funny," Annika said, "since that's what you tried to do with us."

Elidia opened her mouth again, but Judit spoke over her. "You'll be safe on the *Damat*, and when I have a moment to deal with you, you'll be returned where you belong."

Elidia still frowned, but she went with Evie, the man with her still looking around as if he couldn't believe what had happened.

Judit stared awkwardly at Annika, wondering what she should say.

Even Noal looked uncomfortable when Judit expected him to make some quip about the kidnappers' accommodations.

"Are you all right?" Judit asked. She wanted to hear from both of them, but her eyes kept straying to Annika.

"A little shaken up but unharmed," Annika said.

"We're fine," Noal said, "and if you two aren't going to kiss, we need to talk, Judit." He glanced at Annika. "Alone."

Annika's brow creased in pain, and Judit wondered what Noal was going to say before Annika blurted, "I think he wants to tell you about my guardian training."

Judit looked to Noal, and after mashing his lips together, he nodded. She had a sudden flash of her own training: years of combat maneuvering, studying ship's tactics, and learning how to lead a crew and captain a ship. She tried to picture Annika—all glitter and gowns—in her place and failed.

"A guardian?" Judit asked, smiling. It had to be a joke.

"You know my house," Annika said softly. "Built on secrets."

Judit nodded, still not able to get a clear picture, but after another glance at Noal, she knew there was a story here that she wasn't understanding. "Let's go to my office."

"I should clean up first." Annika took off her cap, bringing the green hair into starker relief.

"Okay." Judit didn't want to add that Annika couldn't get back to normal fast enough.

Something in her expression must have shown. Annika smiled, showing a bit of her old self. "You don't like the new look?"

Judit coughed to cover a laugh. "Well…"

"Come on." Noal marched past them. "You can use my quarters to shower."

Judit waited in her office when she wanted to follow them and ask a thousand questions. They arrived together, but Noal's subdued attitude said something off had happened between them. Judit ordered food and made sure the same went to their guests before she sat. "Well, let's hear it."

Noal leaned against the wall, as far from Annika as he could get.

Judit's belly did a little turn. "What happened?"

"In Nocturna, we don't trust anyone," Annika said. "Not even our guardians, and it seems we were right."

"Feric betrayed you," Judit said. "Annika, I'm so sorry." She'd never liked him, but he had to mean something to Annika.

She nodded. "Whether he was someone else's creature from the beginning, or if they found some way to get to him, I don't know. But my grandmother trained me in combat in case something like this ever happened. I was a little surprised Noal doesn't know how to fight."

"I have Judit," he said.

"But I lost you." Judit turned to him. "I failed you, Noal. I'm sorry." She waved his protest away and tried to think. Annika being a secret guardian made sense, though Judit wasn't ready to think about the dead bodies she'd seen on the kidnappers' ship. But now she had to tell Noal she was the real chosen one, and he was already upset by Annika's guardian training. She supposed that was one good thing about her being the chosen one: It would give Noal something else to think about.

"There are plenty of secrets to go around," Judit said.

Noal frowned. "Is there a reason you don't have a Meridian fleet with you?"

"I…wasn't supposed to go looking for you at all."

When they both stared, she took a deep breath, wondering if she should hold something back, but the way she saw it, the only people they had to depend on now were one another.

"Grandmother always suspected that Nocturna would double-cross us. She prepared a secret fleet to destroy Nocturna when that betrayal happened."

His mouth dropped open, his arms coming uncrossed. "And they thought the kidnapping was the double cross?"

She nodded. "They wanted me to lead the fleet, to annihilate Nocturna."

He blinked several times. "And they were just going to leave their chosen one to rot while you did it? Did Grandmother forget the prophecy, or is she ignoring it?"

Judit flinched. "She said…I'm the chosen one, Noal. They would have found a way to strike at Nocturna no matter what, and I was supposed to bring about peace."

"By destroying Nocturna." Annika didn't seem nearly as shocked. Growing up Nocturna, she was probably used to such secrets.

Noal sank into one of the chairs, a stunned look on his face. "I can't..."

Judit crossed around her desk and knelt beside him. Though secrets and lies surrounded them now, she'd never felt as if she'd lost everything, not as long as the possibility of getting Noal and Annika back remained. What would Noal do when they returned home? What future awaited him? "I'm sorry, Noal."

"If you're the chosen one," Annika said softly. "Then that makes you the heir." She lifted an eyebrow, a question in her gaze.

Judit swallowed a wave of desire that fought through the guilt, the confusion. If they were the heirs, they were the ones who should marry.

Annika's mind buzzed with the knowledge that none of them were who the others thought they were. If Judit was truly the mythical chosen one, what did that make Noal? She felt sorry for him, but he could pick himself up, think of a different role for himself. For now, he seemed content to stare at nothing. Annika licked her lips and tried to think of anything but her and Judit and a marriage bed.

"Do you think Nocturna was behind the kidnapping?" Annika asked.

"My crew says no," Judit said. "Not according to the data. For all I know, Meridian organized the kidnapping so that they could attack Nocturna while everyone else was searching for you."

Annika nodded. "Or it could be Nocturna trying to get the rest of the galaxy to attack Meridian."

Judit smiled softly. "What a world we live in."

"What happened to the fleet?"

"No word." Judit sighed. "Which I suppose is good news. If they'd attacked, we would have heard."

"Nocturna will be planning something," Annika said, certain of it.

"Chatter has both houses blaming each other. Soon, everyone will have their ships out."

"Who cares?" Noal said bitterly. "Let them annihilate each other."

"And throw the whole galaxy into war?" Judit asked.

He grimaced. "If one of them can wipe the other out quickly

enough, the other houses won't care. They'll be too busy squabbling over the pieces."

Judit leaned against her desk. "We can't take that chance. We can't let the whole galaxy burn."

Noal mumbled something dismissive.

"If we can end this conflict, we have to." Judit stared at him, her face appalled. She was what Meridian was supposed to be, but in reality, their houses were much the same. "We can't just ignore a bloody battle."

"Spoken like a true chosen one," Noal said. "Why don't the two of you get married and settle it all." He stood, frown deepening, and stormed out of the office.

Annika watched him go, feeling bad for him even if she didn't like how he dealt with secrets. And she agreed with him about Meridian and Nocturna. If the galaxy wanted to destroy itself, maybe they should let it. "Should we follow him?"

"No, let him stew. It's how he deals with stress."

Annika nodded, and as she and Judit stared at each other, her heart thudded hard in her chest. Noal had already suggested they marry. She'd already thought it, and she'd bet Judit had, too. Would it solve anything now?

Annika let her eyes travel along Judit's body. Marriage was only a ceremony. Without Noal in the way, Judit's Meridian proprieties wouldn't hold her back any longer, and they both needed to hold someone at the moment, needed something solid and real.

She took a step, and Judit matched her. Heat rushed through Annika's body. She took another step that was almost a leap, and Judit caught her. They wrapped their arms around each other, knocking together and sliding aside and over and under, searching for any contact as their lips met. For a woman so hard in combat and training and life, Judit's lips were amazingly soft.

The passion lurking behind Judit's stoic exterior blazed to the core as she moaned against Annika's mouth. She licked Annika's lips and then paused as if she wouldn't seek entrance without being invited. Annika opened her mouth and drew Judit's tongue in, and Judit pressed them so close together, it left Annika breathless. To the dark with it; she didn't want to breathe if it meant having Judit farther away from her.

Were it any other lover, Annika would have been tearing at their clothes, but she wanted this fragment in time to last, wanted to savor each second of their first time together. She sensed that Judit wouldn't make any moves unless she did, so she took her time, kissing and caressing, though her hands itched to tear the buttons from Judit's uniform.

She kissed down Judit's neck, feeling fingers in her hair, gliding along her body, exploring her. She slid her hands over Judit's breasts, hearing a sharp intake of breath for her efforts. Enough lingering. She kissed Judit again, deeply, madly, as she undid the first button. As it slipped loose, Annika kissed the inch of flesh that came to light.

Judit forced her head up, and Annika thought she was going to stop them, but she pulled herself onto the desk, then hauled Annika up to straddle her. Judit broke off their next kiss and pulled Annika forward roughly, burying her face in Annika's neck. Annika leaned away and ran her hands along the seam in front of her jumpsuit, opening the fabric with a firm touch. She reached back to pull off the sleeves, trying to shuck the garment quickly.

With Annika's arms trapped behind her, Judit brought her forward again, kissing her breasts, moving her teeth along the sheer fabric of Annika's bra. With a moan, Annika freed her arms and fumbled backward for the catch.

Something buzzed against her skin, and she cried out. She tried to jump away, her thoughts jolted from passion to small explosives.

"It's all right," Judit said, catching her. "It's my comm." She cleared her throat and said, "Say again, Bea."

Annika let out a breath. The Meridians loved their implants. She waited, expecting Judit to dismiss whoever was calling, but Judit's eyes widened.

"I'm on my way," Judit said.

Annika scooted off the desk, putting her clothes back on as an irritated flush crept up her neck. "What happened?"

"Apparently, the houses who run the *Xerxes* have gotten the word out about our little firefight. More joined in their outrage and decided that the larger houses need to be taught some manners." She straightened her platinum hair back into its tidy queue, avoiding eye contact, and Annika bet she had her own flush, though it didn't show. "One of the small houses attacked a Meridian mining post."

Annika sighed. The same thing was probably happening on the

Nocturna side. "Well, I suppose we should sort that out, being the ones who started it."

Judit paused and gave her a shy smile. "I suppose we should."

Annika grinned hugely, and neither one of them had to say that she hoped they'd finish everything else they'd started today, too. They'd have to be on the lookout for an opportunity.

On the bridge, Judit took a fuller report from Beatrice. A lesser house and a group of unaligned ships had captured a small Meridian mining colony, but that wasn't all. Other houses reported similar incidents, sending everyone scrambling for ships and guns. Judit snuck a look at Annika. A marriage contract wasn't going to help that at all, even if it would be very nice. In her office, thoughts of them together had seemed perfect now that Noal was…out of the picture.

By the dark, that was a guilty thought.

She sat in her chair and cursed her lack of patience at the *Xerxes*. As if Meridian and Nocturna didn't have enough problems, now all these other houses and grievances were coming out because she'd thrown Meridian's weight around. She'd been so certain everyone would roll over. That's what always happened when her house got involved. Her grandmother would have been able to get what she wanted with minimum fuss.

The bridge door hissed open, and Noal wandered inside. His expression was neutral, as if he'd somewhat recovered his composure. She smiled. He couldn't sit around and mope while there was a crisis, not when he was so much better at talking to people than she was. She just had to find a way to bring out his sunnier disposition.

If he still had one.

She crossed to him, Annika by her side. "Can you talk to some of the lesser houses, Noal? Settle things down a bit? Now that I've ruffled a few feathers?"

"You weren't the only one," he said with a quick glance at Annika. Before she could bristle, he hurried on. "I don't know where to start. I can try calling Grandmother, but you know she's already got pacification teams in the air. And since I'm not the chosen one"—he swallowed hard—"I don't know if she'll listen to me."

A thin sheen of anger settled over his face, and she forced herself not to try to erase it, to let him work it out. Impatience had gotten them into this mess. When he glanced at her, his face softened, and she knew her guilt must be shining through. "It's not your fault, Jude. Well, not entirely."

She snorted a laugh. "Thanks, I guess."

"From the vibes we got on the *Xerxes*, this sort of thing has been coming for a long time. The big houses have been too wrapped up in their own shit to notice." He snapped his fingers. "We need to talk to Elidia and Spartan."

"The man you brought on board?"

He nodded. "Elidia is from a smaller house. Spartan is…nobody, I think. Who better to give us perspective?"

"But everyone knows the unaligned don't like the houses," Annika said. "What more could he tell us?"

He shrugged, but Judit saw something in his face she'd only glimpsed in the past. He was intrigued by Spartan, maybe romantically, maybe not. A gleeful little thought said that would distract him from her and Annika, making her a little appalled at herself while still being relieved.

She cleared her throat. "Maybe he'll have some insight into how long the unaligned have been plotting with the lesser houses."

"Here's a tip," Noal said sarcastically. "Maybe we don't call them lesser houses to their faces."

Their grandmother wouldn't have bothered, but Noal was the one who'd had the lessons in politics. It was clear their grandmother thought the chosen one only needed to be able to maneuver a ship in a firefight.

And they didn't have any better ideas at the moment. Judit had Elidia and Spartan brought to her office. Noal laid the situation out for them, downplaying the trouble the lesser houses were making and upselling the damage and the deaths that might happen if the violence wasn't stopped. Since Beatrice had told them of the earlier attacks, more reports had come in. Several Nocturna expansions had been attacked by what looked like unaffiliated pirates, but house chatter suspected a conspiracy of smaller houses. And the large houses weren't the only one suffering. Several smaller houses had ceased communicating outside their own holdings, and Roberts couldn't say if they were battening down the hatches, or if they'd quietly disappeared.

When everyone heard this, Spartan kept wiping his lips as if the whole thing left a bad taste in his mouth. "Look," he said when Noal paused. "I'm a regular guy. I'm not part of any house. I worked for some smalltime criminals on the *Xerxes,* and when push came to shove, I helped you." He gestured to Noal and Annika. "I don't want money. I don't want thanks. I just want off somewhere where I can buy passage back home."

"Let both of us go," Elidia said. "You're only making things worse by keeping us here. I can give him a ride home."

"I don't want anyone's help." Spartan's voice choked as if he was struggling to keep his tone neutral. "I can find my own way."

"You have to know this has been a long time coming," Elidia said to Judit, echoing Noal's earlier thoughts. "Power never lasts forever. If the big houses spent more time learning their history, they would know that." Her glance shifted to Annika and Noal. "Did you ever think the galaxy might not want your houses to join? If you were at each other's throats, you left the rest of us alone, but one giant house? If the other big houses didn't see the madness in that, they're crazy. It's all everyone else has been talking about."

Judit didn't bother to correct her about who could now marry and the fact that neither house seemed willing to go through with it. But now they had the rest of the galaxy to add to the list of people who'd try to prevent the wedding by kidnapping the bride and groom.

"So the smaller houses were already planning this uprising before we got involved?" Annika asked. "And the *Xerxes* set them off?"

Elidia shrugged, but there was something off about the way she sat—on the edge of her seat with a back so straight Judit could have used her as a coat rack—that said she wasn't confident. She had none of the smug look she'd displayed when she'd figured out who Judit was really after on the *Xerxes.* She didn't know what was behind the uprising, but she didn't want to admit it.

Annika rubbed her temples. "The takeover of the mining platform, these other disturbances, they're all happening too fast. Our actions on the station couldn't have spread this quickly. There's been no time to organize. Someone was waiting for the right moment."

Elidia stayed silent, but Spartan put his head in his hands. "I've got nothing to do with any of this!"

"With the galaxy in turmoil," Annika said to him, "I'd think you'd be happy to be somewhere safe, not to mention with people who are wealthy. Or have you abandoned your hopes of getting rich?"

He gave her an ugly look. "I'd rather be alive."

"Have you had any word from the *Xerxes*?" Elidia asked.

Judit sent a quick message to Beatrice. "We're getting that Houses Atrius and Flavio are answering for the station and the surrounding sector."

Elidia shifted in her seat. "No word from Munn?"

"Why worry if the other two are your allies?" Judit asked.

The way Elidia's eyes shifted around the room said that any alliance had probably dissolved as soon as the *Damat* left the system. Maybe the other two houses had had their eyes on the station for a long time, and Judit had given them the excuse they needed to kick their third partner out. If they weren't careful, Munn could find themselves disappearing, too, and they weren't the smallest of the houses.

"I say someone is pushing buttons," Annika said. "Everyone wouldn't spontaneously rally like this, and these attacks, these takeovers, speak of careful planning." She looked to Elidia. "And since you don't seem to know, either your house had a council without you, or someone entirely unrelated is pulling the strings." She raised an eyebrow. "There was a Flavio aboard the ship that kidnapped Noal and me."

Elidia's shocked expression could have been faked, but Judit hoped it was real. "I...Munn didn't have anything to do with that!"

Judit rubbed her chin. "So whoever's rallying the smaller houses either got Flavio to cooperate with them, or Flavio is doing it themselves." She shook her head. "Could they have contacted all the smaller houses and gotten them to attack at a moment's notice?"

Noal shook his head. "No, it sounds more as if someone knew when a crisis was going to occur. They arranged a kidnapping and were ready to light a match to the chaos that came afterward, no matter what that chaos might be."

"And we've played into their hands," Judit said.

Elidia's face screwed up in doubt. "And who is this mysterious mastermind? Flavio doesn't have that kind of clout." She lifted her hands. "And I'm not just saying that because Munn is larger than they are."

"I know one place to start looking," Judit said. "The ship where we found Annika and Noal."

Annika nodded. "We didn't have time to go through the computers before."

Judit turned to Elidia and Spartan, happy to have a course. "I'll need you both to stay in your quarters until I send for you again."

"Afraid we're going to take control of your ship?" Elidia asked, a sneer in her voice.

"Not really," Annika said.

Judit gave her a look. Even though her confidence was supremely sexy, it wasn't helping. Then the image of the bodies on the kidnappers' ship came to mind again, and she had to swallow. Somehow, the Annika she'd known for five years had killed an entire crew. Granted, they had kidnapped her and Noal, but something about the easy way she acted now said those deaths didn't weigh on her conscience. They certainly would have weighed on Judit's. Even though she'd been trained to kill in Noal's defense, she'd never had to, didn't even know if she could.

"Evie will take you to your rooms," she said, interrupting their debate. Evie waited outside, and at a gesture from Judit, she moved in. Noal and Annika followed close behind Judit as she headed for the bridge. Annika nearly had to jog to keep up with her, but Judit didn't slow.

"Is something wrong?" Annika asked.

Judit snorted a laugh. "Besides the kidnapping and the galaxy turmoil thing?"

Annika chuckled. "Yeah, besides that."

How could she say what she was really thinking? If being a trained killer was simply part of who Annika was, what could she say about that? Since Annika had never shown any sign of that before being abducted, how many other parts were there?

"There's a lot to think about," Judit said quietly, aware of Noal behind them.

"Like how quickly we can be alone in your office again." She winked, and Judit had to swallow as desire arced through her. In her office, there hadn't been time to think, and that had been as delicious as the actions themselves. She told herself to push the other thoughts down, deal with them later.

❖

Annika noticed Noal turn away as the kidnappers' ship appeared on Judit's screen, the slanted perspective making it seem as if that ship was coming closer and not the other way around. Annika supposed it was natural for him to shy away from bad memories. Ama would have encouraged her to do the same, to pretend the deaths affected her, but now that she'd had a small taste of telling the truth, she found she liked it.

Well, she liked telling *part* of the truth. She'd killed people who were going to sell her or kill her, and she didn't see why she should feel remorse.

Judit touched her arm. "Are you all right?"

So, Judit thought she should be pained by her memories, too. That stung a little, as if both Judit and Noal were saying something was wrong with her. "I'm fine."

Judit nodded slowly as if she didn't believe that. Annika couldn't blame her for being confused. Judit might have a false opinion of who Annika was, but Annika had helped build it. There had to be layers to Judit that Annika had yet to uncover, too. She hoped there was, something to even the field between them.

They went from the bridge to the *Damat*'s shuttle bay, and then the ride to the kidnappers' ship was an easy one. Annika, Judit, tactical officer Evie, and Beatrice, who seemed to serve as both pilot and systems specialist on the *Damat*, all squeezed into the shuttle together.

Once on board the kidnappers' ship, Annika didn't pause at the bodies, but she didn't hurry past them, either, conscious of Judit's gaze. She wondered if she should pretend a little to put Judit at ease. She'd heard that happened even in the most honest relationships. She had to wonder what would make Judit happier: a cheerful lie or a bald-faced truth? Maybe she'd be happiest not even having to consider such a question.

On the bridge, Beatrice dug into the computer, copying what files she could and scanning others. Annika watched over her shoulder. Like all houses, Flavio used codes, but maybe someone on the *Damat* could decipher it. At one transmission record, Annika put a hand on Beatrice's shoulder. She knew that code.

"Feric was here." He'd left orders that she wasn't to be awakened. He knew what she could do. Behind her, she could feel Judit watching, probably wondering the same thing she was. If Feric was giving orders, he was more than someone's tool. And that had to mean Nocturna had been involved in the kidnapping.

Didn't it? Feric had been raised to guard her. He was older than her, taken early from his parents, and raised to serve Nocturna above all else. Maybe mind control really was the key, then. The same techniques Nocturna had invented to control Noal. Maybe she should confess all she knew. Noal already suspected she was more than a guardian. Annika knew her lessons hadn't been the same as Judit's, and she didn't know if Noal would put it down to the differences in their houses or if he suspected something greater. Maybe he wasn't comfortable lying to himself. Ama would never have allowed such a thing inside her own house.

But if she told Noal Nocturna's real plans, he would hate her; they all would. Judit would. She had to keep that secret for all their sakes. Besides, she suspected the worm was involved, but she didn't *know*.

Annika leaned over Beatrice's chair. "Can you find out where Feric went?"

Beatrice shrugged. "I can send the scans to Roberts, see if he can make anything out from telemetry and galaxy-wide chatter."

"Copy everything to the *Damat*," Judit said, "and let's get out of here."

Annika waited while Beatrice worked, her stomach in knots. Part of her had hoped Feric was dead, used and then discarded, but now she had to track him across the galaxy if she wanted to find out what he knew. She should have keenly felt the sting of betrayal, but she kept remembering the giant who'd been a constant in her life, silent and protective. When they were alone together, he'd had this kind little smile. Her first kind smile. He'd never been disappointed in her. He'd never protected her from Ama, but she'd never expected him to. When she'd been a child, he'd held her.

He had to have been tricked. Manipulated. Controlled.

"It'll be all right," Judit said.

Annika took a deep breath, wondering how much of her discomfort had shown. But that didn't matter. This was something she could share with Judit wholeheartedly, making both of them feel better.

"It's Feric. I…" But what was the word for this mishmash of feelings? "When we find him, what will we do with him?" The real Feric, the one she'd grown up with, would never reveal a secret. What would she see now when she looked in his eyes? The blank look he'd had while abducting her? If he'd been working under Nocturna's orders instead of mind control, he had to obey. Annika might now be working against her family's plans. But someone had already disrupted their plans when they'd awoken her early. Whose script was she following?

Judit hugged her from the side, and Annika leaned into the touch.

They hurried back to the shuttle, everyone silent until they were aboard the *Damat*. In Judit's office, they told Noal what they'd found. He cautioned them to wait until the crew had a chance to sift through the data before they shared it with Elidia and Spartan.

When it came time to speculate, Annika was at a loss. "All I can think of are ifs and maybes. Plans within plots within conspiracies. It's making my head ache."

"Now you know how I've felt since waking up in that ship," Noal said. "I mean, was this our houses? I don't know how…" He shrugged and stared at the floor. "I feel as if I don't know anything anymore, as if no one ever *told* me anything."

Yes, he would be feeling that most of all. His house had told him nothing, but a stray Ama thought said he should have been asking questions.

Judit clapped him on the shoulder. "Nothing's as promised. Nothing's as expected, but we still have allies. We still have one another. We can fight."

Meridian thinking. Why bother to expect the unexpected when they could bash their way through every problem? "If we catch up to Feric, and he's working under orders from my house, or if some other house has found a way to sway him, he won't tell us anything. It won't matter what we do to him. Resisting torture was part of his training."

They both stared at her.

"What?" she asked.

"I thought we could…make an appeal," Noal said haltingly.

Judit nodded. "You could talk some sense into him, or if he's being manipulated or threatened, we could offer to help."

"You were thinking torture?" Noal asked.

And even though they were the naive ones, Annika fought a little flush. "Well, I mean…Meridians are always quick to use their guns!"

"We might be bullheaded, but we talk first!" Noal said. "We don't sneak around and stab people in the back. We don't lie!"

"Oh please—"

"Enough!" Judit barked. "We can't turn on one another now. Are we all agreed that we follow Feric once we find out where he's gone? If we find him or not, maybe we can find what he was looking for or discover if he was meeting anyone."

They nodded and settled into an uncomfortable silence. Luckily, they didn't have long to wait. Roberts had analyzed the data from the kidnapper's ship and discerned the transmission gate Feric had headed toward. From that gate's data, he determined several likely destinations—most of them on the edges of colonized space—and sent his conclusions to Judit's private computer.

Annika stared at the data and tried to make sense of it. It was a lot of nothing, several planets that were barely habitable, a deep-space listening post that was several years out of date, and one mining station under the control of a small house that Nocturna rarely had dealings with. Annika supposed they could be part of some conspiracy. There was also an unaligned habitable world, and that could be promising, too.

The last destination caught her attention: the Eye, the hierophant temple, the base of operations for the hierophants who traveled to the center of the galaxy in order to see the future in the time distortions of black holes. The givers of prophecy. Neutral, they normally stayed out of house business beyond officiating various ceremonies, but if Feric had been seeking information…

And information was something she sorely needed, too. "There," she said. Unlike the destinations on the fringes of the galaxy, this one was close to the heart. It felt right.

"The Eye?" Judit asked.

"Even if he hadn't been going there, we could sort through the prophecies for information."

They both looked skeptical, but the hierophants had many prophecies they never released, those they could make no sense of, those that could too easily be misinterpreted. Some who traveled to the center of the galaxy were simply unable to translate what they saw and rambled nonsense that was recorded and archived.

"The hierophants could be keeping a prophecy *they* couldn't make sense of, but *we* might know what it means. If someone saw something about us or about Feric…"

"Seems like a shot in the dark," Noal said.

"Better than going to all these different worlds asking questions and giving our families more opportunities to track us down." Annika's temper spiked, but he didn't back down from her gaze.

Judit sighed loudly. "Noal, any other ideas?"

His nostrils flared as he turned away, and Annika smiled in satisfaction. When Judit gave her a flat look, she shrugged and put the smile away.

"Even if we don't find anything," Annika said, "Nocturna has spies in the temple that are loyal to our house alone. They can tell us if Feric was there."

Noal rolled his eyes. Annika fought down an outburst after Judit gave her a conciliatory look. They seemed so different from each other in that moment: Noal turned to sarcasm, and Judit took everything in stride. Maybe that was the difference between being raised a guardian and a chosen one. Of course, Meridian had known from the beginning who the real chosen one was. In the end, they would have needed someone adaptable, someone with Meridian sensibilities who could still take orders. Noal was raised a brat because they didn't need him to be anything else until the time was right, and then they didn't need him to be anything at all. It made sense to her, but she didn't think Noal or Judit would appreciate it if she pointed it out. They probably thought their own house *couldn't* be so conniving.

And she supposed she should give Noal a bit of a break. She tried to focus on the times he'd made her smile, the times she'd thought of him as a friend, but there was only so much pouting she could take.

When Judit went to the bridge to give the command to go to the Eye, Annika caught Noal's arm. She didn't want to fight with him, despite her lack of empathy. "I'm sorry, Noal, for what it's worth. You would have made a good spouse."

He sighed and ducked his head, but when he raised it, he had a slight smile. "You know, even though I always knew the marriage was coming, I never gave it much thought. I probably would have been terrible. And an even worse ruler."

She smiled and denied it, but the truth was, he wouldn't have been any kind of ruler at all, not if her house had its way. With any luck, he'd never find that out.

CHAPTER EIGHT

Annika tried to get her thoughts in order as they headed for the Eye. Even if they didn't find anything at the temple, fewer people might be looking for them there. Until they knew who had organized the kidnapping, she thought it best to stay away from their families. She didn't want to be abducted again, but more than that, she was tired of being a pawn. A taste of freedom had been sweeter than she'd imagined.

She remembered the first time she'd been let loose on her own: turned out onto the streets of Nocturna Prime at eight years old to live on her own for a week. It had been exciting, thrilling. She'd had many a dangerous thought. She could have gone anywhere, could have pretended to be anything, anyone. It wasn't until years later that she'd found out Ama had been keeping an eye on her, that she would have been rescued if she'd truly needed help. Knowing that had soured the entire memory.

Now, loose on the *Damat*, she felt as if she was making her own decisions for the first time. Oh, she'd made a lot of choices on the kidnappers' ship, on the *Xerxes*, but those had been for survival. Now, as she watched over Judit's shoulder as the Eye came closer, she felt as if she was taking her first steps outside of fate.

Annika resisted the urge to rest her head on Judit's strong shoulder. After they'd come back from the kidnappers' ship, they'd split up to get some sleep. Annika had stared at Judit before they'd parted, wondering which of them would ask the other back to her quarters, but Judit had only bid her good night. Annika had been…relieved, and that had surprised her. She'd enjoyed her time in Judit's office, very much so, but there was too much going on in her mind. She could flirt; she would have gone to Judit's quarters if she'd been invited, but her mind would have kept drifting elsewhere: to Feric, to Noal, to the differences between all of them.

Now, though, with the heady taste of freedom in her mouth, Annika couldn't stop staring at the line of Judit's jaw, at the pale hairs that had escaped their tidy queue. She wanted to trail her fingers up and down Judit's neck, wanted to kiss her, thoroughly distract her from her duties until she pounced.

Instead, Annika told herself to keep her mind on her mission. Nothing had changed between her and Judit save that they were now well rested. It had taken a night and all the next day to get to the Eye, even using a transmission gate. Roberts had fed false ship codes as they passed through the gate, but someone would put the pieces together; someone would track them. Even if Meridian wasn't looking, Ama would never stop.

What would Ama do if Annika went back to her? All her careful plans had come undone. Even if Nocturna had her kidnapped, they couldn't have planned for her escape, for everything she did afterward. Maybe Ama would exile her as she'd claimed to have done to Annika's mother. She'd be Annika of No House, as nameless as anyone from an unaffiliated world.

The thought should have upset her. She was certain it would have upset Noal and Judit. Annika's mother hadn't been Nocturna Blood. She'd been picked to wed Annika's father for her excellent genes, and she'd been well rewarded, but something had gone wrong. The official record, Ama's record, listed her as an exile, but Annika knew the truth. Her mother had fled so she wouldn't become a strategic corpse, a disposable resource in Nocturna's schemes. It happened often; it had happened to Annika's grandfather. But no one knew where she'd gone.

When she'd fled, did she feel this free? Maybe she'd made allies as Annika had. The *Damat* could be her new house now. When Judit smiled at her, Annika knew she'd always have a place here. A comforting thought. It wouldn't have been as nice to be alone. Part of her wanted to suggest they head for the outer reaches and make a home where no one would find them, but the fate of the galaxy seemed to weigh on Judit more than it ever had on Annika. She and Noal cared about the lives of strangers—even if Noal wouldn't admit it—something Nocturna had cured Annika of years ago.

She sighed. That wasn't precisely true. She did care a bit what happened to Spartan. He'd been sucked into a dangerous adventure, though he should have been able to adapt. The thought of an ever-changing situation excited her. They should all be excited. They were free!

Annika smiled as she watched the hierophant's temple come closer still. Carved from a huge asteroid to resemble a ziggurat, it floated like an ancient temple among the stars. Umbilical airlocks trailed lazily underneath it like the tentacles of some giant monster, and the only ships docked were those the hierophants took to look into the heart of the galaxy itself, small shuttles designed for speed and good transmission strength.

The Eye was located as close to the heart of the galaxy as one could get without being slowly drawn in. The only thing closer was the last transmission gate before the black holes themselves. The light from the galaxy's center shone around the Eye as the *Damat* approached, lighting it from behind as if the universe itself was aflame.

It was something of an illusion. The black holes themselves emitted no light; such a massive singularity consumed light as it consumed everything, but that devoured light made the black holes glow before they extinguished it forever. The closer the hierophants came to the event horizon, the more they saw, and they transmitted what they'd seen to the rest of the galaxy. Most returned to find that time had moved on without them. Their prophecies might have arrived too late, and they sometimes returned years after they'd departed but were as young as they'd been when they'd left, preserved in the distorted time of the black holes.

Annika thought of Willa, the hierophant who had prophesied that a chosen one would unite Meridian and Nocturna. She'd had a way of looking at things and speaking of them in ways that everyone could understand, even if they then interpreted those prophecies however they wished. She'd seen the future right until she'd gone over the edge of the event horizon into oblivion.

In her head, Annika went over the Nocturna spies she knew of in the temple. When someone became a hierophant, they were supposed to leave behind house affiliations, but every house had spies in the temple, though the information they gleaned was often the same as everyone else received: the same vague prophecies, the same petty bureaucratic fights that infected any hierarchy. No one house had ever succeeded in taking over the temple or feeding misinformation to the rest of the galaxy. There were simply too many parties at work, and too many hierophants who truly believed in the cause. Since they performed so many official ceremonies, they were welcomed anywhere in the galaxy.

"We need to be careful what we say and to whom," Annika said close to Judit's ear. "There's more than one Nocturna in there."

Judit gave her a curious glance. "Apart from the spies you already told us about? Did any of them give up their house when they joined?"

Annika sighed. "They really kept you and Noal locked away, didn't they?"

"At least we know how to trust people," Noal said from Judit's other side.

Before Annika could retort, Judit cleared her throat. "You two should keep working together. You balance each other out."

Roberts had his hand to his ear, listening. "They want to know our purpose, Boss."

"Tell them we're bringing a new initiate." When Annika gave her a questioning glance, Judit shrugged. "We can't tell them the real reason, right?"

"You're more devious than I thought," Annika said.

"Who's it going to be?" Noal asked.

Judit shrugged. "Go see if Spartan is still as uninterested in creds as he pretended to be."

Noal seemed almost happy as he left the bridge. Maybe he was happy to be of use, even if it was just running Judit's errands.

To his credit, Spartan listened to Judit's whole proposal before saying no. "I've gone as deep in as I want to go. All I want is out."

"This is your chance," Judit said. "If you go aboard the Eye posing as an initiate, and we get the information we want, we can leave you here. It may take you a while to find a ship, but you'd be on your way."

He rubbed his hands through his hair and then smoothed them down his face, stretching the skin. "So, that's your threat, huh? I do this, or I'm stuck on this ship forever?"

"We're not in a position to drop you off somewhere else," Annika said. "And we're not the safest people to be with."

"I know you said it doesn't matter," Noal said, "but we can reward you. You can buy passage on the next ship that visits."

"How soon is that likely to be?" Spartan asked.

They all had to shrug.

He sighed hard. "I guess I have no choice. I'm your new initiate."

Noal clapped him on the shoulder. "Welcome to House Meridian."

They got him ready as quickly as they could, dressing him in something more suitable to a house member and transferring creds into his account for him to access later. He'd be a cousin in Meridian with the others posing as escort and house members who stopped in to pick up new prophecies. Of course, everyone would also suspect them of checking in with their spies, and in disguise as a Meridian guardian, Annika intended to do just that.

Beatrice caught up to them and pulled Judit aside for a whispered conversation. Annika admired the attempt at secrecy even as she wanted to know what was going on. She turned to see Noal watching her. He was frowning, probably expecting her to try to eavesdrop, but she turned to Spartan, who seemed nervous as the *Damat* hooked up to an umbilical from the Eye.

"Ever slid up one of these before?" Annika asked.

He shook his head. "I like the kind of airlocks you walk through."

"You stand under the hatch, take a little jump, and up you'll go. It can be a bit hard on the stomach. Be ready to step out once you're up there and make way for the next person."

Judit crossed over while one of the crewmen secured the umbilical. Annika tried not to ask, even biting her tongue. When Judit leaned toward her ear, Annika breathed out slowly, relieved she didn't *have* to ask. That was both a flaw and a wonderful thing about Judit.

"Beatrice reminded me that as captain, I shouldn't be going," Judit said.

"And you're ignoring her as usual?"

"Someday, she'll hit me over the head."

Annika chuckled. "And you gave her an order to distract her from worrying about you?" When Judit pulled back in surprise, Annika smiled wider. "I've watched you two together. I know you're close."

"Not like you and me. You know that, right?"

Annika nodded. Watching them together, she knew they were friends, not lovers.

Judit gave her hand a squeeze. "I told her to speak with Elidia again. Maybe House Munn can give us more information if she contacts them."

"Aren't you worried she'll give our position away?"

"Roberts will bounce the signal so they won't be able to tell where it's coming from. And Elidia doesn't know exactly where we are. Even if she manages to blurt out something before Evie or Beatrice tackle her, we'll be gone before Munn gets here."

It sounded like a long shot, but that was what life seemed full of these days.

When the umbilical was connected, Judit stepped to the front, but Annika touched her arm. "If I'm your guardian, I'm going first."

Judit's lips pressed into a thin line, but she nodded. Annika wondered what would happen when she finally let go of that tightly wound control, and the thought made her shiver.

A green light flashed. Annika stepped into the airlock and looked to the open door above where the long tube of the umbilical connected. She jumped, and a current of air sucked her upward. The opaque tube wouldn't let her see the surrounding space, but she was ready for the shock of cold. Not enough to harm her, it still took her breath away. She pulled her knees up, ready to land when the docking hallway of the Eye popped into view. She planted her feet on either side of the tube and stepped out of the way, ready for trouble.

No such luck. There was only a contingent of hierophants who'd come to welcome their new initiate. Annika had tied her hair up under a cap again, and she wore a Meridian uniform. They'd disguised her features with makeup, and the hierophants didn't seem to recognize her. They peered around her as if waiting for the real visitors to arrive.

Judit didn't wait for the all clear before she hopped aboard. Noal came next, then Spartan. The hierophants gathered around Noal and Judit, welcoming them and asking questions about their newest initiate. Spartan didn't look like a Meridian, making him a distant cousin, not worthy of much fuss. After the hierophants told Noal and Judit that they were welcome as long as they wanted to stay, the Meridians were turned over to one low-ranking member doomed to show them around.

"We'd like to stay a little while," Judit said, "to make sure our cousin settles in."

"Of course." The hierophant's wide eyes and eager smile said she was elated to be of use and terrified she might piss them off. "I'll show you to some quarters. The very best, I promise!"

"I'm sure," Noal said, all smiles and oozing condescension.

As they walked, Annika pulled Spartan close. "Go through the motions. Keep them busy."

He snorted a laugh. "What do you suggest I do? Light my quarters on fire?"

"Weren't you in charge of keeping people entertained on the *Xerxes*?"

"We had gambling there!"

She shrugged. "Might be high time they had it here."

He gave her a strange look, but the words seemed to make him thoughtful. When they split up for him—Spartan saying loudly that he still needed to make his final decision about staying—he seemed to have a plan brewing.

Once behind closed doors, Annika made a sweep for cameras and found none. "It's almost quaint."

Noal seemed as if he might say something, but Judit put a hand on his shoulder. "What's next?"

"I make contact with the Nocturna spy," Annika said. "He can tell us if Feric's been here. I'll ask about any prophecies the hierophants have been less than forthcoming about or any vague prophecies they haven't bothered to release. He'll probably recognize me, but I'll tell him I'm running a mission."

"That might not stop him from contacting Nocturna," Noal said.

Annika nodded. "We'll have to be quick."

"Be careful." Judit had so much feeling in her eyes, Annika could have kissed her right then, but not with Noal there. She hurried from the room, thinking on all she knew about her family's spy network. The one aboard the temple shouldn't be hard to find.

❖

Judit paced the room for nearly an hour, finding little else to do. Noal watched her with a bored expression. She kept waiting for him to tell her to calm down, but maybe he knew now wasn't the time for calm. She wondered if this was what life was going to be like from now on: Noal waiting for her to act. Since he wasn't the chosen one, he probably didn't know what else to do.

She clacked her teeth together. "Bea?"

"Here, Jude."

This close, they could use their own ship comm, and the chances of someone listening in were far less than with a long-range transmission. "How did it go with Elidia?"

"She's going to send some coded messages rather than trying to speak directly with her house. We figured that would be safer. I've got the computer working on the code, and it looks as if she's asking for info and warning them to stay out of any fights. She doesn't want her house getting into a battle with Meridian or Nocturna, especially not now that her partner houses seem to be squeezing Munn out of their holdings."

"Right," Judit said. "Keep me posted." She clicked her teeth again, cutting the comm.

Noal continued to stare.

"What?"

"You know I can't hear the conversations you have in your head, right?"

She breathed a laugh. "We should get you an implant."

"So someone can blather in my ear night and day? No, thank you." He sat back and toyed with the edge of a cushion. "So?"

She told him about the messages, and he nodded. "Sounds about right," he said. "When she thought she had allies, Elidia was ready to pick a fight, but now that her house might be standing alone, it's a different story. At least now we know she's not a fool."

"I never thought she was. Just headstrong."

"Something you admire," he said, nudging her with a toe.

She let that pass. "What's going on, Noal? What's your take on all this?"

"You mean, from the perspective of the chosen one?" Before she could say anything, he held up a hand. "Don't, don't. I'm feeling sorry for myself. I think Annika's right. Someone started this whole thing, even if it didn't end up as they planned. I think someone's been waiting for an opportunity, pushing buttons."

"Nocturna?"

"That's where the mind wants to go, but I'm not certain." He sat forward and licked his lips. "About Annika…"

"I know what you're going to say."

"You weren't there, Jude. You didn't see her killing people."

"We all do what we have to do."

He shook his head. "You didn't see her face."

She rounded on him, temper getting the better of her. "Now you're going to tell me she's a fiendish killer? That she liked it? Licked the blood off the walls?"

He stood and got in her face, something he'd never done before. It almost made her back up. "She didn't look like anything, Jude. She was *sedate*. She might as well have been a machine reaping wheat." His eyes were intense, unblinking, and she knew Annika had terrified him more than anyone ever had.

She put her hands on his shoulders, trying to hear him but unable to picture it. And Noal could be so dramatic at times. "You still care about her, and that tells me the Annika we knew is the real one. Whatever her family did to her, she's still—"

With a sigh, he sat again, the bored expression pulled back over his face like a mask. "You've got it bad. I knew you wouldn't listen."

The door chimed, and Judit fought her temper down before she spoke. "Come in."

The hierophant who'd led them to their quarters was back, an eager smile on her face. "I thought you might like a tour."

Judit was about to decline, but Noal stood. "We would indeed," he said. "I've always wanted to see the archives. I could spend hours pawing through the fascinating prophecies that were never untangled."

The hierophant beamed. Judit followed as she led the way. She wanted to wait for Annika, but if there was trouble, Noal was the one who couldn't look after himself. Judit tried not to grumble as the hierophant droned about history, tried not to stomp as they arrived in a room in the center of the Eye, the space dominated by a large black surface surrounded by chairs.

"This room stores the unknown prophecies," the hierophant said. "Those too muddy or garbled or that make no sense in the galaxy as we know it."

Noal nodded, expression impressed. "Can we have a moment?"

"Of course! Take your time."

When she left, Judit noticed a hum, as if the whole room was meditating. She wondered if it helped some people. Noal passed a hand over the surface, and it winked to life, small green lights glittering along it.

"Query. How many unknown prophecies are there?" he asked.

The number *7,560,432* appeared as a holo display.

Judit sank down in a chair. "Wonderful."

"They must babble nonstop while they're out there. Query. How many unknown prophecies mention the chosen one of House Meridian?"

The display read *7,000 prophecies mentioning House Meridian. 2,604 mentioning chosen one and House Meridian.*

Judit whistled softly. "Popular topic."

"I guess Willa's prophecy mentioning me...or you...won't be in here, since it's one of the official prophecies."

"And searching by time won't help. What period of time the hierophant saw depends on how close they got to the event horizon and how far time was dilated."

He passed his hand over the console again. "Let's just check. Query. How many of those prophecies were from Willa?"

Zero, the display read. He sighed, a frustrated sound. "Query. How many of Willa's prophecies are labeled unknown?"

Zero.

"I heard she didn't make many," Judit said. "All of them must have been good."

"So, unless you want to sit and read a couple thousand prophecies, this was a giant waste of time."

Judit put her own hand over the surface. "Query. How many prophecies containing references to House Meridian, the chosen one, and House Munn?"

There were only several hundred, so they resigned themselves to sitting and listening to the prophecies or reading them. Most were beyond comprehension, people babbling as they stared into the void, trying to speak about what they saw. Judit had never been near a black hole, couldn't say what the hierophants were seeing and how it was presented. The hierophants had been listening to transmissions made far in the future or watching vid feeds or sometimes staring at stars whose light was hurtling at them before disappearing over the event horizon. Judit grew tired of listening to the shouting and babbling and read instead.

"Anything?" she asked after an hour or so.

"Nope. Maybe we should go find Annika."

She peered across the console at him, hearing the edge in his voice. "Look, Noal..."

He gave her a languid look. "Are you going to tell me to get over it? Which part? The one where instead of being destined to unite two houses, I'm destined for dick-all? Or are you asking me to get over how I feel about not getting married to the person I've been training to be married to for years? Or maybe it's the murder thing? You want me to let that go so you don't have to think about it."

She sat back, feeling slightly sick. "Do you love her?"

"How come you're only asking that now?"

She looked down. "I couldn't bear to hear it before."

"So, now that you feel sorry for me, you can bear it? Now that you're certain she doesn't want me but has always wanted you?"

"By the darkness, Noal! I want us to be okay. You and me."

He stared. He was always so much better at arguing than her. He knew how to cut deep, but the pain in her eyes must have gotten to him. He dropped his gaze. "I did love her, but not like you do. I didn't want to fall in bed with her every time I saw her."

She tried to think of the right thing to say, something that wouldn't bring his bitterness out again, something that wouldn't make him bring up Annika's darker side. "Be angry with our grandmother, Noal. Be angry at the people who thought you were only good as a decoy. I know you're smart and cunning. Your compassion is your strength. Show them."

He held her gaze for a second before dropping it. "I don't know."

She pounded a fist on the surface, and he jerked in his seat, eyes wide. "Show. Them. You will not let them turn you into nothing."

He smiled, and it had more than a bit of the old Noal. "Are you going to marry her?"

She blinked, and a myriad of emotions rushed through her. On the one hand, she'd love to finish what she and Annika started on the *Damat*, but on the other? She'd secretly pictured herself marrying Annika dozens of times, but to say it aloud? And she wasn't certain

Annika would want to go through with such a deed now that she wasn't being forced.

"I wouldn't be sad if you did," he said. "Well, not forever. I'd dance at your wedding."

That felt like a punch to the gut. She didn't know if she could have said the same, but one look at his face said he wasn't trying to wound. She clasped his hand. "Thank you."

"Don't thank me. I'll be drunk. My dance will be so bad, it'll embarrass both of us."

She smiled, touched. "I wouldn't have it any other way."

The door slid open, and Annika walked through. "I looked for you two in your room, but I see you're being productive." She flashed a smile, and Judit considered marriage yet again. Even Noal returned her look with an ounce of his old affection.

"We haven't found anything solid," he said. "Plenty of vague references that might be talking about what's happening right now, but other than that…"

"And your spy?" Judit asked. "Was Feric here?"

"It took a little doing to convince my contact not to report me, but once he agreed, he confirmed that Feric *was* here." She shook her head and crossed her arms as if the idea disturbed her, even though it was what they were hoping to hear. "Feric said he was here to check on a Nocturna initiate, and that initiate left with him."

"Another spy?" Judit asked.

"I don't know. My contact said we'd have to get access to the command center to get a look at her."

Noal shook his head. "But whatever information Feric was after, this initiate probably had it, and now she's gone, too."

Judit sat back and closed her eyes. "And your contact had no idea what the information might be?"

Annika shook her head.

Judit's jaw tingled, and Beatrice's voice sounded in her ear. "Jude, someone on the Eye sent a coded transmission to the nearest gate."

Judit pointed toward her ear so the other two would know she wasn't about to talk to herself. "Any idea who it's for?"

"If I had to guess, with the three of you there, it's either Meridian or Nocturna."

"Someone sent a transmission," Judit said to Annika and Noal.

Noal sat up straighter and looked to Annika. "Sounds as if your contact wasn't convinced not to turn you in."

She started for the door, a deep frown in place, but Judit rose to stop her. "We don't have time. We need to get to the command center and see if we can get eyes on Feric's initiate. Maybe you'll recognize her. Bea?"

"Still here, Jude."

"See if Roberts can send some transmissions to make it look as if the *Damat* already left the system. Buy us as much time as you can."

"Will do, Jude."

They hurried from the room and turned right, heading for the lift that would take them to the Eye's highest level, where the tour guide told them the command center was. "I hope the head hierophant wasn't joking when he said we'd be welcome anywhere on the station."

They headed up, but when the doors opened on a long, unmarked hallway, Judit headed for the first person she saw and spun him around by the shoulder. The hand computer he'd been reading went flying.

"Take us to the command center," she said. His mouth opened and shut. Judit stepped close to him, face angled down, expression grim. "Now."

He babbled then hurried back the way they'd come, past the lift and down a hall to a large set of double doors. Instead of keying them open, he rang a chime, and Judit cursed the fact that she hadn't bullied someone with access.

The head hierophant opened the door. Judit stepped forward and forced him to take a step inside, blocking the door.

"You've been harboring Meridian enemies," she said.

His eyes widened. "We have hierophants from many different—"

"A person who committed crimes against House Meridian fled here, met up with one of your initiates, and escaped."

He paled, and Judit knew she'd hit the mark. Feric's visit and disappearance with one of his initiates had disturbed him. Those who wanted to join the temple took a few days to make their final decision when they arrived at the Eye, but once that decision was made, they didn't leave again until they were full hierophants.

"We...didn't know what he wanted," the head hierophant said. "That man came here under false pretenses."

"Show us the feeds."

He marched toward a display and called up an image of Feric entering the Eye through one of the umbilicals. "The dock is the only place we have cameras."

"Do you have him leaving?"

He chose another file and opened it, showing Feric leaving with a dark-haired, fair-skinned woman. Judit couldn't immediately place her house. She could have been Nightingale, a house with strong connections to Nocturna.

Annika stepped past, eyes glued on the holo image. Her mouth parted, and she breathed heavily as if she was a heartbeat away from losing control.

"You know her?" Judit asked softly.

A terse nod, then Annika strode from the room. Judit stayed with her, not acknowledging the babbling head hierophant who trailed behind them.

"Who is it?" Noal asked as he hurried to keep up.

"My mother," Annika said.

Noal and Judit exchanged a look, and Judit had a thousand questions, but she didn't ask them yet.

"I'm going to tell Spartan we're leaving," Noal said.

Judit nodded. "Quickly."

He peeled off, but they didn't stop as they marched toward the lowest level. As they reached the hallway closest to the umbilical airlocks, Judit turned to the head hierophant.

"That'll be all." He seemed as if he might speak again, but Judit held up a hand. "We don't hold you responsible. We're leaving to look into it now. If you see any of our ships, tell them to meet us in the Panther Nebula."

Which was the opposite direction of where she planned to go. But he nodded and hurried away, and all that was left was to wait.

"You can go ahead," she said to Annika. "I'll wait for Noal."

Annika paced up and down the hall, shaking her head, not speaking.

Judit thought of a thousand things to say but didn't know which would help. Like all of them, Annika hadn't been raised by her parents. The few times they'd spoken of family, Annika had only mentioned her father. Judit had assumed her mother was dead, but when she and Noal had done a little prying, they'd found that Annika's mother had been exiled from House Nocturna. Rumors varied about why.

It had happened when Annika was twelve, so she'd known her mother a little, unless Nocturna had always kept them separate. Neither Judit nor Noal had wanted to ask. Now, from the pinched, angry look on Annika's face, Judit wondered if the falling-out between her mother and Nocturna had involved Annika herself.

CHAPTER NINE

A nnika couldn't believe what she'd seen on that holo. She felt as if it was still hovering in front of her. Her mother, Variel Nightingale-Nocturna, a woman she'd thought never to see again, large as life, escaping the Eye with Feric the betrayer.

She thought of the last time they'd seen each other, shortly after her mother had guided the surgery that resulted in the bone stiletto. It had seemed the perfect gift, a weapon not even Ama knew about, though she had no doubt Ama would have approved. Her mother had taken her aside one day, pulling her out of training, and she'd wondered if there would be another gift. But her mother had led her out of the training facility on Nocturna Prime and told her it was a day out.

Probably another test, but Annika was always happy to spend time with her mother, even if her mother's lessons skewed slightly from Ama's. Her mother was happy Annika had so many skills, but where Ama displayed a willingness to sacrifice others, Annika's mother always encouraged caution. Annika hadn't see the point of thinking before killing someone. Such hesitation might get her killed. That had changed when she'd met Judit and Noal, but by that time, her mother had been gone for three years.

Outside the facility, her mother had made her wait on a street corner, claiming she'd forgotten something, but when she'd ducked back into the building, she hadn't come out again. Her last smile had been tense and hurried, so different from her normal, easygoing look, another thing Ama didn't share.

It was Ama who finally came to collect Annika, saying Annika's mother had betrayed Nocturna and been exiled. It was only later that

Annika had found out the sentence had been passed down *after* her mother had already escaped. Ama said her mother had gotten her out of class as a distraction, that she'd taken Annika outside so everyone would be looking for the Nocturna heir rather than her mother.

For a time, Annika hadn't believed her. In her secret heart, she'd known her mother had been going to take her into exile. And one day, her mother would come back for her. But that hadn't happened, and then it was easier to believe Ama.

Now, though, with that holo image looming in her mind, tiny thoughts long dead began to resurface. Her mother might have had a plan to get her with Feric. Her kidnapping might have been her liberation. The person who'd wanted to meet her on that kidnapper's ship could have been her mother.

Or maybe her mother was just trying to cripple the house who'd betrayed her.

Noal jogged down the hallway, Spartan in tow. Annika raised an eyebrow, happy to have a target for her anger that wasn't in her own mind. "Come to say good-bye to your abductors?"

She meant it as sarcasm, but Spartan shook his head. "Even though I was on my way to getting a good poker game going, I'm not sticking around waiting for your houses to interrogate me. I like my fingernails where they are, thanks."

"Meridian wouldn't…" Noal started to say. He glanced at Annika and cleared his throat. "He wants to come with us."

"Better the darkness you know," Spartan said.

Annika rolled her eyes, but Judit shrugged. "Fine." She gestured for Noal and Spartan to step into the umbilical. "Someone's waiting to catch you on the other end. Annika, you're next."

Even though Annika was probably more capable in a fight, Judit still volunteered to go last. Was that Meridian thinking or simply her nature? Whatever it was, Annika couldn't think too hard on it at the moment, not with thoughts of her mother swirling in her brain.

As soon as everyone was aboard the *Damat*, Judit marched for the bridge, ordering Beatrice to take them out of the system and toward the nearest transmission gate.

"Destination?" Beatrice asked.

Judit hesitated, looking around the bridge. "We need to sort through the info we have, plan our next move. Take us to Xeni."

Annika couldn't help a shocked laugh. "So, one of the favorite vacation spots of the Blood is also your secret planning location?" She'd never been there, but she'd heard tales of pristine beaches and perfect weather, of glorious violet sunsets and light reflecting off the planet's rings.

Judit cleared her throat. "It's mostly untouched. We won't be spotted over some city, and people only go there for pleasure. Would you expect it?"

"No," Annika said. "It's brilliant."

And unexpected. Thoughts of her mother, of all her problems flew away as she stared at Judit and pictured the beaches of Xeni. There were many ways they could lose themselves there, many things to do that didn't require thinking or planning. Even though Judit wanted to plan, Annika was certain she could prove a distraction, at least for a little while.

Her first look at Xeni through Judit's screen did not disappoint. In the light of its twin suns, Xeni looked purple, a hue cast over most of the planets in its system because of the bright white sun and the blue dwarf star circling close to it. The ore in the rocks of Xeni's rings shone like molten gold, and each time one rock smacked gently into its neighbors, it created a shower of golden dust that sparkled like fireworks.

An automated system prompted them for the codes needed to breach the planet's atmosphere, and Judit used a standard Meridian code. There were many coded planets in the galaxy, and Annika had no doubt someone was combing through each and every one, trying to find Annika and Noal, but it would take them a while, and Judit was right. Xeni might be one of the last places anyone would check.

They breached the atmosphere, and Annika watched the ocean go by with the occasional land mass rising out of the water, none of them large enough to be called a continent. It was a series of islands, though some were grand indeed. Each island was encircled by a bright white beach, and the plants inward were a mix of dark green and even darker purple. Blue-green and lavender near the shore, the water surrounding each island deepened to indigo farther out, punctuated by white wave caps.

The automated system guided the *Damat* to a large, empty island. Beatrice steered for a patch of cleared jungle near a deserted beach. Xeni had many such landing pads, reserved for high-ranking members of the Blood, but they were all shrouded by signal-masking satellites. The Blood didn't like to be spied on while sunbathing, and even though Xeni's satellites could be hacked like any others, Xeni would give them somewhere to go to ground.

The *Damat* landed with barely a thud, and everyone seemed to relax.

"Bea," Judit said. "Make a schedule for shore leave. Someone should always be monitoring scanners."

"Got it, Jude."

With a soft smile at Annika, Judit inclined her head toward the exit, and they made their way down before anyone else, exiting the *Damat* from the long gangplank that extended between its landing struts.

It was a quick walk out of the trees to the beach, and Annika pulled off her shoes and buried her feet in the soft white sand. The breeze lifted her hair, and the air smelled of salt mixed with a floral scent. The trees towered overhead, great trunks groaning in the breeze while their dark purple leaves flapped against each other in a waxy, clapping sound.

Along the beach stood little cabanas, wood and gauze with reclining chairs inside, but Annika knew they would be state-of-the-art with light refracting enclosures that could obscure the occupants and provide climate control. They were probably well stocked with provisions. She'd heard that people who visited Xeni preferred to see no one else on their trip, and the house who owned it had gotten wealthy providing just such an experience.

Voices came from the ship as others disembarked. Annika wandered down the beach away from them, watching the ocean, listening to the surf, scanning the horizon, something she didn't often get to see. The sky was a delicate pink, the scarce clouds white, and the air utterly peaceful.

When Judit touched her shoulder, she jumped a little, laughing at the sensation.

"Sorry," Judit said. "You've been quiet since…"

"Just thinking. I've never been here before." She started to walk, and Judit stayed beside her. After a long moment, Annika paused. "Will everyone be all right without you?"

"They'll wander around or get some rest, and if they need me, they know how to get in touch with me." Her eyes held a thousand questions, but Annika didn't want to answer any of them, not yet.

They resumed walking, and Judit cleared her throat, an embarrassed little sound. "When you stopped talking during the trip, I thought you might be upset with me."

"Why?"

"Well..." She waved a hand as if to indicate the whole galaxy. "Judit, none of us asked for this. It's the houses. And once I started thinking about it, it all seemed a long time coming."

Judit nodded.

"Do you ever think about...running away?"

Judit barked a laugh. "Sure."

But Annika knew she was joking. Judit would no more abandon her duty than she'd abandon breathing.

Annika looked back, but no one was in sight. Others from the *Damat* had been wandering down to the water, but no one seemed inclined to come around the corner. Maybe they knew better than to follow so hard on the heels of their captain. Annika led Judit a little farther down the beach and away from the water's edge, into the shade of the trees. Judit had a quizzical look, a little smile that said she was anticipating a secret conversation, but talking was the last thing on Annika's mind.

In the light of the golden rings arcing across the sky above them and the twin suns now hidden by the tree line, Annika kissed Judit gently. Judit deepened the kiss, their lips sliding across each other, but as their mouths opened, Judit pulled away. "Maybe we shouldn't."

Irritation flashed through Annika, but she told herself she wouldn't push. She *would* lay out the facts, though. "We're on a deserted beach on the most beautiful planet within several systems. For a little while, we can just be...us. And I need to forget, even if it's only for a few moments."

Judit paused as if considering. "You're right." She came back in for another kiss, one hand reaching around Annika's waist and the other cupping her jaw, fingers gliding through her hair. Annika kissed her back as passionately and pulled her closer, grabbing her waist. When Judit made a hungry little sound and slipped her tongue into Annika's mouth, Annika let her hands wander to the front of Judit's uniform jacket, unfastening it hurriedly.

Judit spent a few fumbling moments helping before she seemed to remember that Annika was wearing clothes, too. As her arms came free, she reached for Annika again. Annika stilled, letting Judit undress her, enjoying the kisses and caresses and straying hands. When Judit buried her head between Annika's breasts for several seconds, kissing and licking, Annika chuckled delightedly before lifting Judit's head, kissing her again, and continuing to shuck both sets of clothes.

When they tumbled to the sand, Annika endeavored to keep them on top of their clothing but quickly gave up, letting them roll wherever they needed. Judit was a ball of energy that had been repressed too long, and Annika's mind whirled from every hurried caress, every kiss from a mouth that moved like a drowning woman seeking air. She'd never been so thoroughly explored, so enjoyed in all her life by someone who clearly wanted her to enjoy it as much. Judit responded to every moan or cry of yes, applying more pressure or a deeper kiss or a steady pace with fingers or tongue.

Finally, though, when Annika bit her lip through a second orgasm, Judit's energy seemed to flag. Though Annika felt drained, hunger still gnawed inside her, and she turned her attention to Judit's tall, muscular form.

Judit received pleasure more hesitantly than she gave it, occasionally twisting her hips away or trying to coax Annika back to her mouth. Annika did as Judit bid, having to kiss slowly and touch languidly. It would have been teasing to anyone else, but to someone shy with her body, it helped put Judit at ease, get her used to the touching until she went to a place where she could receive pleasure openly. Then Annika gave and gave until Judit sagged as if she could receive no more.

They lay together, breathing hard and staring at the sky, their forearms and fingers touching but nothing else, as if there were too many raw nerves between them for further contact.

"I love you," Judit said softly. "I have for a long time."

"I knew," Annika said. "Because I've loved you just as long."

In that moment, the secrets between them didn't seem to matter, though they would someday, Annika was sure. For now, though, she stilled and enjoyed herself.

They turned to look at one another as day finally gave way to twilight, and Judit's dark eyes picked up the gold of the rings overhead. "Things never turn out this way in stories."

"No," Annika said as she scooted closer so their lips could brush together. "The lovers often run off together."

Judit frowned. "You were serious before, weren't you? When you asked if we could run?"

"I don't understand why the fate of the galaxy has to rest on our shoulders."

Judit turned to look at the sky before she shrugged. "It has to rest somewhere."

Annika supposed that was just a difference between them. "It doesn't matter. I'll go wherever you lead."

"My own personal guardian? I could get used to that."

Annika pushed up on her elbow to give Judit another kiss.

"It's going to be dark soon," Judit said.

"So? Let it be dark."

"You want to sleep…outside?"

So very Meridian. They were always about the technology and gadgets and implants. Nocturna had always embraced the natural, even if they then used it to kill people.

"Come on." She stood and helped Judit scoop up their clothing but stopped Judit from putting it back on.

The skepticism was plain on Judit's face even in the fading light. "I'm close to my crew, but we don't usually wander around naked."

"We're not going back yet." She headed for the nearest cabana. Just a little farther down the beach, and they would have found it before they'd made love, but that would have meant a few more minutes of waiting, and Annika didn't think she could have done that.

When they climbed into the cabana, Judit sighed in relief, and Annika nearly laughed at her. Judit quickly found the controls, and thin panes of glassteel closed around them, darkening slightly. Now no one could see in, but they could still see out. Soft lights came on, just enough to see by.

Annika wrapped her arms around Judit's sandy shoulders. "It's a shame we don't have a shower."

Judit grinned. "Ah, but you only have to wish…" With another touch of a control, waterproof covers slid over the long deck chairs, and a gentle rain fell from the ceiling.

With a laugh, Annika turned her face upward and let the sand wash away. Technology did have its uses, after all. After they showered and ate some of the provisions stored in the cabana's cooling unit, they pushed the comfortable deck chairs together and slept under the stars.

Annika woke with the dawn, and thoughts of her mother bloomed in her brain until Judit's touch grazed her shoulder, and their evening together took center stage in her mind again. They made love, sleepily, slowly, and Annika wondered if their whole life could be this way. Surely no one on the *Damat* would argue if they stayed on Xeni, if they all spent their days and nights eating and sleeping and having sex in the sand.

At least until someone found them.

As if on cue, Annika felt the vibration in Judit's jaw as someone pinged her comm.

"Perfect timing," Judit muttered. She paused for several seconds. "Bea has some news."

Annika sighed as she began to dress in her sandy clothes. They'd shaken them out, but the cabana wasn't equipped for washing clothing. At least the sand was a wonderful reminder of what had passed between them.

Annika's steps dragged as they went back to the *Damat*, and her thoughts turned again to her mother and the kidnapping. If *Nocturna* was behind the kidnapping—and she still thought that likely—that meant they were working with her mother again. *Un*likely. Though if Ama could use someone, she wouldn't pass up that chance over a silly thing like bad blood. She'd pretended to put the past with Meridian behind her, after all. She'd play nice until she had her chance to strike. Annika's mother had to know that, had to expect it.

Everyone on the *Damat* looked a little disheveled and sweaty, as if they'd only started to enjoy themselves when Beatrice recalled them. "Xeni isn't as good a hiding place as we thought, Jude," Beatrice said as both Annika and Judit reached the bridge. Judit hadn't wanted to stop long enough to change, and Annika knew that even with the shower, they had to look a mess. They probably smelled like sand and sex, too. But everyone on the bridge seemed too tactful to notice.

"We need to lay some other false trails," Roberts said. Not a strand of his dark hair was out of place. Like Beatrice, he probably hadn't left the *Damat*, but by the intense way he stared at his station, Annika bet he never took many breaks. "Some of these signals I'm getting are pretty close to us."

"Let me call home," Annika said.

When they turned to stare, she didn't know what to say, didn't even know why she'd said anything. Ama wouldn't admit anything that mattered over a long-range transmission, but Annika needed to hear from her, needed to say a few things, even if she made matters worse.

Roberts rubbed his chin. "It'll take a while to set up a direct transmission, and we'll need to be close to a gate to do it. There are a few stars I could bounce the signal off of, some relays I could put it through. We could look as if we're in several places at once, but you might have to keep it short, and there would be a delay."

Annika nodded. "I'll talk in code. She'll be expecting that."

"Yep," he said. "And we can keep on the move and keep bouncing the signal around, but there's no way to hide forever." He turned to Judit. "It might buy us some time."

Judit looked at Annika with an expression made of worry and sympathy. "Are you sure you want to do this?"

Annika nodded, but though they'd recently been so close, she felt worlds coming between them again. Sex couldn't silence the secrets for long. And talking with her grandmother might let her ultimate secret out, but she didn't think so, not where the whole galaxy could hear.

But she still needed to hear Ama's voice.

"In my office," Judit said. They walked together, and when Annika took Judit's hand, she didn't pull away, even when her crew might see. Annika was tempted to kiss her, but thought that might be flying too far in the face of decorum.

Once they were behind closed doors, Judit gave her a quick kiss. "I'll be outside if you need me."

Annika caught her arm. "I want you here." Everything inside her cried out that she was making a mistake. Her secret was too great, but maybe she wanted it out in the open, before they got any closer, but what was closer than love? "You...might pick up on something I miss."

"I doubt that," Judit said with a fond smile, a look that said she was touched. "I won't be able to understand your code, but I'll stay."

The *Damat* lifted from Xeni, and Annika regretted she wasn't looking at a screen and watching the planet go, but maybe this was better. If she didn't have to watch it retreat into the distance, she could remember it as a canopy of stars overhead and soft sand beneath her naked body.

It didn't take long to get to the closest transmission gate, and then they were on the clock. There was only so long they could stay close to it before someone discovered them. Judit stood against the wall where the holo of Ama wouldn't see her.

"Roberts says everything is ready."

Annika took a deep breath, provided the right codes to get their transmission into the hands of her grandmother, and it was only a few minutes before the console winked to life. A holo of Ama's face appeared above it. "Who has you?" Ama asked.

No hello, no asking if she was all right, but had she really expected that? "What makes you think anyone does?" she said in the same coded language Ama was using.

There was a bit of a delay, the words fed from gate to gate, winging through the stars. "Well, you haven't found your way back." And Ama wouldn't care if Annika told the galaxy who had kidnapped her.

"I'm not dead, either, if that's what you were planning."

Ama's head tilted. "The whole galaxy knows your guardian was brainwashed, probably by a so-called ally of our house that is now part of this coup. Come back now, see the marriage done, and we can start repairing this rift."

She took another breath. "And my mother?"

Ama didn't so much as twitch. "Your mother is in exile."

But even if they were face-to-face and light-years from everyone else, she still might not admit anything. "Ama…" What could she say? Why had she called at all?

"Time is running out, Annika. The lesser houses are attacking major holdings. If marrying into Meridian is no longer an option for peace, I will think of something else. It could be that the lesser houses will destroy Meridian, and then, well, the universe is wide."

A little sniping about Meridian. Anyone who deciphered their code would expect that. As for finding something else for her to do, it could be leading Nocturna, or if Ama thought she was too rebellious, another heir would be found amongst her cousins. And then her new assignment could be "corpse."

Judit held up a hand. If she stayed on much longer, the signal might be tracked to their real location rather than serving as a decoy.

"They can be spared," her grandmother said. "Both of them. If you come back now. Lose any more time, and they will not be so fortunate."

"Good-bye, Ama." She gestured toward Judit.

The transmission cut out, and Judit stepped forward. "Anything?"

Annika considered her grandmother's words. She wasn't a woman to make empty threats, and Annika saw through the offer to spare Judit and Noal. Ama was saying that if Annika didn't come home, she'd kill Judit and Noal to get to Annika. She'd kill them anyway if she got her hands on them. Maybe Annika was supposed to believe that if she went home, Ama wouldn't bother looking for them at all. She might have believed that if Ama were anyone else.

"She threatened you," Annika said. "To get me to come back."

"Annika, no!"

"Don't worry. I thought about it for half a second. But she can't hurt you if she can't get to you, and I'm not letting her lead me anymore." She held her hands out, and Judit took them. "I don't even know why I called her. I asked about my mom."

"What did she say?"

Annika shook her head, feeling sadder by the instant. "My mother left on her own, but Ama told everyone she was exiled. I thought she wanted to take me with her, but Ama said she was using me as a distraction."

Judit kissed her gently. "Maybe she had you kidnapped to save you?"

"From marriage to Noal?" Annika asked with a little smile.

"From house politics."

"She could have asked me if that was the case." Her chest ached a little at the thought.

"Not if she couldn't get to you. This might be the only way she could think of to talk to you." Judit shook her head. "Though if that was true, why didn't she wait on that ship for you to wake up?"

"Maybe she feared what I would do to her," Annika muttered.

Judit's expression turned skeptical. "You wouldn't hurt your own mother."

Meridian thinking again, but Annika found she couldn't argue.

Even with her irritation, she loved Judit in that moment. Hot on the heels of that, though, she felt the weight of secrets again. She wondered if that feeling would ever go away when they had their clothes on.

"What now?" Annika asked. "Where do we go next? Or are we going to become houseless pirates?"

Judit's eyes widened. "We couldn't!"

"It's a joke, Judit. Even if we never go home again, I'm invested in figuring this out now."

Judit's arms dropped from around Annika's waist, and she stepped back, leaning on her desk, her face stricken. "We can't go home again? You really think that?"

Annika's heart went out to her even as she fought the frustration that was always bubbling around Meridians. "Well, maybe you can go back, but not me. I don't want to be part of anyone's schemes anymore." She lifted a hand before Judit could speak. "And please don't try to tell me your house doesn't scheme."

"I'll leave that argument to Noal."

Annika stepped close and lowered her voice. "He can't be as naive as he sounds, can he?"

"He hates secrets, that's all."

"When his house was keeping the biggest one. The identity of the real chosen one."

"That was hard for all of us."

"You're not pleased?" Annika asked with a little smile.

"If it means we get to be together…" She stared with love in her eyes.

They kissed again, the secrets of their houses slipping but never forgotten. As their kiss deepened, Annika was never so happy to have her house far away, nearly on the other side of the galaxy, where its plots couldn't touch them.

For the moment.

Chapter Ten

Judit lost herself in the deep kiss just as her office door chimed.
"You've got to be kidding me!" Annika said.

Judit chuckled. "We should be used to getting interrupted by now."

"A woman can dream of a brighter future." As Annika turned away, a look of pain crossed her face. Her mother couldn't be far from her mind, no matter what she said, no matter what else happened. It would have consumed Judit, though she'd been happy to distract Annika for a little while.

"Come in," Judit called.

The door slid open, and Elidia stepped inside, a wry smile on her face. She'd changed out of the stationmaster's uniform and into a more comfortable-looking pair of slacks and a long-sleeved shirt that hung nearly to her knees. Judit wondered who she'd borrowed them from.

Elidia looked from one of them to the other. "Did you forget about me?"

"No, we haven't…had time," Judit said, not wanting to admit that lovemaking had taken priority. "I see you're wandering around on your own."

"Within limits. Evie gave me permission because of all the help I've given her."

The coded messages. Right. "Find out anything useful?"

"I've heard back from my house. I think I convinced them that someone is deliberately spreading chaos. They've been getting transmissions that *seem* to be coming from near our outer holdings, but when the homeworld dug a little, they discovered that the transmissions originated from the wrong part of space." She frowned hard in what

Judit had come to think of as her natural expression. "And all the rumors they've heard about various attacks can't be true."

Judit had no doubt that many of them were false. Each house had its own news agencies, its own ways of gathering intel and data. Vids and transmissions were easily faked, and it took someone picking through them to discover what was real and what wasn't. The more easily intercepted a news story was, the greater the chance that it was designed to mislead. Nocturna's anti-Meridian propaganda was legendary.

"Which reports have they deemed false?" Annika asked.

Elidia smiled. "One attack supposedly involved this ship, and since I've been aboard the whole time, I could guarantee that one didn't happen. Once I did that, my house looked harder into the others."

Judit rubbed her temples, her anger spiking. Now people were spreading lies about her ship, her crew? Did she even want to know what they'd claimed she'd done? "Well, either it's a complete fabrication, or someone thought we were going to be somewhere else. Maybe Feric hoped to lure us into a fight." She sighed. "Annika, do you still think this is your house stirring up trouble?"

"Sparking rebellion, sneaking around, and shady transmissions?" Annika said. "It sure sounds like us."

"Makes me think it isn't," Elidia said. "It's too obvious now."

"But most people will think it *is* Nocturna," Annika said. "I wouldn't be surprised if Nocturna saw major backlash whether they're behind the chaos or not."

Judit groaned. First, the kidnapping put Nocturna and Meridian at each other's throats, then the agitation of the lesser houses put lesser against greater. Now whoever was behind this would try to turn more of the greater houses on one another.

They needed what they always did: more information. "If I spoke to my family," Judit said, "I don't think they'd tell me anything more than yours did. They'd demand I come back."

Elidia shrugged. "Even with the information I gave them, mine ordered me back, too. Though they knew they'd been manipulated, there was an air of 'we can take advantage of this.'"

"And that's not something you want?" Annika asked, her tone disbelieving.

Elidia gave her a long look. "As much as I despise your houses,

I know that if they unite, they will eventually *annihilate* the smaller houses. Worse still, houses like Munn could get trapped between the houses and the unaffiliated that will rise up against you. Besides, you two and Noal don't seem as if you're trying to burn everything to the ground."

"I didn't think the galaxy would ever come to this," Judit said. "I thought the marriage would solve everything."

Annika shook her head as if she couldn't believe such a thing. "But surely, the history—"

"Hoping the marriage wouldn't happen, fantasizing that you might be mine instead?" Judit shook her head. "That was too painful."

Annika took a step toward her, but after a glance at Elidia, she stopped.

Elidia chuckled. "You two are pretty cute."

Judit rolled her eyes. Of all the things she'd ever endeavored to be, cute hadn't been one of them. "Do you think House Munn will spread the word and get others to see the truth?"

"As I said, I think they mean to take advantage of it. And some other small houses might think the same, but we can try. If we send out a broad transmission with all we've discovered, someone might listen. Maybe other people will start looking for whoever is behind this mayhem, someone with more resources than we have."

That was true enough.

"In the meantime," Elidia said. "I think I should go back. I can keep working on this from my own household."

Annika gave Judit a cautious glance. As Noal had said, though, she tended toward paranoia. Elidia had never hidden her contempt for the galaxy's largest houses. Judit saw no reason why she'd stop being honest now.

She led the way to the bridge. "Bea, locate Munn's nearest holding." She turned to Elidia. "We can't take you to your homeworld, sorry."

"No, that's smart," Elidia said. "I can get a ride."

Judit nodded. They wouldn't announce they were coming, either. Not only did they not want a Meridian or a Nocturna warship waiting for them, they didn't want an unscrupulous Munn to see them as a ship of convenient hostages.

They made for a smaller system with an asteroid mining camp

held by House Munn. The director was a cousin of Elidia's, and she was certain he could get her where she wanted to go. Even folding between gates, it took two days to get there. Munn probably liked staying out of the major traffic lanes. It made them less of a target.

Judit took the opportunity to spend some time with Annika and Noal. Noal had been seeing a lot of Spartan and seemed closer to his jovial self. Maybe the chance to flirt was doing him some good. Annika seemed distracted when she and Judit weren't intimately connected. Judit knew she had to be thinking of her mother, had to be working out a plan or pondering their predicament. Judit pondered it, too, all the possibilities whirling through her mind. When they were together, she tried to serve as a distraction.

She was worried for her house, for the future of the galaxy, but even as they took reports of further unrest, it felt good to be out with the people she cared about the most. They didn't know everything, but they were doing *something*, and she was the chosen one! She wondered what rank she'd be when she went home again, what her new uniform would look like. She shouldn't have been worried about such things, but after so many years of occupying an unidentified space in her house, she finally had a real purpose. Even if she had no real idea what that purpose was!

The thought made her laugh. It couldn't restrain this new giddiness. She was more than the guardian of the chosen one; she was the chosen one herself. Surely she could get something done back home now. She could learn from her mistakes, get Meridian to stop trying to push people around. Maybe that would help with some of the resentment she saw in people like Elidia. And she was her own guardian. Unlike Noal, she'd never need a shepherd. Surely after all this chaos was done, her family would finally listen to her. With Annika by her side, they could create peace.

First step, end this chaos. And the more houses on their side, the easier that would go. To get Munn on their side, they needed to get Elidia home, and that would soon be done. As they approached the mining station, Judit waited on the bridge, looking to Roberts to alert her to the first sign of chatter.

When he caught her eye, he shook his head. "I'm not getting anything. There should at least be a repeating signal warning about mining ships in the area."

Elidia frowned so hard Judit almost expected her to bare her teeth. "What's happened?"

"Ships?" Judit asked.

Beatrice shook her head. "None that I can see, but there are plenty of places to hide."

"A power failure?" Annika asked.

Judit hoped not, for the miners' sakes. Maybe their comm was the only thing down, but Beatrice should have detected their ships. Maybe they'd abandoned the station. "Take us closer."

The mining station had been built inside a huge asteroid, itself mined clear, leaving large gaping holes that Munn had filled or blocked off, creating a livable habitat inside a ball of rock. Judit expected to see the winking lights of the station as they came closer, but all was dark. The drifting asteroid field blocked the light of the nearest stars in flickers and starts, casting dark shadows over the station, and no guiding lights welcomed them in.

"I'm detecting plenty of organics, but there's no way to tell what's alive," Beatrice said. "There's some movement."

Roberts looked up from his console. "Still no signals of any kind."

"If they had power, there'd be lights," Elidia said.

"We need to go look." Judit gestured for Beatrice and Evie to follow and headed for the shuttle bay.

Annika caught her arm. "Are you sure? This could be a trap."

"Who knew we'd come here?" Judit said.

Elidia paused by the door, irritation on her face. "Are we going or not?"

"I'm coming with you," Annika said. "I'm good in zero-G, and if the power's off, that's what they'll have." When Judit paused, Annika leaned close. "I'm not going to let you get into trouble without me."

Judit breathed a sigh, happy to have her along and fearful for her at the same time. But after everything Noal had said about Annika's survival skills, Judit was curious to see them for herself.

They suited up in pressure suits, thin enough to maneuver inside a station and protective enough to keep them warm for a few hours. The suits wouldn't work long in the cold of deep space, but they'd do for an exploratory mission. The docking cables to the station weren't functioning, so they were forced to cram into the shuttle for the ride over. The huge airlock doors were open, but nothing moved inside the cavernous dock. Shuttles had been heaped in the corner as if swatted by a giant hand. Some were floating against the wall as if pulled by the asteroid's slight gravity. Judit's breath caught as she spied several scorched patches of rock: weapons fire or an engine explosion. What the dark had happened here?

Beatrice set the shuttle down near the airlock into the station. As Judit stepped out, engaging the maglocks on her boots, she missed the hum of artificial gravity or the vibration of air reclamators. The whole place felt as dead as the rock surrounding them.

They moved slowly toward the airlock, Judit conscious of the gulf of space behind her. Annika seemed at ease, skating along, engaging her magboots enough for her to half float on the ground. One push too hard, and she would come off the floor and float away, and they might never get her back. Judit opened her mouth to warn against that, but Annika turned and grinned through her helmet, and Judit couldn't tell her to cut it out.

They paused at the airlock. The scanners were dead, as were the cameras. Judit peeked through the window in the middle of the heavy door. A dark shape lay on the floor, something that could have been a person. She brightened the lights on her helmet and saw clothing, but whoever it was had their back to the window.

Elidia stepped up beside her, shining her own light through. "I can't tell who it is. I didn't know everybody here."

"Are they alive?" Annika asked.

"That doesn't look like a pressure suit," Judit said. "And without getting in there, we can't know if there's air." She banged on the door. No movement, not even breathing as far as she could tell. "If we want to get in, we have to get through. Bea, bring the shuttle closer."

They moved the shuttle as close as they could and readied its airlock. If the person was alive, they could whisk them into the shuttle far faster than they could force open the doors into the station. "Ready, Annika?" Judit asked.

Annika nodded. As the fastest, she'd dart inside, grab the person, and leap to the shuttle.

Evie and Judit pulled the lever to manually open the airlock door. Annika dashed inside as soon as it was wide enough to admit her, but when she didn't come out, Judit slipped in behind her.

Annika held a body in her arms, but the tattered clothes were only the beginning. The skin had nasty holes along the torso. Someone had shot him, and as Annika let go, he went floating, his liquefied insides trailing behind him like a comet's tail.

Elidia turned away, and even Judit couldn't stand to look. "Did you see his face?"

"He's not my cousin." Elidia put her hand up as if she might cover her mouth, but when it bumped into the helmet, she seemed to come to her senses.

"You don't want to throw up inside that helmet," Annika warned her.

Elidia gave her a black look. "Thanks for the tip."

Evie took the body and left it in the shuttle bay. They didn't know how many corpses they might find, so they couldn't start stacking them in the shuttle. Beatrice joined them, lugging a portable battery. Judit felt safer having her along for her computer skills than waiting in the shuttle in case they had to make a quick escape.

They sealed themselves inside the station's airlock, but there was no hiss of pressurized air from the inside. The power was still off, and Beatrice read no atmosphere inside the station either. Even if the life support systems had been down for hours, there should have been *some* atmosphere left inside, even if it was toxic.

"There must be a breach," Evie said. "Probably from whoever shot up the shuttle bay."

They forced the interior door, and a long hallway stretched in front of them. Evie clomped forward first, gun at the ready. "The security doors haven't come down," she said. "So the power went out before any breaches."

Judit wanted to take it slow, but Annika bounded up with Evie. "Easy," Judit said through the comm. "If you encounter the breach, you could get sucked outside."

"All the atmosphere is gone, so nothing can get sucked out." Annika glanced over her shoulder. "But thanks for checking." Her tone was teasing, but every time she bounded through the halls, Judit's stomach fluttered. She was right about the atmosphere, but Judit kept seeing her floating into space. Of course, they'd be in the shuttle and after her at once, but once outside, it was easy for something small to get lost very quickly.

Evie gave Judit a look that asked, "Want me to grab her?"

Judit shook her head. Those two getting into a fight was the last thing she wanted.

When they passed the first body floating in the corridor, Annika slowed anyway. A woman, no one Elidia knew, probably one of the workers. She'd also been hit by a pistol, but they didn't have time to linger. They turned the corner and pulled up short. The corridor ahead was filled with floating bodies, all of them still, all of them slaughtered.

"You all right?" Judit asked, looking to Elidia.

After a moment, she nodded, and they continued, brushing past the bodies. Elidia's breathing carried through the helmet comm, and Judit put a hand on her shoulder. Her own heart thudded, and she tried not to look at the ruined husks that used to be people. She'd seen dead bodies before, but never so many at one time. She knew she wasn't supposed to care for those outside of Meridian, not beyond how they could serve her, but so much death and destruction seemed…evil.

Rooms led off this new corridor along with a staircase leading down. A few empty rooms held beds or tables, the flotsam of people's lives floating unattended. They finally came to a closed hatch. Beatrice said it looked as if it'd been shut manually; whoever did it hadn't been able to save the group of people they'd passed, hadn't been able to get the airtight seals in place.

Beyond the door, a jagged hole marred one wall, and sharp pieces of metal bent outward into space. From the looks of a blackened conduit, something had exploded from the inside, but whether it was sabotage, an accident, or an unfortunate coincidence, Beatrice couldn't say.

Many people had probably been blown into space along with the atmosphere. Judit thought it a blessing they had at least died quickly. They found other bodies caught on pieces of metal or conduit. No doubt there were some trapped behind closed doors, but they didn't hear anyone banging to get out. At each door, Elidia knocked but heard no response. When they reached the nerve center of the station, maybe they could restart the power in some sections and contact anyone who might be alive.

The nerve center had been sealed, but someone had cut the bolts keeping the door shut after the power outage. The scene inside was much like the hall. Bodies were hung up on every surface, all of them with those same liquefied holes. Beatrice moved to the main console and affixed her battery, trying to boot up so they could see what the dark had gone on.

The console blinked sluggishly and put up a flickering display. The surface had been cracked, but it was in better shape than most. A hulk of a console in the corner looked as if it had blown completely. Maybe the power had been cut via surge rather than sabotage.

"Okay, looks as if the station has a few closed doors." Beatrice pulled up a locator designed to find employees by the ID chips implanted in their skin. "I've got idents...one is moving!"

"Can you ping their comm?" Elidia asked, moving up beside her.

"Not from here." She clacked her jaw. "Roberts, I'm sending you a signal." She played with the display for a few moments. "Roberts is pinging them. A response!" She turned to Elidia with a hesitant smile.

Elidia breathed a sigh of relief. At least they could save one life. It might even be her cousin. "Where?"

"Roberts says he's trapped in the pantry. We better hurry. He's running out of air."

"Bea," Judit said, "stay here and see what you can piece together. Elidia and Evie, let's go get your man. Annika..."

"I'm so happy you paused before barking orders at me," Annika said with only a slight bit of sarcasm. "I'll stay with Bea."

❖

Annika watched with amusement as Judit left to save the poor soul trapped in the pantry. She was out to save the whole galaxy, it seemed, but self-sacrifice was one of the things that made Annika love her as well as fear for her. She was so darking noble, and someday, it was going to get her killed.

She turned her attention back to the console as Beatrice pulled together the logs of the station, trying to sift through damaged information. The stationmaster liked to drone on about mining schedules and repairs, logging every minor accident and cataloguing the day's ore supplies.

The logs cut off the day before the *Damat* had arrived. Beatrice found the moment when the computer registered a power surge before it blew. The external cameras had caught several ships entering the asteroid field, and the hails from the station were all properly logged, but they never received a response.

Annika peered at the ships, looking for any markings. "That one looks a little cobbled together, don't you think?"

"Probably some unaligned pirate," Beatrice said.

"Stealing ore? After word got out, the other houses would come down hard the minute they tried to sell it."

"Maybe with all the chaos, they've gotten bolder." She leaned so close to the holo, her nose almost poked through. "That other one's not a pirate. I'll have to double-check the register of ships on the *Damat*, but I'd swear that was House Flavio."

"Them again. Looks as if they're not just taking over shared holdings anymore."

"They probably hired the pirates for muscle." She plucked some more controls then clacked her jaw. "Roberts, can you get a good look at the lower levels? Ore processing or holding?"

She waited a few moments. "He says the holding tanks have been blown open. They took the ore."

Elidia, Evie, and Judit came back, hauling a man between them, his feet off the floor as he floated. "Trapped himself in the airtight pantry," Evie said. "All we had to do was find him a pressure suit."

Annika imagined that getting him into it had to be quite harrowing. He was taking deep breaths inside his helmet, fogging up the faceplate as if he'd never expected to breathe again.

"We need to get him to the *Damat*," Judit said.

"I've backed up the records," Beatrice said, unplugging her battery. "I think we've figured out some of what happened."

They hurried as fast as they could to the shuttle. Annika and Evie did their best to clear the way so Elidia and Judit could guide the wounded man around debris or bodies. Once aboard the *Damat*, they gave him to Sewell in the medbay.

"We got to him just in time," Judit said as they waited outside. Evie and Beatrice had returned to the bridge, and Elidia stood inside the bay talking to Sewell.

"How did you get him into a suit?"

Judit shook her head, face disbelieving. "He held his breath, and we opened the door and stuffed him in. He was nearly blue."

Annika could hardly believe he'd survived, but when the will was strong enough...

Elidia joined them in the hall. "Dr. Sewell's got him in a biobed, says he should recover, but since he was stuck in the pantry, I don't know how much he'll be able to tell us."

Judit nodded. "Let's see what Beatrice got from the computer."

They walked to the bridge, and even after the carnage they'd seen, Annika felt lighter. Every little piece of information would lead them toward...

What? Her mother? They had nothing that might lead to her so far. But moving in any direction was better than staying still, she supposed.

Beatrice fed the information from the station into the *Damat's* computers, trying to clean up the camera shots. Elidia identified one of the ships as Flavio, and when she did, her hand curled into a fist.

"What in the dark do they think they're doing?" she said.

"This happened after the general transmissions we made," Beatrice said. "Maybe they took that to mean they had to act fast."

"This is war," Elidia said.

"The station had some news reports from the Munn homeworld," Beatrice said. "Flavio was blaming Munn for several different attacks on some of their holdings. They lost a shipyard, and a colony suffered heavy casualties."

"What?" Elidia leaned over the console. "That's crazy. I need to get home. That's the only way I can sort out what's real and what's fake."

"You might have a schism in your own house," Annika said. "An opportunistic family member?"

Elidia stared at her with a stricken look, as if she didn't want to face such a thing.

"Let's get out of the asteroids, and you can call home," Judit said. "We'll see what they're willing to say."

The Munn homeworld didn't bother to talk in code. They seemed too angry. They acknowledged that they'd lost communication with the asteroid station but said they weren't sure what had happened until they'd received a ransom demand for the stationmaster, Elidia's cousin. It had seemed to come from pirates. With a murderous edge to her voice, Elidia added that Flavio was involved.

Annika winced. Elidia should have found a way to say that in secret so Flavio wouldn't know Munn was coming for them, but Elidia seemed to have a hard time hiding her disdain. Or maybe her house was more like Meridian.

They cut transmission soon after, and Elidia made another fist. "Those bastards are going to pay!"

"I hope your family acts fast," Annika said. "You can bet that once Flavio hears that transmission, they will."

"If they haven't already," Judit said. "We'll take you to the next closest holding."

Beatrice plotted a course, but Annika wondered if they'd find the same thing there.

Later, in Judit's bed, Annika could relax a little, but there was still the question of where they should go after they dropped Elidia off. Lying with her head on Judit's shoulder, Annika stared up at the dark ceiling, wishing it was the night sky of Xeni. "We need to find Feric and my mother. We need another clue."

Judit's shoulders shifted as she shrugged. "Feels like we're chasing our tails all over the galaxy."

Annika thought of what her grandmother said, about how she should come home, how it would make Judit and Noal safe. She thought of her mother's face on that holo, maybe working with Nocturna, maybe not. "We need some real information. If I go back to Nocturna—"

"No."

Annika rolled over to face her. The only light came from the ship's clock mounted in the wall, and even that was a soft glow. Annika could only see Judit's hair and a slight reflection in her eyes. "If I play the cowed runaway—"

"They'd still throw you in a hole."

"There's nowhere I can't get out of."

"They know all your tricks!"

That was nearly true. "Then I'll sneak in," Annika said. "You can make it seem as if I'm still with you, and they won't be expecting me."

Judit pushed up on the bed, and the light came on as she passed her hand over the nightstand console. Annika let her gaze roam over Judit's breasts and wondered if they should just go back to lovemaking before Judit crossed her arms. "You cannot go back to Nocturna."

"Why? It's perfect. I'll take a shuttle, dock on the station or one of the moons, commandeer another ship, and land on Nocturna Prime. With some clever cosmetics, I can play a lesser member of the Blood. They'll never know!"

"If it was that easy, everyone would do it," Judit said.

"I know all the right words, the right gestures."

"You knew them as the Nocturna heir! How often did you go outside of the world they raised you in? Noal and I didn't. Everyone else could operate differently."

Annika sat up, miffed that Judit doubted her abilities and a little saddened she couldn't own up to everything she knew. "I trained outside the security lines all the time and sneaked out more than that. Once, I was gone for three days; it drove everyone mad. I took up with a group of kids in a nearby school and convinced them I was new."

Judit's eyes widened. "I never learned anything like that in my guardian training."

"Different houses, different techniques," she said hurriedly, not meeting Judit's gaze. "I can do this, Judit."

Judit scooted forward and cupped her face. "What if they catch you? They might be expecting you to do something this crazy."

"I promise I will be careful. At the very least, I can make sure Nocturna is or is not the secret power behind the uprisings." And if she could find out anything more about her mother... "And I bet they're processing information like crazy, and we can use that."

Judit's expression fell, and Annika could tell she was wavering. She slumped back against the wall. "You won't be tempted to contact your family?"

Annika barked a laugh. "Not even a little. I'm looking forward to going behind their backs."

"I know what you mean. The only one I'm worried about is my father."

Annika laid her head on Judit's leg, wanting to be close to her since they were talking about parting, at least temporarily. "He's your nonblood parent? Is he privy to all of Meridian's private information?"

"He was there when they told me I'm the chosen one."

Annika smiled as another plan began to take shape in her mind. "Do you think he's still on Prime?"

"I don't know. Why?"

"If he's somewhere less guarded, loyal to you, and he knows what's happening…"

Judit's expression lit up before falling. "I could never get a message to him, not without everyone in the family knowing."

"Not without everyone in the *galaxy* knowing, so find out where he is and grab him."

"Abduct my own father?"

"If he's not on Meridian Prime, he should be an easier target. You'll have to disguise the *Damat*, but it will still be a Meridian ship in Meridian territory." She winked. "Do this the Nocturna way for once."

Judit lifted her and kissed her soundly. Annika responded with the same degree of passion, pulling her even closer. "Are we done talking for now?"

Judit's smile widened. "Absolutely."

Chapter Eleven

Judit had wondered if anything would be as perfect as her time on Xeni, but in her quarters, Annika had proven just as passionate, and she felt as hungry for Annika's touch. Both times, Judit had ignored her own body's needs to bury herself in Annika's skin and be surrounded by the scent of her, to hear her moans of pleasure and feel her fingers in Judit's hair.

Now as they began to kiss again in Judit's bed, Annika didn't seem content to wait. She pushed Judit back against the mattress and straddled her, trapping her. With anyone else, the move would have generated panicky flutters in Judit's stomach, but as Annika's mouth found hers, it didn't seem to matter. Judit let her hands roam, but Annika ducked out of reach and shimmied down Judit's body, kissing all the way until ecstasy roared through Judit like a storm.

Somewhere in the middle, Judit's jaw tingled as someone pinged her comm. She ignored it and the voice that said, "Jude?"

She clacked her teeth to close the channel, not wanting anyone to hear her moans. She didn't think she could manage words, and it was too weird to have someone saying her own name in her ear as she was lost in pleasure.

When Annika climbed up her again, breathing hard, she whispered, "Your comm is pinging, isn't it?"

"How did you know?" Judit asked weakly.

"You were waving at your ear as if trying to make it go away." She smirked. "I'm pretty proud that I robbed you of speech."

"I think it was the bridge. I have to see what they want. Sorry."

"Don't apologize." Her eyes sparkled, and Judit had to kiss her again. "I'm sure you'll give me another something to remember you by before I leave for Nocturna Prime."

The thought of her going made Judit's heart ache, but she pushed the sensation down and checked to see what the bridge wanted. They were close to the nearest Munn station. Luckily, it was still intact and not under threat, though they were on high alert. They wanted Elidia back and the Meridian ship gone as quickly as possible.

After a quick shower and change, Judit and Annika met Elidia and the rescued miner at the airlock while the *Damat* was coming in to dock.

"No time for long good-byes," Judit said, offering Elidia her hand.

With a smirk, Elidia took it. "Would we really want one if there was time?"

"No. That's one of the reasons we're friends."

Elidia looked surprised before she chuckled and took her hand back. "A Meridian offer of friendship that I actually believe. Who'd have thought?" She glanced at Annika. "You two take care of each other."

Annika nodded. "And you. I hope your cousin makes it through all right."

Elidia nodded slowly as if she didn't quite believe Annika's sentiment was as truthful as Judit's, proving she'd make good friends with Noal, too. "Let's stay in touch."

More than an offer of further friendship, it was a promise to keep each other informed. Judit nodded gratefully, and Elidia was gone out the airlock.

The *Damat* headed away from the station toward the nearest gate, always on the move, but it would take them the rest of the night to get there. Judit led the way back to her quarters again, though she reminded herself that they really should try to sleep at least a little this time.

In the morning, Noal pinged her comm, wondering where they were going now. She told him of Annika's idea to sneak back home and the plan to kidnap her father. Before they could send Annika to Nocturna Prime, they needed a ship. The shuttle from the *Damat* wouldn't do. It screamed Meridian. They still had the shuttle from the kidnappers' ship, but Annika and Noal had gutted the inside. It wouldn't do for the long trip.

In Judit's office, Noal suggested asking Spartan, claiming that someone who wasn't affiliated with any house would know a way to get their hands on an unaligned ship. Judit suspected that Noal was trying to find a way for Spartan to be useful. He hadn't said anything about disembarking with Elidia, so he obviously wanted to stay aboard the *Damat*.

They summoned Spartan to the office, and Judit told herself to watch and listen, to see if she could detect some attraction to Noal on Spartan's side that would explain the change of heart.

When Judit asked him about a possible ship, Spartan nodded and stared at nothing, seemingly lost in thought. Noal watched him think with a fond look, and Judit remembered what Noal said about her having a blind spot where Annika was concerned because she was so in love. It looked as if Noal was working himself up to quite a crush, too.

"Noal told me about the Munn mining station," Spartan said at last. "How everyone there was dead."

Judit glanced at Annika, who shrugged.

"Yes," Judit said. "It was horrible." She shut away the memories of the floating bodies but knew they'd keep appearing in her dreams.

"There's nowhere safe left, is there?" Spartan asked. "The whole galaxy's gone mad."

Judit had to shrug this time. "I don't know."

"Did you do this?" he asked, looking between her and Noal and Annika. "Your houses?"

Before Judit could answer, Noal sighed. "I wish I could say no," he said. "I would like to argue that Meridian wouldn't pick a fight with the rest of the galaxy, but I think we brought this on ourselves. We got too big, and if we merged with Nocturna, we'd be even bigger. I know our grandmother assumed that no matter what, the rest of the houses would follow our lead, but part of me wondered if that vision of the future would hold. I suspected it wouldn't."

Judit stared in shock. She knew he'd studied politics and history, but she'd never known he thought so deeply about it. He seemed worlds away from the chosen one who'd complained that his outfit had too many feathers, but if what he was saying was true, this thoughtful person had been inside him all along. She wondered if he'd spoken of it to anyone.

"I thought there was nothing I could do about it until I was in charge," Noal said. "Even if I'd spoken to my grandmother, she would have ignored me, especially since she knew I was never going to be in charge of a darking thing."

"Noal…" Judit said, unable to keep the pity out of her voice.

He chuckled. "Not feeling sorry for myself. It's the truth. So yeah," he said to Spartan, "our houses probably did do this, just by being who we are, but the people in this room are trying to fix it, and we need your help."

Spartan exhaled slowly and gave Noal a smile. Judit wondered what they talked about in private.

"Well," Spartan said, "if nowhere is safe, I guess I'll have to be comfortable here for the moment. And I didn't want to get involved, but if we're the galaxy's only hope…"

A bit overblown, but Judit couldn't argue, not if that was what he needed to tell himself.

"Some dealers on the colony moons of Jaqua sell ships with blank idents, no questions asked," Spartan said. "But they aren't cheap, and if your lines of cred are cut off…"

"We've got plenty of stuff to sell from the *Damat*," Judit said, though she hated the idea of cannibalizing her ship.

He shrugged as if to say that might not be enough.

"I can't get anywhere near Prime in some beat-up unaligned ship," Annika said. "I have to look like someone with business there. If I'm going to pose as a trader, it needs to be high-end goods."

"They might have something," Spartan said with a shrug. "Or maybe someone could give you a ride."

Judit nodded, liking the plan that paired Annika with backup.

"Someone neutral," Noal said. "Maybe even someone who deals in illegal goods."

Judit frowned. She didn't want to trust a criminal, but maybe they'd know how to sneak in and out of risky situations better than a law-abiding person.

Annika's eyes widened. "You're getting good at this sneaky stuff."

He snorted. "There are people in every house who buy illegal goods. Nocturna wouldn't want to call attention to their own by investigating a known smuggler too hard."

Judit glanced at him in surprise. "Meridian doesn't deal with smugglers."

"Oh please!"

"You were doing illegal trading under my nose?" Judit asked. "When? How?"

"Not me, you ass! Uncle Martin is hooked on slice crystals, and our cousin Cana has a taste for Impirion emeralds."

"Martin? And Cana?" She pictured the good-natured uncle who held some low-level position on Meridian Prime, who showed up to all the parties and functions. He'd always had a tipsy look. She'd thought he preferred to stay drunk, but now she knew his mind was half gone from a potent drug that was illegal in every civilized system.

And her half-naked cousin? The one who slinked and flirted and never took anything seriously? She collected emeralds from a world that had been strip-mined, with its entire population wiped out by thugs who only cared about profit?

Noal gave her a pitying look. "Would it make you feel better or worse that once I found out, I told our grandmother?"

"Better!" Then she stopped. "Unless…" Unless their grandmother already knew, which she probably did. And nothing had been done about it. After all, it wasn't hurting Meridian. "But it's so *wrong*."

Now Annika gave her a pitying look, too, one Judit had seen before. "Whatever," Judit said. "I can't…right now."

Spartan rubbed a hand over his eyes. "I know a guy you could talk to, but he's not going to sell you his ship."

"Borrow it?" Annika said. "For a price?"

Judit clamped her lips shut. Now that she knew about her family and their illegal tastes, she didn't want to come near a smuggler. She wanted to suggest they seize his ship, seeing how the man was a criminal, but they'd give her those pitying looks again. Noal was watching, and she wondered if part of him was thinking the same thing, cavalier as he seemed to be about their family's illegal activities. She wondered if any of the more militaristic, upright thinking her teachers had imbued her with had rubbed off on him.

Spartan thought for a moment. "I have no idea how many creds he might ask for, but he is a greedy little darker. He has a price for everything."

"Where can we meet him?" Annika asked.

As Spartan gave options, Judit walked around her desk, trying to fight her nature, wondering how she could meet with a smuggler without shouting for his arrest. She kept seeing her vacant-eyed uncle and her flirty cousin. There had been that party on Prime for Noal's eighteenth birthday, and Cana had worn an emerald necklace; everyone had said how beautiful it was. She'd said she got it on one of Meridian's colony worlds, but she couldn't admit that it was Impirion. Part of Judit hoped she didn't know.

And maybe Uncle Martin thought slice crystals were rock candy.

Judit looked up as her door opened. Spartan was leaving. Annika and Noal stared at Judit with concern on their faces. Annika seemed as if she might say something, but Noal said, "Can you give us a minute?"

"I'll be on the bridge," Annika said.

When the door shut, Judit took a deep breath, ready to tell Noal she didn't need a lecture in the way the galaxy ran, but he headed her off.

"I'm taking this one. It's something I can do."

Judit shook her head to move her thoughts to a different track. "You want to negotiate with the smuggler?"

"Well, I can't fight. I barely know how to fly a shuttle, and I don't know how to conduct a space battle, but convincing someone to do something? Play the rich house offering promises? I could do that for days."

She gave him a look. "I thought you didn't like lying."

"It's not lying, not exactly. It's casting half-truths into a better light." He smiled. "Besides, you shouldn't mind lying to a smuggler. Since you can't arrest him, it's the next best thing."

She was about to point out that his words sounded like something a Nocturna might say, but that wouldn't go over well. And he seemed happy about being useful, even as his mission turned her stomach. She wondered how he'd ever planned to run a new, merged house. Maybe he would have leaned on aides and advisors and Annika.

Before all this, she would have said that Noal thought leading a house would be all parties and fine food and outrageous clothing. That was what his upbringing had led him to believe. Any time their grandmother had let him slack on lessons, Judit thought it was because he was the privileged chosen one. But they were really for her benefit, sitting in with him.

But he'd obviously been watching and listening, and he'd seen a dark of a lot more than she had. And his offer to talk to the smuggler wasn't just him being in his element. He was also doing it so she didn't have to.

"Thanks," she said, giving his shoulder a squeeze. "I could talk to him, but neither one of us would enjoy it."

"We both know you *could* do it, but you definitely wouldn't look as good as me."

"True." But she couldn't let that pass without some teasing of her own. "You and Spartan would make a good team. Or are you a team already?"

He looked away, rolling his eyes, but she knew he was a little embarrassed. Still, his shy smile said it all.

She gave him a gentle push. "Sly dog."

"Shh." He made a show of looking around as if Spartan would hear them. "We've been talking while everyone else has been scheming or running around derelict mining stations."

"Have you…"

"Mind your own business!"

"You *like* him! I can tell. Is that one of the reasons he's staying aboard?" She poked him in the arm. "Huh? Huh?"

"You are so juvenile!" He sighed hugely and leaned on the desk, arms crossed. "Everything is so stupid and complicated and up in the air. I'm not the chosen one, so I have to figure out what I actually am. Our family probably doesn't even want me back."

"Now who's juvenile? Of course they want you back. They want us all back." But she couldn't help thinking of what Annika said, about how they couldn't go home again. It might be true for Annika, but it couldn't be true for her. No matter what Noal said, she knew the people in her house. She knew her grandmother. She would want Meridian to be whole.

"What would they want me for?" Noal asked. "Am I going to be the spare chosen one?"

She didn't have an answer, didn't know what her family's ultimate plan for Noal was, but one thing was certain: He would still make a valuable hostage. Even if Meridian had no plans for him, they weren't going to let a member of the Blood languish in some other house's clutches. But she couldn't tell Noal his only value in life was as kidnapping fodder.

"Sounds like you listened to all your lessons," she said, "and Meridian always needs politicians. According to what everyone has been saying about us, we need them now more than ever, especially since you've been outside Meridian's reach and have seen what the rest of the galaxy is like. You can be the realist in Meridian politics."

He stretched his arms over his head. "Oh great! Couldn't think of a more thankless job?"

She barked a laugh. "No one knows what's going to happen after this dust settles. Will our families be amicable to the merge with Nocturna at all? What if they're wiped out?" She wanted to take those words back as soon as she said them.

"Don't say that. They may have thrown me to the dark, but we're still related." He gave her a sideways look. "Speaking of relations, are you really going to try to abduct your father?"

The sudden change of conversation derailed her. She hadn't given it any thought since Annika had suggested it, but with Annika's departure growing closer, she knew she *had* to think about it. Even that was better than focusing on the fact that Annika was leaving.

"I guess...I guess I should," she said.

"Nice confidence."

"Shut up. I need to make a plan." She sat in her chair and pressed her hands over her eyes until she saw colored spots. "A plan to kidnap my father."

"Maybe he'll come willingly. It'll be nice to see him again. I always liked Tam."

"Me, too." As much as she ever got to see him anyway. "Ever think about your parents?"

He snorted. "I saw mine even less than you saw yours. If they're missing me, I'm sure it's for the same old 'we have to think of what's best for the house' reasons. If we picked them up, they'd try to sabotage the ship."

"Your mom, maybe." Noal's mother Cecily was Blood, but his father was from another house, like hers. "Your dad?"

"You know he's completely under Grandmother's thumb. He'd do anything to keep his comfy appointment." He crossed his arms, not looking at her.

"Could be an act."

Now he gave her a flat look. "I know what I know. Shall we work on the plan to kidnap Tam or what?"

The idea still made her sick to her stomach. She didn't like the notion of yanking anyone out of their lives. It was too much like the events that had pulled her out of her own life, but she tried to focus on how happy her father would be to see her. Unlike Noal's parents, he'd never hidden the fact that he loved her. He couldn't always show it. Grandmother used the people a person cared about as leverage against them. Judit's father had been increasing the holdings of Meridian for years just for the reward of seeing his daughter more often.

"No," Judit said, shaking the thought away. "We need to get ready to meet this criminal."

"Leave the getting ready to me," Noal said. "You do what you always do, prepare to crack heads if something goes wrong."

With a smile, she nodded. "Always."

As Judit suspected, they arranged to meet their unscrupulous target at an unaffiliated station deep in an unappealing section of the galaxy. It took them two days to reach it, and they received more reports about attacks, not just on outer holdings this time. Like the Munn mining station, several other stations had been raided, these deep in house territory. House Donata was reporting raids as close as two systems from their homeworld. Meridian and Nocturna were warning people away from their territory, putting out images of patrolling warships to scare everyone. Meridian and Nightingale, a Nocturna ally, had traded shots in several skirmishes when their patrols came too close to one another. Everyone had fingers on triggers.

Judit was tempted to reread reports, to watch vids of the battles and stew in her office, but as Annika pointed out, they were doing all they could. Judit eventually let herself be tempted away. Showing Annika how much she would miss her was time much better spent.

When they reached the system with their target station, Judit called for a halt at a distance, wanting to watch the traffic come and go and see if anyone was looking for a fight. From the bridge, the *Scipio* seemed busy, with many ships flocking around it. Roberts picked up more chatter about unrest in other systems. Many ships were putting out short-range signals requesting news. Judit didn't want to take the *Damat* into the heart of that, not when people might be blaming

Meridian for the recent trouble. There was no disguising who they were. Even if they changed their ship signals, even if they erased all the outside markings, the shape of the *Damat* would give them away.

"Are we close enough to send a private signal?" Judit asked.

Roberts nodded.

"We should ask him to meet us somewhere else," Judit said. "If we barge in there—"

"No," Noal said. "That's exactly what we should do."

Judit raised an eyebrow. Standing beside her chair, Annika and Spartan looked at him, too. "You remember all the trouble barging into a situation got us into last time?"

"You could have handled that with more finesse, but now we have to prove we have weight to throw around. Head on in there, Meridian flag flying. Trust me."

She did, especially since he seemed to have fully recovered the old Noal swagger. "All right, Beatrice, take us in. And the cannon?"

"Let's not heat the guns yet," Noal said. "We just want to look capable of punching someone in the face; we don't need to walk in with our fists raised."

With tense shoulders, Judit watched as the *Damat* cruised closer to the station. She could almost feel the other ships' scanners oozing over her. Several ships turned and exited the system quickly and quietly. All gave way. Some had impressive cannon, but their ships were cobbled together, pirate crap. Even though they'd gotten several reports of unaffiliated ships banding together against houses, these didn't seem like those types. Most seemed determined to stay away from one another. Still, Judit let various scenarios play out in her mind, picturing their course should someone attack and determining which ships posed the greatest threat and needed to be dealt with first. She had a string of maneuvers lined up in her head, but no one moved to accost them.

"The chatter's gone quiet," Roberts said. Judit noted a hint of smugness in his voice. Everyone was sitting a little straighter. "I'm detecting a few signals, but everyone's gone private, ship-to-ship."

She bet they had. A few ships detached from the station and eased into space with all the nonchalance a ship could muster. The station itself was larger than the *Xerxes*, with several tall pylons jutting from the top: berths large enough for the *Damat*.

"An automated system has cleared us to dock at berth three," Roberts said.

Beatrice nodded. "Got it."

"We better ping our contact," Spartan said. "Let him know we're here."

Noal chuckled. "Oh, he probably knows."

"Nevertheless," Spartan said, giving Noal an affectionate smile.

Judit resisted the urge to tease and led the way to her office. When Annika tried to follow, Judit leaned close. "It's going to be a bit cramped."

Annika frowned. "You know how I love being left out."

"I promise I'll tell you everything."

With a sigh and a shrug, Annika stayed behind.

"You should make contact," Noal said to Spartan. "Since he heard from you first."

"You want me to speak for your house?" Spartan asked.

"Large houses sometimes use intermediaries—"

"When they don't want to get their hands dirty," Spartan said.

Judit nearly barked at him to just do it, but Noal touched her wrist.

"If we're going to play a part," Noal said sweetly, "we might as well play it all the way."

With a sigh, Spartan nodded. Even though Judit didn't know if she could wheedle someone like that, it worked like magic. Noal gave her a wink when Spartan wasn't looking.

"Now," Noal said, "Spartan, you and I will stand here where the holo can see us. Judit, back there against the wall where you can hear, but you'll be out of the way."

"Tell me when you're ready," she said.

Noal spent another moment arranging Spartan's hair and straightening his own jacket before he said, "Ready."

Judit clacked her jaw. "Roberts, open a channel to my office."

"Done, Boss."

Judit nodded to Noal. Spartan punched a few numbers into the console. "I'm pinging the personal comm he gave me."

Judit gave them both a warning look, hoping to remind them to be careful with what they said.

They both gave her looks that said they weren't stupid. Heads tilted, expressions disbelieving, they looked remarkably similar, and she wondered if it was from spending so much time together, or if they were just that alike. The holo blinked on, and Judit looked at the holographic projection from the back, seeing through it.

The smuggler was older than expected. All holos made people a little green, but his skin had hints of purple that meant he had roots near Munn or Flavio, not enough to be considered important, or maybe he'd run from his responsibilities in order to be unaligned.

He also had a beard, very out of fashion, and like his hair, it was dotted salt-and-pepper; his eyes were a blue so light and piercing, they seemed to shine out of the projection.

"Mr. Antiles," Spartan said with a nod. "Spartan Roulege here. As you've no doubt heard, we've arrived."

The holo chuckled and waved a hand. "It's just Antiles. I never go for titles. And yes, you made quite a splashy entrance. Now that you're here, what can I do for House Meridian?"

"We'd like to discuss that in private on the station," Spartan said coolly. He'd always seemed so nervous before. Maybe Noal had been giving him lessons. "Somewhere completely...discreet." And he said it with the right amount of sneer. Definitely some lessons.

Antiles opened his arms as if to say the galaxy was theirs. "The *Scipio* is nothing but discreet, Mr. Roulege."

"We were thinking of our ship."

Antiles inclined his head. "While I do acknowledge that Meridian is a mighty house, quite used to having things its own way, I must decline. Your house, while powerful, is also one that has not hesitated to arrest individuals such as myself in the past."

Except when they needed them, Judit thought, imagining slice crystals and Impirion emeralds.

"You understand my reluctance, of course."

Spartan made a show of looking to Noal, who'd spent the whole interview looking bored, examining his fingernails, seemingly in a hurry to get the preliminaries out of the way. Noal waved a hand.

"There is a restaurant aboard the *Scipio*," Antiles said. "All automated, no staff, sound-dampened booths, low lighting, and no weapons allowed. I'm sure whatever business you have can be conducted there?"

The thought of meeting this man anywhere made her skin crawl, but Judit had to nod. If it had been her in charge she would have demanded Antiles come to them or she'd blow his ship up, maybe even the whole station. But stealth was what they needed right then. Noal was right.

They arranged a time, then all they had to do was dock and wait. Luckily, it wasn't long. Judit hoped Antiles wasn't giving himself enough time to set a trap, that he was simply being cautious. Dealing in illegal goods, he would have to be. He might have had dealings with Meridian before, though it turned her stomach. She fought the image of her drunk uncle and her jewel-covered cousin. He might have been the ones to peddle those very goods. Would it be rude to ask? But she wouldn't be doing the asking. And she wouldn't be left behind, either.

"Annika and I are coming with you," she said as soon as the transmission closed.

"I wouldn't have it any other way," Noal said. "I've heard of these types of places before, soundproof and whatnot. I plan to have you with us in case anything turns nasty."

"Antiles might not like meeting four people when he thought there'd be two," Judit said.

Spartan snorted. "Oh, he'll have muscle. I know the type. You might not see them. And he'll probably assume we have more people than we're showing."

"Let me do the talking, Jude," Noal said.

She sighed. "Fine. But if he starts throwing threats around…"

"Merchants don't threaten potential customers," Noal said. "That's not how sales works. By the dark, Jude, have you ever bought anything?"

She opened her mouth to say of course she had, but the more she thought about it, she couldn't remember when. She usually told someone she needed something, and it showed up. "Have you?"

"Oh please. I've been buying my own suits for years. You can't make sure about the fit unless you talk to the tailor face-to-face, or at least face-to-holo."

She thought she remembered him doing that several times, but she tuned out any discussions related to clothing. "Well. Good."

He gave her a patronizing smile that she wanted to flick his ear for, but she wouldn't do it in front of Spartan. "Let's get ready to go," she said. "We want to get there first, right?"

Noal grinned. "Now you're getting the hang of it."

CHAPTER TWELVE

They docked quickly, and Judit, Annika, Noal, and Spartan gathered near the hatch on the bottom of the *Damat*. They'd have to descend a ladder into the station airlock, which would be a bit tricky if they had to leave in a hurry.

Judit had filled Annika in while Noal and Spartan had gotten ready. Since the primary function of the *Damat* had been to ferry Noal from place to place, he had quite a wardrobe on board. He was dressed in what he probably thought of as a modest suit, electric blue, but it had a thin covering of nanosheen that changed color ever so subtly. It might take an hour to make the transition to emerald green, the color of his cravat. A large diamond pin held the cravat in place, and similar diamonds winked from the cuffs of his jacket.

Instead of the ragtag suit he'd been wearing when he came aboard, Spartan was now in one of Noal's suits, a comfier affair with wider legs and shoulders, probably to accommodate his slightly larger frame. His shirt hung open at the collar low enough to show a smattering of blond chest hair. He'd rolled his sleeves up almost to his elbows. To Judit's unpracticed eye, he looked sloppy, but Noal had no doubt dressed him to send some sort of message. Maybe it was "This is my slovenly— though expensively so—associate who handles my initial contacts."

Judit stayed in uniform. When he saw her, Noal sighed but didn't say anything aloud. He gave Annika a grateful nod. She didn't have any of her elaborate gowns on board, but she'd paired the military trousers Judit had loaned her with a bright pink shirt she borrowed from Dr. Sewell. She wore her hair down but fashionably swept to the side, and she'd taken Noal up on his offer of cosmetics and jewelry. She wore a platinum earring that curved around her left ear and a sapphire stud in her right. The makeup was subtle, like Noal's, but it softened her cheekbones and features. Maybe such artistry was why Judit had never considered her dangerous before.

A disturbing thought.

Evie accompanied them to the station. She would wait outside the appointed restaurant, though the sound dampening would also deaden her comm. She was another pair of eyes to look for trouble, and someone who could fight if it came to it. Noal seemed confident they wouldn't need any help, but Judit would only take so many chances.

When they were all aboard the *Scipio*, Annika hooked her arm through Judit's as if they were taking a stroll. She hadn't added anything to the plan, and Judit wondered if she'd have played it the same way, or if she would have threatened her way through. She had too many qualities of both Noal and Judit to be sure.

The restaurant was on the topmost floor of the station, halfway between the *Damat*'s pylon and the bay where smaller ships docked on the *Scipio*'s side. Strategically, it was the sort of place Judit would have chosen, and she bet Antiles picked it for the same reason. Everyone had a quick way out if things turned sour. She wondered how often that happened to Antiles, how often his customers turned on him, but maybe that wasn't what he was worried about. He probably worried that people like Judit would be waiting to ambush both him and his customers and arrest the lot. Or maybe he liked being in a position to flee once business was concluded.

Thinking like a criminal was hard.

Judit wondered if she and Annika should take a booth near Noal and Spartan, but they wouldn't be able to hear, so they let a little service bot—little more than a cube on wheels—guide them to one booth cut into a half circle with a table before it. If Antiles didn't like speaking to all of them, they'd have to find another criminal to deal with, painful as that was. Judit did not want to start this whole process over.

The booth had a high back, fairly comfortable, upholstered in dark red leather. In front of their table, a massive window showcased a view of the stars. The closest planet was an orange ball that looked about the size of a fist at this distance. The lighting was dim, and if Judit leaned forward, she could only see the backs of other booths or the hint of a side, a sea of dark wood rising from the blue carpet. Protective glassteel surrounded many of the tables she'd passed on the way in, shielding the occupants like the cabana on Xeni. Whoever owned this station, this restaurant, had gone to a lot of expense to make sure their visitors felt protected. It should have made her feel better. It would make a criminal feel better, but all she could think was that everyone in the room had something to hide.

Annika squeezed her leg. "Relax."

"You should keep a fork handy," Noal said. "So you can jab her before she tries to talk."

Judit glared at him. "I won't say a word."

"I have all the faith in you," he said.

"Like dark you do."

That got a little smile from all of them, and Judit joined in. Barely.

They waited to put up their barrier, and a different service bot came to take their drink order. This one was about three feet tall, rectangular in shape with a holo display on top that showcased a variety of drinks.

Judit ordered water, making Noal roll his eyes again. Annika and Noal ordered elaborate alcoholic drinks with fruit and straws and umbrellas. Spartan stuck to water, too, and Judit nearly clapped him on the shoulder in solidarity. Noal didn't roll his eyes at Spartan's choice, and it was all Judit could do not to point that out in a teasing tone.

They made idle chitchat, talking about the décor or the stars or nothing in particular. Judit almost laughed at the four of them talking idly when they had so much else to discuss, but without the barrier, they couldn't know who might be listening. Judit didn't add much, and Annika gave her more reassuring squeezes.

Antiles came around the corner soon after, following the service bot. Instead of a suit, he wore a flowing robe with billowing sleeves. The front parted to reveal a modest black jumpsuit underneath, but the robe itself was a riot of colors, an intricate pattern that hurt Judit's eyes if she stared too long. Maybe that was a negotiating tactic.

"Sorry I'm late," he said, looking at all of them in turn. He had a mellifluous voice, and his blue eyes were even lighter than the holo suggested, nearly as pale as the whites. She had to struggle to meet them. "I don't believe we've all met."

Spartan activated the glassteel shield before he spoke, and any ambient sounds faded away. "Nicholas and Veronica Meridian," Spartan said, indicating Noal and Judit. "And this is our friend Calliope."

"Charmed," Antiles said, bowing from his seat. "Well, well, two members of the Meridian Blood, and…" He stared at Annika before grinning. "Their beautiful companion."

Judit had no idea if he was fooled by the names; he didn't give anything away. They lowered the shield enough for Antiles to order his own drink. Once he had it, and the shield was up, he leaned back in his chair and took a long sip.

"Now, what can I do for you today?"

Judit held her tongue; she was already tired of his oily smile, his confident demeanor. She didn't dare pick up her own glass, not trusting her hands to keep still. She tried to remember her chosen role as bodyguard. The muscle didn't do the talking.

"To put it bluntly," Noal said, "we'd like your ship."

"Interesting," Antiles said. "Am I allowed to know what for?"

"We need to pose as you or one of your close associates and take Calliope to Nocturna Prime or one of its moons."

Antiles stayed silent, and Judit wondered about his calm expression, if he'd gone frozen. "Even more intriguing," he said at last. "Would you need any stock to sell?"

"We'd just need the ship."

"Well, that begs the question, why does the lovely Calliope need *my* ship? I mean, obviously you can't take the Meridian ship parked outside, but surely there are others for sale."

Judit wanted to snap at him to mind his own business. Even though she hadn't liked him before she'd ever met him, she hadn't known he would affect her so strongly in person. Maybe it was his cologne, a light scent that made her recall leather and some kind of spice. She hated colognes of any kind, and she found his particularly annoying.

Noal toyed with the flotsam on his glass. "Secrecy is key. We need to look like someone familiar with the area who's beyond suspicion."

Antiles gave a delighted little laugh. "And you think that's me? Why in the galaxy would I be able to get close to Nocturna Prime?"

"Reputation," Noal said, using his oiliest, most charming smile, the one he normally reserved for the press.

"Of course." Antiles sipped his drink. "And what are you offering in exchange for my ship?"

"Oh, I think your imagination can be relied on to think of something," Noal said. "And if creds don't leap automatically to mind, surely there's something else?"

Antiles thought for a few moments. "For my ship, nothing. It's not for rent. It's not for sale." Before Noal could say anything, Antiles held up a hand. "But I am willing to be transportation." He nodded to Annika. "For the right price."

"And that is?"

Antiles gave a little shrug. "I will admit, I have been…near Nocturna Prime before. I'll tell you right now, I won't have my property involved in any assassinations. And if we *can* come to some arrangement, and I *do* transport you to Prime, someone will be looking for my return, with a handy transmission to the Nocturna government all queued up in case I never make it back."

"No assassinations," Noal said. "If all goes as planned, no one will even know Calliope has been there, and you'll be free to conduct whatever business you see fit while you're there."

"Even more intriguing than before. And all I have to do is decide what I want from you."

"Within reason. I can't promise you the galaxy on a string."

"Hmm." Antiles looked at each of them in turn. "Well, if you're not after the blood of the Blood, you must be after an object or information. How about this, if it's an object, I get a cut or an object of similar value. If it's information, I want access."

Noal glanced at Annika, but she kept up a bored façade. "That… will depend on what information we happen upon. We won't give you anything that might lead to the death of a Nocturna Blood."

Judit glanced at Annika, who shrugged. Judit frowned, not liking that Annika could dismiss the possible assassination of a family member so lightly, even if the gesture was fake.

"Fair enough," Antiles said. "But trade secrets are fair game, like any high-cred deals you happen to uncover. Maybe a little insider information on this uprising, like, what Nocturna plans to do about it. Any advance warning on places they might attack or pacify so that a certain someone could make sure his goods and associates are far gone when it happens."

"Deal," Noal said.

Judit bristled at feeding information to a criminal, but she supposed they had little choice. And she was sure Annika would find a way to vet the information before she handed it over.

Antiles turned his attention to Annika again. "Do you speak, dear Calliope? Or shall our voyage be a silent one?"

"I'll speak if I have something to say," she said, smiling.

"Splendid. I assume you need time to get your bags together? What's your timetable?"

"As soon as possible," Annika said.

Judit felt herself stiffen. She wasn't ready to send Annika with this darking criminal.

He took another look at all of them, and by his smile, Judit knew in her gut that he recognized them. He might have always known who Noal was. He might have discovered it after they'd first spoken, but he knew, and he was smart enough not to say anything.

Noal leaned forward. "It probably goes without saying, but discretion is key in this...mission."

"For Meridians in Nocturna space, I should think so."

But something about the way he said "Meridians" reinforced Judit's conclusion that he knew who they were.

He swirled his glass again. "Aren't you a little afraid I might sell you out? Not that I will," he said quickly. "But why trust a stranger? Meridian must have many resources."

"We need someone who's only interested in what we can give him," Noal said. "And you don't seem as interested in creds as you do in information."

Antiles flashed a smile. "Smart, very smart. Well then, Calliope, my dear, shall we?"

"I'll meet you at the docking ring in an hour."

He stood, bowed deeply, and Noal lowered the shield so he could leave.

They waited until he'd cleared the restaurant before they left, meeting Evie in the hall.

Judit clacked her teeth. "Roberts, Antiles left. I want you monitoring his comm hard. Anything coming from his ship, even static, I want it recorded and analyzed."

"On it, Boss."

They waited until they were back aboard the *Damat* before Judit said anything more. "Nice work, Noal."

He grinned. "I thought it went well. And nice work to you on not killing him."

"You were very tense," Annika said.

Spartan nodded. "Nearly vibrating."

Judit frowned. If they'd all noticed, Antiles probably had, too. "Bodyguards are supposed to be tense."

"Well," Annika said. "Now all that's left to do is pack and say farewell for now."

Judit felt a pit open in her stomach. "Is that better than good-bye?"

"Much. Noal, I'd like to borrow some makeup and clothing. I'll need to do whatever I can to disguise myself."

"I've got some hair dye, too."

Annika nodded.

Noal took her hand. Judit raised an eyebrow. Maybe it took her putting her life in danger for that old affection to come back. "Take care of yourself."

"I will," she said, her own smile like the old days. "You too."

Spartan gave her a nod, and he and Noal walked toward Noal's room. Judit followed Annika to the quarters she was using. Even though they spent a lot of time in each other's company, Judit thought it important they have their own space. It gave them room to think.

She sat on the bed as Annika packed a small bag with borrowed clothing. "Tell everyone I'll have their things back as soon as possible, if I don't have to leave them in a hurry."

"There's no bit of clothing that can't be replaced." She fiddled with the edge of the blanket, her whole being crying out for her to demand Annika not go. There had to be another way. There was always another way. "Are you certain you'll be all right?"

"I can take care of myself," she said as she sat beside Judit. "If Antiles upsets me, I'll knock him unconscious, and he can wake up when we get back. I'll give him his information, and hopefully he'll be so happy, he forgives the bump on the head."

Judit chuckled. "Good to know." She took Annika's hand. "We've been through a lot, but we've had each other through all of it."

"I know, but my guardian trainers assumed I would be by myself. I am very prepared."

"You're still taking a weapon."

"If you insist."

Annika smiled as Judit gave her a personal comm and a small shock stick, easily hidden in her clothing. The comm wasn't powerful enough to send a signal to the *Damat* across space, but she could keep in touch with Antiles. The shock stick wasn't as powerful as its longer cousin, but she wouldn't need it at all. She could incapacitate someone with her hands much easier. Her bone stiletto was her emergency weapon. Noal had probably told Judit about that, but she didn't need reminding.

"I'll get back here as fast as I can," Annika said.

"We'll be on the lookout for Antiles's ship."

"If I have to steal another for some reason, I'll give you a shout." She paused, thinking of all the possibilities. "If I have to stow away on another ship, we need a signal so you'll know I'm there."

"How will you get a ship you stowed away on to come here?"

That was a tricky question, one she'd have to work out later, but she could see she'd planted more doubt in Judit's mind. "I trust you to find me."

Judit looked pained. "Annika—"

"I'll tinker with their engines. Give them a leak in one of their systems. If I'm not back in a week, look for lame ships."

"In the whole galaxy?"

Annika kissed her gently. "I'll try and get them to head out of Nocturna territory as quickly as I can. I'll be fine!"

Judit didn't look comforted, but she nodded all the same, miserable look in place.

Annika didn't want a hurried round of lovemaking before she had to depart, so she and Judit simply held each other, kissing occasionally, until it was time to collect her cosmetics from Noal and head to the docking ring. Judit followed her all the way to Antiles's ship.

"Even though I don't want to," Annika said at last, "I have to let go of you now."

By the myriad expressions crossing Judit's face, it was clear Judit was fighting the urge to grab her and run for the *Damat*.

Annika gave her a quick kiss. "Back before you know it."

"I know it already. I love you."

"I love you, too." She fled before Judit could fall apart, knowing Judit hated to get emotional in front of others. She risked one look back, and Judit was staring as if trying to memorize her features. Annika felt her own eyes get a little misty, so she hurried faster.

Antiles was waiting inside the airlock of his small vessel. He gestured for her to follow and closed the door behind them. She tried to take everything in, anything to keep from remembering Judit's stricken face. The area nearest the airlock was filled with containers and crates, and she was certain there was other, hidden cargo. She noted an emergency pressure suit on one wall and another container colored deep red. That one probably held an oxygen tank or fire suppressor.

He led her deeper into the ship, and they passed a richly appointed bedroom with a smaller bedroom across the narrow hall. Beyond that was a washroom, then a small galley with a single table and two plush chairs. She saw a basket of fresh fruit and guessed the cold stores would be well stocked. Antiles finally stopped at a round cockpit on the other side of the ship with a glassteel dome looking into space. There were two chairs in front of the blinking console, and he took one, gesturing to the other.

She took another slow look around as she sat, trying to memorize where different controls might be. A large hatch near the rear of the cockpit had a pull handle, and she guessed it led to the engines.

"Are you looking for traps or other travelers, Calliope?" Antiles asked.

"Just getting the lay of the land. I'm surprised you don't travel with guards. Though the fact that you don't makes me certain you're going to wait for your information rather than sell me to Nocturna." Because he couldn't incapacitate her on his own.

"Information is a lot less messy." He gave her a grin. "And I'm pretty sure you won't try to cheat me seeing as how I'm your ride home."

Smart, but he didn't know what she was capable of, even if—as Judit suspected—he knew who she was.

CHAPTER THIRTEEN

Sitting in her office, Judit tried not to think of Annika and failed with every breath. She'd watched Antiles's ship depart, all the while hoping Annika would run back to her. She knew it was a silly fantasy, like those where the galaxy magically went back to normal. They went hand-in-hand with those where Nocturna and Meridian insisted Annika and Judit marry in order to unite their houses under an umbrella of peace that would stretch across the whole of space.

Both dreams would have made her grandmother vomit. She'd only agree to such an arrangement if that peaceful umbrella was made of Meridian weapons and no one else in the galaxy was allowed to fight back.

Judit had never had such thoughts about her own house before, and Noal's words came back to her about the great houses being responsible for the unrest. She should have been looking harder at the people around her while she'd been in a position to do something about it. Maybe her father had been looking harder than she had; maybe he could tell her a few things she didn't know.

But she had to get to him first. On her console, Judit dismissed the view of nearby space. Antiles's ship was long gone, and she trusted Roberts was keeping an eye on telemetry, making sure Antiles headed toward Nocturna. That was the best they could do. Judit tried not to think how difficult it would be for Annika to escape Nocturna space and turned her attention to finding her father.

His usual appointment was on Freemen, a planet on the outskirts of Meridian space. When she was younger, Judit thought her father had been sent out so far because he'd displeased her grandmother, but she'd since discovered he was very good at his job. He negotiated new holdings on different worlds, slowly expanding Meridian space. He oversaw the building of new stations and mining operations—not in person, but the reports came through his office, and he compiled them for Meridian Prime.

As Judit looked through the paths to Freemen, her worry grew. Looking like a Meridian ship was no longer the problem. It was looking like the *Damat*. Their name wasn't written on their hull, and Roberts could change their registry, their comm signals, but the *Damat* was recognizable in other ways. Roberts and Beatrice had put out false leads that had them currently in another system, but going anywhere near Freemen would make her feel as if she had a target across her bow.

She brought Noal to her office to get his advice, wondering when exactly she'd decided to seek him out rather than him asking for her. But then, the only thing he'd ever asked her about was security or what kind of outfit to wear, and she suspected the latter was so he could laugh at her choices.

"There's nothing more we can do to disguise ourselves?" Noal asked when she laid out the problems for him.

"Not that I can think of."

"Then we'll have to continue as we are."

She gave him a flat look. "Thanks, very helpful."

He shrugged. "We have to hope no one notices. As for sneaking onto Freemen to get Tam, I can help with that. After I'm finished, no one will recognize you."

She knew what that meant: cosmetics, hair dye, the works. She didn't bother to hide her frown.

He only laughed, clearly a heart without pity.

There was nothing to do but head for the nearest transmission gate and then through that to another that would transmit them closer to Freemen. Then it was a day's journey into Meridian space, but at least it was still on the fringes. Judit tried to spend the time pining over Annika, but Noal forced her into several conversations and card games, roping in Spartan and whoever was off-duty at the time. When she tried to refuse, he teased until she relented. It did give her time to catch up with the crew.

But none of that stopped her from rushing to the bridge when they finally neared Freemen. Judit watched their approach from her command chair. She felt as if everyone's eyes were on them again, and it made her twitch as it had on the *Scipio*, but her instinct this time was to run rather than fight. In her head, she plotted several courses that would get her ship to safety as quickly as possible. She could return to the *Scipio* where she was supposed to meet Annika. She half wanted that to be her only option. Maybe she should take Beatrice's seat at the helm so she could turn them toward the nearest transmission gate at a moment's notice. Then she wouldn't lose seconds giving the order.

They had more to fear than the threat of meeting someone who knew them. Even though her grandmother was systems away, Judit expected to hear her voice at any moment. She feared she'd go into autopilot and do whatever her grandmother commanded; she'd been obeying orders for so long. It'd been easy not to think about her recent disobedience when she'd been hurrying from one goal to another, but entering the proverbial lion's den brought it all rushing back. She *was* disobeying, had been doing so for weeks. She was a fugitive. More than that, in her grandmother's eyes, she was a criminal. Not as bad as Antiles, but when it came to disobedience, her grandmother didn't bother to rank the people she punished.

"How are we doing?" Judit asked quietly, knowing there was no need to lower her voice but unable to stop.

"Quiet so far," Roberts said, his tone as soft. "Lots of background coming from the surrounding planets and ships. Some from nearby stations, all regular chatter."

In Meridian territory, even on the fringes, it would be safe. Other Meridian outposts may have been attacked, but Freemen always had cruisers nearby, ready to defend the surrounding space. It also had a defense grid for the planet itself. And now it had more ships than usual in the surrounding space. Everyone was on high alert.

But as Roberts listened, he reported that some of those ships were traders seeking sanctuary; others were Meridians from outer colonies who'd fled to the closest stronghold, fearful of attack. Some wanted escorts or sought a place to offload harvested ore or other goods that had yet to be processed. They didn't want to be targeted by pirates. To Judit, it seemed everyone wanted to feel safer however they could. Maybe being one more ship would be easier than she thought.

"Anyone paying us a lot of attention, Bea?" Judit asked.

"Not yet, Jude." Beatrice leaned close to her screen. "No one's giving us too wide a berth, but no one's headed straight for us. If we're unlucky, we might pick up some of the baby ducks who don't have weapons and are looking for a mama."

Judit tuned in to some of the chatter and heard patrolling warships warning civilians to stay clear. The lists to dock on Freemen station and take a shuttle to the surface were probably long indeed. People who'd fled their colonies or stations wouldn't want to live on a ship for long. They'd be looking for somewhere more stable, somewhere to stretch. If they couldn't have that, they'd want to stay close to a ship bristling with guns.

"Our diplomatic signal should keep everyone away," Roberts said. The *Damat* usually put off such a signal in Meridian space; they'd needed it to warn other Meridian ships of their precious cargo while shuttling Noal across the galaxy. Now, they weren't the only diplomatic runner in the area, but they put out a lower priority signal, hoping to be mistaken for a ship carrying a lesser member of the Blood.

The other ships stayed out of their way, and Roberts answered every hail as smoothly and seamlessly as he always had. Her crew had never wobbled in their duty. It made her feel a little better about leaving the bridge.

"I'll be with Noal if anyone needs me," she said.

Time to work on her disguise. Like Annika had planned, she was going for a look that said she was a member of the Blood, only a lower rank than she really was. There weren't that many pure Bloods around but quite a few with diluted Blood, enough so that a scanner would register them. Judit hoped she and Noal would look like just two more.

She tried not to squirm as Noal added streaks of red to her platinum hair, making it look as if it grew that way naturally, like those with a muddier pedigree. She changed from her uniform into a more elaborate outfit, a silver suit that flowed like liquid over her body. Noal dug into his closet and pulled out a fascinator that partly covered her face with silver mesh.

Noal looked her up and down. "Very nice. Now the face."

She frowned hard. "I hate makeup."

"Oh, we're going to need more than that." He opened a case and pulled out some temporary prosthetics. She remembered one awful season when everyone in Meridian had been sporting extremely pointy chins and heavy brows. She supposed they were lucky Noal never threw anything away.

He put some small pads on her cheekbones and forehead, then covered the whole thing with a thick layer of cosmetics. Hopefully, it would be enough to fool any facial scanners. With luck, she wouldn't have to go into any areas requiring a deep DNA scan. Any cursory scans would reveal that she was indeed a member of the Blood, but anything deeper might reveal who she was.

"Now for me." Noal changed into a kilt and blouse combo in bright, peacock colors, added streaks to match in his own hair and then used makeup and prosthetics to make his face rounder and his eyes heavier. His skill with cosmetics also gave him fuller lips.

"Nice," she said, "reminds me of the old days."

"Except in your case," he said, sitting on his bureau. "You haven't been out of uniform since you were what, five?"

She rolled her eyes. "I don't sleep in it, you know."

"I wouldn't be surprised if you did. I hope you took it off for Annika."

She bit back a retort, feeling instead a rush of anxiety.

He sighed hugely, and she knew something must have shown in her expression. "I'm sorry. Didn't mean to make you worry. I'm happy for you two, really."

"If you say that a hundred more times, I might believe it."

"I know you would have tried to resist her if she and I had married. You would have torn yourself up and told yourself you were going to live in misery the rest of your life when what you wanted was well within reach. But I do believe it would have happened, Jude, sooner or later. I'm no fool. And I wouldn't have been upset. I'm not upset about it now. I'm upset about a lot of things but not that. I'm at peace there."

Joy overrode her worry. She rested a hand on his knee. "Thank you. She's…" Her cheeks burned, and she couldn't look at him. "She's wonderful."

He grinned and leaned forward. "You're embarrassed."

"Shut up." She sat back, all sympathy evaporating.

"Judit has a lover," he said in a singsong. "And her name is Annika."

"Shut up! I take back ever feeling sorry for you."

He made kissing noises, and she knew part of it was for her teasing him about Spartan at the *Scipio*. She shoved him off the bureau.

He caught himself and pushed her shoulder slightly, chuckling. "I'm happy you two morons have each other."

"If she and I ever get married," she said, "I want that engraved on our wedding silver."

He put his hand in the air as if tracing it. "Annika and Judit, morons together. Forever."

"And you and Spartan?" she asked, unable to resist a punch back. "Been moronic, yet?"

"We're having a nice time going slow, thank you very much." He lifted his chin, determined not to take her bait, it seemed.

"During all this madness? You were the one telling me to hurry up and grab what I wanted!"

"What's good for you is not for me. I like slow." He shivered a little, and she wondered if he was thinking about what came after slow. Where the anticipation had felt like a hot knife to her, it was obviously good for him.

Her jaw tingled. "Jude, we're getting close."

Judit returned to the bridge, Noal with her. They'd drifted closer to Freemen, the place her father called home. They'd never had much time to speak, just the random visit now and again. She'd gotten the idea that was one of the reasons he made sure to excel at his job: so he could see his daughter more often. He'd never said that, but she'd had the thought before, and it had made her both happy and guilty. Of course, she'd also thought he worked hard because he wanted Meridian to succeed. They all did.

She'd ask him when they had time to sit down on the *Damat*. They'd talk about a lot of things. He was always interested in what she had to say. She'd noted a keenness in his eyes when they'd spoken, the same rapt attention he'd given her in her grandmother's office. And it had never felt as if his interest stemmed from what she could do for her house or the prestige she might provide. He'd once asked her if she liked being Noal's guardian, and she'd had no idea how to answer. Now she'd have time to ask him some questions, too.

The station above Freemen let them dock with minimal fuss, and Judit and Noal simply had to step across the airlock to come aboard. They didn't take bodyguards. They couldn't afford to attract attention, and lower members of Meridian Blood wouldn't need them, not in Meridian space. People of no rank moved aside as they ventured farther into the station. When Judit spotted one of her distant cousins walking toward them, she almost met his eyes, but Noal pulled her to the side of the corridor.

"We have to make way for full members of the Blood," he said quietly.

Judit nearly laughed. She'd never had to make way for anyone before. They'd always made way for her. But they couldn't take the chance that anyone would see through their disguises. "Good catch. I'm glad you're paying attention."

He winked, and they passed beyond the docking ring into the busy station. Unlike the *Scipio*, the corridors here were bright, the paneling and carpeting white or gray, and recessed lighting illuminated every corner. There was no place to hide on a Meridian station, and Judit felt exposed while at the same time, the décor urged her to relax. The two feelings merged into a vague disquiet that made her shoulder blades feel as if they were trying to climb into her neck.

They passed bars, restaurants, and waiting areas, all packed with Meridian affiliates, citizens, and employees. Judit spotted a few members of the Blood, but most of them would be in private waiting areas, away from the wash of colors and voices. Some gray military uniforms moved briskly here and there, and station personnel wearing light yellow jumpsuits pushed through crowds with irritated looks.

Noal and Judit headed to the innermost corridors, to the shuttle docks. A large waiting room guarded the paths to the actual shuttles. A queue threaded through plastic chairs to where station personnel took the names of those seeking to go to Freemen. A holo display showed the shuttles completely booked for the next two weeks. Judit bit back a curse, but Noal continued forward with a casual air. He ignored the queue and headed for a small door to the side of the booths, guarded by a man in military gray. As they approached, the officer looked to a scanner. Judit hadn't seen it before, but now it stood out starkly, a globe of blackness that shone from the wall like an evil eye. When it flashed green, the officer stepped aside so Noal and Judit could pass, their DNA confirming them as Blood.

On the other side of the door was a waiting room of a different kind. Plush couches in silver and white dominated the brightly lit space.

Soft music played from hidden speakers, and several palm-sized vid screens were stacked neatly on a heavily polished table. As Noal and Judit moved to sit, a server appeared from a recessed door and offered them champagne. Another came out a heartbeat later and set a tray of canapés on the table.

Noal took a bite and then a sip. Judit tried to copy him, but her stomach was in turmoil.

"Honored guests," the second server said. "How may we be of service?"

"We need two seats on the next shuttle," Noal said.

"Of course." She smiled before hurrying away to bump someone out of their seats. It made Judit frown, even though she knew it was the way things were supposed to be. With the *Damat* under her charge, she'd never had to worry about it.

Noal gave Judit a languid smile, but his eyes widened a little as if warning her. The room might have cameras. She sipped her champagne and tried not to grind her teeth. Too many emotions were piling on top of her. She worried for Annika, she wanted to sneer at the surroundings—she'd made fun of too many fawning courtiers to enjoy them—and she was impatient to be moving. And the damn silver mesh covering part of her face was really starting to annoy her.

Luckily, they didn't have long to wait before being escorted down a hidden hallway and led to a waiting shuttle. A small curtain around their seats gave them privacy. Several nonblood looked their way as they sat, and she wondered if they were thinking of those who'd been bumped. They should count themselves lucky. If she and Noal had been riding under their real identities, the shuttle would have been emptied for their trip.

Once everyone was seated, the crew gave a brief announcement about safety, and everyone buckled restraining harnesses over their chests. After a short countdown, the shuttle dropped from the station with a stomach-turning lurch. They glided smoothly for a few seconds until they entered Freemen's atmosphere, then the entire craft shook and rumbled as if being rattled by a giant hand. Noal clutched Judit's arm. The ride down to a planet on a small craft was much rougher than the *Damat* and not as smooth as a space elevator, though those took longer. But Noal had never liked G-forces, and she patted his arm, feeling her protective urges rearing up along with the other darking feelings. He shut his eyes, and she wondered who else was wishing they were somewhere else.

Vids played on the wall in front of them, designed to distract, even for the short trip. There were no windows, but one of the vid feeds was an external camera. Judit watched as the large forests of Freemen came closer, a sea of dark greens with the Meridian buildings lost among them, but the shuttle dock was a huge platform that stuck up from the foliage like a giant's dinner plate. She pressed forward against her restraint as the shuttle pulled up hard on the dark surface of the platform, but they settled within moments, and the sound of the engines dulled as they powered down.

"We're here," she said.

Noal let out a breath. "Sometimes, I wish I had your courage."

She nearly barked a laugh. "Earlier I was wishing I had your patience."

"Oh." He stared, seemingly touched, then leaned against her shoulder. "No matter what, we stay together."

She leaned her head against his briefly, knowing she'd love him no matter what, too. "I never once pictured one of us without the other." It was the way it had always been, would always be.

"Well," he said as he unbuckled his harness. "Let's go add one more to our team."

The shuttle held the other passengers while Judit and Noal disembarked, so they had the elevator into the docking base to themselves. The Freemen base looked much like the station above with its white walls, but the light on the planet came from enormous windows rather than artificial sources. And unlike the windows on Meridian Prime, these seemed real, letting in the dazzling sunlight that shone above Freemen's forested canopy.

Signs for the tram system led them down a grand staircase, and as they passed below the level of the canopy, the light dimmed. The view from the window changed from a sea of green leaves to lines of massive brown trunks with few branches below their crowns.

The trams departed and arrived from the lowest level of the base. People lined up in front of doors that would lead into the cars as they stopped. Another small crowd stood before a holo showing the day's schedule with a map of all the stops. The deep roots of the trees made building belowground difficult, so the tubes ran between the massive trunks, and the bulk of the buildings were built high in the branches. Pride added to all the emotions already beating against Judit's defenses. Her people went with the flow of each planet they owned, not wanting to detract from any natural beauty. They knew how to adapt, at least with their buildings. With their neighbors? Not so much.

"Tam works in the main government building?" Noal asked as they approached the schedule and map.

Judit thought fast. She knew what her father did. She knew what planet he did it on, but what building? "I've never been here before, and I don't know that he ever said."

"Hmm." He glanced around and headed for another holo kiosk labeled Information.

Judit looked for anyone paying them too much attention and for the platinum hair of Blood. People stayed out of their way as they were, but if they'd been traveling under their real identities, they would have had an escort, someone to clear the way. Noal might have been mobbed by well-wishers, maybe those searching for autographs. It had happened before, though Judit had never felt he was in danger. Now people barely looked at their faces, just shuffling out of the way because of Meridian hair and features. She tried to keep up the imperious look Noal sported, but she feared she simply looked angry.

Noal fiddled with the directory. "Here he is: building four, garden district. I guess they have to put the gardens high since the light doesn't reach the ground." He swallowed visibly. "So we'll be really, really high up the whole time we're here. Goody."

"I don't know how someone who spends so much time in space can be afraid of heights," Judit said as she scanned the crowd.

"And I won't bother to explain the difference again. Now, stop watching everyone like a guardian. I'm going to look up a few more people to cover our tracks."

"Sneaky. Is Annika rubbing off on you?"

"She has good ideas, but she's far too paranoid."

"Makes sense with her guardian training."

He snorted, not looking away from the kiosk.

"What?" Judit asked.

"I've said everything I have to say on the subject of her training. You know how I feel."

She just couldn't reconcile it with her own thoughts, her own memories. She'd never seen Annika in action. And she hoped Noal would suddenly forget what he claimed to have seen, though she didn't know why that mattered to her. "Nocturna," she said slowly, "has different ways of training, that's all."

"If those people on the kidnappers' ship were her first kills, I'm a purple otter."

She shook her head, determined not to think about that if she didn't have to. "Hurry up, will you? Some of the trams are arriving any minute."

He swallowed again, and she knew he was thinking of all the air between them and the ground. "Done. Come on."

Standing before their designated door, they could see through the tube that held the tram. Judit's eyes followed the line of a huge tree trunk, but it sank beyond her vision, nearly into blackness, reminding her of a vid she'd seen of the deep sea.

Noal avoided looking down, staring instead at where the station was anchored to several massive trees, their bark visible through one wall. Judit took a step closer to the edge, trying to see farther down, and Noal made a strangled noise in his throat.

Judit stepped back with a smile. "Sorry."

"You're not," he muttered, still not looking.

The top half of the tram was glassteel, offering breathtaking views, with the bottom half covered in the same white metal and plastic as everything else on Freemen. Chairs faced forward and backward in a row along one side of the car, leaving the other side as an aisle. All the chairs were plastic except for the first two, and those were upholstered in soft purple fabric. Judit moved toward them, hoping no other Blood came aboard. She'd hate to have to present her fake credentials in a fight to prove who was most important.

As she began to sit, Noal said, "Wait."

When Judit looked over her shoulder, she saw pure platinum hair, a full member of the Blood. She made way, but when she focused on her cousin Cana's face, she froze.

Noal poked her in the side, and she got moving again. Cana didn't even look at them as she took one of the first seats. There were no backward-facing seats behind the purple ones, and the second row made way for Judit and Noal. Judit sat and stared at the back of her cousin's head. What if she turned? Were their disguises good enough?

Noal gripped her hand, and she wondered if his heart was thundering as loudly. It was a wonder the whole tram couldn't hear it. Cana wore a white sundress without ornament or cosmetics. Blood could afford to be bland, but the fabric still looked marvelous against her dark skin. Judit thought of the Impirion emeralds, wondered where they were today, if her cousin had brought them for her visit to Freemen.

Noal clutched her tighter, and when she looked at him, his eyes were wide in warning again. She knew she was frowning, unable to help it. He must have known how badly she wanted to say something.

The tram slid noiselessly forward, the trees whizzing by; sunlight flashed through the dense canopy above. Judit's stomach began to knot, and she couldn't take her eyes of the sweep of Cana's hair, wondering when she'd turn.

No, she had to look away, to think of her father. She'd never been nervous to see him before, but now she wondered what she'd say to convince him to come with her. As far as abducting him went, there was no way they could wrestle him through the tram, the shuttle base, and the station in orbit. Besides, she didn't want to take him by force.

The tram made its first stop. Cana stirred, and Judit's heart leapt into her mouth, but Cana didn't stand.

"One more," Noal breathed.

Passengers changed. The tram slipped forward again. Noal didn't even wait for a full stop before he stood; he wasn't the only one, though people got out of his way. Judit resisted the urge to look over her shoulder and heard an impatient sigh.

Cana. And she needed to get past them to leave. Judit's belly turned to ice. Slowly, she drew back into the space between the seats, towing Noal with her. From the side, his face looked as terrified as she felt.

Cana glanced at them as she passed, her gaze flicking up and down their bodies, and then she was gone without a hint of recognition in her eyes.

Judit breathed out slowly. Noal seemed as if his knees might buckle. Judit hauled him up and hurried them to the door before the tram could move, and several other passengers had to hurry even faster.

Noal clutched Judit's arm as Cana walked up a stairway, exiting the station. "By the dark," he muttered.

"No kidding. You okay?"

"I had several heart attacks, but I'm probably fine."

She patted his hand. "Your cosmetics skill passed the ultimate test."

"If we're caught, I want that in my eulogy."

The garden district was built close to the canopy, with rays of sunlight dappling its buildings, walkways, and fountains. Building four was the tallest, though only two stories. Its curved roof nearly pierced the canopy itself, and its white façade stood out blindingly as the wandering sunlight struck it.

Inside, Judit realized they needed another plan. Beyond a large, carpeted foyer, staircases stretched to the second floor, but they were guarded by gray-uniformed military. A huge wooden desk sat between the two staircases, but instead of holos to guide visitors or confirm appointments, receptionists smiled at those who entered. One looked up eagerly at Noal, clearly ready to please.

Judit stood back while Noal turned up his charm to one hundred and fifty. He claimed he and Judit had a meeting in the building then implied that the receptionist's good looks were worth skipping a meeting or two. By the time Noal was done, the man was babbling and blushing and giving Noal all the information he wanted. With a wink, Noal said they'd be back when the receptionist got off work and led Judit outside.

"For someone who isn't interested in having a stable full of lovers," Judit said, "you certainly could if you wanted."

"I feel a little bad that I won't be here for our dinner."

She grinned wickedly. "What if we are? I mean, what if this takes longer than we thought, and you have to show? He might want to bring you home."

Noal rolled his eyes; his cheeks were probably on fire. He tried to give a nonchalant shrug, but she bet he had no idea what he'd do if backed into a corner. Not to mention that Noal was the most monogamous member of the Blood she'd met besides herself. He wouldn't cheat on Spartan even if they weren't yet a couple.

"So, did you get us an appointment?" she asked.

"I figured going to Tam's office should be the last thing we do. I discovered instead that Tam Ada-Meridian takes his lunch in the same garden at the same time nearly every day."

Of course he did. Her father loved the outdoors. That she did know, and it lightened her heart that he got to work in surroundings that made him happy. They made their way to the small garden and waited, passing a stressful two hours. Judit rehearsed many speeches in her mind, but when her father turned the corner of the little garden near his building, a cold, nervous feeling spread through her. All the speeches blew out of her mind.

The sun brought out the copper in his hair, making it bright as a halo. He strolled, one hand in the pocket of his long blue jacket, the other holding a small case, no doubt his lunch. He looked out into the trees with a happy smile.

"Hello, Dad," she said.

He pulled up slowly, as well versed in schooling his expressions as any of them, but when he focused on her, his mouth opened slightly. "I don't…" He stepped closer. "Judit? Noal? What?" He looked around, but they were alone. When he looked back to them, his eyes shimmered slightly, but he didn't cry.

"Jude," he whispered. He looked toward the camera she'd already spotted, the one she had her back to. He took a step and lifted his hand as if he might touch her dyed hair. "Are you all right? They don't know you're here, do they?"

"No, and I don't want them to." She took a deep breath, trying to bring her emotions under control. "We're all right. But we need you to come with us, Dad, come with me, back to the *Damat*. We need your help. You can tell us what you know about the chaos that's been going on and help us sort this mess out."

He took a deep breath. "You came all this way to get me?" He seemed pleased by the fact until his smile turned sad. "For the information."

"We turned to you," Noal said, "because we need family right now, and we knew you wouldn't order us to turn ourselves in."

He took another shuddering breath. "I may not be as in the loop as you think."

"Better than we are." Judit's heart began to sink at the thought that this wouldn't work. "Please, Dad. You need to decide right now. We can't wait."

"Have you been in contact with your grandmother? Your parents, Noal?"

"Grandmother, no," Noal said, "and I've seen even less of my parents than Jude has of you."

Her father sighed. "This isn't the life I wanted for you, either of you. You have to know that. I argued and pleaded—"

Judit held up a hand. She wanted to hear everything, but instead of feeling so open, the trees of Freemen felt as if they were closing in. "Please, Dad, we can talk later. Will you come with us?"

Another breath. "No."

As little as she knew him, it still felt like a stab. She couldn't catch her breath, then she let her training take over, schooled her face to neutral. There'd be time for crushing disappointment later. "Fine. Noal, let's go."

Her father caught her arm. "Jude, wait. I love you, but I also love your mother, and I can't abandon her now. She needs me here, what with all the raids and the panic. I'm keeping things cool." He shook his head, his expression stricken. "I would love to go jaunting off with you, to get to the bottom of what's going on, but I also need to put out the fires. Please, understand."

That was what she'd been doing all her life. "You made your decision. Let me go."

His face fell as if she'd told him she'd never loved him, but he didn't let go. "Give me a few minutes, and I'll get you a data chip with some information. Then your trip won't have been…wasted."

He strode back toward his building. Judit turned farther from the camera and leaned on the railing, tempted to leave, but she knew she'd be fleeing from her emotions more than anything else. She needed that chip if she couldn't have him. She'd been so certain he'd say yes. Maybe they really should have grabbed him.

"You okay?" Noal asked.

She shrugged when she wanted to mope. "It's not as if we know each other. I should have expected this."

"He's going to give us a chip. That's something."

"Right."

"It doesn't mean he loves you any less than you thought."

"Right." But she'd been picturing them finally getting to know each other while traveling on the *Damat*, finally feeling close to someone in her family other than Noal. She supposed it could be worse; she could be sneaking across Nocturna Prime at the moment, trying to steal what her father was freely giving.

CHAPTER FOURTEEN

Antiles couldn't land on Nocturna Prime itself, not without a good reason, and Annika didn't want to attract such scrutiny. She guided him to Caligo, the largest and busiest of Nocturna's moons. Luckily, he'd been there before, though he didn't elaborate on what he'd sold or to whom. Annika didn't press. The fewer questions she asked, the fewer she expected to answer.

The moon itself was green and silver, a fairly unassuming ball of rock for the most part, but peeking through the craggy exterior, Annika spotted metal, glassteel, and piping, all of it hinting at the underground installations that ran beneath Caligo's surface. Ships crisscrossed the air above it, and Caligo's technicians guided them to landing surfaces that took them briskly underground and stowed them until the owners were cleared to depart. A quick getaway was nearly impossible.

In the distance, Nocturna Prime glittered like a blue and gold jewel. Annika could barely make out the winking light that was Luna station, suspended above the capital city of Presidio, where great space elevators moved large amounts of people and freight.

"How shall I introduce you?" Antiles asked as Caligo guided them to one of the docking stations. "My assistant? My new partner?" He winked. "A young person wishing to make some extra creds by selling her time?"

She avoided rolling her eyes, wondering if he'd ever actually sold anyone's…time. "Assistant will do, if you must. I don't want to attract attention."

"Of course not." He hadn't batted an eye when she'd disguised herself with Noal's cosmetics, changing the planes of her face and dying her hair a vibrant purple. She liked brightly colored dyes. They made people look at her hair rather than her face.

After their ship landed, a platform slid it sideways to rest with other ships behind an airlock-sealed wall. As darkness closed around them, Annika let out a slow breath. She didn't let herself think about getting caught. Best to focus on the job. When that was over, she could think about everything else, but from this point forward, she had to put even Judit out of her mind.

Difficult as that was.

When she and Antiles walked out of the darkened docking area and onto one of Caligo's busy thoroughfares, she relaxed. The atmosphere wasn't chaotic like the *Xerxes*. Lighting on shops and restaurants was tasteful and not too bright. The ambient light was provided by old-fashioned streetlights, and the occasional glimpse of starlight far above gave the place a feeling of perpetual evening. People hustled to and fro, but no one pushed or shouted, and the hubbub of conversation never climbed above comfortable levels.

"There's a bar I know," Antiles said. "Always my first stop."

She nodded and followed. She'd only been on Caligo once, and she remembered the general layout, but she needed a moment to formulate a plan. She still had a long way to go. His favorite bar was a cheerful affair: A striped awning hung out front, and illumination designed to look like warm candlelight shone from within. The ceiling was decorated with murals of fantastical creatures frolicking in a garden, and the gentle light passing over it gave the illusion of movement.

They sat in a quiet corner and ordered drinks. Annika tried to wrap her mind around the momentous task in front of her. She'd been so confident during the journey, but something about being lowered into Caligo's shadowy depths had sapped her self-assurance. Even though she was close to home, she felt as lost as when she'd first stepped aboard the *Xerxes*. She wished she had Judit beside her or even Noal, or both. Then they could lean on one another.

Ama would have sneered at her. Her training had taught her to depend on herself. How quickly she'd forgotten it.

"Well," Antiles said. "May I ask what your plan is now?"

She tried to get her mind in order. Start at the beginning. She needed information, so she needed access to a computer. "Maybe I can break into one of the computers here," she said, looking around. "If not, I'm going to have to find a way onto Prime."

"Risky, but I bet the rewards are great. Anything more I can do?"

She would have been suspicious of his offer of help, but the more information she got, the more for him, too. "Cover for me. You came here with an assistant, so people are going to expect you to have one."

He stroked his beard. "I'm sure I could find a reasonable facsimile to play your part. And if not, I'll invent a story about how you're laid up with a nasty illness. Only the finest, of course."

She chuckled and decided she might miss him when this was over. He was delightfully unmoved by position. She thought Noal would have gotten on well with him given time. Judit would have killed him by now.

Annika threaded through the bar, listening for gossip. Many Nocturna allies had come to Caligo in an attempt to keep safe from the chaos in the galaxy. She spotted an increase in the number of guards, too, both in uniform and without.

She left the bar and began wandering the thoroughfares, trying to look like a visitor passing time until her business was concluded. Areas of the station reserved for Blood were unmarked, but easily spotted because of nearby guards, all with hand scanners.

The scanners would read her DNA, but she wasn't sure that passing into restricted sections was the way to go. She'd be watched too closely. Her people remained forever suspicious. Judit would probably be able to whisk her father away without any trouble, but it was going to be near impossible to get near the command center on Caligo.

She could request an audience with whoever was in charge, talk her way into the command center. No, that would draw too much attention, and they might want more than a DNA scan. As silly as it sounded, she began to think her chances of finding a computer on Prime might be easier.

She headed toward one of the shuttle bays that ferried people to the station, the other moons, and Prime itself. She added her false name to the list of Blood who wanted a seat, but there were many, all of whom she'd have to stay away from. She wondered if Ama had begun calling the family home. Maybe she was passing out new assignments, or maybe she wanted to make her house into fewer targets. Either way,

Annika couldn't push in, not with her disguise. There were some high-ranking members on the list, far above her fake name.

Antiles got rooms at a modest hotel and began to conduct business as usual. Annika wondered if she should go with him but decided it was better to be cautious and stay in their room. His clients included Blood, and she didn't want to take the chance of being recognized. No, better for him to make excuses and for her to lie low, waiting for the shuttle.

Even with her status, it took three days, and she wondered if she could get the names of anyone she'd been bumped for. Maybe she could pay them a visit when she was on Prime, but she couldn't afford the luxury of even small vengeance. She imagined Judit being appalled at the dark thought, but it wasn't as if she'd kill anyone. She just wanted to scare them a little.

When the summons came, she took her bag and headed for the shuttle bay. Her fake name was at the top of the restricted list, but she spotted several high-ranking names below hers. She paused, waiting for the screen to change. If those names had just been entered, it might take a moment for the list to reset, but it stayed the same and then blinked, and where she expected to see the names reappear above hers, they were gone.

She took a deep breath and forced her heart to still. A glitch? Possibly but unlikely. A mistake? Equally unlikely. Those chosen to serve the Blood rarely made such mistakes. A change of plans from the higher-ranking Bloods? But why had their names been below hers in the first place?

Only one explanation made sense: Someone wanted to make certain she was here, now, so she'd gone to the top of the list. And the rest of the Blood were being kept away in case a fight broke out.

Were there more guards than before? A few had scanners. Looking for her? Or was she being as paranoid as Noal accused her of being?

She backed up slowly. There were reasons to be paranoid. Her family was one of them. She looked toward the vids and holos, trying to seem nonchalant as she edged toward the exit. She'd go to the restaurant where Antiles said he'd be, and they'd make their way to the ship as quickly as possible. He'd tell everyone her illness had gotten worse, and he needed to get her to a treatment facility.

Her heart began to pound so she could hear it in her ears. She forced herself to look calm but purposeful, as if returning to her room for something she'd forgotten. As she rounded a corner along the promenade, she slowed. A group of people lingered outside the entrance of the restaurant. They didn't seem as if they were waiting for a table, just talking, but their gazes darted through the crowd, and she didn't like the way they stood. She saw past their airs of nonchalance to the way their muscles gathered like coiled springs.

Annika paused, looking in a shop window. After a heartbeat, she turned down another street. Back to the hotel? Try to sneak aboard Antiles's ship? Leave him if she had to? She took the personal comm out of her pocket. If whoever was waiting for her had Antiles, they might have his comm as well. There might be a way they could track her. And if they didn't have him, if they weren't sure he was connected to her, signaling might give him away.

She put the comm back in her pocket, trying to think of something else. Maybe the guards knew her name was fake, but they didn't quite know who she was. Maybe she'd managed to fool the cameras, but station personnel were on the lookout for whoever claimed the name she'd used.

Or maybe they knew that Annika Nocturna was aboard the station, but they weren't sure where. Even now, facial recognition programs might be trying to find her but were thrown off by her disguise. If some secret scanner had given her a deep scan without her realizing, they could know who she was. It wouldn't even take a drop of blood. Maybe she'd lost a hair, and it had gotten whisked into some vacuum and into a scanner.

Why in the dark would her people do such things? Why couldn't they be lax like the rest of the galaxy? Why were they all so darking paranoid?

Then she reminded herself that she was running from a kiosk with a glitch and a bunch of loiterers outside of a restaurant. If that was the case, she should be able to get to Antiles's ship with no problems. Then she'd know for certain. Then she could laugh at herself in peace.

She tried to walk calmly but quickly, thinking of what she could do when she got to the ship if she had to leave in a hurry. But there *was* no leaving in a hurry. She'd known that from the start. And now everyone she saw began to look suspicious. All conversations seemed false. Everyone looking at a vid also seemed to be looking over their shoulders. She saw one man turn, look at her, then look away.

She didn't slow her stride, didn't even glance at him as she passed, but when she was about to round a corner, she peeked and saw him putting a hand into his pocket and drawing out something that might be a small comm.

She went faster, wondering if she dared risk a run. A man at another vid turned and took a step toward her, his hand raised. She launched a fist into his windpipe, cutting off his air, his eyes bulging. She kicked his knee and sent him toppling then continued her course. She could lose herself among the ships. She could sneak onto one that had clearance to depart, even if she had to cram herself in beside the landing strut. She had to get out of these halls, she had to—

The disembarking lounge was full of people, all of them watching the hall. No one waited in the seats or stared at the board for their clearance to depart. The elevator doors were shut. These were guards, waiting for her, not even bothering to pretend. She felt more of them come down the hall behind her, cutting off her retreat. She almost expected Ama to thread her way through them, but of course, Ama would never come herself.

Annika dropped her bag at her feet. At least she'd been right. "Well, who wants to be first?"

"Please, cousin." Ricardo, one of her more annoying cousins, stepped forward. She'd only spoken to him a few times. She felt a little insulted they hadn't brought someone she liked better. Well, at least she wouldn't hesitate to punch this one. "Your grandmother requests your presence down on the planet."

"Requests, does she?" Annika asked, tickled by the thought. "Please, tell her no on my behalf. Oh, and throw in some flowers to soften her disappointment."

They didn't laugh, but she didn't expect them to. Ricardo smiled and stepped aside, one hand out. He'd dressed all in black, and she wondered if he thought it made him more intimidating. "If you will, my private shuttle awaits."

How hard should she make it for them? There were enough that they'd eventually bring her down, but should she make them earn it? How close would they come to killing her? A few had shock sticks, and she had the one Judit had given her in her pocket. Since weapons were some of the things traded on Caligo, they couldn't forbid them, though anyone who wished to carry them usually had a license.

But was now the time to use it? Did she want to be carried to Prime unconscious? Did she want to wake up in a medbay bound to a bed?

She picked her bag up and walked toward the elevator. Several guards turned to go with her and Ricardo, but they couldn't all fit on a shuttle. There would be opportunities.

Ricardo held up a hand. "If you wouldn't mind a small search, cousin?"

She lifted an eyebrow. "How could I refuse?"

They searched her bag and her person, finding the shock stick and the comm and taking both. They scanned her and pronounced her clean, giving her back the bag with the clothing. She supposed if all else failed, she could strangle her cousin with a shirt, but with her bone stiletto, she wouldn't need to. She wondered how long Ama would spend wondering what in the dark she could have stabbed Ricardo with.

It was a small shuttle, and Ricardo was the only one to follow her aboard. She couldn't hit him yet, had to wait until they'd cleared Caligo, then she could pummel him, take the ship, and do as she pleased; whoever was monitoring them wouldn't know she'd taken over until it was too late. Something about the way he moved told her it wouldn't be that easy, though. If he hadn't gotten her exact training, he might have gotten something close.

"She knows what you're up to," he said as he took the pilot's seat.

"Who?" It was a standard Nocturna shuttle, and she had no doubt she could fly it.

"Our grandmother, who do you think?"

She eyed him again, trying to remember anything significant about him and coming up empty. "She's your grandmother, too? I didn't know we were that closely related."

He gave her a wan smile. "No one ever knows everything, but you should know that. You went off on that Meridian ship. By all the rumors, Grandmother knows you're trying to get to the bottom of the little…rebellion. If that's what the lesser houses and the unaffiliated are calling it."

"It's not so little out there. If you'd seen any of it, you'd say the same."

"Well, she approves of what you're doing."

Annika couldn't speak. Ama...approved of her disobedience? "She ordered me home."

"She would have to say that, and she thought you might come here looking for information, so she's going to give it to you."

Annika sat back in her seat, floored. "She's going to tell me what she knows?"

"Yes, and then you're going to go back to the Meridians, use the information however you can to bring them under our power, and by the time the dust settles, the new plan for our joined house can go ahead as scheduled."

Just like that? They thought she could so easily go back to being Noal's monitor, his soon-to-be assassin? If they were hoping for everything to be as they'd planned, they obviously didn't know that Judit was the real chosen one. She saw no reason to correct them. But did her grandmother hope she would implant the worm in Noal before the wedding?

Well, they could forget it. She didn't even have to think hard about it. She cared for Judit and Noal too much to betray them now. But part of her wanted to hear Ama out, to take whatever information they fed her and do as she pleased. But would Ama let her go again without the means to control her? One look at Annika's face would tell her grandmother that she'd fallen from the fold. There was no tricking that woman. Maybe she had a worm with Annika's name on it, too.

Annika lashed out a fist, but Ricardo blocked her. His eyes widened, but if he was more than a little surprised, he didn't show it. He turned sideways in his chair as she came for him again, but he'd received training similar to her own. When he brought a hidden stunner out from underneath the console, she pinched her arm, making her bone stiletto slide free. He seemed shocked. She didn't know why he was so surprised. No one got to know everything, as he'd said.

She slashed his arm, and the stunner thumped to the deck. He backed off, holding his wound closed. She feinted forward, and he slammed into the console. She dropped, grabbing the stunner in one hand and his leg in the other. Already off balance, he was easy to yank forward. He slid down the console between the seats, kicking with his free leg, but it did nothing but make him fall faster. That was good. When she stunned him, he didn't have far to drop.

She went to the controls. He'd already programmed the shuttle to land at one of Presidio's government buildings, but she suspended that, trying to see how good the link was to the Nocturna net. Cursory, as she half expected. No, if she wanted information, she'd have to land. Problem was, her grandmother was expecting her, and she'd have quite the welcome party waiting.

Annika could run, take the shuttle and meet Judit at the rendezvous. Maybe Judit's plans had gone better, and this whole trip wouldn't be a waste. She clenched a hand, hating that thought. Her grandmother had anticipated her, but she couldn't do so forever. And Annika had proven she could fool the facial recognition scanners, at least for a little while. The whole of Nocturna Prime stretched out below her, and there were plenty of places where she might access the net and find what she was looking for. And she had to move quickly. As soon as her grandmother suspected she was on the planet, she'd lock everything down tighter than it already was. Outlying areas would complain when they couldn't access the net, but her grandmother would listen to their complaints for days if it meant trapping her granddaughter.

Maybe that was the answer. She *could* go to Presidio, to the heart of information, but make her grandmother think she was somewhere else entirely. Annika programmed the shuttle to enter low orbit so it would be harder to spot. Then she took it in at an angle, heading for the outskirts of the capital city. She programmed it to set down in one of the remote landing strips on the planet, up north near the pole. Hopefully, that would give her time.

She moved behind the seats, searching the area around the small airlock. A standard Nocturna shuttle had the standard emergency gear. Before she could think too hard about it, Annika took the low-altitude emergency chute, suit, and helmet and slipped them on, clipping her traveling bag around her waist. The shuttle would be going on without her.

The shuttle neared the outskirts of Presidio, the city stretching far below her. Annika took a deep breath and popped the hatch. The wind whipped around her, and she dove into it, not able to suppress a cry that was half joy and half terror. She let her training take over, kept her arms tight, and flew toward the ground like a dart. Her heart was pounding, but she had to keep herself from crying out again, this time in pure happiness. She hadn't been skydiving since that part of her training two years ago, and she'd missed it.

When the suit's alarm beeped in her ear, she spread her arms, deploying bat-like wings to slow her descent. When she was close enough to the ground to be inconspicuous, she deployed her chute. The whole thing went as her training had, like clockwork, and she was happy she'd insisted that Ama include skydiving in her list of skills. Her grandmother hadn't seen the point at the time, but she had capitulated. Every skill might someday be useful.

She aimed for a clump of forest, and the chute tangled in the trees, dangling her about ten feet off the ground. Annika detached, rolled when she hit, and was up and running as fast as she could in the direction of the city. If anyone had seen the shuttle or the chute, she needed to be long gone from both.

There were all sorts of things to consider as she moved: how she would break into the net, how she would get access to a computer in the first place, how she would get off the planet once she had what she was looking for. But all those considerations got lost in the joy she felt to be using all her training for something she believed in. She'd used her combat skills when she'd been kidnapped, to get herself and Noal to safety, but that had been tempered by Noal's disgust and the way she'd had to lie to him, never mind that the lying was for his own good.

But now, running through the trees, she could do as she wished, as she was always meant to do. Judit would finally see how valuable an asset she was.

And why was that so important? She and Judit loved each other, but even at the time she'd said it, Annika hadn't really known what it meant. She'd cared about what happened to Judit, cared about her feelings as well as her body. At the time, that had been love. Now, though, she wanted to be important to Judit, to be an asset. Maybe that was part of love, too. Judit's opinion was important, more important than anyone else's.

Even Ama's.

That *had* to be love, even though Annika couldn't think of anything to compare it to. She could get her heart pumping harder just by thinking of the moments they'd shared, that they'd continue to share if all went well. And she could chill herself to the bone by thinking of Judit in danger.

Love, then. Truly. And since it *was* love, Annika supposed she had to fully commit herself to this plan to help the galaxy come back from chaos. So far, Judit had been the one with the ship, the plan. Annika had been more than willing to leave their problems behind, to run away if they had to, but now she saw how she could help; she could do things Judit couldn't or wasn't willing to do. She supposed she should have realized that when she'd first volunteered for this mission, but part of her desire to come to Prime had been to see if she could break into the net of her homeworld. Now the cause itself was important because Judit was important to her.

Funny, it only took jumping from one little shuttle for her to realize it.

CHAPTER FIFTEEN

Judit's father was taking too long. She could feel time ticking away as she and Noal waited in the small garden. Her father hadn't gotten to eat, probably wouldn't get to that day. She tried to shake off the guilt, then chuckled at herself. If missing lunch was the only thing that went wrong, they could count themselves very lucky.

Judit had given up pacing and sat with Noal on a bench made to look like stone. Where stone would have been cool, this was slightly heated, situated as they were in shade. She tried to think of all the materials it might be made out of but couldn't distract herself for long.

"How much time now?" Judit asked.

"Since he's been gone? Thirty-five minutes. Since you last asked? Five minutes."

That didn't help her worry. "He should have been back by now. He said a few minutes."

"He probably got pulled into some meeting, and he can't tear away, or it will look suspicious."

"For this long?"

"Maybe people feel they can waste your time if you're not Blood."

The thought made her cringe. "He's close enough."

"Okay, then maybe everyone wants some of his time." But he sounded less sure. He'd never been one for pacing, but he'd given up all attempts at idle conversation. He hadn't even tried teasing her in fifteen minutes.

"We should go." As much as it pained her to leave, it couldn't hurt more than her father not wanting to come with her in the first place. "We can't wait forever."

"Give him a few more minutes."

"Why would a few more minutes make any difference?"

He paused. "You don't think…"

"What?"

"He wouldn't tell anyone, would he?"

She jumped to her feet, her belly gone cold. Turn them in? Could he do such a thing? Might if he thought it was for her own good, for Meridian's own good? Or maybe he'd accessed the wrong database in his quest to give them information. Maybe he'd gone about it in the wrong way and attracted attention.

Now that the idea had been presented, it stuck. "Let's go."

This time, Noal didn't argue. She forced herself to walk toward the tram, holding on to Noal's arm as if they were strolling. Their path would take them past her father's building; she wanted to see if anything was out of the ordinary. If her father had gotten into trouble over her, she wanted to see if she could help him, even if it meant risking herself. Even if he'd hurt her, he was still family.

But the outside of the building seemed as normal as ever. If she wanted to know more, she'd have to go inside.

"Go on to the tram," she said quietly. "I'll find out what's going on."

"You're not going anywhere without me."

Her temper flared, but she tried to keep a pleasant face. "One of us has to make it back to the ship."

"Fine. You go, and I'll see what's happened."

She fought a snarl. "Who's had the guardian training, you or me?"

"Who's actually the chosen one?" He gave her a sharp look. "It's your ship, Jude. And as you've pointed out, you're more equipped than I am to handle a firefight."

Judit looked to the building again. No horde of guards loitered out front; no one loitered at all, just as when they'd first approached. Judit looked to where the tram waited to take her to the shuttle bay, but when she tried to separate from Noal, she couldn't do it.

He gave her a look, but before he could speak, she said, "It's both of us or nothing."

After a sigh, he nodded. "Think casual. Let me do the talking." He took a deep breath. "And at the first sign of trouble, pick me up and get us both out of here. I'm terrible at running."

She snorted a laugh and coughed over it, fearing the tension had made it too loud. "Done."

They sidled into the lobby, trying for nonchalant. A few people filed in from lunch, all dressed in business suits. The receptionists were still on the desk. Security still guarded the staircases. Nothing appeared out of the ordinary. There didn't seem to be any secret guards hiding in the potted plants.

Noal turned to Judit. "Maybe it *is* just taking longer than he thought." He took a slow look around. "Maybe we can get up to see him. My receptionist is still on duty."

"We could go back to the garden," Judit said, not knowing if she should be irritated or relieved. Probably both. "Wait some more."

Noal shushed her as her father crested a staircase. Relieved, definitely. She'd been too impatient again, that was all. She took Noal's arm to lead him outside but froze when two people in military uniforms followed her father. They walked too close to him, and one had her stare pinned on his neck. His hands were unbound, but Judit had no doubt he was in their custody.

Her father's gaze raked the small crowd in the lobby, and when his eyes met hers, they widened, and he shook his head ever so slightly. She couldn't help staring, but luckily, she wasn't the only one. Her father had been caught. She tightened her jaw to keep her mouth from falling open. Waves of cold passed through her, and she thought she might be sick.

People made way for the guards and their prisoner, and their passage sparked pockets of quiet chatter. Many people on Freemen would know who he was, but they couldn't know what was going on, and speculation had to be flying wildly. She heard one frantic whisper of "Has the system been breached?"

An enemy intrusion would send the military running for her father, but by the calm way he walked, Judit didn't think that was so. If she could have transformed this situation into that one by sheer will, she would have. At least then he'd have been safe, even if she didn't get the information she was looking for.

Her father and the guards passed through the doors. Noal and Judit waited a heartbeat before following along with several others. They were taking her father to the tram, and a desperate part of her said this was the last time she'd ever see him. She should have been nicer to him, should have said something better!

Noal mumbled something about staying calm, but all Judit wanted to do was rush the two guards and grab her father. It could work. They wouldn't be expecting an attack. A few well-placed kicks and punches, and she could take them out. Then they could sprint for the tram.

No, too slow.

Noal's grip on her arm tightened. "Don't even think it."

There was more security in the building, probably around every corner, and her arrest would mean Noal's arrest and that of her whole crew. She and Noal would be all right, but everyone on the *Damat*?

Her father stumbled, and the guards steadied him, but she saw something wink as it fell from his hands to the grass, and then they were walking on.

Judit's eyes fixed on the grass, her whole body numb as if attached to a biobed. Her father had nearly disappeared into the tram station. She could separate from Noal, send him to the *Damat*. Then she'd take her father and find a place to hide here on Freemen until they had a chance to get away.

"Jude," Noal said softly. "You can't help him now."

"He's my dad. I have to try."

"He warned you off for a reason."

But watching him go was the hardest thing she'd ever done, harder than watching Annika's and Noal's engagement. She took a step.

Noal's fingers felt like claws. She'd have to shake him off or convince him to let go.

"Get to the *Damat*," she said. "You can pick us up later."

"You cannot help him. You'll be caught! Where will that leave the rest of us? Where will that leave Annika?"

Judit froze. If the *Damat* was busy trying to retrieve her or running from Meridian warships, Annika would be stranded. What if she needed help? "Darkness, Noal," Judit whispered.

"I know."

When her father and his guards had gone, Noal coaxed her forward, neck craned as if still trying to catch sight of an intriguing scandal. He stopped at the spot where the glittery thing had fallen and turned to her. "Are you all right?"

She couldn't speak.

"No, I know you're not, but I need to say something so it looks as if we're having a conversation." He pulled a wrapped candy out of his pocket and offered it to her.

She reached for it woodenly, knowing what he was doing, trying to play along.

He dropped it before she could grab it, and when he bent down then straightened, she knew he had whatever her father had dropped. It disappeared into his sleeve, and the candy was offered to her again.

She took it this time, knowing the other thing had to be a data chip. Her father had managed to hide it in his own sleeve before they'd caught him. Even being arrested, he'd still thought of her.

"We have to do something," she said.

"Yes, we have to leave."

"Maybe Beatrice can break into the Meridian net."

"If she could, she'd have done that in the first place," he said more sternly. "Things will only be worse for your father if they find us here. He risked his safety to get this to us."

"He wouldn't have had to risk anything if—"

"Jude, someone clearly found out what files he was accessing. If we leave, he can make up some excuse, but if they catch us…"

"They'll know he planned to give the information to us without authorization."

He nodded slowly. "Best thing we can do is nothing at all. He's smart. Give him a chance to talk his way out of this."

He was right, and at the moment, she hated him a little for that. She let him lead her toward the tram, but she kept running scenarios and then discarding them when she factored the odds of success. Her father was good at negotiating. She had to trust that he could do it again. It was the plan that had the greatest chance of working.

It was an uneventful trip back to the shuttle station. Judit parked herself in front of one of the vid feeds as they waited, scanning for any story that would give her a clue as to what had happened, but if her father had been charged with anything, it hadn't made the news yet. She was tempted to tip off one of the news agencies so she could find out more, but she didn't want to force anyone's hand. Maybe after a bit of questioning, they'd let her father go. He did have clout, and he had her mother to speak for him, the woman he wanted to stay and help more than he wanted to help his own daughter. That had to count for something besides making a bitter taste flood her mouth.

"I got someone else bumped," Noal said as he came back from the passenger kiosk. This waiting room was small enough that it didn't have a special section for Blood, but they'd still taken the most comfortable chairs.

"Good."

He stared at the vids. "Anything?"

She shook her head, her stomach sinking with every passing moment. "There had to be a way to help."

His sigh spoke volumes. "Could you have beaten up every guard between there and here? And everyone in this station? In the space station above? When all it takes is one call to the planetary defense grid to disable or destroy the *Damat*?"

A nasty voice inside her said that she'd hesitated only because she wanted to see Annika again. She'd had a chance to act, and she hadn't done it because she was selfish at heart.

"Come on," Noal said. "Our shuttle's here."

She let him lead her again. Judit buckled herself into her seat, not noticing anything except Noal trying to keep up their casual façade. She ground her teeth as he flirted with the attendant who put the curtain around their chairs, but she kept her face turned to the side so no one could see her expression. Let him keep up the fakery so she wouldn't have to. It was what he was best at.

Once on the station, she nearly ran to the *Damat*. Only Noal's hand hooked in her elbow slowed her pace. If he tried to argue with how fast she was walking, she didn't hear him. The moment they were aboard the *Damat*, she stopped in the hall, letting the familiar smell and feel of her ship surround her. Evie was waiting, staring at her expectantly, looking out at the station as if wondering why Judit had stopped.

Judit closed the hatch behind her, then kicked the side of her ship hard, causing Noal to draw back, but he wisely said nothing.

"Get us out of here," Judit said, barely able to talk through the tightness in her throat. "Noal, give that data chip to Beatrice. Tell Roberts to scour the feeds. Find out everything you can about what's happened to my father."

She could have spoken over her comm, but she didn't want to talk to anyone else. Noal hurried away, but Evie paused, watching her, and

Judit could see the questions in her eyes. Judit had never been as close to her tactical officer as she was to Beatrice. Evie didn't seem to mind. Her expression seemed sympathetic with a bit of caution, as if Judit was a wounded animal rather than a captain.

And Judit couldn't go on like that, couldn't let her ship down as she'd let her father down. She took a deep breath. "My father…is not coming. We need to go to the rendezvous point."

Evie nodded slowly. "Do you need Dr. Sewell?"

Judit blinked, momentarily perplexed out of her angst. "Why?"

Evie pointed to Judit's chest, and Judit realized she was holding her clenched fist tight to her abdomen as if trying to keep her guts from pouring out. Or maybe it was keeping more emotional outbursts inside.

"I'm fine," Judit said, straightening and lowering her arm. She couldn't fail her ship, and she wouldn't fail Annika either. "Please, go to the bridge, Evie, and make sure we get under way. I'll be right behind you."

❖

As she raced toward Presidio, Annika was glad she'd thought to bring her bag along. She couldn't walk around the city dressed in a flight suit. As soon as she'd gone some distance from the chute, she put on a regular outfit, a dark green jacket and trousers. She checked her face in a small mirror to make sure her implants were where she wanted and added heavier eye makeup and a bold lip. She fixed her purple-dyed hair on top of her head. She'd still have to avoid any deep scans, but there wouldn't be any random checks in a place as big as Presidio. Though they might be a problem when she tried to gain access to the net.

The edges of Presidio were still occupied by single houses, dwellings for those who eschewed city life but wanted to be close to its conveniences. A tram ran on a narrow track between rows of houses, and Annika headed for the nearest stop. The architecture was limited only by the owners' imaginations. She passed mansions that resembled castles and fashionable houses with nary a right angle. One resembled a large circus tent, and she saw its neighbors—their house a dazzling collection of stained glass—staring at it in disdain from their lawn. If others on the street felt the same way, she couldn't imagine the tent house would last long. Of course, those who lived out here could no doubt afford to change their houses as easily as they changed their minds.

At the tram stop, Annika sat on a plastic bench, trying to look like a bored commuter. She needed to be closer to Presidio's heart in order to strike. Ama had no doubt locked out her personal codes, but Annika had memorized many from her forays into Nocturna's computers, and Ama couldn't possibly have changed all the codes Annika had memorized. That would cut too many people off. And Ama couldn't lock everyone out for long if she decided to go that route. There was too much that needed to be done.

When the tram arrived, Annika stepped inside, not bothering to jockey for anything restricted to Blood. When the doors closed, the tram slid down the rail while a computerized voice listed the upcoming stops, and holo ads called from the ceiling.

Annika kept her eyes on her bag while she listened to the stops, trying to think of which she should use. She needed access to somewhere with a terminal, somewhere that wouldn't have as much security as a government building but nothing so low in the food chain that it might have an outdated system or restricted access.

As the sun came out from behind the clouds, Annika took Noal's shades from her bag and unrolled them, holding the flimsy-looking plastic up to her face so it could form around her head like nanosheen, covering her eyes and perching over her nose before it stiffened. It dampened the light amazingly well, and she barely felt the weight of it. Noal always had the best toys.

As the tram continued, Annika began to change her mind about her destination. Maybe the city's heart wasn't the best place to go. Maybe she needed to be in what the locals called Off Center, a cluster of buildings not quite in downtown, but still with an affluent, important air. Access with less attention. She waited through two more stops, then disembarked with a horde of others, trying to look as if she had a specific destination in mind.

She passed many upscale shops, real merchandise or rotating holos in each window. She slowed and glanced around as if considering a day of leisure. When her eyes passed over a squat, discreet building behind the others, she slowed. Some kind of distribution warehouse, probably catering to many of these shops. It had its own shuttle bay sitting atop it. It wouldn't be a main warehouse, just a drop-off for these high-end places, but it would need to organize merchandise with off-world suppliers.

And that meant it would have to hook into Nocturna's main net, at least peripherally.

Annika ducked inside one of the shops and demanded an empty box with the store's logo. The clerk babbled at her, glancing behind his counter, his eyes wide. The store's DNA scanners would be telling him she was Blood, so she barked that he wasn't being fast enough. He handed the box over with something like a sob. Annika strode from the store as quickly as she'd stormed in.

From her bag, she selected an extravagant scarf and wrapped it around her head before marching to the small warehouse, the box held before her.

After sounding the chime, she yelled, "Hurry up! I have an incorrect delivery that needs to be fixed immediately!"

No doubt they scanned her, too, and the door opened quickly. There weren't many members of the Blood who acted as shopkeepers, so they had to conclude she was an owner, and any owner in that area had to be rolling in creds.

"Dama," the man who opened the door said. His eyes were wide, skin tight and waxy. "If you had but called—"

She pushed past him. "My merchandise is too important to use comms. I can't have my competitors knowing that I'll be the last ones selling this season's fashions because you and your staff are incompetent."

There were more people on the floor, gawking. Off to the side, a set of stairs led upward.

"Dama," the man said, "perhaps if you let me see the box and the order slip?"

She yanked it out of reach. "Fool! I'm not letting this merchandise out of my sight until I see this error corrected. I demand you show me the order in your system immediately."

He blanched and bowed, a custom that hadn't been in vogue for twenty years. "Dama, of course. I would be happy to. Anything I or my staff can do to make your errand easier—"

She leaned close and pitched her voice dangerously low. "*Now.*"

He nearly jumped out of his skin and led the way upstairs. It was almost too easy. He led her into a small office and closed the door, and then there were only three of them. She let him lead her close to a console. One of the workers stood so she could have his chair, and she hit him in the face with the box. While he reeled, she kicked the manager in the knee. He fell, and as he drew breath to cry out she kicked up into his chin, silencing him. The other was plastered to her seat, eyes wide in terror. Annika slammed her hand into the neck of the one she'd hit with the box, and he fell, too.

"Da...Dama?" the last worker said. Her face had gone bloodless, but she hadn't made a move to alert anyone.

Use her to navigate the system? No, too great a chance she'd come to her senses and sound an alarm. Annika placed her box on the ground. "Face the console. I need you to access some files."

With hesitant, wooden motions, the woman obeyed, but before her hands moved, Annika hit her as she'd hit the other, then caught her before she could pitch forward over the controls. She leaned the woman over the seat and gently pushed the chair away.

Annika locked the door and sat, passing her hand over the console to bring up the holo display. She saw the connections to Nocturna's system that allowed the warehouse to move merchandise from one place to another on Prime as well as off-world. The console also had access to the news vids. She found some reports of a net outage near the area where she'd sent the shuttle. As expected, her grandmother cut ties to some of the outlying sectors of the planet, thinking Annika would be trying to access the net there. So now Ama knew she was on the loose but couldn't yet know where she was. She'd have to work quickly.

She wouldn't be able to access her grandmother's personal files, not from anywhere except her grandmother's computer, but with the right codes, she could access some of the intelligence Nocturna had gathered. She didn't have time to sort through it, but even at a cursory glance, there was a lot to see. Nocturna's spy network was extensive, but until that moment, she didn't realize how large it was, how much information was being fed into their system every single day. Not just reports but camera feeds and entire logs from listening posts. It could have been every single transmission from anywhere in the galaxy. It took entire teams to go through all the data on Nocturna; how in the world would Judit and her crew manage it?

She'd have to narrow her search to the past month. Annika copied the information onto a data chip. She moved to shut down her link to the system just as it blinked off on its own. She was out of time. She took the chip, picked up her box, and stomped imperiously down the stairs, walking across the floor as if she had every right to be there. The guard at the door even opened it for her, his eyes averted.

Once outside, Annika picked up speed, dumping the box in the nearest trash receptacle and taking off the scarf. Her grandmother might have located the console she was using, or she might have cut off access to the whole street, maybe to all of Presidio. Annika didn't know, but she couldn't stick around to find out.

Once she joined the regular traffic on the street, Annika tried to walk as she had before, an important person with purpose, above the notice of those around her unless they happened to stumble into her path. Now all she had to do was get off the planet, no easy task. But taking off was always easier than landing when it came to Nocturna Prime.

She considered the space elevator. Too risky, too many opportunities to be caught. And if she managed to make it aboard, she'd be stuck for the ponderous journey up to the station. No, better to aim for a shuttle, and not a passenger vessel this time. Shuttles carrying goods came and went all the time: to Caligo, the other moons, and various stations where they would be transferred to larger ships. She'd sneak aboard one before Ama had time to shut down the shuttle port.

Annika jumped on one of the trams and kept near the door, feeling the seconds tick by keenly, as if there was a clock under her skin. She tried to picture what her grandmother was doing, how computers and people were sorting through footage, looking at faces or strides, looking for people acting out of place before they looked even deeper. When the tram stopped, she was at the doors along with a crowd of others. She crossed the lane to another stop, one that would take her to the port where the bulk of the shuttles landed. Guards lounged around this station, rifles hung across their shoulders, the kind she never saw in space because of the damage they could do to a ship.

These guards didn't seem on high alert, but they were scanning the faces of everyone who went past. Annika changed direction smoothly, heading away from them. Unlike on Caligo, there was more than one way to get to the shuttle port here. She remembered a fence that guarded the cargo entrance, but she could find a way around that. As she strode down an alley, she risked a look back and spotted someone from the crowd peeling off to follow her. All her senses on alert, she listened to his footsteps, the way he was talking urgently into the comm curling around his ear, something about trading futures and shares. She didn't believe the ruse. Noal might call her paranoid, but she'd been right on Caligo. And this wasn't Noal's planet.

At the end of the alley, she ducked into the doorway of a shop, hand to her own ear as if making a call or listening to one.

In the reflection of a pane of glass across the way, she watched for the man to come out, waiting to see who was right, her or Noal. The faux-businessman stepped out, and for the blink of an eye, she thought maybe she was wrong. He didn't seem to notice she'd gone. Then he paused, looked both ways down the street, and then back the way he'd come. He was still talking, but his chatter began to make less sense, as if he thought the most important thing was to keep talking, no matter what he said.

When he turned and scanned the street again, she knew he was looking for her, and the satisfaction of being right about him was almost enough to combat the aggravation she had about either having to lose him or take him out.

There were too many people on the street for option number two. He began easing in the opposite direction, craning his neck to see into doorways. She slipped out and sidled behind him, hurrying back down the alley until she was far enough away to break into a run. She didn't look over her shoulder but sprinted for the street. Before she reached it, she slowed, getting her breathing under control so her heart rate could climb down from the heavens.

Once clear of the alley, Annika glanced back but didn't see the faux-businessman. She wasn't naive enough to think herself in the clear, though. She wondered if he was following her because he suspected her or if Nocturna spies practiced following people all the time. She wasn't going to wait and find out.

Annika turned up a few more streets, working her way to the shuttle port cargo entrance. A line of self-driving trucks waited to get through a security checkpoint that scanned each as it went by. She wondered what the scans were looking for. Weapons? Stowaways? Not many people sneaked *off* Nocturna Prime.

Except her. And her mother. She had a sudden thought that her mother had been in this same situation years ago. Had she taken this route? Hidden in a box of vegetables so no one would find her? Or did she have confederates waiting to sneak her off-world? Had she known them personally, or had she bought their help?

Annika shook her head, focusing on the trucks. She supposed the scanners *could* be looking for people. Criminals perhaps. But such people were caught and dealt with hurriedly on Nocturna Prime. There was always someone watching, and Annika suspected she'd gotten as far as she'd had mostly because the scanners acknowledged her DNA. There were no prisons on Prime, no reason for someone to want to get off the planet covertly unless they were practicing, as she'd done a time or two.

Or if they wanted to leave their family forever, as her mother had done.

Annika told herself to get it together. One truck passed through the checkpoint, but unlike the others, this one had a man riding in the cab. He leaned out and spoke to the guard minding the scanning equipment. They had a quick conversation, then she waved him on.

The alarms hadn't sounded. Good news. Annika could grab hold of one of the trucks and hide, ride through the scanners, but just because no alarms went off didn't mean the scanners *weren't* looking for living organisms. If a person fell asleep or unconscious in a truck, no one wanted them to be shot into space in an unprotected cargo hold. And Nocturna wouldn't risk sending bacteria or animals to a planet that wasn't ready for them, like a new world that expected only sanitized equipment or building materials.

Annika turned away from the gate and walked through the grass along the fence, staying well away as she scanned for weak spots. Cameras clustered near the gate, but along the fence, their little black eyes didn't shine as frequently. She paused at one section between two cameras and hurried forward, kneeling at the base of the fence. It would be covered in sensors, but it didn't look electrified or shielded. She supposed no one would risk pulling a robbery in the shuttle port. Nocturna dealt harshly with all lawbreakers, especially thieves. Well, those who weren't working under the house's orders, anyway.

She could vault over the fence, but she needed cover once inside. Just because the guards weren't having to combat crafty thieves didn't mean they wanted random people wandering their shuttle port. She'd need a better disguise than any she had on her.

Annika smiled, remembering the guard at the entrance. She gave the fence a few harsh kicks. As expected, an alarm sounded from the nearby guard booth. Annika lay in the long grass, waiting. The guard on the gate would close it securely before coming to check, but she would come, Annika had no doubt. It was probably the most interesting thing that had happened all day.

When Annika heard footsteps, she darted up, smacking the guard in the face and neck until she fell. Annika dragged her into the grass and stripped her quickly, then donned her uniform and took her belt, palm computer, and keycard. She didn't bother to go back to the gate but strapped her bag over her shoulder, vaulted the fence, and walked toward the gate from the inside, looking at the palm computer as if checking something.

In the distance, a group of attendants drove a little cart toward where Annika had kicked the fence. Some central system must have registered the strikes, too. "False alarm," she shouted, waving them away.

They waved back but went on to look at the fence. She shrugged as if she couldn't care less. From the inside, they wouldn't see the guard in the grass, and once they'd made sure the fence was all right, they'd go back to whatever they'd been doing.

Once at the gate, Annika opened it again, letting the machinery do its work, but instead of monitoring it, she took the cart parked outside the booth and drove toward where the shuttles waited on the tarmac beyond.

Now all that was left was to find the best place to hide. On a larger shuttle, she couldn't remain in the cargo hold. She didn't know which ones would keep the atmosphere flowing and the temperature controlled. A smaller shuttle would do, but it would have fewer places to hide. Maybe she could sneak aboard a large shuttle and hide in an escape pod or some kind of emergency space. She'd need something fast, capable of long-distance travel, but with a small crew she could easily subdue. And she had to pick one that was going to launch before the guard was discovered, and the shuttles were placed on lockdown.

A siren sounded through the field, and Annika cursed, not

knowing what caused it, not knowing if it was normal. She pulled to a stop near the closest shuttle. The ground crew stood around talking while maintenance bots loaded cargo into the hold. She crept along the shuttle's side, trying to get close enough to hear what the crew was saying.

She spotted movement in the distance, another of the carts trundling down the tarmac. She tried to keep tighter to the shuttle, thinking she could run from one ship to another, but another cart was coming from the opposite direction. They had to be looking for her. She was out of time. Again.

Not daring to think too hard, Annika sprinted for the shuttle's open hatch and bounded in as the crew called out to her. The hold was full of equipment, and in the dark, she stumbled across it, looking for a door to the cockpit. She spotted it and tried the panel. Unlocked. But why *would* anyone bother locking it when it was on the ground? The thought almost made her laugh. Were these still her mother's footsteps?

She dashed into the small cockpit and flung herself into one of the seats, gaze raking the controls as she figured out how to prime the engines and shut the doors. There was a clatter from behind as the cargo door slid shut, and the maintenance bots fell away. Someone banged on the outer door, but she'd engaged the locks.

Her heart pounded hard, but she felt almost giddy. She didn't have clearance. She'd have to bull her way through Prime's defenses. She could already picture bursting through the lines of waiting shuttles and hurtling into the sky, flying close to someone else to make her a less desirable target before she finally—

The cockpit door squealed open behind her, locks overridden by brute force. She was up in an instant, launching a kick before she even saw who it was. Her heel banged off the side of a maintenance bot. She yelped as she spun away, her foot throbbing. She saw the stun stick aimed around the bot and tried to dive to the side, but the cockpit was tiny. The stick rushed forward, the attacker's face in shadow, and the blast hit her full force. The sounds of the shuttle flickered and died around her.

CHAPTER SIXTEEN

Once she was on the bridge, Judit didn't know what to do. They were under way. The data chip was in Beatrice's hands. Evie was back on her station. Noal had gone, maybe to see Spartan, maybe to change. All of a sudden, Judit was acutely conscious of the makeup and the prosthetics still on her face. The clothes felt heavy, too, as if they were made of steel instead of the finest fabrics. "I'll be in my quarters."

She heard a chorus of acknowledgments, but she was already thinking ahead. In her quarters, she stripped off the implants and the costume. She took the streaks out of her hair and stepped into the shower to let the hot water cleanse the makeup and soothe her tired muscles. She kept seeing her father's face as he turned her down and walked bravely to his fate. She should have tried one of the many scenarios she'd imagined: leaping at the guards, smuggling him into the tram. She could have used the *Damat* to rain terror onto the planet and confuse their pursuers. She could have had her father break into the planetary defense grid and take the whole thing down. They could be on her ship right now, laughing and talking about what a great adventure they'd had.

But, a dutiful voice inside her said, if she'd done all that, how many people would have been injured or killed? How many lives would she have destroyed trying to save her father from a fate he could get himself out of, as Noal said? And have the *Damat* fire on Freemen, fire on House Meridian? Where had that thought even come from? One rejection from her father and she was ready to shoot her own people? But what good was being the chosen one if she couldn't actually accomplish anything?

The alarm in the shower pinged, and the water shut off. She'd used up her allotment. It was a rule in space even a captain had to abide by. Judit leaned against the wall, glad she'd scrubbed her face, unable to remember if she'd washed the rest of her, but at the moment, she didn't care. She lifted her head and breathed deep. She couldn't stay there, couldn't afford to wallow. She'd already told herself that. Annika was counting on her; the crew of the *Damat* was counting on her. She couldn't afford self-pity. If she'd made the wrong choice, she'd have to live with that, have to spend the rest of her life making up for it.

Maybe there was *something* she could do for her father. Roberts could make it seem as if the *Damat* had been somewhere else all along. Then no one could accuse her father of helping her. But who would they think he'd been compiling information for? That didn't matter. He could convince the authorities he'd been putting together a report for someone official, and that his arrest was a big misunderstanding.

Judit toweled off, trying to think of a better strategy, when her jaw tingled, and Beatrice's voice said, "Jude?"

"What is it?"

"You'd better get up here. We're getting a message over the Meridian feed."

Judit donned her uniform hurriedly and raced to the bridge. Noal was already there, everyone watching the main holo display where Judit's grandmother was standing behind a podium in front of the Meridian seal. Judit knew that seal. It decorated the wall on the bottom floor of the main government building on Meridian Prime. Judit's mother stood beside her, and though her expression was still unflappable, Judit thought she detected a bit of tightness around the eyes that outsiders might miss.

"It is with great sorrow that we announce a traitor in our midst," Judit's grandmother said solemnly. "One guilty of supplying information to our enemies and furthering this rebellion against our long established, magnanimous power."

Judit gripped the arm of her chair, knowing what was coming and unable to stop it. "What are they doing? They can't do this."

Noal took her arm. "Jude—"

"Quiet!"

"Today," her grandmother said, "we arrested one brought into our family, accepted into our hearts only to turn his back and betray us all. Tam Ada-Meridian—"

Judit slammed her hand down on the arm of her chair. "No!"

Noal gripped her arm harder. "Wait, wait!"

"—will be put to death, executed tomorrow for treason and crimes against our House. That is all." Without another word, her grandmother turned and left the podium. The feed went dark, though Judit bet the news agencies were still speculating.

The bridge erupted into gasps and whispers. "What about a trial?" Evie said.

"They can't do that," Beatrice said.

Noal had a hand to his mouth. "They must be operating under war protocols."

"Lying, dark eating bastards!" Judit said. "Open a channel to Prime!"

Roberts nodded. "I'll set up the signal to bounce—"

"Now!"

Noal pulled on her arm. "Jude, they'll track us."

"I don't care! My father didn't supply information to any enemies. He gave it to us!"

Noal pulled harder, swinging her around. "We are enemies in Grandmother's eyes, Judit! We became the enemy the moment we didn't come home."

"I can say something. I can persuade them. The only reason he didn't go with us is because he didn't want to betray his house!"

"They'll only tell you to come back," Beatrice said as she stood. "Maybe tell you they'll spare his life, but only if you turn yourselves and Annika in. This whole thing could be a bluff."

Was her grandmother that devious? Judit put her head in her hands and tried to think. It couldn't be true, couldn't be happening. It was all a mistake, and she only had to make them *see*!

"We can bounce the signal," Noal said at her side, "but you know what will happen. She won't say anything of substance."

Her grandmother might even be waiting for Judit to ride to her father's rescue so they could all be snatched up in one go. "We'd never get back to Freemen alive, would we?"

"Not even close. And we'd darking sure never get anywhere near Prime."

Judit shook her head. "Bounce the signal. I'll take it in my office." Before anyone could argue, she said, "I have to try."

In her office, she paced. They had to get to the nearest transmission gate and wait while signals were sent. Roberts would be using their codes to try and put her through to her grandmother's office, but they wouldn't have the latest codes. By the time he was done, everyone on Meridian Prime would know she was calling, and someone would probably be able to track their signal. She was about to tell Roberts to forget it when her jaw tingled.

"Boss? I've got your mother on the comm."

"Got it." She keyed her console on. Her mother wasn't bothering with a holo. She hunched over a screen in what looked like the command center on Prime. Her face filled the view as if she was trying to hide her screen from everyone else.

"Judit, about time you called." Her voice was imperious, nearly toneless, as if even the impending execution of her husband couldn't rattle her. She spoke in Meridian code, and Judit had to struggle for a moment to remember it all.

"I need to talk to Grandmother. She can't execute my father!"

Her mother's left eye twitched. "He gave information to Nocturna. Nothing can save him." She glanced away. "Nothing should save him."

Judit couldn't speak for several seconds. "No, he didn't! He gave information to me! And I'm still a member of this family. Annika isn't..." She was about to say that Annika wasn't on the ship, but she had to remember that everyone could be listening. "It was just a few hours ago—"

Her mother held up a hand. "We have evidence."

"No! It's a mistake. It was me!"

"Come home."

"Will...will he be all right if I do?"

Her mother's head tilted, and her expression seemed as if it might crack. Was she thinking about lying? Did any part of her want to save her husband? A hand landed on her mother's shoulder, turning her roughly aside, and then Judit's grandmother's face appeared on the screen.

"Tam's fate is sealed," Grandmother said. If anything, she seemed sterner than ever. "Return home, Judit, and you can save your family further embarrassment."

"Promise that my father will be spared if I do." It might be childish, but it gave her hope. She'd go home alone. Noal and Annika could carry on without her. Maybe she'd find some way to help them from inside Meridian. "I won't lead a fleet, but—"

Her grandmother sneered. "Your cooperation isn't necessary. One way or another, we will achieve peace, and if we have to truss you up on some other captain's bridge in order to garner your participation, so be it. Come for him, Judit. Try and save him."

The feed cut out.

Judit clenched a fist, rage boiling inside her. If her grandmother wanted a fight—

"Don't play into her hands," Noal said from the door.

Judit leapt out of her seat. "What are you doing?" She looked past him, but he was alone.

"You were so focused on that old bag, you didn't hear me come in." His voice was calm, but there was sorrow in his eyes. "Don't let her bait you."

"She's going to execute my father, Noal! She's…framing him somehow, saying he's fed information to Nocturna, but that's not right!"

"I know."

"She's going to kill him."

"Whatever she's going to do, she wants you mad enough to try to ride to his rescue. You can't fight the Meridian fleet."

"I can go by myself."

"Then she'll have you and still execute your father."

She grabbed a palm computer from her desk and threw it against the wall. "I can't sit and do nothing!"

"You have to. If you're going to stay with us, stay free, and help everyone like you want to, you have to do nothing."

"Like the dark." She strode past him and headed for the bridge. "Roberts, I want a wide, long-range transmission. We're going to tell everyone who will listen that my father is innocent. Meridian thinks he betrayed them to Nocturna. We know that's not true. We need to make everyone else see it. Maybe with enough pressure, my grandmother will give in."

It was a long shot, but if it was all she could do, she was going to do it.

"On it, Boss," Roberts said.

Judit walked from the bridge, waving behind her in case anyone tried to follow. She needed to be alone. In her mind she was still calculating the risks of a return to Freemen, an assault on the military there. They wouldn't fire on her, not on their chosen one. She could use herself as a shield. And they would subdue her, and she'd be the chosen one from a prison cell, helpless.

She spent the night in her quarters, glued to the vids, waiting for news. Roberts gave her the occasional update. Many people acknowledged their message; many protested her father's sentence. It seemed as if quite a few people in the galaxy had been following the exploits of the *Damat* ever since the kidnapping. Elidia had been singing their praises. Judit and Annika were fast becoming the galaxy's favorite couple, especially since people saw them as rebelling against their houses.

All the Meridian news outlets were talking about the impending execution, acknowledging the protests and speculating about how Judit's grandmother would answer them. Many were just tearing her father to shreds, and she screamed at them in impotent rage. There was a feed from Freemen that was a view of a square, no commentary, just a countdown until the execution was to take place. Judit imagined her grandmother watching the same feed, waiting for Judit to come rushing in. Some of the other feeds switched to that view occasionally, speculating as to what sort of execution it was going to be, how it could have been prevented, and what it might mean for the future.

"Nothing," Judit said with a growl. She clutched a plastic bowl. Someone had brought her dinner some time ago, but she'd thrown it at the wall along with many of her other possessions. Now she threw the bowl again for good measure. "She has to listen!"

Her door chimed.

"Go away!" she shouted.

"Let me in," Noal said, "or I'm going to get Evie to force the door, and then she'll see the mess you've no doubt made of your room."

"Fine, come in, but shut up."

The door opened, and he walked in, mumbling something as he stepped over the chaos on the floor. He sat on the edge of the bed, behind her chair, and she felt him there, could almost hear him breathing. It made her want to shout at him to leave, but she couldn't take her eyes off the feed of the empty square.

Finally, the timer expired. Judit's stare fixed on the row of zeroes, and she began to count her breaths. One, two, three...

Her father appeared on the screen, walking into the square, wrists shackled in front of him. He stood surrounded by an escort. Under other circumstances, it might have been an honor guard.

"No," Judit said softly. "No, she can't. She has to listen."

"By the dark," Noal whispered.

A holo in the square winked to life, showing Judit's grandmother and mother with a sea of Meridian faces watching stoically in the background. They'd set up a holo so they could watch from Prime. Judit's father's face was pale but set, as if he'd come to terms with what was happening to him. There wasn't a microphone anywhere near him, but the square was absolutely silent. Judit wanted him to cry out about what he'd done, to beg for mercy in the hopes that her grandmother would grant it, but he said nothing, merely stared into the camera. His face leapt large as the camera zoomed, and his eyes bored through all of space and into Judit's heart.

"Don't," she said. Noal reached for her shoulder, and she gripped his hand hard. "Please, Noal, make it stop. Make her listen."

"It's not your fault, Jude."

Her grandmother went over the charges again. She said that treason could never be forgiven, that Meridian answered to no one. Judit clenched her hands into fists.

The guards unbound her father's hands and left him to stand on his own. Judit begged in her heart for him to run, to at least make them work for it, but he stood still.

Her grandmother finished her speech with "...death by neuro-toxin."

Judit gripped Noal's hand so hard it probably pained him, but he said nothing. On the vid, her father's expression didn't change. Neurotoxin. Sometime during his incarceration, he'd been fitted with a small device to his neck that would inject him with a powerful poison. He wouldn't have known when it was put there or by whom, but she bet his neck had been itching all day, that he'd felt around it more than once, but the device would be so thin and small he'd never have found it.

One heartbeat passed, then two, long enough for Judit's hopes to rise. The first thing her grandmother would do was cut the feeds. Since her plan to lure Judit hadn't worked, she wouldn't want any evidence that—

Her father inhaled sharply, and his eyes widened before they relaxed. The most blissful smile spread over his face before he crumpled to the ground.

Silence. Judit held her breath. He didn't move.

"Get up," Judit muttered, her body gone cold. "Dad?"

Utter silence reigned in the square and on the vids. Then a crowd began murmuring, some applauding, but maybe the rest were shocked by a gesture that hadn't been necessary in years. A commentator on another feed began speaking in a low voice, but Judit couldn't understand him, couldn't understand anything but the body of her father lying on the platform as the doctors pronounced him dead.

The noise of the crowd swelled, and the commentator had to raise his voice. On the holo, Judit's grandmother made the pronouncement that justice had been served before she turned and walked away. Judit's mother stayed rooted to the spot, holographic eyes on her dead mate. Judit knew she'd loved him at least a little, maybe never as much as he'd loved her, but there was something like sorrow and regret in those eyes. And Judit bet there was a lot of blame there, too, all of it laid at Judit's feet.

The holo blinked out, and the feed cut to the commentator. Judit turned it off, and the silence of her quarters surrounded her. She'd let go of Noal's hand somewhere along the way, but she could feel the weight of his stare. He'd probably take his cues from her, but she didn't know what to give him.

"It could be a trick," Noal whispered.

She'd never wanted to hit him so much in all her life. She forced herself to sit still. Their family didn't play games like that. Their grandmother would turn her nose up at such deception.

"I can't believe..." Noal put a hand over his mouth. "Jude, I'm so sorry."

She nodded and turned to him, and her desire to strike evaporated in the face of his grief. She'd never seen such sorrow in her family, and it broke through her walls. She wrapped her arms around him and dragged him forward. He hugged her as tightly, and they both wept.

❖

Annika was aware of the pain first. She'd been hit with a stunner as part of her training, so she'd know the sensation. People always looked so limp afterward. Now she ached from the tip of her head to her toes, as if she'd overtaxed every muscle in her body.

Still, she stayed silent. A slight weight rested across her shoulders, her midsection, and both hands and legs. Cloth restraints. And the surface beneath her felt soft but not as much as a proper bed. Probably a medical or prison bed.

"I know you're awake," a woman's voice said. Despite her training, Annika felt her hands twitch. She knew that voice, knew it in her core, though she hadn't heard it in years. "You can control your body but not your brain waves."

She felt it then, the whisper of weight that meant two electrodes were attached to her temples. She opened her eyes. If the game was up, there was no use pretending. "Hello, Mother."

Her mother smiled down at her, and anger boiled up inside her. Her mother seemed older and not simply in years. Gray dotted the temples of her brown hair, and she had some lines in her pale skin, but her eyes were as brightly green as ever. Annika had a sudden memory of a woman who always seemed on edge, always looking over her shoulder.

Annika felt a tug inside, sorrow mixing with anger and trepidation. She tried not to let it show, not to let her mother rattle her. This was just another enemy. That had to be why she was restrained.

Her mother smiled wider from where she sat on the edge of the bed, and unless Annika was much mistaken, she had a look of pride on her face. Feric stood near the wall, and his presence caused another bloom of fear and betrayal. He smiled, too, looking as proud, but he didn't speak, couldn't when Nocturna had taken his voice.

"So, you're both working for my grandmother?" Annika asked. "Which government torture chamber is this?"

"No," Feric signed. "We've always been working for you."

She frowned and tried to think past the lump in her throat. "Having me kidnapped and stunned? That's working for me?"

"We had you set free to fulfill your destiny." Her mother smoothed her hair, and Annika forced herself not to lean away. "And you've done beautifully."

"What are you talking about?" She nearly vibrated with rage. As happy as she was not to be on a path where she'd have to hurt Noal and Judit, she didn't like being forced into anything. "Are you trying to tell me you wanted me free? Then why didn't we work together? You could have told me what you were planning. You knew I wasn't happy, Feric." She jerked against the restraints and felt them tighten in response. With a deep breath, she forced herself to relax.

"Yes," he signed. "I knew you'd always do the right thing, but you couldn't be prompted."

"What the dark does that mean?"

"It means you won't be under your grandmother's thumb ever again," her mother said. "After the explosives we set off on Prime, she might not even realize you're still alive."

Annika went cold. "What explosives?"

Feric put a hand on her mother's shoulder as if warning her to keep quiet. She glanced at him and shrugged. "What does it matter now?"

He sighed and dropped his hand.

"What explosives?" Annika asked again. She jerked against her restraints. "Tell me!"

"By now, Judit's father will have been executed for treason. The Meridian leader will think he was smuggling secrets to Nocturna, and now forces on Nocturna will think their homeworld has been attacked by Meridian infiltrators after several explosive devices detonated in Presidio, killing hundreds."

Annika blinked, trying to process all of that. Judit's father? Hundreds dead? What the dark was happening? "You...you killed..."

"Soon," her mother said as she stood, "Nocturna and Meridian will turn on each other while the rest of the houses and the unaffiliated continue to undermine them from the outer reaches. They will annihilate one another, and the houses will continue to fall." She smiled. "The galaxy will be reset to its proper form, and you will be free."

"Let me go," Annika whispered. Her chest felt too tight, the room too small and hot. She kept hearing hundreds dead. She'd killed people, people who'd been trying to kill her, but to use explosives, to kill without discrimination... "Let me go."

"Don't worry," Feric signed. "You'll see Judit soon enough. We're so proud of you, Annika."

"Proud?" She was shaking, but she tried to control it, to calm herself. She could hear Ama telling her to breathe, force the universe back into order. "Proud of what? I didn't bomb anyone!"

Now Feric's hand came up to her mother's shoulder again, and this time, she nodded. "I wanted you to know that you're doing so well."

"With what?" Annika yelled. "What the dark are you talking about? Why would you bomb people? Why was Judit's father executed? Where have you *been*?" She was breathing hard, nearly hyperventilating. The pounding of her heart drowned out Ama's voice.

"Shh," her mother said, bending close. "I never stopped loving you."

"You..." She had a flash then. She'd seen her mother leaving the Eye with Feric. At the time, she'd thought it meant her mother had been pretending to be a hierophant initiate, but what if she wasn't? What if she was proud of Annika for fulfilling some prophecy? What if she was trying to fulfill one herself? But hierophants were supposed to watch the future; they weren't supposed to change it.

"What have you done?" Tears were gathering in Annika's eyes, and there was nothing she could do to stop them. Her mother had bombed people. And it was all supposed to be for Annika? And Judit's father? Did Judit know? Had she been captured, too? Whatever had happened, she needed Annika now more than these two ever could.

Annika jerked against the restraints, feeling the tears slide down her face, but rage was overtaking disbelief and sadness. "Let me go!"

Feric pushed her shoulders down. She glared at him, even more of a betrayer than her mother. When her mother left, had they been working together? Had she always trusted him to one day kidnap her daughter and hold her on some darking ship?

"If you're going to kill me, do it!" Annika said.

Feric looked pained, but behind him, Annika's mother's face went still. By the dark, they weren't done with her yet, whether they were going to kill her or not. At least Feric seemed as if he didn't want to. Annika's stomach shrank into something cold and dark. "Let me go," she said again, softer.

"You still have a part to play," her mother said.

"From this bed?"

This time, Feric smoothed her hair, and she pulled away from him as much as she could.

"We'll talk more soon." Her mother stepped toward a door.

Feric hesitated, and she wondered if he doubted this part she supposedly had to play. That was the chance she needed. "Feric, please." He'd know if she tried to trick him, so she summoned every good feeling she'd ever had about him and forced it into her voice. "Please."

His forehead creased, and he looked as if he wanted to say something, but his hands dropped as soon as he lifted them.

Annika moved her fingers as much as she could, brushing his. "I know you care about me, Feric. You don't want to leave me tied to this bed. You...you should scan yourself! Scan yourself for the worm!"

That would explain everything. The worm could turn loyalty and duty to anything it wanted. Her mother could have found a way to steal the worm from Nocturna, or maybe they'd implanted one themselves, and her mother had found a way to subvert it.

Feric frowned harder. "I'm not under anyone's control," he signed.

"You wouldn't know if you were. They wouldn't let you know. Scan yourself."

He frowned, the beginnings of anger stirring on his features. "I don't need to."

"*She* won't let you."

"Come along, Feric," Annika's mother said from the doorway.

Feric followed her to the door.

"Try, Feric. Just try it," Annika called as they walked from the room. "There might be a way to fight the worm!"

The door shut behind them, and Annika cursed. She didn't even know if it *was* possible to fight the worm, didn't know if she could plant doubts in his mind. Whoever was controlling him could make it seem as if Feric's own assuredness kept him from wanting to be scanned. Whichever it was, worm or blind faith, it didn't seem as if she was going to get through to him anytime soon.

And her mother? Annika was still thinking about the cold look on her face. Feric hadn't wanted to kill her, but her mother didn't seem to mind the idea. That hurt, but Annika didn't want to feel that pain right now. Maybe her mother thought all Nocturnas had to die, or maybe Annika had to die to further her mother's agenda. Whatever the reason, the result was the same: Annika had to find a way off this ship before they came for her again.

Annika relaxed against the restraints and let them ease before she tested them one by one to see how fast they could react. Each held, including the one across her chest. That made sense. Feric knew almost everything she could do. She'd never told him about the bone stiletto, but her mother knew about that. It was probably gone from her arm.

If they were working off a mad prophecy, they had some idea of what to do next, but she had no idea where they were taking her or how her death would help them. She tried to think of what they could have seen in the future. If the current chaos in the galaxy was because of them, maybe they had a step-by-step guide of how to throw everything into ruin.

Of course, based on what Spartan said, the galaxy had been heading there already. The unaligned were tired of having houses at all, and most of the houses were tired of Nocturna and Meridian, especially when it seemed as if those houses might unite. But a full-scale war between them would put the lives of everyone else in jeopardy, too. Huge battles always had collateral damage.

Annika's mother said she wanted the galaxy to reset. She wanted the houses gone. That would mean a lot of lives lost, maybe so many planets bombarded that the houses *couldn't* go on, that they couldn't rebuild. They wanted not hundreds of deaths, but hundreds of thousands. Maybe even millions. Billions? How could someone contemplate having that many deaths on their conscience even if they thought the galaxy would ultimately turn out better than before?

Funny, Annika had never thought the idea of death would bother her this badly.

Apparently, Feric and her mother thought of themselves as the real chosen ones, and they were using Annika, Judit, and Noal to unite the galaxy in their own way, first under hatred and then under grief. Well, she wasn't going to help them anymore, not quietly. In the beginning, she'd wanted to run from this conflict, but now they'd darking well pissed her off.

Maybe that was part of the prophecy, too. Maybe this whole part of the plan was to make her so angry, she... What? What was it they wanted her to do? They'd been fine with her running around on her own so far. Or maybe they hadn't. According to the computer from the kidnappers' ship, Feric had left orders that she was supposed to stay asleep until someone came to collect her. Then someone else had "wanted to meet her," so the crew had woken her up early. Who was that? If they hadn't wanted her to get loose, had they been chasing her since then? What was it they'd wanted her to do?

She sighed loudly. If she kept worrying about what they wanted her to do, she'd never get anything done. She pictured the hierophants in their temple. Were any of them simply watchers? The idea chilled her as she pictured them manipulating history, the whole of time and space to get what they wanted. There was at least one in every house. But it couldn't be all of them! The Nocturna spies inside the Eye would have reported such a thing. And if the hierophants were the real masters of the galaxy, they would have made a move long before now.

She had to remember that her mother was telling her only what she wanted Annika to hear. Annika needed to bring this information to Judit and Noal if they'd managed to stay free. They might have a better take on it than she did, might be able to find out what they should do next instead of what they were "supposed" to be doing.

She looked to a nearby console. No way to reach it, very little she could do, especially without her stiletto. But she didn't actually *know* it was gone. She flexed her arm and felt it move.

She frowned. Her mother hadn't taken it. Because she wanted Annika free? But no matter what, Annika needed to be free in order to act. She'd have to be careful of her actions from then on, but she couldn't do anything strapped to a bed.

With subtle flexes, she pushed the stiletto out, guiding it through the scab. She rolled and flexed until the stiletto slipped down into her palm. Slowly, carefully she turned her hand so the knife lay between the restraints and her skin. Then it was a matter of patiently working it back and forth. The blade cut into her slightly, but she blocked out the pain, using the discomfort as a motivator. Blood trickled down her wrist, and she slowed her cuts so the trickle wouldn't become a flow.

When one hand was free, she went to work on her chest before starting on the other hand. No one came to check, and she wondered again if they meant her to free herself. They had to have heard what happened on the kidnappers' ship. They had to know how hard she could make it to keep her prisoner.

She freed herself at last but kept the electrodes at her temples in case they were feeding someone information. She eased the machine along with her as she searched the cabinets and drawers in the small medbay. She found a few strips of instaskin and pasted them onto her arm where the stiletto had cut her. She was still wearing the stolen uniform she'd gotten on Prime, but a look in the polished surface of a steel tray revealed they'd cleaned her face. That was fine. She wasn't going to be hiding.

She turned to the machine monitoring the electrodes. If she shut it off or pulled free, there could be an alarm. To the dark with it. She couldn't wait around in indecision. She peeled the electrodes off, then hurried for the door in case she triggered an alarm.

No one came. She put her ear to the door and listened but heard nothing. It was a small medbay, but the fact that they had one at all suggested a ship of some size, a crew of more than two unless they were running minimally, like the ship that had kidnapped her. And the door was unlocked.

She stepped back and scanned the room for cameras but didn't see any at first glance. What the dark was she supposed to do now? She took another look through the cabinets and drawers, searching under and behind machinery.

Under the bed, crammed into a darkened space, she pulled out the bag she'd had on Nocturna Prime. She went through it quickly and found the data chip hidden in the lining where she'd put it. All she could do was stare. They wouldn't have missed that. Why had they left it in the room with her?

Ama's voice insisted it was because they wanted her to escape. They wanted her to take the chip to Judit. Somehow, it was part of their plan.

But they had to know she'd suspect that. And then she was lost in a "they know you know" style argument. What else could she do besides take the opportunities they'd given her? Sit and wait? Judit wouldn't be content to wait. If she was free, she'd be trying to find Annika, and if she wasn't free, she needed Annika's help.

Nothing for it, then. She tucked the data chip into her bra and opened the door. They shouldn't have made it so easy, but they clearly wanted her gone. Why not set her on some planet? Why this elaborate ruse? Why take her at all? They could have let her escape from Nocturna Prime!

It was making her head hurt. She slid the door open and looked outside, but no one waited in the hallway, no one guarded the door, and no one seemed to be hurrying down the corridor to check on her.

She sighed and wondered if the ship was empty, if she was supposed to take it somewhere. Maybe she'd blow it up and find her own darking ship. Maybe she should look for Feric and her mother and stab them both.

The hallway ended in a heavy, single door, a pressure door, and the controls beside it were dim. Annika listened but couldn't hear anything through the thick steel. Time to throw caution to the wind. She tried the controls, but they were as dead as they appeared. She tried to pry off the panel to access the wiring, but it had been welded shut.

Well, now she knew why there were no guards. They'd barred the heavy door from the other side, and no bone stiletto was going to shake it loose. If they meant her to escape, they hadn't made it as easy as she'd thought.

Annika headed back to the medbay. She'd already found some water and rations. Hidden behind a panel was a toilet. Maybe they knew she'd get loose from the bed, but after that, they planned for her to stay awhile. Then why leave her bag with the data chip? Maybe she'd need it when they let her out? Maybe someone was supposed to find it on her corpse? She sighed and put her hands on her hips. All the panels in this room were welded shut, too. Even the lights were secured in the walls. There was nothing she could force. She inspected the bed, looking for something that could be used as a pry bar, but it was a single piece except for the useless straps.

It seemed as if she was stuck here until someone came to see her, and with the food and water they'd left, she doubted anyone would. Perfect. All her worrying for nothing.

CHAPTER SEVENTEEN

Annika was late for the rendezvous. Judit tried not to let it worry her, but worrying was so much better than grieving. Her every emotion felt turned up to the max, especially the bad ones. With each hour that passed, her anxiety and dread doubled until her insides felt like a bundle of knots, and she couldn't shake the feeling that every horrible thing that happened would spawn other horrible things until life became nothing but a ball of misery ending in death for all of them!

Judit collapsed in her office chair and sighed. When had she gotten so melodramatic? Noal must have been rubbing off on her. She wondered if she should call him, and they could be melodramatic together, but after they'd wept, he'd retreated to his room, and she didn't want to disturb him.

Since the execution, protests against Meridian had gotten louder. Some of their allies had cut off communications, though several messages of encouragement had been sent to the *Damat*, open signals everyone could hear. Judit wished they could make her feel better, but she feared nothing could.

Her nerves were so taut, she jumped from her chair when her office door chimed. Until she heard Annika was safe, she didn't think she'd welcome any news. "Yes?"

Beatrice stepped inside. When she looked at Judit's face, she shut her mouth on whatever she was going to say and cleared her throat. "Our listening outposts detected several networks going dark in Nocturna territory. Roberts says that usually means they found a security breach and are looking for the source."

With Annika going to Nocturna space, it couldn't be a coincidence. Maybe they'd caught her and were looking for confederates. All of Judit's other emotions stilled, poised. "Does Roberts know if they caught her?"

When Beatrice didn't bother to argue that it might not have anything to do with Annika, Judit could have kissed her. "We don't have any information *that* detailed," Beatrice said. "Nocturna hasn't made any official announcements about...her. And we haven't heard from Antiles, either. We're trying to keep ears on all ships leaving Nocturna Prime's system."

"Wait. You said they haven't made any official announcements about *her*. What have they made announcements about?"

Beatrice shifted. Even that small delay was enough to make Judit's skin crawl. "There've been some bombings on Nocturna Prime. Word got out through unofficial channels before the Nocturna government put their official spin on it, and now they're saying it was Meridian terrorists."

Judit's belly went cold. "Does Meridian have ships in orbit? How the dark did they get that close to Nocturna Prime?" Had her grandmother launched the fleet without her? Had Annika and Antiles been able to get out in time, or had they been there when the bombs dropped?

"The reports say it was a ground-based attack," Beatrice said.

Judit frowned hard. "Why would Grandmother put boots on the ground when she could rain death from orbit?"

"A terrorist attack, Jude," Beatrice said. "In secret."

"That's not possible!" As much as Judit hated it, the execution of her father made sense, at least as far as her grandmother was concerned. She'd realized that as she wept with Noal. But secret terrorist bombings? Her grandmother would call that cowardly. Surely Nocturna had to know that.

Would it matter if they did? "Do they have proof?"

"They claim to," Beatrice said slowly, and by the way her gaze wouldn't meet Judit's, there had to be more to the story. Beatrice knew Meridian couldn't be behind the bombings, so why was she so nervous?

Judit bit her lip. Secret bombs were the sort of thing a Nocturna would do if she had to—maybe if part of her *wanted* to—as angry as she was at her own house. "You think Annika did this."

Beatrice's lack of eye contact spoke for her. She thought Annika had bombed her own people, maybe to create a distraction; maybe she'd had to do it in order to get away. Or maybe she'd done it out of revenge. Those were the reasons the crew would be betting on.

"No," Judit said. "She didn't do it."

Beatrice didn't argue as Noal might have, but her nod was lackluster.

Judit pounded a fist on her console. "She didn't do this, Bea! I may not have known about her training, but I know *her*. She kills in self-defense. She wouldn't blow the dark out of a bunch of random people. She wouldn't risk taking innocent lives!"

It was what her heart told her, but now a tiny part of her mind was saying, "You don't know." She curled her hand into a fist. "Keep looking for her," she said aloud.

"We will."

And when Annika got back, she could tell everyone what had happened, and the crew would love her as much as Judit did.

Beatrice cleared her throat. "I've been sorting through the data that...you collected. There are lots of reports of unrest and fights, like cracks running across the galaxy. We're trying to find a main cause, but several incidents appear to have incited the others. If someone was planning all that's happened, they unleashed several strings of violence at once."

"And still no idea of who that someone is?"

"Your father and his contacts had a lot of different ideas. Some of them are good. And more interesting, he had some notes about searching through the hierophant database."

"They were looking for prophecies?" That didn't make a lot of sense. Judit and Noal had looked through the prophecies out of desperation, but her father had so many other resources. Had something led him there? Meridian believed the prophecies like everyone else, but they clearly hadn't let that stop them from doing whatever the dark they wanted. They'd even taken the famous prophecy about the chosen one and twisted it to mean that peace between the two houses was best achieved if Meridian wiped Nocturna out. If they were looking through prophecies for clues, it had to mean they thought they had a good chance of finding something.

Beatrice touched her jaw, telling Judit she was getting a message.

Judit wondered why the bridge hadn't contacted her directly. Maybe they thought she was too fragile. She stiffened her spine as Beatrice listened. They had to know they could still depend on her.

Beatrice finally nodded. "Understood. Jude, we've caught wind of several ships leaving Nocturna space that don't have a Nocturna signature."

Judit's heart leapt even though there was little to hope for in that statement. "Any clues?"

"Roberts is sorting through the data. One of them appears to be heading this way, no house signal."

It could be an unaffiliated trader or a mercenary. A pirate. But it was dangerous to go about with no allegiance in house-held space. "It could be her."

Beatrice frowned. "It could be a lot of things. If we leave the *Scipio*, we might miss her." Judit clenched a fist until it hurt. Beatrice looked as if she was about to say something when she put her hand to her ear again. "We're getting a message. It's Antiles."

"Where is he?" Judit asked.

"On his way here. He couldn't say much."

Because anyone could be listening. "Find his position. We'll meet him." She strode past Beatrice and headed for the bridge. If Antiles was sending a signal instead of coming to the *Scipio*, something had gone wrong. And the *Damat* was faster than his little ship. They'd be able to get to him before he could get to them.

And even though it could be very bad news, at the moment, it seemed like a piece of good luck. They were under way at least, and any direction was better than standing still. When Judit arrived at the bridge, she was happy to see her crew busy at their stations. Beatrice walked past her and took the helm.

As the *Damat* headed for the nearest transmission gate, Judit leaned back in her chair and tried to contemplate all the possibilities. Any number of things could be happening. Perhaps Annika was on Antiles's ship, but they were being followed. In that case, Annika would want the *Damat* with her for the extra firepower, especially if the ship following them was faster than they were. Maybe Annika had caught a ride on a different ship, following closely behind Antiles. Maybe she'd had to sneak onto a ship going in an entirely different direction, and Antiles was summoning the *Damat* to tell them where she'd gone and why. Whatever the problem, Judit had to believe it was one she could solve. Darker thoughts knocked at her consciousness, but she refused to let them in. Fate wouldn't be so cruel to take two people who loved her within days of each other.

She wanted to stay on the bridge, but as it was, they were at least a day away from meeting Antiles, and that was if he didn't get delayed. Judit longed to call him again, to hear what was happening, but they couldn't risk anyone else knowing, especially if Annika was somewhere she could be captured. She'd still make a valuable hostage, both to Nocturna and to Judit. Meridian would pay well for her if only to have something to hang over Nocturna's head. They'd probably find a way to execute her for treason, too.

Judit's stomach cramped at the thought. It was too soon for such comparisons, and they would only lead deeper into shadowy thoughts.

When Noal pinged her comm to ask her to dinner, Judit nearly refused, but she needed something to distract her even if she'd be horrible company. When she arrived at his quarters, she found Spartan there as well. He stood as she entered, as if he were under her command. She tried not to chuckle at the thought and waved him to his seat. Noal had wrangled an extra chair from somewhere. It stood at his small table laid with bowls and cups. A steaming pot of noodles sat in the middle, and he'd found a bottle of wine. He probably had them stashed in many different places. He never seemed to run out.

Judit had a sudden flash of memory. She and Noal had been dining with Annika while Feric guarded the door on the small satellite where they met. Annika's grandfather had died not long before, and Annika had been downcast and thoughtful for the whole visit. Feric had remained by the door, stoic as always, and Judit remembered being angry with him for not comforting his charge.

After trying to cheer Annika up and failing, Noal had given Judit a stricken look, but she didn't know what to say. It didn't seem the time for jokes. They'd already given her their condolences and offered to listen if she wanted to talk, but she'd declined with a smile and then picked at her plate.

"Let's have a picnic," Noal had said, putting his napkin down.

Annika had blinked at him. "A what?"

"Come on." He'd gathered up all the food and plates and took them into the living space.

Judit and Annika had exchanged a glance, but Judit trusted Noal when it came to the cheering-up department. With a smile, she'd followed suit, and Annika did the same. Feric had followed but stayed by the door as always, staring straight ahead. Noal had lit some candles and turned the lights down. He'd called up a star map on the holo and projected it on the ceiling so it looked as if they were under the night sky on some faraway world.

Even then, Noal had secured more than a few bottles of wine, far more than he should have been able to get since they'd just turned sixteen, but the chosen one got his hands on a lot of things he wasn't supposed to have. Since none of it was illegal, Judit usually didn't care, but when he kept pouring that night, she'd given him a few warning looks. But Annika seemed to relax, and there was even some joking and giggling while they'd eaten with their fingers under an artificial sky.

Now, in Noal's quarters on the *Damat*, Noal and Spartan were staring at her, and Judit realized she hadn't been paying attention to anything they'd said or done. Spartan's eyes were wide, apprehensive.

"I'm sorry, what?" Judit asked.

Noal tried a hesitant smile. "Did you fall asleep sitting up?"

"I was thinking. Remembering."

He nodded but didn't press, probably thought she was reminiscing about her father.

"I'm sorry about your dad," Spartan said. "I lost mine a few years ago. It's rough."

She blinked at him. She'd forgotten the rest of the galaxy had fathers, too. "Thank you."

"And I'm sure Annika is okay," he said. "She's…really tough." He rubbed at his throat and looked at nothing as if lost in his own memory.

"So I've been told." And she was grateful then for all of Annika's training. If it frightened the dark out of anyone who'd seen it, she was probably okay.

They ate slowly, quietly, and Judit was reminded of state dinners. She much preferred the intimate little dinners with Annika, Noal, and the silent Feric. But as Noal and Spartan started talking, letting Judit decide whether or not she would participate, she began to relax. They spoke of normal things, a bit of their pasts, but it sounded like any old conversation, and Judit could sigh and let it happen around her. No decisions. No talk of the future, of plans, of what-ifs and maybes. When she left after dinner, she was glad she'd gone.

The next day, they were close enough to spot Antiles's ship on long-range scans, and Judit kept a close eye from the bridge while Evie scanned for other ships, other threats. Roberts listened to chatter. Antiles's ship seemed as if it was alone, but they couldn't tell who might be aboard. Judit nearly dug her fingers into her armrests as her stomach roiled. By the time Antiles was close enough to speak ship-to-ship, Judit's hands had cramped into claws. She had Roberts put Antiles through on the bridge comm, and his face appeared on Judit's screen.

He seemed worried, that was her first thought. She didn't know him well, but the smug, slightly suspicious look he'd sported every time they'd met had been replaced by a wrinkled brow, a tightening of the eyes.

"Where is she?" Judit asked.

He took a deep breath. "Straight to the point, eh? Last I heard of *Calliope*, she was looking for a way off the moon Caligo and onto Nocturna Prime." He arched an eyebrow. "But I did hear a rumor that Annika Nocturna, heir to the house, was captured on Caligo, then escaped to Nocturna Prime."

Escaped. Judit let out a slow breath, unable to hide a smile. Of course she'd escaped. "Anything else?"

"Oh, so you do care what happens to Annika Nocturna? I thought your two houses were at odds?"

She wished Noal would hurry to the bridge. What did this odious man want from her now? "She's not aboard this ship, if you're looking for payment. And since you no doubt still want information, it's in your best interest to tell me everything you've heard about Annika Nocturna."

He gave her a pitying look. "You're not nearly as smooth as your cousin Noal."

Well, she'd suspected he knew who she was. She hadn't even thought to put on a disguise before taking this call. "And so?" she nearly growled.

He sighed as if disappointed she wouldn't dance, but his nervous look came back. "I have to assume she made it to Prime. You heard about the bombings?"

"That wasn't her."

He lifted his hands. "Never said it was. Just that there was trouble. And quite a few ships fled the system after that unfortunate incident. Rumor has the Nocturna heir on one of them."

"Any idea which one?"

"I have a few ideas." He sat back in his chair.

Judit waited, impatience growing. "And?"

Noal arrived at the bridge, breathing hard as if he'd been running. He limped to Judit's chair, holding his side.

"Ah," Antiles said, looking to him. "Finally, the negotiator."

"Negotiating for?" Noal asked.

"For the data I have on the ships that left Nocturna space, those most likely to be carrying the Nocturna heir."

Judit's hands curled into fists, and the cramps came back with a vengeance, making her snarl. "You son of a darking—"

Noal pushed her back in her chair. "Easy."

"We had a deal!" Judit cried.

Antiles waved a hand. He seemed more relaxed by her anger than worried by it. "A deal for transportation that I still haven't been paid for."

"You can get paid when we find her!"

"Judit, let me take over!" Noal said.

She stabbed at the console. "Tell him—"

"In your office," he said. "Alone." He waved at Roberts to transfer the comm.

Roberts looked to Judit, who turned to Noal in disbelief. "I have to be there!"

He leaned close. "To do what? Make this worse? You trusted me to speak with him on the *Scipio*. You just have to do the same thing now that you did then."

But then she'd *been* on the *Scipio*, able to listen. Noal had needed her physical presence in case he got into trouble. She took a deep breath. He didn't need that now. And if her temper had gotten the better of her on the *Scipio*, she could have tanked that deal. She could easily dark this one up. She already wanted to shoot Antiles out of the sky.

"Fine," she said.

Noal hurried from the bridge, and Judit went back to mangling her armrests. She kept her eye on the ship's clock; the next twenty minutes felt like hours. She wondered what Noal was promising Antiles. She should have insisted on going with him, she should have—

The door to the bridge opened, and Noal walked in. He gestured to Beatrice. "Antiles's ship should be sending you some intel."

"Got it," Beatrice said.

On Judit's console, Antiles's ship began moving away.

"Wait!" Judit said. "Where's he going?"

"We finished our deal," Noal said.

Evie was looking to Judit. "Want me to stop him?"

Noal put his hand over Judit's. "Trust, remember?"

She gritted her teeth. "He gave us the information on the ships leaving Nocturna space?"

"Yes."

"And you're sure he gave us all he had?"

"It's commerce, Jude. That's how it works."

Judit waved at Evie to let Antiles go. "Beatrice? Roberts?"

"Looking at the intel now," Roberts said.

Beatrice nodded. "I'll move us closer to the nearest transmission gate."

Judit turned to Noal. "What did you promise him?" she asked softly.

"I gave him some of the information your father gave to us. It will help him make some deals, maybe tap into some new markets. I also told him we're spreading the word that your father wasn't a traitor. He said he'd pass it on."

Judit felt a catch in her throat and a headache starting in her temples. On the one hand, she loved the idea of more people knowing her father wasn't a traitor. On the other, a criminal like Antiles spreading the news left a bad taste in her mouth.

Noal put a hand on her shoulder. "Don't worry. I didn't give him anything that should directly hurt our house, though why you still care, I don't know."

"It's not that," she said. "It's…" She didn't have the words to explain. Her own feelings for her house were so complicated, she couldn't think the words, let alone say them. "Thank you."

He nodded and smiled.

"Anything?" Judit asked Roberts. All this reminded her of the search for the original kidnappers' ship, but she'd been looking for Noal then, too. At least she'd managed to hold on to one of them.

Roberts frowned at his console with the same intense look he always sported. "There were a lot of ships leaving the Nocturna system after the bombings. Those leaving right before seem like normal traffic except for two. Most ships leaving Prime stop at the station or one of the moons. Since Antiles left right before the bombings, he recorded two other ships leaving Prime, and neither stopped anywhere; they headed right out of the system."

"Why is that unusual?" Judit asked.

He blinked at her. "Because the data says it is."

So he didn't know the real reason why, just that it went against the norm. Well, she hadn't chosen him for her crew because of his imagination. "Go on."

"One of the ships went to a transmission gate just outside of the system, the main Nocturna gate. The other looks as if it was headed toward the next nearest gate, which would have taken it at least two days to reach. If they weren't headed there…" He fussed with his console again. "There are a few systems in the way, all held by Nocturna."

Judit leaned back in her chair and tried to think. The *Damat* wouldn't be able to get close enough to Nocturna's main transmission gate to get any intel about the ships passing through. The other was still within Nocturna territory but might be less guarded.

"You cannot be thinking of going in there," Noal said.

It would be a hard fight, especially with Nocturna blaming Meridian for the bombings on its homeworld. "What gates are closest to the one two days from Nocturna Prime?" she asked. "Where could they be jumping to?"

Roberts pulled up the gate system and sent it to her console. There were three gates closest to the targeted destination and four closest to the Nocturna main gate. And an infinite number of other gates farther away from either point. But smaller ships couldn't go forever, especially not one that seemed smaller than Antiles's ship. It would need to restock fuel and provisions regularly. It couldn't hold much water. The air reclamators would need to go offline to be cleaned. There was a reason people used larger ships for longer journeys. They had redundant systems so one could be shut down for maintenance, and the ship could keep running.

"How far could both of those ships get before they needed to stop for supplies?" she asked.

Roberts turned in his chair. "Depends on the size of the crew. Fewer people would equal a greater distance."

"Not necessarily," Beatrice said. "A smaller crew would have to go off duty more often. Someone's got to drive the ship."

"Well," Roberts said, "with automated systems—"

Judit held up a hand. "I'm just looking for some possibilities so I can find the love of my life, if you please."

They both turned back to their consoles. "I can come up with some possibilities," Roberts said. "But if we could get closer to either of the gates and collect more data about which ships went through recently and where they were going, it would help."

And they wouldn't have to go into Nocturna territory to get information. They could get data from the gate network itself, but the closer they were to their target gate, the better. But first, Judit would have to pick a ship to follow. Their two suspects seemed to be headed in opposite directions.

Judit looked at the scans again, studying each ship. Odds were good that Annika was on one, and she'd said that if she had to escape on another ship, she'd leave Nocturna territory as quickly as possible. And the one heading away from Nocturna was going slower. It would be easier to catch. "Let's focus on the ship that left for the farther gate."

"You got it, Boss," Roberts said.

Judit went to her office to wait while Beatrice took them toward the nearest gate, and Roberts fiddled with the numbers. It was a long bit of waiting, of searching. Nocturna had become a stirred-up hornet's nest, and Beatrice reported several times that they needed to hide from Nocturna warships. Judit didn't want to be drawn into a firefight.

At last, after several long, tedious hours of picking over data that had already been picked over, Judit went to the bridge again. They'd found several ships on long-range scans that fit the specs Antiles had given them. It wasn't long before they'd narrowed that down to one that fit exactly. When Judit compared it to the shot Antiles captured, it seemed like a match.

"They can't have a crew over five," Evie said. "And it's got one cannon, but nothing to compare with the *Damat*."

"They're not talking," Roberts said. "And they must know we're here."

And Annika would be hailing the *Damat* if she was in charge. "You're sure their comm is working?"

He shook his head.

"Well, they're not slowing or turning to meet us," Beatrice said. "And they're too small for us to dock with, even with the shuttle. If they want us to go somewhere, they'll have to find a way to send a signal."

And Annika would have thought of such a thing. She'd told Judit she'd find a way to damage the engines and leave a trail.

"Try another hail," she said as they got closer. The crew might not even know Annika was aboard; they might be anyone going anywhere. Maybe if she got them to talk to her, she could bully them into stopping.

"No response," Roberts said.

Judit waited to see if the ship would change heading or speed, but it did neither, simply continuing its original, leisurely course.

"Bring us in closer," Judit said.

When the *Damat* loomed over the smaller ship, it kept the same course. Its speed was even more curious now, cruising along in no particular hurry. It put Judit in mind of animals who ambled through life because they were either too tough to kill, or no one could stand their taste.

Noal joined them on the bridge, and Judit filled him in. "I'm thinking trap," he said.

"Of course you are. Everyone here thinks everything is a trap. If that ship was going to blow up or something, shouldn't it have done so by now? If they wanted us to come aboard, wouldn't they have made it easier?"

Judit went through possible scenarios. They could disable the engines, but with a ship so small, any shot might blow it to bits. She studied the view of it on her screen. She could see the airlock door on the side, but they had no umbilical to connect to it.

"If I got onto that hull, I could cut in through the airlock," Judit said.

Noal stared as if she was crazy. "If you *got* on the hull? How do you propose to do that?"

"Big cutter from engineering would cut through," Evie said. "Slice the bolts holding the door closed, then you could seal it behind you with a maglock."

Judit nodded. "I'll have to jump from the shuttle. I'll get suited up."

A chorus of murmurs erupted. "You can't, Jude!" Noal said.

"Can't storm in to save the woman I love? Sounds like 'have to do it' territory to me."

"It's crazy!"

"If they've got Annika—"

"Then they'll have both of you? How is that better?"

"Fine, come along if you want, but I'm not sending a team over there, then waiting here for news. I don't care if it's stupid. I can't sit around and do nothing but think about my dead father!"

Everyone fell silent, but Noal continued to glare. Judit turned from the bridge.

"Wait!" Evie said.

Judit turned back with a sigh, lining up arguments in her head.

"I've got a Nocturna warship entering the system," Evie said. "Contact in twenty minutes."

Judit felt the blood drain from her face. That far out, they wouldn't be able to tell anything about the ship until it got closer, just that the signal it was putting out was all Nocturna and all business. And Judit didn't know whether they were tracking this ship or if it was bad luck.

"We'll have to hurry," Judit said.

"Jude, no!" Noal said. "We have to get out of here."

At her slow pace, the smaller ship couldn't outrun the *Damat*, but Judit would have to get over there and back before the Nocturna ship caught up. "Bea, you're my pilot. Evie, cover us with the *Damat*'s cannon. Get Browning up here on the helm."

"Are you really doing this?" Beatrice asked, staring at Judit as if she was mad, but she stood anyway.

"I'm getting aboard that ship one way or another."

"Not without me," Evie said. "Slattery can cover tactical on the *Damat*. I'm going with you."

Judit was about to argue, but Evie shook her head, more serious than Judit had ever seen her, and she was serious most of the time.

"I'm going to watch your back, Boss," Evie said. "It's my right."

Judit couldn't argue with that. And maybe two could get the job done faster than one. She nodded and started out of the bridge, Beatrice and Evie with her.

Noal followed on their heels. "This plan is very stupid."

"It's simple. The shuttle's going to get close to that ship. Evie and I are going to jettison over there in evosuits and cut our way in."

"It's *insane.*"

"So is love."

He stayed on her heels, trying to edge in front of her with a frown in place. "I can't let you do it."

"Better than staying here and crying on your shoulder again."

"Don't pull that shit on me. Making me feel sorry for you is not going to put me off. Let Evie go alone."

She glanced at Evie, who didn't add anything. Apparently, she was happy just to be a member of the party.

"I can go with her," Beatrice said. "Any of us would risk our lives for you, Jude."

Judit gave Beatrice a proud, embarrassed smile. "Thank you, really. But I have to go. I love her, Noal. I can't wait while someone else goes to help her."

He snorted. "I'm surprised she's not in charge of that ship already. Well, I'm coming with you on the shuttle." When she looked at him in surprise, he held his hands up. "Don't worry. I'm not going on the wacky, suicide portion of the mission. I'm making sure you get on your way safely and land on that ship. Then I'll be waiting with Beatrice to pick your sorry asses up."

She laughed. "Our sorry asses will be very happy to see you."

"Definitely," Evie added.

Chapter Eighteen

Annika felt the ship tremble around her. It was the second rumble within moments. She supposed the ship could be going through a debris field or something, but why wouldn't they go around it? No, it had to be weapons fire.

She hoped it was Judit and then cursed the fact that she couldn't do anything to help. She paced up and down her hallway, and when an alarm sounded, she pressed her ear to the sealed door. It was a shrill alarm, the kind that promoted utmost urgency. Something had breached the hull, probably a shot. Emergency doors would be coming down, but since she didn't feel a change in air pressure, her door provided protection. Her mother wouldn't want the prize damaged, after all.

Annika went back to the medbay and searched it for the hundredth time. She'd already looked in every nook and cranny. She'd pried up anything she could. She'd taken the doors off cabinets and tipped the bed over. Didn't the designers of medbays ever think the patients might have to sneak out? What if this ship was under attack, and one of the crew managed to lock herself in the medbay? She'd be trapped!

But then, no ship was equipped with secret passages and bolt-holes. She told herself that if she ever built a ship, she'd make sure she could get out of every room. But then any prisoners could escape. Ah well, it was better to kill one's enemies than take them prisoner anyway.

Annika turned to the small camera she'd found while searching for secret conduits. She'd covered it already, but no one had come. Maybe if she made them think their safety door had failed? Would that make them send someone? She could start a fire by breaking open the camera and stuffing instaskin around the wires, but if no one noticed, she'd die of smoke inhalation. A mortifying thought.

As she was about to make another trip up and down the hall, she heard a clank from near the sealed door. Someone was coming. From inside the medbay, she didn't have time to get into an ambush position in the hall, so she crouched behind the overturned bed.

"I don't care what he says, I'm not dying for this," someone said from the hall. "If you want to fight that maniac, go ahead."

Which maniac, Annika didn't know, but she'd soon find out. The door made another noise, but she couldn't tell if someone shut it or not. She heard slow footsteps. They were being cautious.

As if that would help them.

"Come out," the same voice said. "We know you're loose."

But Annika wasn't going to make it easy. She stayed silent and peeked around the edge of the bed. The barrel of a pistol came into the medbay first, followed by an arm. Annika readied her bone stiletto, and as soon as she saw a head, she threw.

The body collapsed. Annika was up and running before it hit the ground. She heard a gasp from a second person as she dove for the weapon. The deep thrum of a pistol filled the small space. Annika twisted and tried to curl away, but the edge of the blast clipped her arm, burning the curve of her bicep like acid. She cried out, the door splashing with blood as a feeling like fire rolled from her arm and across her core. She clenched the pistol she'd captured and slid toward the bandages strewn across the floor. A shadow leaned into the doorway, and she fired two shots. Someone scrambled back, cursing.

Annika tore the bandages open with her teeth and fixed them over the shoulder, covering her clothing too as she tried to staunch the bleeding. They hadn't left her any painkillers, but she slowed her breathing and tried to focus, picturing the pain rolling through her body and out her feet, leaving her behind.

She could still feel her arm, could move her fingers, though it was agonizing. She didn't think the shot had hit bone, but it had definitely sloughed off skin, maybe all the way to the muscle. She wouldn't be using her left arm for a while, but that was all right. She was equally good with the right.

"Come…come out," a shaky voice said.

"That didn't work for the other guard, and it won't work for you," Annika replied, hearing a tremor in her voice and swallowing to try to get rid of it. She wondered if she had time to put on instaskin but didn't think her new friend would leave her alone that long. "And now I have a pistol." Her stiletto was still in the body, but she'd get it back soon enough.

"S...so?" the voice asked.

"So, throw your gun in here, then step into the door with your hands up, and I won't hurt you."

"I hurt you already! I can see your blood on the floor."

"This is a medbay, friend. I've fixed your little love bite."

A few heartbeats went by, and Annika heard the clatter of feet. The woman was running for the heavy door. Annika leapt up and sped after, ignoring the throbbing in her arm and the woozy feeling trying to take over her head. The woman rapped on the door in a complicated pattern, and as the door eased open, Annika gained speed.

The woman turned, mouth open, eyes wide as she tried to bring her pistol to bear, but Annika was on her quicker than that, pushing her through the door. Annika fired at the one face she saw when the door opened, turning it into mist. She fell on top of the woman, jarring her injured arm, but she went with the pain, turning it into useful anger that drove her head forward to crack the guard between the eyes.

The guard grunted and went limp, her eyelids fluttering. Annika pushed up and knocked the other pistol away. The guard shook her head and blinked. She gasped at the headless body, but before she could react further, Annika pointed the pistol at her face.

"Prove your usefulness, or you're joining him."

With a grunt, the guard slumped, breathing hard, eyes unblinking. "What do you want?"

"Is someone firing on this ship?"

She nodded.

"Who?"

"I...don't know."

"Like the dark you don't."

"I'm just a hire! No one tells me anything."

"Hired to do what?"

"Make sure you don't get out of that hallway. They said you were dangerous."

And maybe she hoped to flatter or maybe not, but Annika didn't move. "So, you aren't useful?"

Her eyes went wide. "I can show you to an escape pod!"

"I'd rather see the bridge. Get me past any checkpoints, and you might stay alive." Though Annika would have preferred to find her own way, Feric and her mother would have good security. But they might not predict that Annika would use someone to help her. Nocturnas killed whoever was in their way and sorted everything out afterward.

The guard nodded hurriedly, and Annika stepped back so she could get up. Annika bent and retrieved the other pistol, then waved for the guard to face the wall for a quick pat down. Her arm throbbed, but Annika breathed the pain away. The guard didn't resist, but Annika knew she had to be working on a plan to escape. Who wouldn't be?

"What's your name?" Annika asked.

"Melise."

"What house?"

"None. I'm...none."

So she probably had been at one time, and she'd left. Not Blood, then, at least not that Annika could recognize. "Where is this ship going?"

"I'm not the pilot."

She probably knew, but Annika didn't have time to sort through any lies. And whoever was firing on them wouldn't let them get there anyway. If it was Judit, the faster Annika could take the ship, the better. "Come on."

She marched Melise back to the medbay and made her wait while she put instaskin under the bandages. She forced herself to look at the injury and assess it. Part of her muscle had been exposed, and the instaskin kept wanting to slide off. With the bandages, Annika finally got it to stay in place, and the bleeding stopped, though the pain was still very much there.

Melise watched her with wide eyes, her pale skin a little green.

"What?" Annika said. "Don't like the look of your handiwork?"

"I've never seen someone put their arm back together before."

"It's not as bad as it looks." She flexed her fingers, clenching her teeth through the pain, trying to seem as if she wasn't as wounded as she was. She couldn't have Melise thinking her left side could be used against her.

"Bridge," Annika said, gesturing with the pistol. "And on the way, you can tell me about any security this boat has."

❖

Inside the *Damat*'s shuttle, Judit and Evie donned evosuits. Larger and bulkier than a pressure suit, the evosuits were better equipped to handle the cold of space. They included a backpack with air jets as well as a full oxygen tank. On the wide, bulky belt, Judit strapped a hand scanner and a pistol. Evie donned a pistol as well as several grenades. Judit looked crossways at the large weapons. If she punched a hole in the ship...

Evie saw her looking and shrugged. "You never know."

Judit also strapped on a large laser cutter they'd borrowed from engineering. Now all they had to do was aim for the ship and hope they made it. And thinking about that was the most difficult part. Judit was certain Annika would have been looking forward to it, would have gleefully jumped into the abyss, but Judit couldn't help focusing on the yawning chasm of space outside the door.

The shuttle rocked slightly. Judit and Evie held on near the closed airlock. They'd already shut the cockpit off from the rest of the shuttle and secured anything that might vent into space. Noal was watching through the small window, his face creased in concern.

"Get ready, Jude," Beatrice's voice said in her ear. "The *Damat* is moving to shield us from the Nocturnas if they get here before we return. I'm going to get as close to the other ship as I can."

"Copy that." Judit tried to sound surer than she felt. She and Evie held on to a bar overhead and faced the airlock door. It had a tiny window, too, and the other ship whirled and raced outside. She didn't dare look too hard for fear she'd throw up.

"I'm turning off the gravity," Beatrice said. "Noal and I are buckled in."

"Copy that."

"Magboots," Evie said, nudging Judit's arm.

"Right." Judit engaged her boots and told herself to get her head in the game. She tore her eyes off the window and took deep breaths. Her ears felt the change in gravity, but with her boots, her feet didn't come off the deck.

In the airlock window, the enemy ship leveled off as the shuttle matched its course and speed. Judit braced herself, but before they could get close, the enemy ship's cannon glowed red.

"Hold on," Beatrice shouted.

The shuttle rolled away, and the shot went wild. Beatrice fired a short salvo, and Judit bet the *Damat* was swinging around to defend them.

"We can't risk destroying that ship!" Judit said over her comm.

"We can't let them shoot us out of the sky either," Evie said.

"They can evade! Bea, tell the *Damat* to only fire warning shots." Judit knew Slattery was a good shot, but he wasn't as good as Evie. By the dark, things were going sideways faster than she'd anticipated.

"Tell the *Damat* to draw their fire," Judit said. "And bring us around for another pass."

"The *Damat* is firing," Beatrice said. "There's an opening."

"Take us in."

The shuttle swung around, and Judit saw a blast fire in the opposite direction. The enemy's cannon wouldn't penetrate the *Damat*'s armor, so Judit tried to put her ship's safety out of her mind and focus on the hull of the enemy ship as it slid back into sight.

The shuttle cruised closer, and Judit tried to judge the distance, waiting for their chance. Evie put a hand to the door controls.

"Wait. Wait," Judit said. "Get ready. Now!"

Judit released her magboots as Evie opened the door, and the bit of atmosphere in the shuttle's cargo hold blew them into space. They hurtled toward the enemy ship as if rocketed from a cannon, but Judit knew distances could be deceptive. She engaged the jets on her pack and angled herself to fly boots-first at the enemy hull. She'd done a similar maneuver once in practice, and it had scared the dark out of her then, too.

Now her heart hammered, and her brain kept up a shrieking litany of all the bad things that could happen, not the least of which was what might happen if she missed. She was small enough that the shuttle and the *Damat* could lose track of her in a matter of moments, and she could drift anywhere, could crash into something or burn up or run out of air. There were so many ways to die in space.

And now the ship was flying at her even faster.

"Evie, use your jets to push away!" Judit cried. "We're coming in too fast!" Every part of her was crying out to do the opposite, to land as fast as she could, but she might break her legs *and* bounce off to die in space. As she got closer, Judit slowed, the jets pushing her away, but if she gave them too much power, she'd push away from the ship completely.

"Now, Boss?" Evie asked.

"Yep." Before the jets could push them away, Judit engaged her magboots and pulled toward the ship again.

The shock of landing was still enough to make her knees buckle. Her feet stuck to the hull as she fell backward, bouncing hard enough to whip her head forward. Her neck throbbed, but her feet were stuck, and for a moment, that was enough. She took half a second to breathe, to feel that she wasn't injured, that she'd reached her target, and that she wasn't floating alone in the blackness of space.

"You okay, Boss?" Evie asked.

"Good. You?"

"A bit shaken, but I'll straighten out." She leaned into Judit's view, *smiling* for dark's sake. She couldn't be enjoying herself, could she? Judit didn't even want to ask.

"Let's get moving." They lessened the pull of their boots so they could walk, hurrying as much as they could toward the side of the ship, to one of the airlocks. The forward cannon glowed before it unleashed a volley at the shuttle, a bright flash without sound. Judit went flat on the deck, even though the shot didn't come near her. She felt the concussion as the bolt streaked past, and a slight weight bounced off the top of her: Evie, covering her.

A nice sentiment, but if that shot had hit them, the cover wouldn't have mattered at all. Evie twisted around to watch the shot, but Judit tugged her onward. "Come on! That Nocturna ship will be here soon."

When they reached the airlock, Judit began cutting the bolts. Evie crouched, waiting to push inside. The crew of the ship would detect the breach, but that would happen no matter where they cut. At least this way, Judit and Evie couldn't automatically vent anyone into space. Well, Judit didn't want to vent Annika into space. Anyone else, she didn't care about, though she knew Noal would censure her for that thought.

The door popped open. Evie swung inside with her pistol drawn and dropped to the floor, held by the ship's gravity. She peered through the small window before signaling.

Judit stepped in, secured the airlock door with a large maglock, and scanned the controls. "I'll give us some atmosphere. See anyone?"

"There's a shadow at the end of a hall, but it's not moving, so I can't tell if it's equipment or a person."

"I'm opening the inner door." They took cover on either side. As soon as the door hissed sideways, the deep thrum of a pistol shot came through the inner door and dissipated against the outer.

The nearness of the shock sent cramps through Judit's muscles. They couldn't hope to get through the door quickly enough to avoid a hit.

"Return fire?" Evie asked.

"Think you can hit anyone?"

"Without being a target?" Inside her helmet, she shook her head.

Judit looked to the maglock she'd placed on the outer door. She grinned. "Get ready. I'm giving our friends a bit of fresh air."

"Copy that, Boss."

Judit engaged her boots and pressed hard to the wall. She loosened the maglock just enough for the door to slip open, and the effect was immediate. The atmosphere whistled past her so quickly, it turned to fog as it hit the cold of deep space.

"Lock it up!" Evie said.

Judit redid the maglock. Evie dashed into the corridor, and Judit ran after. The shooter had been pulled around the corner by the escaping atmosphere and lay along the floor. Judit smiled again. It was about time the vacuum of space worked for her rather than just scaring the dark out of her.

Evie thundered toward the shooter and kicked her hard in the midsection. The woman grunted, and her pistol dropped as she curled into a ball. Evie punched her hard, and she went still.

Judit grabbed the dropped pistol. The woman likely wouldn't recover from that hit in the next twenty minutes or so, and Judit planned to be long gone by then. When they poked their heads around the next corner, two people scrambled away, taking cover and drawing pistols of their own. Evie let off a shot, but they fled around a corner and fired back. Hopefully, Annika was tucked somewhere safe instead of getting fired on by every guard on the darking ship.

Judit tapped her helmet's external speaker. "I want Annika, your prisoner," she called. "We can part without bloodshed."

A volley of shots answered her.

"Have it your way." She switched to personal comm and gestured to Evie's array of weapons. "Any of those stun grenades?"

"They all are." Evie pulled one loose, her eyes wide with surprise. "I'm not a monster. Did you think I was packing frags? That I'd risk blowing a hole in this ship?"

"I...well..." She felt her cheeks grow hot.

Evie pursed her lips and muttered something about trusting a tactical officer to know which weapons to use.

"Sorry."

"Covering fire in three seconds, please, Boss," Evie said. "Then take cover. Don't look at the *stun* grenade." She gave Judit a reproachful look, pulled the pin, and counted, no doubt estimating the distance of the shooters based on the sounds of their weapons.

Judit fired around the corner. Evie lobbed the grenade, then both turned away. A bright flash and a crackling sound echoed around the corner, but it was the stunning discharge that made Judit's hair stand on end, even from a distance. The attackers didn't have time to call out.

Judit poked her head out and saw a leg sticking into the hallway. She sprinted forward and found both attackers unconscious. The stun would keep them out for an hour, maybe more.

They needed to find Annika, and Judit felt time slipping away. She peeked into several rooms, but they looked like standard crew quarters. When she tried a door and found it locked, she paused.

"Well, only one way to find out who's in there." She knocked.

When a shaky voice asked, "Who is it?" she blinked in surprise that anyone answered. A man's voice, but he might have information.

"Everything's all right, sir," she said, using her most soldierly, official voice. "We're moving everyone one corridor over, just in case."

The door opened, revealing a man in the dark red robes of a hierophant. She grabbed a handful of his robe and hauled him into the hallway, banging him into a wall to stun him.

Evie peeked into his room. "It's clear." She took up position at Judit's side, pistol out as she kept watch.

The hierophant squealed, and Judit clapped a hand over his mouth. "I'm not going to hurt you." She leaned close as his eyes rolled. "I'm not going to hurt you! I'm looking for someone. Tell me where she is, and I'll put you back in your room; you can lock the door behind you."

He shuddered, and she repeated herself more calmly until he seemed to settle. "I don't...I don't..." He looked closely into her helmet, staring at her face. "You...you're..."

"Running out of patience!" Judit said. "Was someone brought aboard this ship? Are you holding her prisoner?"

He laughed, and Judit was afraid he'd lost his mind. "I didn't think it would be me. I thought it would be one of the others, but..." He sighed. "If I have to die for the cause, I'm ready."

"What the dark are you talking about?"

"Boss," Evie said, "we can't stay still for long."

"Tell me where she is!" Judit barked.

"She won't be hurt and neither will you," the hierophant said. "You're both too important."

"Too important to whom?"

"To fate. You don't know that yet? You're the chosen ones."

Judit rocked back on her heels. How did he know that? Did Meridian release a statement? No, she would have heard. And chosen *ones*? Was he talking about Annika? She'd always been the Nocturna heir, but when the prophecies mentioned the chosen one, they were always careful to say the title belonged to Meridian alone. Was there another prophecy she didn't know about? And this man was a hierophant. Surely he would know. Was that what her father had been looking for?

"She's waiting for you on the bridge," the hierophant said. "Now that you're here in person, I'll tell the guards to stand down."

Judit shoved him into his room. If Annika was on the bridge, Judit didn't need this man anymore, didn't need his crazy theories. And if he was telling the guards to stand down, it didn't matter the reason. Judit would take all the good fortune she could get.

"What the dark was that about?" Evie asked as they continued down the hall. She moved cautiously, and Judit was with her. They couldn't depend on the promises of one crazy hierophant.

"Who knows?" Judit said. "After we get Annika back, we can take the darking ship somewhere else and question everyone at our leisure."

❖

Annika glanced down the hallway, but no more guards waited for her. She'd expected a whole cadre of them. "Where is everyone?" Melise shrugged. "There's a sealed door ahead."

"Can you get us through?"

Melise shrugged again, but Annika had seen her gaze linger at every door or corridor they'd passed. She was looking to bolt, and a sealed door would be the perfect place to try. Whether she ran or not, it was clear she wasn't going to make this easy.

Annika pushed her hostage down the corridor to another hallway. She wondered if she should favor her left arm, but she feared stiffening up. The use of an injured arm was better than one that might fail when she needed it.

This next hallway ended in a door, but instead of being sealed, it stood open a crack. "Now's your chance," Annika said. "Get me through that door, and you're one step closer to freedom."

Melise didn't look as if she believed that. Annika gestured at her with the gun. "I'll have a clear line on you the whole time. Talk fast." She stayed behind Melise as they turned the corner, but they hadn't gone ten paces when the sound of a pistol echoed ahead, and Melise collapsed with an oozing hole in her chest.

Annika scurried back down the corridor.

"Nice try," her mother's voice said from the other side of the door. "I understand you're trying to take control of the prophecy. It's one of the reasons you were chosen. But it's not quite time yet. I told them not to go in and check on you, but Feric insisted."

Warning lights flared to life in the corridor, and a low siren began, a steady, electronic whine.

"I've begun scuttling procedures," Annika's mother said. "We're under attack by a Meridian warship, and I'm not letting them get their hands on you."

"You're going to kill me instead?" Annika shouted. "What did Feric have to say about that?"

"There's a shuttle two decks down. If you hurry, you can make it."

A door to Annika's left slid open and revealed the inside of a lift car. The sealed door began to roll closed. If she sprinted...

She cursed and got into the lift as the ship was jarred by another hit. She didn't know what her mother and Feric were up to, but she doubted they'd let her die in a Meridian attack. They needed her for something, but she intended to be the only one on the supposed shuttle. Well, the only conscious one, anyway. And it was a better plan than trying for the bridge. Even if the ship managed to survive an assault, Annika wouldn't be able to override any scuttling codes. This ship was a lost cause, and there was something to be said about living to fight another day.

The lift door slid open two decks down, and as promised, a sign pointed to the shuttle bay. Annika took off at a jog as the ship rocked again. A few of the escape pod bays stood empty. She wondered if Feric had gotten away and didn't know which idea bothered her most, that he had or hadn't. Part of her still cared about him, but a louder part of her wanted to hunt him down herself.

When she got to the shuttle bay door, it stood closed, but scorch marks said someone had tried to burn their way inside. There was no control panel, only a DNA scanner, and Annika wondered how she was supposed to get in if several desperate attempts to cut through had already failed.

The scanner flashed green as she came near, and the door slid open. She paused, looking down the hall. She hated being led, and this was so obviously what her mother wanted her to do. Had this been part of her mother's bizarre plan this whole time? But who could have planned to be attacked by a Meridian warship? Was there even a warship or a scuttling going on? Or did her mother want her to get in this shuttle for some other reason?

Annika reminded herself of a thought she'd had in the medbay: If she second-guessed every decision she made, she'd be forever paralyzed. And there were alarms, and if the rocking of the ship wasn't caused by weapons fire, something bad was still happening. If she was in the shuttle, at least she'd be on her way to freedom.

Annika poked her head inside the bay. Nothing there but a waiting shuttle. She hurried to it, and the door opened. She stepped inside gingerly, wondering again what the plan was. Could her mother have beaten her here? The shuttle seemed empty, but any of the walls could be a secret compartment. She slipped into the shuttle's emergency pressure suit, easing it over her injured arm. She'd get away from this ship, vent the atmosphere, and see if any hidden assassins could breathe in a vacuum.

She keyed open the main bay doors and guided the shuttle out and away as fast as she could, turning and weaving, evasive maneuvers. A look from the cameras showed the ship she'd been on in a firefight with another, larger ship. It did indeed look like a Meridian design. She had a brief thought that it might be Judit, but the ship seemed bigger than the *Damat*. Still, her heart began to pound at the thought that she might be running away from her beloved. As she reached for the controls to make the camera zoom, light-headedness swept over her. Clearly, all her recent escapes were making her giddy.

But no, now her hands wouldn't stop shaking, and she could no longer reach the controls. Lethargy overtook her, and she slumped in her chair. Even panic was ebbing away. The air inside her helmet. Something was wrong. She fumbled for the catch, but her gloved hands wouldn't work right.

Feric stepped into view beside her, a smile on his face. "I set a few traps in here," he signed, "but something told me you'd pick the suit."

She couldn't be angry with him. Blissful peace spread through her limbs. Her arm ceased to throb, and she felt as if she was floating in zero-G. That was good. She was good in zero-G. If only she could move...

"Don't worry," Feric signed. "I'll take care of you, and when the time comes, you'll be safe to meet your destiny."

Annika smiled at him and tried to tell him that when the time came, she'd kill him, but the words wouldn't come. Her eyes drifted shut, and existence became as dark as the blackness of space.

CHAPTER NINETEEN

As the hierophant promised, Judit and Evie saw no one until they reached the bridge. The door to the nerve center of the ship stood open, and guards lined the walls, but their weapons hung by their belts. A lone figure stood at a center console, her back to the door. She was dressed in the same red robes as the other hierophant, but long silver hair cascaded down her back, as bright as Judit's own.

Judit's breath caught. A Meridian? But the woman turned, showing skin far lighter that was beginning to line with age. Her smile seemed kind, if sad. She clasped her hands in front of her.

"Welcome, chosen one," she said.

Judit was struck with a feeling of recognition. She had a flash of sitting with Noal during one of his lessons. History maybe. The tutor had played a litany of prophecies, including Willa's clear prophecy of the chosen one. The tutor had shown them holos of her, too, stressing that she'd sacrificed her life for her peerless prophecies by traveling past the event horizon of a black hole.

"You can't be Willa," Judit said. "She died over forty years ago!" And she'd been in her fifties when she'd made her famous prophecy. This was no ninety-year-old woman!

Willa tilted her head and smiled wider as if she could read Judit's mind and was amused by it. "The closer you come to a black hole, the more time slows. Within it?" She shrugged. "Time is nothing. I died and was reborn. As for all the things I've seen?" She shook her head. "I fear that if I told you, you could not even comprehend, much less believe. And I barely scratched the surface of time."

"So you knew," Judit said, stepping forward, "that I was the real chosen one? Did you know about the plan Meridian had in case Nocturna betrayed them? Did you know about the original kidnapping?"

"The things I know would astound you, but those are not the questions you came here to ask."

Judit hadn't come to ask questions at all, interesting as this was. "Where is Annika?"

Despite everything that was happening, Willa's blue eyes seemed kind. "On the path to her fate, as you are, as we all are."

"Did you have her kidnapped again? Are you behind all the chaos in the galaxy right now?" Anger burned through Judit's temples, and she resisted the urge to point her pistol at Willa's chest. "I thought hierophants were supposed to observe the future, not make it."

"My journey taught me better than that," Willa said. "It showed me that I have the opportunity to put the galaxy right, to truly unite humanity instead of dividing it."

"We have to go, Boss," Evie said over their personal comm. "That Nocturna ship will be here soon."

"Give Annika back to me," Judit said.

"Certainly."

Judit nearly took a step back. She hadn't expected that. "Well... okay." She waited half a heartbeat, but no one moved. "Now!"

Willa waved. Judit turned, expecting to see someone bringing Annika inside, but the thrum of a pistol sounded from behind them. Judit ducked and spun, going for her own weapon. Her muscles clenched as the shot landed close to her, and there was only one place it could have gone.

Judit turned in time to see Evie crumple, her face a mask of surprise. A crimson hole tipped a red river down her side, and the look of wonder didn't leave her face until it slackened.

Judit caught her. "Evie, hold on!" She brought her pistol to bear on the guard who'd fired and pulled the trigger, but he rolled away from the blast.

"Bea!" Judit called. She fired again. "We need—"

Something pushed into her back, and she went rigid, lights exploding in front of her eyes. Her head whipped back, and she lost all thought.

❖

Annika woke to the smell of charred meat. She breathed deep, trying to determine the source and wondering how many times she was going to wake up after being knocked unconscious. So far, she'd been strangled, hit with a shock stick, and gassed. Did the different circumstances mean there was less chance of brain damage?

At least she was getting plenty of practice taking stock of her surroundings with her eyes closed. Besides the smell, she heard popping and buzzing, maybe a damaged console. Someone was muttering, but they were too far away to hear. Though the meat smell was strong, she could also smell ozone and scorched plastic, damaged electronics. If she was still on the shuttle, it might have come under attack; the burnt smell was probably a person who'd been injured or killed.

Feric? Possibly, but who was muttering? Her mother? Had she been aboard the shuttle, too? Maybe she'd never been in that hall, never been anywhere on the ship, and Annika had been imagining her the entire time.

It nearly made her laugh, and she wondered if the gas was still in her system, making her foggy and light-headed. She flexed her muscles, and nearly cried out as her injured arm came alive with pain. She was lying unrestrained on a hard surface, probably a floor. At least she was lying on her right side so she wasn't resting on her injury. By the crinkling sound, she was still wearing the pressure suit, but the helmet was gone. That was good; they couldn't gas her again.

After the slight sound, she paused to see if anyone noticed. A small weight rested on her forearm, maybe someone's hand. Annika stiffened, ready to move, but the hand gripped her.

"Wait," a soft voice said in her ear. "Not yet." It was her mother's voice, and she didn't know why it made her hesitate, but the next words stilled her. "They'll want to kill you, to make a martyr that will draw more people into the fight, but I won't let them, Anni."

What the dark did that mean? Emotions she'd thought long dead reared in Annika's mind. She thought she'd never again feel the safety of a parent's arms. She was certain she no longer needed it.

"I couldn't say anything with Feric around," her mother said. "He's a true believer, but I joined their cause once I knew you were at the heart of it. I wanted you to be free, so I had to go along this far, but I won't let them hurt you or Judit, I promise."

Judit was there, too? Annika risked opening one eye. It looked like the control room of the Eye, but it was in ruins; several consoles had shorted out, and bodies were scattered around the room. She didn't see Feric, but a few other people in hierophants' robes gathered near one of the live consoles. Her mother must have been behind her.

"I know you don't trust me," her mother said. "The dark knows I've given you enough reasons not to, but it was all for the good, I promise. Nocturna was going to kill me, so I had to leave, and this was the only way I could get you back."

Annika's heart thudded, and she shut her eyes again. A huge part of her wanted to give herself over to her mother, but the galaxy was full of tricks. Ama was not always wrong.

Someone stepped over her, and her mother knelt into view, bending low. "When I say, come up swinging, but not yet, not until Willa is here. If one of us can get to her, it'll all be over."

Willa? The prophet responsible for the prophecy of the chosen one? That *was* a surprise, but as she thought about it, who else would lead the rebellion of the hierophants than their most famous daughter? Annika opened her eyes again and looked at her mother before blinking once.

"Good girl. Do you have the data chip you took from Prime?"

Annika blinked again.

"I added a few things to it before you woke up in the medbay. I knew you'd find it. When you get loose, broadcast it to everyone within reach, anyone that will listen. People will find out they've been manipulated, that the hierophants commanded the bombings on Nocturna Prime. The hierophants also told House Meridian that Tam Ada-Meridian was giving information to Nocturna spies. Then everyone should start to calm down, at least enough to listen. Then you and Judit can marry, unite your houses, and get everyone to see sense."

Annika nearly snorted a laugh. At this point, wasn't peace between Meridian and Nocturna nothing more than a fantasy? Ama would say so.

Her mother leaned close. "Hopefully, it will be easier than you think."

"Variel?" someone in the room called. "Is your daughter all right?"

"Still sleeping," Annika's mother said over her shoulder.

Someone sighed. "I know it will be a great sacrifice, but you have to let her go."

Annika's mother managed to make her voice sound calm, even happy, as she said, "If it's for the good of the cause, I'm at peace with it."

Annika tried her best not to shudder. A short time later, a door opened, and Annika heard several people enter. She risked a look and nearly twitched in surprise. Two people carried Judit, both of them in hierophant red. Several others surrounded them, and the woman who led them seemed familiar, a face out of the history holos: Willa herself.

Annika waited until they laid Judit down. She was dressed in an evosuit, but like Annika, she wore no helmet. Well, if the atmosphere evaporated from the room, at least their bodies would be protected. All the hierophants began to move to the center of the room. Annika didn't need the prod of her mother's toe to know it was time to act.

She was up in a moment, her right side tingling where she'd laid on it, the wound aching in the other arm. She ignored both and the slight fog in her brain and leapt for Willa, her right arm ahead of her, palm flat so she could slam it into the side of Willa's neck.

The hierophants reacted faster than Annika thought. One launched a kick and caught her in the side. She went with the motion, but it was still enough to send pain arcing through her ribs and making her wounded arm scream all over again.

With a roll, Annika was up in an instant, hands forward to strike at anyone who came near, but the hierophants assumed defense positions of their own, and she knew they were more than they seemed to be.

But she'd worked as a distraction. Her mother eased around behind them, closer to Judit. If she could wake Judit as she'd awoken Annika, the three of them might have a chance.

"We knew what you were going to do before you did it," Willa said.

"Did you always know you were going over that event horizon?" Annika asked, anything to keep them focused on her.

"I knew it was my destiny," Willa said. "On the other side, I knew what had to be done. The opportunity to reshape the galaxy as it was meant to be, not divided by houses but united by our very humanity."

"At the cost of so many lives? You bombed a city!"

Willa spread her hands. "It is only from ashes that we may spring anew."

It sounded like cryptic nonsense. Annika's mother bent over Judit, injecting her with something. Annika felt a flutter of fear. Her mother might be poisoning Judit, could be doing anything, but why would she bother to hide?

When Judit's eyes snapped open, Annika's mother put a hand over her mouth and whispered in her ear.

"What do you want us for?" Annika asked loudly. "Why us?"

"You know why," Willa said with a smile. "You're the chosen ones, born at the right time, groomed to take the actions we knew you would take. There were a few bumps in the road, but with the bits of the future I was able to see, it's all gone as planned."

"And how does it end?" Annika asked as her mother helped Judit up. "Have you seen that?"

"No one ever gets to see their entire future, just enough to know what's right, what's true."

Annika nearly rolled her eyes. No one was going to tell her what she could or couldn't do with her future. Behind Willa, her mother gave a nod. Annika struck at the two guards in front of her while her mother and Judit attacked them from behind. Judit felled one with a giant swing to the back, and her mother wrapped an arm around the neck of another.

Annika launched a fist at one of her foes while angling a kick at the knee of the other. He'd been watching her fist, and the kick struck him hard. He went down, uttering a cry of pain. Annika ducked the counterswing of her original foe and slammed a fist into his stomach. She put one hand on the ground and swept her leg into his, sending him tumbling. She stayed down, kicking his face when it was level with hers. Then she switched position and kicked up at the other man, planting her heel in his chin.

They had all four guards down quickly. The other three hierophants hugged the walls, leaving Willa alone in the middle of the floor.

She watched them with an amused smile.

Annika's mother stepped up behind Willa and grabbed her arm. "Now this ends. Annika and Judit will unite their houses, and there can be peace without death and destruction."

Willa kept her smile. Judit stepped around them, heading for Annika, and Annika met her halfway, their hands clasping, though Annika kept her left arm free.

"Are you all right?" they both asked at the same time.

Annika chuckled breathlessly. "I'm a little banged up, but I'll be okay."

"Me, too."

Annika turned back to her mother, wondering what they were supposed to do now. Did she introduce her lover to her mother or wait until later? Was her mother going to kill Willa or arrest her? She'd said that without Willa, the hierophants' plans would end, but the hierophant guards were subdued. Yet Willa was still smiling.

Annika's mother arched an eyebrow. "Are you going to tell me you saw this, too, Willa? That all this is going according to plan?"

"Yes," Willa said.

Annika looked to the cowering hierophants. "So, we should kill them?"

Judit clutched her hand. "We should arrest them. Once the galaxy hears what they've done…"

"Right," Annika said. "We can use their console." One of the hierophants set a foot in her way, and she backhanded him hard, sending him spinning to the ground. She gave a look to the others, and they moved farther away, their expressions terrified. If they'd seen this future, they weren't too certain of it.

❖

Judit tried to process everything that had happened; her emotions were hammering at her to stop, to ask questions, to try to get everyone to explain what was going on. She had Annika by her side, so that was a point in the positive column. But she also had the woman she recognized as Annika's mother, Variel. She'd awoken Judit and told her that if she attacked the guards, they had a chance to stop the chaos, and since Annika had seemed in the process of doing that, it sounded like the best idea.

So Variel was on their side? And they seemed to have won, but Willa still had a creepy smile, and Judit didn't know what to make of that. If Willa was responsible for the chaos, that meant she was also responsible for Judit's father's death, and she was definitely responsible for Evie's death. Judit wanted to punch her, but they had her subdued. Judit looked forward to turning her over to the Meridian authorities as soon as she and Annika united the galaxy.

Whatever that meant.

Annika inserted a data chip into one of the consoles, but the controls were locked. She turned to the hierophants. "What's the code?"

They shrank from her, shaking their heads.

"They don't know," Willa said. "Did you think I wouldn't know you'd try this?"

Annika turned to her with a murderous look, and for once, Judit wanted to support her almost as much as she wanted to see Willa in prison.

"Give her the code," Variel said, and Judit knew where Annika had gotten that dangerous growl. Annika's childhood couldn't have been easy.

Willa folded her hands and said nothing.

Variel shook her slightly. "You want to die?"

"If that is my fate, so be it."

Now Annika stepped close as well, removed her glove, pushed up the sleeve of her suit, and slipped something from her arm, a bone knife. Judit stared at it in horror. The short white sliver was a little bloody where it had slipped through her skin. Judit had to swallow back a wave of bile. She hadn't believed Noal when he'd told her.

"Does your fate have you whole or in pieces?" Annika asked.

Judit's stomach turned a little more. "It's over," she said. "You want peace? That's what we want, too, and we can make it happen without so many deaths."

"There have already been too many," Annika said. "You bombed Nocturna!"

Judit let out a breath. Well, she knew it hadn't been Annika.

"Not personally." Willa's gaze cut to Variel, who scowled at her.

"I did what I had to do to get my daughter back!"

"You?" Judit asked. How could she trust someone willing to do such a thing, no matter the reason?

Variel glanced at her. "They wanted Meridian and Nocturna at each other's throats."

"They framed your father, too, Judit. I'm so sorry," Annika said.

Judit leaned against the console. It felt like the room was closing in. She couldn't breathe. She tried to tell herself she couldn't fall apart now, but the people responsible for killing her father were in this room, and if she wanted, she could end them now. It was clear that Annika and Variel wouldn't mind.

Willa smiled as if all the deaths in the galaxy wouldn't affect her. Judit saw flashes of her grandmother in that face. It was probably Annika's grandmother, too, and all the people in the galaxy who didn't want to change except to get worse. They'd believed in their own causes for so long, there wasn't room in their minds for anything else.

And she didn't want to become them. Judit glanced at the console again. "If we can't unlock this, we need to find the *Damat*." If they had escaped the trap she'd fallen into, they'd have followed her. Everyone but Evie.

No, the grief would have to wait until later. Judit cleared her throat. "If Willa wants us here, we need to be somewhere else. Let's get in a shuttle."

"We can't leave her alive," Variel said, thrusting her chin at Willa.

Judit didn't want to talk with Variel, didn't even want to look at her. She wanted to arrest both of them. "Then we take her with us. She belongs in prison."

Annika and her mother frowned in exactly the same way.

"We cannot appoint ourselves executioners," Judit said. "Fighting for our lives is one thing. Cutting down an unarmed prisoner is another."

"Judit—"

"No, Annika," Judit said. "If we're going to be together, you have to see my point in this." She put all the feeling she had into the words, not only love but grief and anger and so much fatigue it was a wonder she didn't pass out.

Annika stared before she nodded. "I might not understand your point, but I can see it's important to you. So, that means I'm willing to learn, right?"

Judit nodded, happy she agreed, but how happy would she be when Judit arrested her mother? "Let's get out of here before whatever Willa thinks is going to happen happens."

The four of them hurried down through the Eye. Scorch marks and bodies littered the way along with blown doors and shattered consoles. The hierophants who wanted to shape the universe seemed to have crashed into those who wanted to watch it as they'd always done. Mass killings had already started here, and Judit didn't want to see them spread across the galaxy.

Annika warned off any living hierophants by saying she'd hurt Willa if they didn't back off. Judit thought they were going to proceed all the way to the shuttles unmolested, but as they rounded the last corner before the umbilicals, Feric blocked the hall.

Annika stopped cold, a myriad of expressions crossing her face. She glanced at Variel, who shook her head. "It's over, Feric."

He frowned, and a look of near hatred passed over his face as he stared at Variel. He made a few gestures with his hands.

Annika held the bone knife to Willa's neck. "Get out of the way, Feric."

He gestured again.

"I don't have a destiny!" Annika cried. "It was all a bunch of shit! I got loose. I got your leader, and I've got my mom back. I've won, and you've lost, you darking traitor!" Anguish filled her voice, and tears hovered in her eyes but didn't fall.

Judit wanted to reach out to her, but she turned to Feric, readying herself in case he rushed them. He shook his head. Annika pushed the blade against Willa's neck, and a line of blood welled around the sharp edge.

"You know your destiny," Willa said, her face calm.

"Shut up," Annika said, eyes locked on Feric.

Judit's jaw tingled, and she jumped. When Beatrice's voice said, "Jude?" in her ear, she nearly whooped.

"Here!" Everyone glanced at her. "The *Damat* is here."

"Jude," Beatrice said, relief thick in her voice. "We've got to get you out of there. We've got Meridian and Nocturna ships entering this system."

"We're in the shuttle bay. We'll come to you." She turned to the rest of them. "Time to go. Our ride's here."

Feric took a step forward, and he seemed to get wider as he pulled his shoulders back, a stance clearer than any words.

Willa smiled, even with the blood running down her neck. "They're coming, aren't they? Nocturna and Meridian?"

"We'll be gone before they get here." Judit took a step toward Feric, but Annika cried out in shock.

Time seemed to slow like on the edge of the abyss. Willa had rammed her head forward, forcing Annika's knife into her neck. Her eyes bulged, blood pumping around the bone. She coughed, splattering scarlet drops along the floor, the wall.

Feric charged. Annika's mother ran to meet him, screaming for Annika and Judit to get out. Annika let Willa's body fall, then stepped toward where her mother and Feric wrestled in the hall. Footsteps pounded down the corridor, and without Willa as a shield, they were going to be overwhelmed. Whatever Willa had set in motion would come to fruition.

Never. Not while Judit could draw breath. And they weren't going to get caught because of a darking killer. Judit leapt at Annika and tackled her into one of the umbilicals. They fell in a tangle of limbs, the flow of air slowing them as they dropped into a hierophant shuttle, but neither of them was facing the right way, and they fell half on top of each other.

"Mom!" Annika cried, but Judit was already reaching for the console. "Judit, wait! We have to get my mom."

"When she sees we've gone, she can make her own escape," Judit said. "I have to save us."

Annika lunged for the console, but Judit grabbed her. Annika stiffened as if she might counterattack then stilled. "Let me go, Judit," she said quietly. "I have to get my mother."

"It's too late. We're disconnected. I'm sorry, Annika; I had to. Once she sees we're gone—"

"You left her there to die!"

It would be no more than she deserved. The shuttle lurched. Judit glanced around Annika at the console. An automated system had engaged. The shuttle raced forward, and both of them fell. Judit scrambled up and reached for the console, but nothing would respond to her touch. Annika tried, too, but nothing worked for her, either. She turned to Judit with fury in her eyes. "You locked me out!"

"I haven't done anything!" She clicked her teeth. "Bea?"

She heard a faint response, but according to the screen, they were moving away from the Eye at top speed, away from the *Damat*.

Judit searched for the shuttle's destination, her belly going cold as she sorted through coordinates. The hierophants might have preprogrammed all the shuttles in case she and Annika escaped, or maybe all their shuttles were this way. The Eye usually sent its people to one place, after all, and the hierophants might not know how to fly. For where they were going, a computer would be a better pilot anyway.

Annika looked at her with wide eyes after she scanned the information scrolling across the console. "We're...we're headed for..."

"The black holes at the center of the galaxy."

CHAPTER TWENTY

Annika slumped in front of the console, trying to think. One moment it had seemed as if she had everything worked out, everything going according to plan. Now the woman she loved had forced her to abandon her mother, the key to unraveling the hierophants' plan was dead, and she was headed for a massive cluster of black holes at the center of the galaxy.

What a day.

Judit hunched over the controls, stabbing at them with frantic energy. "The comm will only let me send messages back to the temple. Maybe the *Damat* will intercept them."

"But you won't be able to hear them." Annika felt still, as if all the emotions inside her had compressed and left her numb, her own little black hole.

Judit banged on the console. "Maybe the *Damat* can disable this shuttle's engines." She put her gloved hands to the sides of her head. Her hair stuck out crazily. "No, we're too small. Cannon fire could destroy us. Evie will know that…" She paused, and a stricken look came over her face.

The sorrow there broke through Annika's numbness. "Oh, Judit. What is it?"

"Evie is dead," she said quietly.

So they were both down a parent and a friend. Even though she was still hurting, still angry, Annika raised up on her knees and pulled Judit toward her, holding her fiercely. Judit hugged her back, making Annika's arm throb, but she clamped her teeth on that pain.

Judit pushed back, inhaling deeply and wiping her cheeks. The gloves left smudges in her tears.

"There's got to be a toolkit on board," Judit said. "Help me find it."

But the numbness had come back, and Annika stayed where she was as Judit found the kit and pried the panel off the console. Annika stared at the wires and chips inside, unable to decipher what they were. Nothing was labeled; the shuttle was different from any she'd seen. She had a random thought that maybe she could figure out how to turn the gravity off, but when it threatened to make her laugh, she thought of anything else.

"Do you think my mom is dead yet?" she asked, wanting to shock herself back to reality.

Judit turned, face sorry and angry at the same time. Annika didn't even know how she wanted Judit to respond. "I am sorry, Annika, but she... I knew they were coming, and we had to get out of there. I couldn't let you be captured or killed, and I...reacted." She clenched a fist. "And we can't get back there if we can't turn this darking ship around!"

Judit turned back to the controls, a tool gripped in one hand as if she might start randomly stabbing at things.

"Don't," Annika said. "If you damage the life support, we'll die even quicker."

"We are not going to die!"

"This must be what Willa wanted," Annika said, "what she'd seen. The rest of them will make up some story about us going out here, maybe how we were trying to see into the future so we could help."

Anger began to bubble inside Annika's chest, breaking her calm again. Every time she or Judit had thought they'd been rebelling, they'd been following someone's script. Even Judit's "rescue" of her, tackling her into this ship, had been part of someone's plan. They'd been led through their whole lives as easily as someone who had the darking worm!

Her gaze slid to Judit again. They'd miss so many things together. They had so many memories to share, and there was still a giant secret between them.

"Okay," Judit said, staring at the console again. "So, we know where we're going, but the shuttles don't automatically go over the event horizon into the black holes. Most hierophants come back. So there must be a way to fly the shuttle when they get there. Maybe it's automated this far so the hierophants can't change their minds before they get out there." She took a deep breath, frowning. "So, instead of going into the black hole, we might come back and find out time's moved on without us. That will solve all our problems. The galaxy will probably have exploded by then." She put her head in her hands. "But if Willa knew this would happen, she probably programmed this shuttle to hurtle into oblivion!"

"Judit," Annika said softly.

Judit put her hand up. "We're approaching the last transmission gate. Maybe the *Damat* will be able to disable it, but I don't know where they are because I can't get the darking sensors to work!"

No, she couldn't wait any longer. "Judit."

"Just a second." She clicked her teeth. "Bea? Slattery? Anyone on the *Damat*, can you hear me? They're either too far away or something on this darking shuttle is blocking me."

The shuttle had no window, no way to look out except for the feeds from the cameras, and those only showed the forward view as they approached the gate. The shuttle slowed, and Annika shut her eyes as the gate caught hold of them. The shuttle sent an automated transmission, and then came that feeling of being stretched, laid thin over the whole galaxy. It passed quickly, and they were through the gate closest to the galaxy's heart, into the one area of space that had never been contested.

A dark filter slid over the view from the screen, but the cabin still filled with the light from all the stars being eaten by the black holes, the epic singularity that would consume the entire galaxy one day as similar clusters would consume the whole universe.

Judit's mouth opened, and a look of wonder came over her face as it was bathed in light. It covered her, and she looked every inch the chosen one, a bright star all her own, the woman Annika loved with all that was left of her heart.

And she didn't deserve all the lies she'd been told.

"Judit," Annika said. "I have to tell you something."

Judit turned to her, and the wonder deepened as she smiled. "I love you, too. I hope you can forgive me."

"Well, since you mentioned forgiveness..." She paused, not

knowing how she could put this into words, but if they were going to die, she had to say it. "My house never intended my marriage to Noal to be...a happy one." She sighed a laugh, but it had no humor in it. "Their plan, our plan, was for me to use biotech to take over Noal's mind, to slowly separate him from his family, and one day, when he'd fulfilled every purpose Nocturna had for him, to kill him. I was supposed to kill you, too, if you got in the way."

Judit blinked, face blank as if she was a computer trying to process Annika's words. "You..." She swallowed. "But after you got to know us, you changed your mind, right? It was what your family wanted. You weren't actually going to..."

Annika breathed deeply. "Honestly, I didn't want to."

"Didn't *want* to?"

"But it was what I was trained to do." Her heart hammered, and she had to wonder if it'd been a mistake to say anything. She might be spending her last few moments alive with Judit hating her.

"You were going to kill us, to kill me? You said you loved me before you were kidnapped."

"I did...I think."

"You *think*?"

"Judit, please! You have to understand. Love...I had no idea what that meant, not really. I loved my mother, but she left, and my grandmother said she abandoned me, and my grandmother never showed me love, not like you do, not like Noal does. I thought I loved Feric, but now I don't know. I never met anyone like you and Noal. You...you changed me."

"But you would have killed us anyway?" She stood, anger shining from her face. Annika stayed on the floor. If Judit wanted to strike her, well, at least she could understand that.

Annika felt tears gathering and not from grief. She tried to summon what she'd been like before this whole adventure started, tried to remember how she'd felt, but it was like a different time, even though it wasn't long ago at all. She let the tears fall and hoped Judit saw the truth in them.

"I can't be that mad at Feric, at the other hierophants," Annika said. "They set me free. It wasn't until I realized that the marriage was off, that I might never go home again, that I could open myself. I realized what it meant to love you, to be loved by you. Would I have gone through with Nocturna's plan? I don't know." She lifted her hands, dropped them. "That's the most honest answer I can give you. I didn't want to do it; that's the truth. But it's what I'd been trained to do ever since I can remember, and that's a hard thing to break free of, a hard thing to abandon. And if I hadn't done it, if I'd tried to warn you, if I'd tried to do anything but run, Nocturna would have found another way to get what they wanted. Even if I'd defected to your house, they would have found a way."

Judit didn't move, and Annika wondered if she was waiting for more, but Annika didn't know what else to say. Well, maybe there was one more truth.

"I love you," Annika said. "Now. I loved you then in my own sorry way, but I love you now with everything I have. I'd never hurt you or Noal now. And whether we survive this or not, I swear to you that there will always be truth between us."

Judit took a shuddering breath, then another and another until she seemed able to breathe normally. Annika wanted to beg her to say something, no matter what, but she forced herself to be patient. A light on the console blinked, and they both turned to look.

"Transmission sent," a line of text read.

Annika drew a sharp breath. Everything she'd said had been sent to the galaxy at large. She'd forgotten they were aboard a hierophant shuttle, and that every word got recorded for the hierophants to pick apart. Indeed, the light was still on, waiting for more speech, more clues about the future.

So, now everyone would know. No more lies. The idea should have scared Annika, but it filled her with a wondrous sense of peace. She looked back to Judit, who watched the light, too. Maybe she was thinking of what Noal would do when he heard it.

The shuttle still had them on course for the black holes, no indication that control would be returned to them. Maybe this was all Willa's doing after all, and they would serve some cause whether they believed in it or not.

"Our houses did this." Judit took a seat at Annika's side, but Annika didn't dare touch her, not yet. She couldn't stand the thought of her touch being rejected. "My house had a plan, a secret fleet built to annihilate Nocturna if they put a foot wrong in the marriage plan. If the marriage had happened, Meridian wouldn't have dismantled that fleet. Whatever happened, they would have found a reason to use it. It's not…exactly like your family's plan, but they weren't willing to take a chance on peace, either."

Annika nodded. Nocturna had planned to absorb Meridian. They would assassinate key players, but they'd never planned to bomb entire planets, unlike Meridian. She didn't point that out, certain Judit wouldn't see the distinction, not when the assassinations would start with Judit and Noal.

"But you weren't involved with the secret fleet," Annika said. "The moment you found out about it, you were appalled. Unlike mine, your family didn't teach you to be just like them."

"They didn't trust me or Noal. They knew *we* would have told *you.*" She gave Annika a look of pure accusation.

Annika nodded, knowing she deserved it even if Judit didn't understand what would have happened if Annika had told her and Noal about the plot. Annika would have been removed as heir, and one of her cousins would have been promoted to the role. If Judit and Noal had taken the news to Meridian, the secret fleet might have been launched. Whatever had happened, the two of them wouldn't be together.

"I'm sorry, Judit," Annika said. "I don't know what could have been different, if I could have been different, but I'm sorry I kept this from you for so long, even after I knew it wasn't going to happen."

"Why tell me now?" She gestured at the transmission light. "Because you wanted everyone to know they shouldn't trust your house?"

Annika sighed, wanting to think about her answer. "Since there's a good chance we'll die soon, I wanted you to know how much you've changed me, and I couldn't do that without telling you where I started. That's the power you have, Jude. That's why you're the chosen one."

Judit leaned her forehead against Annika's as if breathing her in. "It must be true love if I can adore you and be very angry with you at the same time."

Annika laughed and clasped their hands. "You must love me if you can't say the word 'despise.'"

"I could never despise you."

She reached for Annika's cheek. Annika turned her gloves over, ready to take them off. She wondered if their suits would protect them inside the black holes. Willa had survived somehow. Annika wondered if her shuttle had survived, too, or if they'd found her floating in deep space.

Floating…

Annika sat back. "Judit, we're dressed for open space."

Judit blinked before looking down. "I am, but you—"

"A pressure suit will do for a short time. Let's jump!"

Judit stood and nearly leapt away from her, face horrified. "What?"

"You said the *Damat* is probably following us. If we jump, they can pick us up."

"We…" She swallowed. "We don't know that they're out there."

Annika leaned close to the console. "*Damat*, if you're listening, we're going to jump." And for good measure, she fed her data chip into the shuttle's computer, setting it to transmit. Soon, the whole galaxy would know how rotten Nocturna, Meridian, *and* the hierophants were. "If you've got the info from Meridian," she said, "broadcast it. The galaxy needs to know who the real problem is. Meridian and Nocturna need to stand down."

Judit bent beside her, and though she still seemed frightened, she spoke without a quiver in her voice. "It's time for them to be split into smaller houses, and Annika and I will start the first one."

Annika gasped and nearly wept again. Even after what she'd confessed, Judit still wanted to marry her? She had to kiss her but pulled back quickly. The black holes were getting closer. They didn't have much time.

"We don't have helmets," Judit said.

"There's always something." Annika rooted around in the ship until she found the emergency pressure suits, designed to keep a person alive inside the shuttle. She took a glove to replace the one she'd lost, and the helmet fit perfectly around her own suit, but they had to rig one onto Judit's.

"I should put the other pressure suit on," Judit said.

Annika shook her head. "You have a greater chance of survival with the evosuit."

Judit caught her hands where they were fixing the helmet. "That means you have less of a chance!"

"I'm used to surviving in extreme conditions. I'll be fine."

Judit looked stricken. "What if you're not? This is crazy, Annika!"

"Not any crazier than a Nocturna assassin and a Meridian guardian falling in love."

She finished with the helmet, and they got the air flowing. Annika switched out her tank with one of the other suits, and they did the same for Judit. They had enough air, but the pressure suit wouldn't keep Annika warm for long. If the *Damat* wasn't with them, neither of them would survive.

On the forward view, the cluster of black holes came ever closer. They were supposed to be looking backward, searching through a special catcher that sifted through transmissions and images coming from the rest of the galaxy. They were supposed to be searching for the future, but Annika didn't want to search anywhere but Judit's face.

Annika bound them together with a long tether. "I love you."

Judit readied the shuttle door. "Ready. On three."

"One."

"Two."

As they both said "three," Judit opened the door, and the loss of atmosphere blew them into space.

❖

As soon as they were free, Judit clicked her teeth together. "*Damat*? Come in! Bea?"

The openness of space lay before them, the shuttle flying away at high speed. Judit clung to Annika's hands. In space, they'd be tiny dots. No one would ever find them, even if they were close enough.

Annika gripped her tightly, eyes wide inside her helmet. "It's all right, Judit," she said over their helmet comm. "Just look at me."

Judit tore her eyes from the galaxy, the wheeling stars and the nebulae, the hideous cold that wanted to engulf her. They were spinning, and the light from the black holes came and went inside her vision, blinding her over and over even through the helmet's tint. It made her sick, but she told herself she was imagining things. There was no gravity to act on her stomach.

She tried to keep her gaze locked on Annika's beautiful, stormy eyes. That was all the infinity she needed right there, and all she had to do was focus. "I love you, too."

Annika smiled. Was her face a little paler? She'd be feeling the cold more acutely. Even with the rate they were moving, she seemed to be shaking. Judit had thought to insist on giving her the evosuit, but then she'd have to watch Judit die first instead of the other way around. As much as the idea hurt, Judit wanted to spare her that. It would be the last gift Judit could give her.

"I'm all right," Annika said, but it sounded a little breathless. "I'm okay."

"Bea?" Judit cried. "Please, come in. *Damat?*"

Silence answered her. Should she take shallow breaths or deep ones? If she used up her air, maybe she and Annika would die at the same time.

"I'm okay. You're okay." Annika's eyes looked heavy. The cold would put her to sleep before it killed her.

"Stay with me," Judit breathed. "Stay awake."

Annika smiled languidly. "I should have worn something warmer."

They should have stayed on the darking shuttle! "Bea!"

"I see you, Jude!" Beatrice's voice echoed in her ear.

Judit cried with joy, and her stomach did cartwheels. In the reflection of Annika's helmet, Judit watched the *Damat*'s shuttle coming closer. It maneuvered around them, into their trajectory, and hovered, open airlock waiting.

Judit heard Annika laughing and joined in. They were going to live! Going to get a chance to be together, to grow old together.

The thought didn't bring her as much joy as she wanted. When she'd thought they were going to die, it had been easy to forgive Annika, but now, she wasn't sure that wave of forgiveness had been real. She'd pushed what Annika had told her to the back of her mind, focusing on all the good things that had happened between them since death was so soon in their future.

Now, as she stared at Annika's still beautiful face, she thought of every filthy trick Nocturna was going to use her for. They hadn't planned to simply kill Judit and Noal. They wanted to take over his *mind*. That was so very Nocturna, and it filled Judit with both hatred and fear. If Annika had considered going through with that plan, what else was she capable of? Judit had seen exactly what her mother was capable of, after all. They might not be so different.

A frightened, animal part of her said to cut the tether, let Annika float away. She was already falling asleep. She wouldn't even notice. Judit's pack had the jets; she could maneuver into the shuttle alone. Judit clutched Annika tighter and nearly sobbed at the most cowardly, inhuman thought that had ever crossed her mind. She used her jets to move them both into the shuttle feet first.

"We can use the magboots to slow us," she said.

"All right," Annika said sleepily.

Judit's boots pulled her to and fro as they neared the shuttle, as if the magnets couldn't decide which surface to stick to. She and Annika ended up thudding into the inner wall of the shuttle in a tangle of limbs, and the artificial gravity dropped them to the floor. Annika grunted as Judit did; there'd be more than a few bruises between them. The outer door hissed closed, and atmosphere filled the room along with a blast of heat. Judit scrambled upright and wrestled her awkwardly fitting helmet off, then helped Annika do the same.

"Are you all right?"

Annika nodded, only a little wobbly as Judit helped her up.

The cockpit door hissed open. "Welcome back!" Beatrice called from where she piloted the shuttle alone. "Sorry for the bumpy landing."

"Thanks. Really, Bea." Judit went forward and hugged her around the shoulders. "I'm so happy to see you."

Beatrice grinned. The forward screen showed them already under way toward the *Damat*.

When Judit turned, Annika kissed her soundly. "We're alive."

"Yes." And she wanted nothing more than to sink into Annika's embrace, to let everything go as she'd done on the shuttle, but doubt jangled in her mind, and she didn't know how to get rid of it. She sat in the second chair. "Is everyone all right, Bea?"

"A little banged up. After that ship accelerated with you on it, we gave chase, but the Nocturna warship caught up to us. We got into a firefight and had to flee. Roberts figured out where your ship had gone, and then we were on your trail." She glanced at Annika. "But I guess you two made it out okay?"

"I don't think I was ever on any ship you found," Annika said. "Feric laid a trap for me and destroyed the ship we were on."

"And Evie?" Beatrice asked. "Is she back at the Eye?"

Judit's breath caught, and her stomach lurched as she relived Evie's death, the surprise in her eyes, the hole in her side. "She's dead."

Beatrice sucked in a breath and stared, and Judit was flooded with guilt for saying it so bluntly, so cruelly. She wouldn't be the only one mourning.

"Willa killed her," Judit said. "She killed a lot of people."

"Willa? The Willa?"

Judit nodded. "I'll explain it to everyone at once, if you don't mind."

"It was the hierophants," Annika said. "They were trying to use us to bring about war, but we've thwarted them now. We won't be their martyrs. We'll be their ruin."

For once, Judit was glad to hear the cold-blooded killer in her voice. They needed her now if they were going to see the corrupted hierophants destroyed.

Once aboard the *Damat*, Judit was left with what to do first. Go back to the Eye? Tell the crew about Evie's death? Her body was probably aboard some ship docked at the Eye, the same one that had brought Judit. If they got her back, they could have a funeral. Judit would have to plan it, and the thought made her stumble. She'd never lost a crew member before.

Noal met her outside the shuttle bay and hugged her, but when he looked to Annika, Judit knew there was more to think about than just their next actions.

The way he stared at her, as if he'd never met her, Judit knew he'd heard the transmission. Spartan was behind him, and he put a hand on Noal's shoulder as if ready to pull him away from Annika at a moment's notice.

Annika opened her mouth, then closed it as if thinking better of what she had to say.

Noal put up a hand. "I understand, but I'm not ready to talk to you yet."

Annika nodded, looking pained, but she didn't argue. She looked to Judit, and a question lingered in her eyes. Now that they were safe, what did Judit want from her?

Time, Judit decided. Time to think about what she should do. "Have we heard from anyone else about our transmissions?"

"Not yet," Beatrice said.

And the Meridian and Nocturna ships Beatrice had detected were probably waiting at the Eye. "Tell everyone we're going to the Eye," Judit said, heading for the bridge.

"Everyone?"

"In the galaxy," Judit said. "Put it out there, then bring us in slow."

Annika gasped, and Judit knew what she was thinking. If they went in fast, maybe they could get her mother out alive. Anger flared in Judit again: at Annika, at her mother, at Nocturna, at Meridian, too. Variel would have to survive on her own for a little while longer.

On the bridge, Beatrice moved to get them under way, having a word in Roberts's ear first about announcing their destination.

Judit sat in her chair and adjusted her comm so she could speak to the whole crew. "Attention, *Damat*, as your captain, I'd like a moment of your time."

The bridge crew turned to her, and Beatrice's eyes still held sadness. Now Judit would have to watch the rest of the bridge crew cope, see their pain, but this wouldn't wait. It shouldn't.

"It is with great sorrow that I tell you of the death of our tactical officer, Evie Benson, cruelly ambushed by hierophants of the Eye, the same people who engineered the chaos now facing our galaxy." Judit paused, gripping the arms of her chair for support. Noal wrapped an arm around her shoulders.

"She died bravely," Judit said. "Always doing her job without hesitation, and it is in her name, in the name of my father and all who have died in this chaos, that we will put an end to it. We will seek out the hierophants who have engineered this crisis and see them brought to justice." She nearly growled out the last word and felt it settle inside her like the prophecies of old.

Chapter Twenty-one

Annika listened to Judit's words, but even the thought of revenge gave her no comfort. While they'd floated in space, Judit's face had gone from frightened to distant. That had been easy to see even through the lethargy that wanted to take over Annika's body. When she'd spoken later, her voice had been calm, almost deadly. Annika's confession had affected her more than either of them thought. Maybe the words had only just sunk in.

Noal had certainly absorbed them. He could barely look at her; if she moved suddenly, he'd probably jump out of his skin. But she couldn't worry about him now, or any of Judit's crew, no matter how they looked at her. She had to focus on defeating the hierophants once and for all.

Judit wanted to imprison the hierophants responsible for the chaos, and Annika now realized that included her mother, if she was still alive. She'd participated in the plot to disrupt the galaxy, she'd planted bombs on Nocturna Prime, and she'd had a hand in Judit's father's death, all so Annika could be free.

No wonder Judit had left her behind. She was a criminal, and Annika knew she deserved punishment, but part of her hoped her mother had already fled, maybe leaving a note that promised to get in touch soon.

As Judit finished her speech, the bridge crew mourned together, some shedding a few tears. Annika looked to Judit, wondering if a hug would be welcome. Noal still had his arm around her shoulders, and Annika didn't think he'd welcome the contact.

Annika sighed. She'd begun thinking of the *Damat* as her new house, her new home. She'd been overjoyed when Judit told the galaxy they'd marry and start a new house, but now Judit might reconsider. That offer might have been an empty promise, made only to give the rest of the galaxy something to focus on, something Judit planned to die thinking about.

She might be Annika of No House for the rest of her life. Maybe she should run away with her mother.

The thought stabbed at her, and she clenched a fist, nearly groaning. No, she could never flee as her mother had, could never hurt Judit like that. If Judit was angry, fine. She wouldn't stay angry forever. And Annika would repay years of deception with decades of honesty, with giving. There could be trust between them.

And Annika knew where it could start. She would help catch her mother, as much as the thought pained her. The punishment didn't have to come from Nocturna or Meridian but someone more neutral. Her mother would have to pay for what she'd done, even if a court decided she had to pay with her life.

That was a hard truth to swallow. Annika had always considered the law to be mutable, something for show, to be bent as needed. But to Judit, the law was a thing of beauty, the stitch that held the galaxy together. And Annika's mother had broken it in the worst way. If Annika wanted a life with Judit, she would have to see justice served no matter how much it hurt.

When they traveled back through the transmission gate to the Eye, Annika kept her eyes on Judit's screen. The area was swarming with ships, both Nocturna and Meridian. They all bore damage, but they'd stopped fighting for the moment, maybe waiting for the return of the *Damat*, maybe to blow them out of the sky.

"I can't believe the hierophants engineered this whole thing," Spartan said. "I mean, they're watchers. That's what they do. They watch and they report."

"And what they saw led them to this," Noal said. "To resetting everything. They saw themselves as the catalyst. Maybe some of them even thought it was about time."

"It wasn't all of them," Annika said. "They'd been fighting amongst themselves on the Eye."

Noal and Spartan stared as if they'd forgotten she was there. Maybe after her admission, they'd forgotten she was on their side. It hurt her more than she thought. At least Judit didn't look at her that way, even if she didn't look at her at all.

Spartan cleared his throat. "Then maybe there are some out in the galaxy who are still watchers. They'll be able to tell us who was in on this plan, and who wasn't."

"Whatever happens," Judit said quietly, "we're off script now. Willa thought Annika and I were going to die in that shuttle."

The Eye came closer, and from the outside, it looked the same as always, a ziggurat carved from an asteroid. The umbilicals floated below it, two still attached to shuttles, but the rest stood empty, waiting. Annika had imagined them as the tentacles of a monstrous sea creature before. But they didn't hang empty in space; they extended across the whole galaxy.

"We're getting hails from both Meridian and Nocturna ships," Roberts said.

Judit looked over her shoulder at Annika. "Ready to send a message?"

And what would that message be? Were they going to present a unified front that Judit didn't feel anymore?

Judit stood and waved Annika to her side. "Make a holo of us and get ready to send it to everyone," Judit said.

"Ready," Roberts said.

"Judit," Annika said quietly, "can you forgive me?"

"I still love you." Judit's expression twisted as if she was feeling too many emotions to focus on one. "I can't ever see not loving you, but…I'm going to need some time."

Annika nodded. "And the new house? Is that what we're going to announce?"

Judit took a deep breath, and Annika's heart froze, wondering if she was going to say no. She had a flash of anger. She'd never cared about anyone this much before, and it was so darking painful. Judit couldn't open her up like this and then say good-bye. It wasn't fair!

"We have to," Judit said, "for the good of the galaxy."

"For the good of the galaxy," Annika repeated, and she knew it sounded bitter. So, she was going to get her political marriage after all, only this time, there wouldn't even be friendship within it. Her stomach cramped around the thought.

Judit gestured to Roberts, and a holo camera in the ceiling flashed, bathing them in green light. "This message is for all of Meridian and Nocturna, for all of the galaxy. I, Judit Meridian..."

Annika clenched her hand. "And I, Annika Nocturna..."

"Pledge to begin the first of the smaller houses that will be created from those formerly known as Meridian and Nocturna."

Annika nodded, knowing what she had to say, what Judit needed her to say. "We ask the rest of the galaxy to cease attacking one another. Now that you know you've been manipulated by the hierophants of the Eye, we ask that you turn your attention to the galaxy's two largest houses and extend your pressure and influence to force them to dismantle or else face destruction."

Judit gave her a glance, but Annika only squeezed her hand again. Threats of force were the only thing their houses would understand. Sometimes, fire had to be fought with an even larger fire. And threats had stopped the war in the first place; they'd just had the wrong plan to stop it forever. They didn't need to unite. They needed to disperse. And maybe with Willa dead and the largest houses in tatters, they could finally see peace.

❖

The *Damat* was bombarded with transmissions from different sectors of the galaxy, but Judit took the hail from the Eye. Variel smiled at them from Judit's screen.

"The hierophants who weren't in on the conspiracy helped me retake the Eye," she said. "All the conspirators are either dead or in custody."

Judit nodded, but anger burned in her. Who was this woman to talk about conspirators and custody? She'd been part of this plot, never mind her reasons.

Before she could speak, Annika said, "We need to get over there, Judit, so you can take custody of the prisoners yourself."

Judit lifted an eyebrow. That sounded like a good idea, but a new, suspicious Judit had been born in the time since Annika's confession, and she wondered if Annika only wanted to go to the Eye to help her mother escape.

She tried to fight the new voice down, tried to remember everything Annika had said and done, not just the confession. She was a different person. Love had changed her.

But Judit had to give her new suspicious side a little peace of mind, too. She summoned a contingent of crew to act as guards, missing Evie keenly. Slattery protested as she got ready to leave the bridge. Judit nearly snapped at him about thinking he could take Evie's place, but he was doing a job, one Evie had trained him for.

"If we dock at the Eye, we'll be vulnerable," he pointed out.

True, but Judit didn't want to take a shuttle for the same reason. And so far, the ships didn't seem to want to fire on the Eye or the *Damat*. Maybe they realized that if any one of them pulled the trigger, it would mean death for everyone.

"I've got more ships entering the system." Beatrice turned to Judit with a happy look of wonder. "It's House Munn and a fleet of unaffiliated ships."

"Getting a transmission from Elidia," Roberts said. "It's open, so everyone can hear."

Judit turned to her screen. "Put her through."

When Elidia blinked onto the screen, she had that same smirk as when Judit had first seen her on the *Xerxes*, a woman in control who knew she was going to get exactly what she wanted. It made Judit smile, even as the suspicious voice said that Elidia had come to mop them all up.

"I've continued to follow your little love story," Elidia said. "Everyone has. So I thought I'd come help."

All the Nocturna and Meridian ships had gone quiet, probably listening.

"Good," Judit said, "you can cover us as we dock with the Eye."

"My pleasure." Elidia had quite a fleet, and Judit felt certain the other ships would behave if they knew they'd be facing not only Nocturna or Meridian, but Munn as well. "The rest of the galaxy likes the way you've been so open with your info, and House Flavio has been keeping a low profile since we found out they were helping the hierophants. I don't think you're going to have any trouble getting everyone to help you dismantle Nocturna and Meridian. Hierophants are being ousted from every house as we speak."

Judit smiled. At least something was going her way. The hierophants had only been able to engineer the chaos because they were welcome everywhere. She bet even the legitimate ones would have a hard time finding welcome now.

The *Damat* docked with the Eye, and Annika and Judit boarded with the guards. Variel waited for them. This was it; this was where Annika pushed her mother into a shuttle and helped her escape. Judit had to stop her. Annika was going to prove that her every word had been a lie; she hadn't changed. She was Annika Nocturna through and through, a murderer at heart, and she would help her murdering mother escape justice.

"Mom." Annika reached forward as if for a hug. Her mother's arms lifted, both of them awkward as if they didn't know what the other wanted. They both paused, laughed nervously, and ended up clasping hands.

Angry as she was, Judit's heart broke. Everything Annika had said about love was true, at least. Even now, she and her mother didn't know how to show it. But Annika had figured out a way to show Judit. And Judit's suspicious half couldn't blame that on Nocturna training.

"Mom," Annika said, tears in her voice. "I have to place you under arrest."

Judit held her breath, wonder and surprise coursing through her.

Annika's mother blinked several times. "You..." She glanced at Judit, but her expression remained unreadable.

"It's not something I'm saying just because Judit is here." Annika's lip wobbled, and she pressed a hand to her cheek as if trying to get her face to obey. "You killed people, Mom. You helped Feric bomb Nocturna Prime. I know you did it for me, and I want to keep you alive, but you have to pay for what you've done. You have to give yourself up."

Her voice broke on the last word, and she looked an inch away from tears. Judit wanted to hug her but didn't want that to break the dam.

"You'll be turned over to House Munn," Judit said. If she kept Annika's mother out of Nocturna and Meridian hands, she was more likely to remain alive. Judit waved several of her crew forward. "Secure her aboard the *Damat* with every courtesy."

They nodded. Variel took a deep breath and looked hard at Annika before she nodded and placed her hands on Annika's shoulders. "I understand."

Annika nodded back, but it seemed she couldn't speak. As the guards led Variel past, she leaned close, and Judit expected an entreaty to treat her daughter right, but she whispered, "Feric is imprisoned in one of the rooms nearby."

Judit nodded, and Variel cast one more look toward Annika before she was gone.

When they were alone, Judit took Annika in her arms. "It's all right. Let go."

Annika sobbed into her shoulder, her arms wrapping Judit tightly. Even when she'd been injured, even when someone had died, Annika had never cried in front of her like this. Judit joined her, weeping for her father, for all the dead, for a little Annika who didn't know how to hug a parent, for everything their houses had done to them.

"I believe you," Judit whispered when she could use her voice again. "I believe you." And it felt stronger than "I love you." As Annika smiled through her tears, it seemed she thought so, too. They kissed, lips wet and salty, truth passing between them.

EPILOGUE

The planet of Fortuna was much easier to sneak onto than Nocturna Prime. Annika didn't even have to engineer a disguise. It had taken weeks to find Ama's hiding place. The vultures of Nocturna had wasted no time picking their house clean as everyone grabbed for power. It was almost funny, but Annika couldn't take real joy in it. It was hard to watch the house she'd been raised in fall apart, even if they deserved it.

The streets on Fortuna were abandoned. Perhaps Ama had kicked everyone off the small planet. Perhaps they'd left on their own. It wasn't much to see, anyway, a craggy ball of rock that Nocturna used for heavy manufacturing. Annika hadn't even known it was one of Ama's bolt-holes, but she'd figured it out eventually. She supposed she should be grateful that all the factories were dark. She didn't have to explain herself. She was a bit worried when she didn't see any guards, but like everyone else in Nocturna, they'd gone with whoever could pay them the most, and at the moment, that didn't seem to be Ama.

A hand scanner led her to the one building with power. Instead of barricades or guards, Ama had posted signs promising radiation damage to anyone who entered. Annika's scanner confirmed the presence of radioactive particles, but she knew that trick. She took a small EMP grenade from her belt and lobbed it over the fence. She jogged out of range of the small blast, unseen but felt by the surrounding electronics as it knocked them out. When she approached the fence again, the radiation signal was gone.

She scaled the fence and spotted several concealed weapons drooping from recesses on the building's side. The EMP had taken them out, too, but no backup generators resuscitated them, and no guards came rushing to see what the outage was about, further proof that Ama had no one left to protect her. And she was using the power for something else.

Annika ignored the doors and approached the air vents. Ama would be hidden behind secret doors, and Annika didn't want to spend all day searching. But Ama would need air, and so the vents would lead to her eventually. Annika cut the wire inside the main intake vent and climbed inside. Ama used traps, but she'd never really worried about assassins. Of all those who'd tried, none had come through a confrontation with her alive. It both pained and tickled Annika that she might be the first.

Annika followed the power signatures to Ama's office inside the walls, climbing around the bots that kept the vents mostly free of grime. She paused, watching as Ama strode from console to console, all of them scrolling with different data. Her hair was a mess, and the neck of her blouse stood open. Annika had never seen her looking so frazzled.

Ama stopped and pressed the comm hanging around her ear. "Then find someone else!" she screeched. "Don't bother me with petty problems."

Annika dropped soundlessly to the floor. "You're coming apart at the seams."

Ama whirled and blinked as if seeing a ghost. "What are you doing here?" She glanced left and right, no doubt looking for a weapon. A stack of crates stood in one corner, some of them unpacked, items strewn about the floor. In another corner was a cot, some ration packs, and many bottles of water.

"How long have you been hiding here trying to glue your empire back together?" Annika stood on tiptoe, trying to see what else Ama was hiding, and spotted a large jar. She gasped, shocked at seeing the worm. "What in the dark did you save that for?"

Ama smoothed her hair, and when she straightened, she had the regal bearing Annika remembered. Even with all Annika's confidence, it still created a pall of dread inside her. "Have you come back just to ask stupid questions?"

"You never begin a conversation by asking me how I am," Annika said. "Did you know that other people do that? Do you hate wasting time, or do you simply not care?"

Ama turned back to her consoles. "If you're not going to kill me, either help me or go away."

Annika barked a laugh. Dread was quickly morphing into pity.

"If you want to help, take whatever ship you came here in and go to Caligo," Ama said. "We need to take the shipyards back from Ricardo."

"Huh. I didn't think he had it in him. I didn't come to help you, Ama."

Ama turned again slowly. "Then why?"

"To see whether or not I should kill you."

"And?"

"It doesn't seem worth it. You're a spent force."

Ama sneered. "Or you're a coward."

It didn't even hurt. Annika wandered over to the worm. "What are you going to do with this?"

"I thought it might come in handy when I finally get my hands on our enemies."

Annika stared into her grandmother's eyes and thought of every nasty thing she'd been taught. She tried not to recall every childhood grievance, too, but they reared inside her mind without her permission. She smiled slowly, enjoying the way her grandmother tensed as if waiting for an attack. The fear in her eyes was nice, too. Even Judit might have enjoyed it.

"Feric was never your creature," Annika said. "Maybe he was mine in the beginning, then he belonged to the hierophants. He believed in fate." She'd had several long conversations with Feric. She'd scanned him for a worm but had found nothing. Of course, the worm was designed to be undetectable, but if he did have one, maybe Ama didn't know about it. "You lost this fight a long time ago, and you didn't even know it. You couldn't even control one bodyguard who'd been raised to obey you."

With one smooth, motion, Annika knocked the jar over, spilling the fluid across the floor. When her grandmother gasped, Annika ground the worm under her heel. "You're too pathetic to kill."

With a screech, Ama leapt, as out of control as Annika had ever seen her. Annika ducked out of the way, easily avoiding her grandmother's strikes. Ama slipped in the fluid and banged into one of the crates, knocking it into several others. She crashed to the ground, sputtering in anger.

Annika walked back to the vent and crawled inside. "Enjoy the house you've built, Ama. I know I will."

❖

Judit had never waited on this side of the ship before: getting ready in her quarters while someone else guarded the door. She pictured Beatrice shooing away well-wishers and smiled sadly. It should have been Evie, but then, Judit's father and Annika's mother should have been there to wish them luck, too.

Judit looked in the mirror and straightened her uniform. She'd worn Meridian gray for so long, it unnerved her every time she saw the dark blue cloth that covered her now. Blue, Annika's favorite, and a shade unclaimed by any of the other houses. It was only fitting that the first house to come out of the deconstruction of Meridian and Nocturna, House Penumbra, had its own formal military color, even though its current military consisted solely of the crew of the *Damat*.

It wouldn't stay that way for long. Many Meridians and Nocturnas had volunteered to be part of the new house, though Annika had warned her that some Nocturnas would be spies. Both houses would have to be watched to make sure they didn't try to recombine sometime down the road. Some members of other houses had offered to join Penumbra, too, including several Munns and Spartan. Judit wondered how many of the newcomers thought that being part of the galaxy's hot new house would give them prestige, but Judit planned to put them to work. Everyone in Penumbra would have a job. No more lazy Blood doing nothing but bumping passengers from shuttles.

Judit straightened her uniform again. The gold buttons shone, and she wished she'd pushed harder for a more unobtrusive metal.

Noal stepped up beside her. "Stop fussing. You look good."

"I shouldn't have let you talk me into the gold."

"Gold is nice. It attracts attention."

"I don't want attention." She sighed, knowing how surly she sounded but unable to help it. She tried to focus on the fact that everyone would be looking at Annika anyway; she was the beautiful one.

Over the two months since the chaos had died down, both Judit and Annika had to have some difficult conversations with their families. Judit's grandmother had made several "over my dead body" threats about the future of her house, and then refused further conversation. But several days after that, Judit's mother had contacted her and said that Grandmother had stepped down as head of House Meridian, naming Judit's mother as her heir.

Judit had desperately wanted to ask what had happened to her grandmother, but since her mother assured her that the old woman still lived, Annika convinced Judit not to ask. After all, it wasn't her house anymore. It wasn't her responsibility. That had hurt, and she'd tried to turn her attention to all the work they still had to do.

Judit sighed and turned. When she saw the box of cosmetics in Noal's hand, she pointed at him. "No."

He rolled his eyes. "It's for me, thank you very much. Now, if you'll quit hogging the mirror."

She stepped aside, and he sat, opening his box and getting to work. To her surprise, he also wore the dark blue of the new Penumbra military, but he'd added a bit of shine to the material, and some of his buttons had the sparkle of gemstones. He didn't dye his hair, though, and she wondered if that was a nod to his Meridian heritage.

"Thoughts?" he asked.

She sighed again, a far different sound as she thought of Annika. Their future together made her giddy and terrified at the same time. "I love her."

"Good."

"You still don't trust her."

He shrugged. "I keep telling myself that was her then; this is her now."

"You were the one who said she's still capable of awful things."

He put his brushes down and stared at her. "Do you think she'll hurt you, Jude?"

She nearly drew back. "No."

"Me? Someone else you care about?"

She shook her head.

"Then I can deal," he said. "It took me a while to admit, but she wasn't the only one who lied to us about who she is."

Judit tried to parse that sentence and failed. "What?"

"She told us that she showed us only some of her true self, but you know who supplied the rest? Us." He poked a finger at her and then at himself. "We built her up in our heads, made her someone she isn't: the perfect princess. Maybe she did the same thing, but she isn't holding that against us. We can't blame her for not living up to these false expectations we had."

Judit smiled widely. "I'm glad you feel that way. I'd hate to have to find an errand for her every time you want to speak with me."

He laughed and went back to his makeup. "Well, as a bystander, I can be as resentful and bitter as I want to be. I can come to all your dinner parties and make snide comments."

She had to smile. "But you're clearly over it."

He winked. The thought that Annika had guardian training hadn't upset Judit because it was something she could understand, and because Annika knowing how to kick ass was really hot. But even after Annika had arrested her mother, it had taken time to put the new, suspicious Judit away. Knowing Annika was capable of the amount of lying she'd had to do, capable of smiling to their faces while planning to kill them, even if she didn't want to...

Judit shook her head. The fact that Annika didn't *want* to hurt them was the crux of the matter. If it had come down to it, Annika *probably* would have done something else. The moment she'd gotten out from under her grandmother's thumb, she'd saved Noal's life and confessed her love to Judit. All it had taken was a few hours outside of Nocturna's plans, and she'd reverted to the woman she'd always wanted to be.

"Time to go." Noal stood and held out an arm. "Shall we?"

"I need a minute alone."

He gave her a long look before he nodded. "All right, but hurry up. House Penumbra waits for no one."

"Let's make that our new motto."

He chuckled, kissed her on the cheek, then stepped outside her quarters. Judit checked herself in the mirror again, wondering at her sudden reluctance. She knew all her fears would blow away the moment she set eyes on Annika. They could do this. They could build a house together. They'd already laid the groundwork. Meridian was in good hands dissolving under Judit's mother. Nocturna had split up surprisingly fast as all the Blood made grabs for power.

Someone knocked lightly on the door. Judit turned, ready to

snap at Noal that she was coming, but pale fingers waved at her from between the slats of the air vent on the wall.

"What in the dark?"

"Can I come in?" Annika's voice called.

Judit brayed a laugh. "What are you doing here?"

The vent swung outward and Annika popped out. She wore a yellow jumpsuit that was covered in stains from her trip through the vent. She had a scarf tied around her hair and dragged a black bag behind her. "I thought Noal would never leave," she said as she grinned.

Judit reached to help her down, but Annika waved her away. "I don't want to get your uniform dirty." She winked. "Well, not yet."

Judit chuckled again as desire swept through her, but she forced herself to stay back. "Are you getting married in that jumpsuit?"

Annika patted the bag. "I thought we could get ready together. Sorry I'm late." She leaned forward for a kiss before slowly undoing the jumpsuit, bottom lip between her teeth. Judit whirled around, not trusting that she could keep her hands to herself. Annika's chuckle was low and throaty, and Judit clenched her hands into fists.

"I thought I'd come check on you," Annika said amidst the rustle of fabric. "Make sure you weren't having second thoughts."

"Never," Judit said. "How in the dark did you sneak onto the *Damat*?"

"I have my ways. You can turn around now."

Judit swallowed. Did she hope that Annika was clothed or naked? On the one hand, everyone was waiting for them. On the other, everyone could wait.

Annika looked...comfortable. That was the only word Judit could think of. Well, she was beautiful as always, but by her own admission, her clothing was usually functional, if only to elicit admiration or desire in the viewer. This dress was Penumbra blue, made of something lightweight, maybe even cotton. It fitted through the midsection and flared into a full skirt below her hips. It had long, fitted sleeves and a plain V-neck. She wore her red-gold hair down, cascading over her shoulders. Her face was bare and so lovely, Judit almost couldn't look at her.

She turned slowly. "What do you think? I decided not to go military. I figured we should all wear what we want today."

"It's perfect. You're beautiful."

With a grin, Annika kissed Judit again. "So are you. I've never owned anything comfortable before. I think I love it."

"And I love you."

"Not as much as I love you."

Judit lifted an eyebrow. "Is that a challenge?"

"Oh yes, most definitely yes."

As they kissed again, Noal banged on the door. "Are you two done in there, or do I need to find some entertainment for the waiting crowd?"

"He helped you sneak in here, didn't he?" Judit asked.

"My lips are sealed." She took Judit's hand. "Let's go get married. Our future's waiting."

Judit clasped her hand, kissed it, and they stepped to the door together toward a brighter fate than either had ever hoped for.

About the Author

Barbara Ann Wright writes fantasy and science fiction novels and short stories when not ranting on her blog. *The Pyramid Waltz* was one of Tor.com's Reviewer's Choice books of 2012, was a Foreword Review BOTYA Finalist, a Goldie finalist, and made Book Riot's 100 Must-Read Sci-Fi Fantasy Novels By Female Authors. It also won the 2013 Rainbow Award for Best Lesbian Fantasy. *A Kingdom Lost* and *Thrall: Beyond Gold and Glory* won the 2014 and 2016 Rainbow Awards for Best Lesbian Fantasy Romance, respectively. *Coils* was a finalist for the 2017 Lammys.

Books Available From Bold Strokes Books

A Lamentation of Swans by Valerie Bronwen. Ariel Montgomery returns to Sea Oats to try to save her broken marriage but soon finds herself also fighting to save her own life and catch a murderer. (978-1-62639-828-3)

Between Sand and Stardust by Tina Michele. Are the lifelong bonds of love strong enough to conquer time, distance, and heartache when Haven Thorne and Willa Bennette are given another chance at forever? (978-1-62639-940-2)

House of Fate by Barbara Ann Wright. Two women must throw off the lives they've known as a guardian and an assassin and save two rival houses before their secrets tear the galaxy apart. (978-1-62639-780-4)

Planning for Love by Erin Dutton. Could true love be the one thing that wedding coordinator Faith McKenna didn't plan for? (978-1-62639-954-9)

Sidebar by Carsen Taite. Judge Camille Avery and her clerk, attorney West Fallon, agree on little except their mutual attraction, but can their relationship and their careers survive a headline-grabbing case? (978-1-62639-752-1)

Sweet Boy and Wild One by T. L. Hayes. When Rachel Cole meets soulful singer Bobby Layton at an open mic, she is immediately in thrall. What she soon discovers will rock her world in ways she never imagined. (978-1-62639-963-1)

To Be Determined by Mardi Alexander and Laurie Eichler. Charlie Dickerson escapes her life in the US to rescue Australian wildlife with Pip Atkins, but can they save each other? (978-1-62639-946-4)

True Colors by Yolanda Wallace. Blogger Robby Rawlins plans to use First Daughter Taylor Crenshaw to get ahead, but she never planned on falling in love with her in the process. (978-1-62639-927-3)

Undercover Affairs by Julie Blair. Searching for stolen documents crucial to U.S. security, CIA agent Rett Spenser confronts lies, deceit, and unexpected romance as she investigates art gallery owner Shannon Kent. (978-1-62639-905-1)

Unexpected by Jenny Frame. When Dale McGuire falls for Rebecca Harper, the mother of the son she never knew she had, will Rebecca's troubled past stop them from making the family they both truly crave? (978-1-62639-942-6)

Canvas for Love by Charlotte Greene. When ghosts from Amelia's past threaten to undermine their relationship, Chloé must navigate the greatest romance of her life without losing sight of who she is. (978-1-62639-944-0)

Heart Stop by Radclyffe. Two women, one with a damaged body, the other a damaged spirit, challenge each other to dare to live again. (978-1-62639-899-3)

Repercussions by Jessica L. Webb. Someone planted information in Edie Black's brain and now they want it back, but with the protection of shy former soldier Skye Kenny, Edie has a chance at life and love. (978-1-62639-925-9)

Spark by Catherine Friend. Jamie's life is turned upside down when her consciousness travels back to 1560 and lands in the body of one of Queen Elizabeth I's ladies-in-waiting…or has she totally lost her grip on reality? (978-1-62639-930-3)

Taking Sides by Kathleen Knowles. When passion and politics collide, can love survive? (978-1-62639-876-4)

Thorns of the Past by Gun Brooke. Former cop Darcy Flynn's heart broke when her career on the force ended in disgrace, but perhaps saving Sabrina Hawk's life will mend it in more ways than one. (978-1-62639-857-3)

You Make Me Tremble by Karis Walsh. Seismologist Casey Radnor comes to the San Juan Islands to study an earthquake but finds her heart shaken by passion when she meets animal rescuer Iris Mallery. (978-1-62639-901-3)

Complications by MJ Williamz. Two women battle for the heart of one. (978-1-62639-769-9)

Crossing the Wide Forever by Missouri Vaun. As Cody Walsh and Lillie Ellis face the perils of the untamed West, they discover that love's uncharted frontier isn't for the weak in spirit or the faint of heart. (978-1-62639-851-1)

Fake It till You Make It by M. Ullrich. Lies will lead to trouble, but can they lead to love? (978-1-62639-923-5)

Girls Next Door, edited by Sandy Lowe and Stacia Seaman. Bestselling romance authors tell it from the heart—sexy, romantic stories of falling for the girls next door. (978-1-62639-916-7)

Pursuit by Jackie D. The pursuit of the most dangerous terrorist in America will crack the lines of friendship and love, and not everyone will make it out from under the weight of duty and service. (978-1-62639-903-7)

The Practitioner by Ronica Black. Sometimes love comes calling whether you're ready for it or not. (978-1-62639-948-8)

Unlikely Match by Fiona Riley. When an ambitious PR exec and her super-rich coding geek-girl client fall in love, they learn that giving something up may be the only way to have everything. (978-1-62639-891-7)

Where Love Leads by Erin McKenzie. A high school counselor and the mom of her new student bond in support of the troubled girl, never expecting deeper feelings to emerge, testing the boundaries of their relationship. (978-1-62639-991-4)

Forsaken Trust by Meredith Doench. When four women are murdered, Agent Luce Hansen must regain trust in her most valuable investigative tool—herself—to catch the killer. (978-1-62639-737-8)

Letter of the Law by Carsen Taite. Will federal prosecutor Bianca Cruz take a chance at love with horse breeder Jade Vargas, whose dark family ties threaten everything Bianca has worked to protect—including her child? (978-1-62639-750-7)